ONE WEEK WITH THE FRENCH TYCOON

BY
CHRISTY MCKELLEN

MILLS
BOON
&

First Published in Great Britain 2016
By Mills & Boon, an imprint of HarperCollins*Publishers*
1 London Bridge Street, London, SE1 9GF

© 2016 Christy McKellen

ISBN: 978-0-263-91986-8

23-0516

Our policy is to use papers that are natural, renewable and recyclable products and made from wood grown in sustainable forests. The logging and manufacturing processes conform to the legal environmental regulations of the country of origin.

Printed and bound in Spain
by CPI, Barcelona

Formerly a video and radio producer, **Christy McKellen** now spends her time writing fun, impassioned and emotive romance with an undercurrent of sensual tension. When she's not writing she can be found enjoying life with her husband and three children, walking for pleasure, and researching other people's deepest secrets and desires.

Christy loves to hear from readers. You can get ahold of her at www.christymckellen.com.

This one's for my beautiful, witty and fiercely clever sisters-in-law, Kat and Buffy. Thank you for being the sisters I never had and welcoming me so warmly into your family. I love spending time with you. Here's to spending many more fabulous weekends in London together.

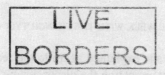

CHAPTER ONE

Arriving in Amalfi—a most lively and dramatic town in which to begin your journey...

WHEN INDIGO HUGHES had spent long hours daydreaming about her walking holiday along the Amalfi Coast of Southern Italy, *this* wasn't exactly what she'd envisioned.

Luggageless—after the airline had inexplicably sent her backpack containing her carefully organised walking gear to goodness knew where instead of Naples—and apparently dispossessed, because of a foul-up on the computer with her hotel booking, she was now facing the reality of spending the first night of her much anticipated holiday sleeping rough on the streets of Amalfi.

Whilst she wasn't averse to roughing it—she'd travelled to enough festivals and partaken in enough camping trips for that not to be an issue—she'd been looking forward to falling into a comfortable bed after a crazy week of late nights and early mornings, and was not in the mood to laugh this off.

'But my ex-boyfriend booked a room in this hotel

months ago,' she explained again to the receptionist, her voice now projecting the disconcerting characteristic of a crow with a sore throat.

The intimidatingly poised receptionist pursed her blood-red lips and tightened her arms across her impressive cleavage. 'I'm sorry, *Signorina*. As I said, I have no record of your booking and we are fully booked. If you had the documents to prove it, or even the credit card it was booked with, I could perhaps do something for you, but as it is…' From the look on her face, she clearly wasn't keen on having someone as scruffy as Indigo messing up her beautifully appointed five-star hotel reception desk whilst also challenging her competency.

Panicky heat rushed to Indigo's face. 'As *I* explained, my *ex*-boyfriend booked the room so I don't have the credit card or documents. I assumed a booking reference number would be enough.'

The woman's helpless shrug, then her overemphasised shift in eye contact to the next person in line, tipped Indigo over the edge of frustration into fiery indignation. But before she could draw breath there was a movement behind her and a tall man in a beautifully cut casual suit stepped forwards to stand next to her at the desk.

'Pardon, mademoiselle,' he interjected smoothly, his fresh, spicy scent hitting her nose at the exact same moment his eyes locked with hers.

Indigo had never related to the expression of being 'swept off her feet' by a man before, but that was exactly how she felt right now. As if the power of his presence had physically lifted her into the air, her internal organs quivering as if she were in free fall. She gazed up at him, his unusual combination of whisky-brown eyes and sandy-blond hair keeping her transfixed as her pulse beat an enthusiastic rhythm in her throat. But apparently she didn't capture his interest in the same way because, after giving her a curt nod, he turned sharply away, bringing her back down to earth with a thump.

'I have a reservation,' he said to the receptionist in a deep, smoky, French-accented voice, which made Indigo think of the actors in the Gallic art house films she'd been so in love with during her college days.

Lounging against the desk, he held up his smartphone so the receptionist could see the screen and type the booking reference into her computer.

Indigo looked from one to the other in disbelief. She seemed to have been well and truly dismissed.

Something she'd become rather too familiar with recently.

Before she could open her mouth again to point out that they were both being utterly rude and that she wasn't going to be ignored like this, the receptionist shook her head and looked up at the Frenchman, her expression projecting a lot more contrition than when she'd dealt with Indigo.

'I'm sorry, *Signor*, I don't have a record of your booking.'

'That's not possible. Check again, please,' the man replied in a tone that clearly brooked no argument.

Indigo watched with a sense of self-righteous vindication as the receptionist typed the number in again, then checked something else on another screen, her shoulders stiffening as she finally accepted there was a problem with the booking system.

She seemed a little pale when she looked back up at him. 'My apologies, *Signor*,' she breathed. 'I don't know what could have happened. It appears there was a glitch with the computer and I've given your room away. I only have the honeymoon suite available now, but it would be my pleasure to let you stay there tonight. We will correct the mistake by tomorrow and I will have your original suite available for you then.'

Indigo frowned as she twigged what was going on.

'Hang on a second. Why didn't you offer *me* the honeymoon suite? I was here first!' she protested, feeling a cocktail of humiliation and umbrage warm her face again.

The woman's gaze slid to hers. 'Because the gentleman booked a *suite, Signorina*, so this room is more in his…*category*.' She gave Indigo a tight little smile as if to say, *That's not the word I was grasping for, but you get the message.*

'Okay—' the Frenchman began in his smooth, lyrical accent.

But even the strength of his charisma couldn't keep the bubble of anger from rising through Indigo's body.

'*Really?*' she spluttered, taking a step back to run a critical gaze over his long, lean body. 'You're *really* going to take the room when you can plainly see that *I was here first!*'

He turned to look at her again, his expression giving nothing away as his heavy-lidded gaze swept over her face.

She felt exposed, almost naked under his scrutiny, and had to fight not to wrap her arms around her body for protection against it. Locking her jaw, she stared him out, knowing from experience that not backing down was the only way she was going to get what she wanted. Or, in this case, what she needed—a comfortable bed for the night. Which had already been paid for!

A muscle twitched in the Frenchman's jaw as he kept his gaze fixed on hers. He really did have the most striking face, with prominent high-set cheekbones and a broad masculine brow above those mesmerising eyes. What was it about French men that made them so unutterably sexy? The ones she'd met throughout her life had all had the same confident, direct gaze that made her feel simultaneously appraised and giddily unnerved. It was as though he was scrutinising the whole of her exterior whilst also looking deep inside her.

The feeling of being so thoroughly examined made her whole body tingle.

She stared harder at him to combat her dip in concentration.

Something flashed in his eyes and the corner of his mouth lifted fractionally. Was he amused by her determination to win?

Scowling as frustration pricked at her skin, she opened her mouth to restate her case—but he beat her to it.

'You're right,' he said bluntly. 'You must have the room.'

Indigo blinked at him in surprise, snapping her mouth shut. This, she had not expected.

'Oh! Okay.' She frowned, a little dazed by how easy that had been. 'Really?'

Sighing, he ran a hand over his clean-shaven jaw. 'To be honest, *mademoiselle*, I'm too tired to argue. It's been—' he winced, his expression turning troubled '—an *intense* day for me and I want to relax before starting my walk tomorrow.'

'Wait—you're walking the coast too?' she asked in surprise. Looking at him, standing there in his expensive suit with his designer bags sitting prettily at his feet, she'd imagined he was here to do some upmarket sightseeing in the town, or perhaps conduct a high-powered business meeting in the hotel.

His eyes crinkled at the corners as he half frowned, half smiled. 'Is that so unlikely?' he asked, his voice tinged with playful irony.

The bottom fell out of her stomach. 'No! No, I guess not.'

'Anyway, what kind of a man would I be to leave a lady stranded in a strange town in the middle of the night?'

Something about the way he said this, with a twist of wry humour, stopped her from telling him she didn't need a *man's* help—that she'd managed perfectly well on her own for the last three months without one, despite the challenges she'd faced.

'But, *Signor*, there are no other rooms available in Amalfi!' the receptionist cut in before Indigo could form a reply. 'It's a busy time and all the hotels in the town are booked up. I know this because I've already phoned around for another traveller.'

The Frenchman turned to face her. 'You're telling me you can't find me an alternative room for the night?' he stated with unnerving calm.

She shrank away from his gaze, suddenly seeming a lot less self-assured than she had a few minutes ago. 'Yes, *Signor*, I'm so sorry,' she said, her swallow appearing to catch in her throat. 'I'll be able to give you the suite you booked from tomorrow, but tonight there aren't any other rooms available—'

'This is unacceptable,' he said quietly, but with a girder of steel to his voice. 'I do not expect this level of incompetence from an establishment like this. Fetch your manager.'

The receptionist's shoulders tensed as if she'd balled her fists and her eyes widened. 'I can't disturb him—he is sleeping right now and has given strict instructions not to be woken—'

'I don't care. Get him.' He leant forward, pressing his hands against the desk. 'Now.'

'Please, *Signor*, I'll lose my job,' she whispered. 'I'm new here and I can't afford to make any mistakes.' Her brow tensed as her eyes took on a look of abject panic.

The desperation in her voice made Indigo's stomach tighten as a wave of pity washed over her. She could see by the way the young woman's eyes had pooled with impending tears that she was both terrified of her boss and totally inexperienced in dealing with this level of cold assertiveness from a customer.

'Describe the suite to me,' Indigo blurted to the receptionist before the Frenchman could respond.

The receptionist turned to stare at her in surprise

before recovering quickly, using the question as a lifeline to pull her professional self back to safety. 'There is a beautifully appointed bedroom with a super king-sized bed and an en suite bathroom—'

'Does the bedroom door have a lock?' Indigo asked.

Out of the corner of her eye she saw the Frenchman turn to stare at her in baffled disbelief. She ignored him.

'Yes, *Signorina*,' the receptionist replied, looking confused to have her patter broken into with such an odd question, 'and the separate living area has the latest entertainment system—'

'And a large sofa?' Indigo cut in again.

The receptionist blinked hard and frowned, then her expression softened with a mixture of relief and gratitude as she realised where Indigo was going with this. This time she didn't falter with her answer. 'Absolutely! It is very comfortable—large enough to fully stretch out on. There is also a separate bathroom with a whirlpool tub and a waterfall shower.'

Indigo nodded decisively. 'Okay then, we'll share it.'

'What?' The word jumped from the Frenchman's mouth as if he'd not been able to stop it.

She took a breath and turned to face his incredulous gaze. 'I'll take the sofa in the living room, you can have the bedroom; that way we both get to sleep tonight.'

The Frenchman's brow crinkled in disdain. '*Non*. Thank you, but I don't think that's appropriate.'

She raised an eyebrow. 'I don't bite, you know.'

His mouth twisted into a wry smile. 'I'm sure you don't, but it seems improper to ask you to share your room with a strange man.'

'You don't seem that strange to me.' She cast him a smile, which he begrudgingly returned, one eyebrow raised.

'But, seriously, it's fine,' she said. 'I don't mind sharing and I'd hate to feel responsible for this woman losing her job.'

He flapped his hand, dismissing her concern. 'It wouldn't be your fault.'

She looked him hard in the eye. 'But I'd still blame myself and it would ruin my holiday. Anyway, it doesn't sound like you have a better option.'

He gave a gentle snort and shook his head, wearily rubbing his hand over his forehead, as he appeared to give her suggestion some serious consideration. 'Are you sure you're happy to do this?' he asked, his eyes dark with indecision.

'Yes, of course!' she said brightly. 'When life throws problems at you, you have to do whatever you can to make the best of a situation.' She produced a firm smile. 'Anyway, what kind of a *woman* would I be to send an exhausted man out into the night to sleep on the streets in such a beautiful designer suit?'

He looked at her intently for another few seconds, as if giving her the chance to change her mind, and when she resolutely kept her mouth shut he gave a sharp nod.

'Okay, but you take the bedroom so you can lock the door; that way you have no reason to feel unsafe. I'll take the sofa. I'll be up and out early in the morning so I won't be in your way.' Without waiting for her response, he bent down to scoop up his luggage.

'I'm getting up early myself,' she said to the top of

his head, her cheeks heating a little as she realised how defiant that sounded. For some reason she didn't want him to think she was some kind of lazy slob.

'Then we'll each have to pretend the other doesn't exist,' he said with a flash of droll humour in his eyes as he looked back up at her, pushing a hand through his hair as he righted himself.

An impossible feat, Indigo thought, her eyes following the movement of his long fingers and the way his hair fell perfectly back into place, as if it didn't dare defy him. There was no way a man like this could ever be ignored.

Turning back to the receptionist, he held out his passport. 'If you'll give us two key cards we'll find our own way up to the room.'

With an air of sombre apology, the receptionist checked the passport, then picked up Indigo's—which was still lying on the reception desk—and tapped something into her computer. After swiping a couple of key cards through a machine, she handed everything back to the Frenchman. 'There are extra blankets and pillows in the wardrobes. I hope you will be comfortable,' she said sheepishly, before scurrying away to serve someone who had just arrived at the other end of the desk.

Handing Indigo her passport and key card, he turned abruptly on his heel and, without another word, strode away from her, bags swinging from his hand.

Clearly he was a leader, not a follower.

Indigo paused for a moment, staring after him, suddenly feeling a little unsure of herself.

Had she really just offered to share a suite with a complete stranger?

She was so used to figuring out quick fixes at work it hadn't struck her exactly what she'd committed to until it was too late to back out of it.

As she watched him reach the elevator and jab the button to call it, exhaustion from the mad scramble to get her community café in good shape so she didn't have to worry about it whilst she was away hit her like a wallop to the gut. The last three months had been tough, filled with worry about whether the funding she'd applied for in order to keep it running would materialise, and it all seemed to be catching up with her now.

Ironically, this week away was supposed to be a break from the stress of it. Initially it had struck her as ridiculous to come on holiday when she had the possibility of losing everything hanging over her head, but she'd dropped the ball and made a few silly mistakes recently that, while fixable, had meant she'd cost the café some money it could ill afford. As her friend Lacey had jokingly pointed out, it would probably do both her and the café some good to have some time apart.

Added to which, all the travel and accommodation for this week had already been paid for and was non-refundable, so it would have been a waste of money *not* to come.

Wastage was something she felt very strongly about.

Anyway, it was too late to change her mind now—even if she let the Frenchman have the suite to himself. She didn't have the money to pay for a room in another hotel, let alone the energy to face the monumental task of finding one.

This was her only option.

Hurrying after him, she caught him up just as the elevator door opened with a smooth *swish*.

'Okay, let's do this,' she said, her words coming out a little breathlessly after her dash across the room.

He just smiled in a perplexed sort of way that made the skin prickle on the back of her neck, and gestured for her to walk into the elevator before him.

'No, no, after you,' she said, sweeping her own hand in an exaggerated arc towards the centre of the car.

Shaking his head in amusement, he stepped inside and moved to the back to allow her plenty of room to follow him in.

Once she was safely past the doors, he hit the button for their floor and the doors closed on them with another gentle *swish*.

Heavy silence fell between them.

Indigo shifted from one foot to the other.

Well, this is awkward.

'Perhaps we should introduce ourselves, since we're going to be suite-mates,' she said, raising a questioning eyebrow at him. 'I'm Indigo. Indigo Hughes.'

'Julien Moreaux,' he replied, catching her off guard by stepping forwards and kissing her gently on both cheeks.

Being English, she'd forgotten about this traditional French greeting and almost jumped away in shock, only managing to hold her nerve at the last second. His scent hit her nose again, even more intensely this time due to his proximity, and instinctively she breathed him in, intuiting cool nights after hot days, the crisp tang of cold wine in the sunshine and the musky scent of warm skin.

Delicious.

After he'd stepped back it took her a full couple of seconds to pull herself together again. She gave him a friendly smile, but what she really wanted to do was pull him back towards her, bury her face in the scoop of his neck and drag his scent deep into her lungs again.

What was wrong with her? She'd never had this kind of visceral response to a complete stranger before, but there was something so commanding about this man. He made her feel safe, somehow.

Oh, get a grip, Indigo!

The honeymoon suite was exquisite, decorated in those amazing heritage colours that Italians employed so effortlessly, the furniture simple but refined, with an art deco theme tying the room together. Romantic aspiration seemed to ooze from the walls, as if they'd been infused with the happiness of all the newlyweds that had stayed there over the years. She felt sure this place had to have been included in every *World's Best Honeymoon Suites* article written for the glossy magazines she judiciously avoided buying these days.

After thoroughly investigating the suite with her eyes, she turned to look at Julien and realised that he hadn't even glanced around him and was instead staring down at the screen of his phone.

Clearly he was already *au fait* with the finer things in life.

Shaking her head at his lack of interest, she went to

explore the bedroom, which was just as overwhelmingly beautiful as the rest of the suite. This whole experience was like stepping into a fantasy.

Despite her protests about it being a waste of money, Gavin, her ex, had insisted on booking the first night of their stay in this expensive hotel—he'd wanted to start the holiday in style—before spending the rest of the week moving between smaller, more basic places. So this would be her only chance for luxurious pampering.

She was going to have to make the most of it.

After grabbing a blanket and pillow for Julien from the wardrobe, she floated back out of the bedroom and dumped them on the sofa before turning to find he was still staring down at his phone, lost in his own world.

'Stay in the honeymoon suite a lot, do you?' she asked, edging her voice with dry amusement.

He glanced up at her and for a split second a dark expression flickered across his face. 'Only once.'

His change in demeanour unsettled her. 'You're married?' she asked to cover her discomfort.

'Not any more.'

She could have sworn the temperature dropped a few degrees.

'Oh. Sorry to hear that.'

He flipped her his teasing grin again, breaking the tension. 'You English are always sorry for something.'

'I was just being polite,' she said, bristling.

His grin deepened.

She cocked an eyebrow back at him.

He looked at her for a moment longer with amusement in his eyes before turning away to drop his bags next to a mosaic-tiled coffee table in the middle of the room. 'Well, I'm going to—what do you English say?—*crash out*,' he said.

That was her cue to leave. And not a moment too soon. Her whole body felt hot and tingly with the awareness of being alone with him.

'Me too,' Indigo said, backing towards the bedroom. 'So I guess I won't see you in the morning.'

'Probably not,' he said, flopping down on to the sofa and stretching his arms above his head.

She came to a halt in the doorway and watched with fascination as he put everything he had into the stretch, the pleasure of it rippling across his face as he released the tension in his muscles. Forcing herself not to run her eyes up and down the powerful length of his body, she gave a stiff bob of her head, then turned to walk into the bedroom, shutting the door firmly behind her, pushing away the ridiculous urge to lie down on top of him—chest to chest, thigh to thigh—just to feel the solid strength of him beneath her.

It brought it home to her how much she'd missed being touched, being held, just being physically close to someone since Gavin had left her. Now she had the time and space to think about it, the after-effects seemed to be coming out in the strangest of ways.

She turned the key decisively in the lock, hearing it click.

Flinging herself at Julien was definitely not the way to deal with things.

Okay, time to put the sexy Frenchman out of her mind and get practical.

Striding purposefully away from the door, she dropped the small rucksack she'd used as hand luggage on to the bed. Thank goodness she'd had the forethought to pack a few essentials into it for just such an occurrence.

Even so, after spending a lot of time planning for this trip, it was unnerving to find herself without all her carefully thought-out trekking gear. She didn't even have her walking boots with her, so she would have to walk for at least five hours each day in the trainers she'd changed into at the last second at the airport because her feet were so hot. What an unfortunate decision that had been.

Hopefully the airline would find her bag soon and send it to one of the hotels on the route. She'd left her details and itinerary with the lost luggage desk at the airport and they'd promised—after what seemed like hours of form-filling—to send it on once it had been located.

The biggest problem she faced was that she'd put half of her money and her emergency credit card into the lost backpack too, not wanting to carry it all in her hand luggage in case that was stolen. At least her breakfasts were already paid for, so she could eat heartily in the morning and maybe skip lunch in order to eke out what little cash she had to feed herself in the evenings. Just until her backpack turned up. Which would be okay. She was used to budgeting and eating frugally.

It would all be part of the adventure.

Emptying out her rucksack on to the bedspread, she took an inventory of what she had with her: one extra pair of knickers and one pair of socks—that she'd have to alternate with the ones she had on and wash each day—a toothbrush and a tiny tube of toothpaste, a spare T-shirt and a short cotton skirt which she'd interchange with the shorts and vest she had on, a pack of mints, a mascara that promised to give you 'Hollywood eyes' and her trusty liquid eyeliner, a packet of painkillers, her wallet and passport and a book on walking the Amalfi coast. She didn't even have her mobile phone with her, she realised with a lurch, because she'd packed that into her missing luggage too, determined to only use it for emergencies on the trip so that she'd make the most of the scenery and social life and not be constantly diverted by the online world.

After packing everything carefully back into the bag, she took a refreshing shower in the floor-to-ceiling marble bathroom, lathering herself with the zingy-smelling complimentary shower gel, before sliding between the crisp cotton sheets of the bed.

What luxury!

Stretching herself into a starfish shape, she brushed her fingertips over the smooth mahogany headboard and sighed hard, painfully aware of how much empty space there was on either side of her.

The cruel irony of staying in the honeymoon suite had not been lost on her.

In a parallel universe—where Gavin hadn't fallen in love with another woman—she'd be tumbling into bed with him right about now.

What would he have said about staying in this room? She pictured them laughing about it, ribbing each other about how much sex they should be having to keep up with all the former inhabitants. Out of nowhere a feeling of utter desolation hit her right in the chest. It had been three months since they'd split up and she'd not allowed herself to fall apart since the day it had happened, keeping herself busy and using this holiday as a bright spot to look forward to when she felt glum. But the realisation that this was it—that she was here now, on her own, and this was the reality of her situation suddenly brought her low.

She thumped the mattress on either side of her. She was *not* going to let it get her down.

As she'd learnt from an early age, crying and whinging didn't get you anywhere. That was what growing up in an all-male household and having four smart, alpha, and now highly successful older brothers would teach you. She'd never won an argument or topped a challenge by turning on the waterworks or asking for special dispensation, and that was the way she preferred it. Everything she'd achieved had been on her own merits. She'd fought just as hard—if not harder—than her brothers for her successes and she was proud of what she'd achieved.

Unfortunately, Gavin hadn't understood that drive to succeed on her own, and had cited her desire to pour too much time and energy into making her café a success and 'excluding him from parts of her life where he wasn't necessary' as the catalyst for their breakup. According to him, she treated him like one of her projects and acted as if she had more love for the strangers who frequented the café than for him. That had been particularly gutting to hear because she liked to think of herself as a perceptive and caring partner.

Pushing away the threatening gloom, she sat up and punched her pillows back into shape before flopping back down and wriggling further into the sumptuous bed.

Well, from this point on she was looking after herself.

Whilst she was here she was going to get some fresh air and exercise, meet people outside of her small sphere of work and recharge her batteries before returning home feeling refreshed and more positive about her future.

As she lay there, willing away the lingering tight feeling in her chest, something about her earlier head-to-head with Julien suddenly occurred to her. He'd conducted his whole conversation, even the bit with the receptionist, in English. Had he done that so as not to exclude her? Or was he just better at English than Italian? From her experience with him so far, she got the impression he'd be good at everything he did—he certainly exuded that kind of confidence.

Except for that moment when he'd talked about how *intense* his day had been. There had been a vulnerability to his voice that hadn't been there for the rest of the time.

Whatever could have affected him so deeply? Could it have something to do with his failed marriage?

Perhaps he, too, was here to get a new perspective on life after a bad breakup.

She knew first-hand how demoralising it could be

going through a divorce. Gavin, her ex, had been an utter mess when he'd first moved into her spare room— which she'd offered to him as a favour to a friend of a friend after his wife demanded they separate. At that point it had been six months since her father had passed away and she was finding it very lonely living in their empty family home without him, so it had been nice to have the company.

She'd found comfort in taking care of Gavin: making him healthy meals when she discovered he wasn't eating properly and sitting with him, listening to him talk through his pain and humiliation for hours and hours.

At the time, she hadn't anticipated it turning into a relationship, but there it was. In retrospect, it seemed inevitable now that something more would have developed between them, especially when they'd grown so emotionally close.

A prickle of disquiet ran up her spine.

She really should have asked Julien if he was okay when he'd mentioned his divorce. In her experience, whenever people brought up things like that it was usually because they wanted to talk to someone about it, but she'd blithely ignored his prompt, more concerned about rebutting his teasing. It was possible she could use her experience to help him out in some way, though. As one concerned human being to another. Considering he was here on his own, she wouldn't be surprised to find he didn't have anyone at home he could talk to about what he was going through.

Turning over and letting out a huge yawn, she told herself that if she saw Julien again on the walk she'd make an effort to check that he was okay, just to set her mind at rest. But that would be it. The whole experience with Gavin had made her very wary of getting romantically involved with a divorcee again—she never wanted to be someone's rebound relationship ever again.

So for now, she was going to put the sexy Frenchman—unnervingly close on the other side of the door—out of her mind.

CHAPTER TWO

The Ravello Circuit. A tricky walk with lots of steps. We recommend breaking the walk at the magnificent Villa Cimbrone gardens before visiting Ravello, then stopping for a scenic lunch break in Pontone...

JULIEN MOREAUX AWOKE to find the sun streaming in through the large windows of the honeymoon suite. He rubbed a hand across his bleary eyes, forcing his thoughts into some kind of coherent arrangement.

He was here, in Amalfi. Finally.

It hadn't mattered to him exactly where he'd end up when he'd asked his PA to book this break for him—all he'd stipulated was that he wanted somewhere where he could move from one place to another so he didn't feel trapped into having to see the same people in the same place every day—and he was pleased with her choice.

This walking holiday had been marked in his mind for some time as the beginning of the return to the way things were to be, and he'd been looking forward to losing himself in the monotony of hard exercise and self-imposed solitude.

Not that the solitude part had worked out well so far.

He grimaced as the events of the previous evening came back to haunt him. Sharing his suite with a bohemian idealist with an overblown zeal for life had not been an ideal start, but after sensing Indigo's desperation to fix the situation amicably and seeing the earnest pleading in her eyes, he'd known there was no way he could refuse her suggestion.

And he was tired of being the bad guy.

A huge yawn hit him and he rocked his head back against the soft cushions of the sofa, giving his body a long, hard stretch to wake up his cramped muscles.

Considering the way he was feeling this morning, he suspected, if he allowed himself, he could easily spend the whole week sleeping. Not that he was going to do that. He'd come here for a change of scene and a reprieve from the pressures of life and there was no way he was wasting his time in Italy staring at four walls. Even if they were as magnificent as the ones in this hotel.

This observation led his thoughts back to Indigo's wry comment about him being familiar with staying in the honeymoon suite.

A cold prickle ran across his skin.

The last time he'd been in a room like this he'd thought his life had been on the up and up, but look at him now, barely two years later, holidaying alone only hours after signing his divorce papers, with the ink of his signature still drying in his mind.

Swinging himself into a sitting position on the sofa, he stifled another yawn behind his hand and rubbed his face hard to get the blood circulating.

He really needed to get up and out before Indigo emerged; he didn't think he had the mental energy this morning to deal with another awkward scene with her.

Glancing towards the bedroom door, he was surprised to see it standing wide open.

Huh, weird. He checked his watch. Seven o'clock. So she hadn't been joking when she said she'd be up and out early too.

Hauling himself off the sofa, he went to investigate further.

'Indigo?' he called gently, so as not to startle her in case she was still in there.

There was no reply.

Poking his head around the doorway, he saw that the bed was empty, with the sheets pulled haphazardly back and the door to the en suite bathroom flung open.

She was gone.

That was a relief.

Feeling the tension leave his shoulders, he went back into the living area and pulled out the clothes he was going to wear for his walk today, before heading off for an invigorating shower.

There had been something about her that intrigued him, though, he mused as he felt the soothing water cascade over his aching back—her determination and bolshie confidence perhaps. She certainly wasn't his usual type, with her leggy, voluptuous figure and short, feathery bobbed hair in a shocking shade of red, which had reminded him of the colour of the sea of poppy fields behind the house in Provence where he'd grown up. Historically, he'd always been attracted to petite women, usually blondes, with more of a delicate air about them, but there was something incredibly alluring about Indigo, with her wide, open smile and playful gaze.

She was sexy.

He shut off the water and reached for a towel, drying himself vigorously. If he was being honest, she'd probably only captured his interest because it had been refreshing to meet a woman who didn't want to take something from him and just walk away for once. He was used to being the one to sort out other people's problems, and it had been a long time since someone had done something benevolent for him.

It would be better if he didn't see her again, though, he told himself, flinging the towel into the bath. He wasn't in any state to be sociable at the moment.

After shaving off his morning stubble, he pulled on shorts, a light breathable T-shirt and the brand new walking boots that his PA had sourced for him, and gave himself a nod in the mirror.

Okay. Now he was ready to face the day and whatever it might bring.

He checked his email on his phone as he travelled down in the elevator ready to grab some breakfast in the restaurant, pleased to find there wasn't anything that needed his urgent attention. That was sure to change by the end of the week, though.

After dropping by the reception desk to confirm they'd have the suite that he'd booked available for him when he returned from his hike, he was about to walk away to get his breakfast when curiosity about Indigo's situation stopped him. He should probably check whether he was likely to come across her again, just so he could prepare himself for it.

He turned back.

'Did you find another room here for the woman I shared the honeymoon suite with last night?' he asked the receptionist.

Confusion flickered across her face, until recollection seemed to strike her. 'The lady from your suite checked out, *Signor*.'

That must mean she wasn't doing the Ravello circuit and coming back to Amalfi today, which meant there wasn't any danger of bumping into her again.

Good, that was good, because he'd feel compelled to acknowledge her if they saw each other again, which would encroach on his much anticipated alone time.

'Okay, thanks,' he said, giving the receptionist a nod before heading over to the breakfast room at the other end of the lobby.

Considering it was still pretty early, the place was already buzzing with guests, and he grabbed the only spare table near the back wall. After seating himself, he took a look around him, soaking up the animated vibe. Quite a few of the guests seemed to be dressed in walking gear, like him. Clearly the coastal walk was a big draw to the area. Hmm, perhaps it wouldn't be as solitary an experience as he was hoping, he reflected with a twinge of annoyance.

A flash of bright red on the other side of the room

caught his eye and, heart thumping, he quickly leant back, using the couple sitting at the table next to him as cover. Grabbing the menu in front of him and holding it to hide most of his face, he gradually leant forwards again to take another look. As he suspected, it was Indigo, standing at the breakfast buffet with her back to him, her hair damp and gleaming and her small rucksack slung over one arm.

She looked refreshed and energised this morning, her skin glowing with health and her posture relaxed. His gaze followed her as she moved smoothly along the buffet, seemingly checking over her options before making her choice. She grabbed an apple and a couple of bread rolls from the display and he stared in baffled amusement as she slipped them into the gaping opening of her bag. After a quick check around, she seemed to discern that no one was watching her and popped a couple of slices of Parma ham and a small bottle of mineral water from the cooler section in there too. Next went in a pat of butter and a little package of cheese.

Evidently deciding she had enough food stashed away, she strolled nonchalantly away from the buffet, slinging her bag over her shoulder and shoving her hands deep into the pockets of her shorts. He half expected her to start whistling *Food, Glorious Food* as she made her getaway.

She was staying in a five-star hotel, but she was too cheap to buy her own lunch? What was that about?

He allowed himself one last look at her long, shapely legs as she disappeared out of the room, then turned to gesture for the waitress to bring him some coffee.

And that, he guessed, feeling an odd twinge in his chest, would probably be the last he'd ever see of Indigo Hughes.

Indigo had thought she was in pretty good shape. She went to the gym at least a couple of times a week and opted to walk around London as much as possible instead of jumping on public transport, but by the time she'd climbed what seemed like a thousand steps leading away from Amalfi—pausing on her journey to walk through the ancient brick-walled walkways hung with canopies of vibrant greenery in the Villa Cimbrone gardens—then on to the quaint little town of Ravello, she realised her fitness levels were nothing like as good as she'd imagined.

Still, she'd made it here without incident, and after wandering around the quiet streets crammed with cool artisan shops and visiting the simple but atmospheric cathedral, it was a relief to walk downhill to the little village of Pontone and stop for a rest and to eat her lunch.

Sitting on a wide grassy viewpoint which looked out over the dramatic drop down to the coast, she was just about to take the final bite of the sandwich she'd made out of the food she'd filched from the breakfast buffet when she noticed a familiar figure making his way across the grass in the direction of the *trattorias* that, according to her guide, were favoured by walkers on the route because of the incredible views from their balconies.

After spending the whole morning trying not to think about the sight of Julien lying bare-chested on the sofa, looking utterly divine in repose as she tiptoed past him, she was disconcerted to see him again in the flesh. Not that she was going to let that stop her from being friendly. She'd made that promise to herself to check he was okay here on his own, so that was what she was going to do. Just because he was ridiculously sexy and ever so slightly intimidating it didn't mean she couldn't have a friendly chat with him.

'Hi there,' she called as he came level with where she was sitting.

He didn't appear to hear her.

'Julien! Hey, Julien, over here!' she shouted this time. She could have sworn she saw him flinch before turning to look over to where she was sitting. He raised a hand and gave her a nod of acknowledgement, before turning back and continuing on his journey.

Huh.

Perhaps he assumed she wouldn't want to be disturbed whilst eating her lunch. Yes, that must be it; he couldn't be deliberately avoiding her.

Could he?

No—she was being paranoid.

Jumping up and grabbing her daypack, she made after him, having to pick up her pace in order to catch up with him before he strode out of sight.

'Hey, Julien, wait!' she called, a little out of breath by the time she reached him.

He turned around and gave her a look of expectant concern. 'Are you okay?' he asked, his gaze flicking behind her as if he was worried she was being pursued.

'I'm fine,' she panted, 'just wanted to check you're

enjoying your day. You seemed a little—er—' she flapped a hand at him '—stressed yesterday.'

He took a small step backwards and let out a sharp snort. 'Yes, I'm enjoying it so far.' A small frown flickered across his face. 'Thank you.'

There was a pause while she waited for him to ask if she was having a good time too.

He didn't.

'Okay, good.' She clapped her hands together awkwardly. 'Well, I just wanted to say hi. So, hi!' she blurted, sincerely hoping he'd assume the blush travelling up her neck was a flush from the sun and her mad dash across the grass.

'Hi,' he replied flatly, folding his arms across his chest.

There was another heavy pause where he blinked at her, as if waiting for her to make her excuses and leave. Well, she wasn't going to. She'd learnt over the last year whilst working at the café that just because someone seemed unfriendly when you first spoke to them, it didn't necessarily mean they didn't want to talk to you. They were probably just distracted by something they'd been thinking about, or they were hungry, or concerned about the tightness of their trousers or something. Not that it appeared as though any of his clothes weren't fitting him perfectly. In fact, he looked as if he'd just stepped off a page in one of the hiking gear magazines she'd pored over whilst preparing for the holiday, before realising she could afford exactly none of the items in it.

'Did you like Ravello? All those steps up to it nearly

killed me!' she joked, cringing inside at the hint of desperation in her voice.

He didn't even break a smile. 'Yes, it was an interesting place.' His brow creased into a frown. 'They told me at the reception desk you'd checked out. I didn't expect to see you on this circuit today.'

She stiffened, wondering why on earth he seemed so irritated about her walking the same route as him.

'I have another hotel in town booked for tonight. A better organised one, I hope,' she said, shrugging off her discomfort and forcing a smile on to her face.

'Okay. *Bon.*' He took a deliberate step backwards, then froze as her words seemed to sink in. 'Do you mean you're staying in Amalfi again tonight?'

Another wave of warmth began to creep up her neck. 'Yup.'

His brow crinkled in confusion. 'Then why are you moving hotels after only one night?'

She shifted uncomfortably. 'I like to change things up. It keeps me on my toes.'

And I can't afford to stay in that hotel again, not that I'm admitting that to you, Monsieur Moneybags.

He nodded slowly, his gaze searching hers as if he was trying to rootle out a lie.

She just raised both eyebrows at him, determined not to give in and blurt out the truth, trying to ignore the way her pulse had sped up.

Letting out a sharp huff of a laugh, Julien broke eye contact and glanced behind him as if looking for an excuse to leave. Not that she could blame him; the conversation wasn't exactly flowing well and she was tempted to slink away herself. But she wasn't going to; she was going to see this through to the bitter end, as a matter of personal fulfilment.

'So, are you going to try one of those *trattorias* for your lunch?' she pressed, nodding in the direction he'd been heading.

He closed his eyes for a second and pulled in a sharp breath, then smiled politely. '*Oui*. I didn't have the forethought to bring any food with me.' He gestured towards the remains of her sandwich, which was still clutched in her hand. 'Where did you get your lunch today?' The dry irony in his tone suggested there was more to his question than a simple polite query.

He must have seen her take the food from the buffet. The realisation sent a prickle up her spine. Normally she would never have done such a thing, hating the idea of stealing anything from anyone, but with the limited funds she had available until her bag turned up, it was necessary to bend her rules a little.

'I purloined it from the breakfast buffet,' she admitted, forcing herself to keep her chin up and her gaze locked with his. 'I thought the least the hotel could do was gift me a lunch after their mess-up with the room last night. Anyway, a place like that always puts out more than is consumed. I was helping with their wastage problem,' she finished, aware that her tone was edged with defensiveness.

His eyes crinkled at the corners as his wry smile deepened. 'Don't worry; your secret is safe with me,' he murmured, leaning closer and enveloping her in his delicious scent.

It was all she could do not to take a great gulping breath of it through her nose. What was it that made his smell so enticing to her? Was this what people called the pheromone effect? She'd never experienced it before.

'Thanks,' she deadpanned.

He gave her a curt nod. 'Well, I'm going to go and eat.'

'Okay, enjoy,' she said, disappointed that he was leaving now. Despite his standoffishness, she'd enjoyed chatting with him after spending her morning alone. All the other English-speaking walkers she'd encountered on the route seemed to be part of a group, which she hadn't had the courage to try and break into yet.

She watched him stride away, trying not to stare at the way he moved his large, fit body with such powerful grace.

Judging by his troubled mood, she guessed he must be struggling with some serious emotional turmoil, which she knew from personal experience could make for a pretty lonely existence. She hated to see people in pain, especially if she thought she could do something to help.

Well, she'd just have to keep an eye out for him, just in case he fancied some no-strings company later.

CHAPTER THREE

*Back in Amalfi. Make sure you take advantage of
the wonderful selection of restaurants and eateries after visiting the imposing cathedral in the
centre of the town...*

AFTER THOROUGHLY ENJOYING the solitude of his walk
earlier in the day, Julien had been looking forward to
finding a place to grab a peaceful lunch when Indigo
had run over and accosted him.

It had taken everything he'd had not to be rude and
pretend he hadn't heard her calling out to him, then
continue with their stilted conversation when it became
clear she wasn't going to let him get away without ex-
tracting some kind of information out of him.

He wasn't sure why she'd been so keen to chat. Perhaps she was lonely and hadn't found any other English speakers to buddy up with. He hoped she'd got the
message that he preferred to holiday on his own now
though, and wouldn't bother coming over to talk to him
should their paths cross again.

A niggle of shame twisted in his gut. He felt bad

about being so unfriendly, but she'd picked the wrong time to try and get to know him.

If that had been her objective.

Perhaps she was looking for something more. If that was the case, she was bang out of luck. After the train wreck of his marriage, he wanted nothing to do with women and relationships again for a very long time.

Even spirited ones with legs that went on for miles and eyes you could get lost in.

When he got back to the hotel, he took a long cooling shower then a refreshing nap before striking out for dinner, strolling through the centre of Amalfi on the way to the restaurants on the marina that the hotel receptionist had recommended he try.

Diverted by the magnificence of the *Duomo* in the town centre, he climbed the wide steps and walked through the Arabic style Cloister of Paradise, looking out through the grand archways at the panoramic view of the town, with its pastel-coloured stone buildings wrapped with iron balconies.

He knew what he was looking at should have blown him away, but ever since his life had fallen to pieces he'd had trouble finding pleasure in things. He felt desensitised to beauty, as if he was viewing it from inside a plastic bubble. Nothing seemed to touch him any more.

Shaking off the building tension at the base of his skull, he was just about to turn and walk back to the steps when a bright flash of red caught his eye.

Was that Indigo again?

Craning his neck, he tried to see past a crowd of tourists blocking his view and catch another glimpse of her so he could make sure to walk in the opposite direction, but she seemed to have disappeared. Was his brain playing tricks on him? No, it must have been her. That hair colour was so unusual it couldn't be someone else with the exact same shade—and he knew for a fact she was staying in Amalfi tonight.

Walking slowly down the steps, he forced himself to take a deep breath and relax, telling himself it was unlikely they'd cross each other's paths when it was so busy.

Reaching the Popolo fountain in the middle of the piazza, he sat down on the stone edge of it and ran his fingers through the water, enjoying the cooling effect on his skin. What was wrong with him today? His heart seemed to be racing and his palms felt sweaty.

The heat must be getting to him.

Someone sat down next to him and on impulse he glanced round to see who it was.

'Fancy seeing you here,' Indigo said, with a mischievous lift of her eyebrow.

He snorted and shook his head at his terrible luck. What was it about this woman that kept drawing them together?

'It's a small town centre; I guess we were bound to bump into each other at some point,' he said wearily.

She leant back on her hands and studied him. 'Are you off to forage for some supper?'

He raised his eyebrows, bemused. 'Forage?'

'Looking for a place to eat.'

'Oui.'

'On your own?'

'Oui.' He tensed, anticipating what was coming next.

'You're welcome to join me if you'd like,' she said brightly, confirming his fear. 'I was just about to grab a slice of pizza at one of those small family-run eateries just off the square.'

'You mean the cafés with the plastic tables? *Non—*' he began to say, but she cut him off.

'You'd be doing me a favour,' she said. 'I've been on my own all day and I'm beginning to have conversations with myself out loud, which is never a good sign. If you don't come and have dinner with me there's a good chance I'll be arrested by the end of the night and taken to a secure facility.' She sat up and folded her arms. 'Anyway, you owe me.'

He frowned, perplexed. 'What for?'

'For letting you share my room.'

'Your room?'

'I was there first, remember?'

He sighed, fighting a smile. 'How could I forget?'

'So what do you say? Can I tempt you with a slice of pizza?' She looked so hopeful it made something twist in his chest. But he needed to stay strong.

'I'm going to try out one of the restaurants down on the marina,' he said, giving her an apologetic look. 'Apparently they have fantastic à la carte menus with a good selection of locally caught fresh fish and seafood. Word has it the lobster spaghetti is not to be missed.'

Her eyes seemed to glaze over as if she was picturing the food he'd described. 'Sounds awful,' she joked, flashing an impertinent grin. 'Anyway, those places are a total tourist rip-off.'

'And the pizza joints aren't?'

Spreading out her hands, she gestured around the square. 'They're part of the local colour. You can eat overpriced gourmet food in Paris, or wherever you're from. Come and support the underdog for once.' She stared at him hard, like she'd done the previous night, dipping her head to one side and looking up at him through her thick black lashes, and something twisted again inside him—then broke.

Despite his earlier determination to keep to himself tonight, he realised he had no choice but to go and eat a huge greasy slice of pizza with this woman. Maybe then she'd leave him alone.

'Sure.' He threw up his hands in surrender. 'Pizza sounds good.'

'Great!' she said, breaking into a huge smile.

He hoped she wasn't going to read too much into this. Whilst he was prepared to spend the next hour with her, he didn't want her thinking he wanted to buddy up for the whole week.

As they walked away from the piazza towards one of the back streets that housed the pizza outlets, they passed a homeless person slumped on a filthy-looking rug next to one of the souvenir shops. Out of the corner of his eye, he saw Indigo reach into her pocket, then discreetly drop a handful of coins into an empty hat by the side of the man, before strolling on as if nothing had happened.

As soon as they'd ordered their slices of pizza and drinks from a very jolly waiter at a café with red plastic tables and chairs arranged out on the pavement, Indigo excused herself and went inside to find the bathroom and splash some cool water on to her face.

Maybe insisting on bringing Julien here had been a little extreme, she deliberated as she patted her face dry with a paper towel. He'd not exactly been enthusiastic about taking her up on the offer of company—but she couldn't shake the concern that it would have been a miserable experience for him, eating dinner on his own, and she was pretty sure if she was patient he'd thaw out eventually.

Sometimes people put up barriers for whatever reason and you had to coax them out of their shell. She'd seen it a lot throughout her time running her café and evening classes. People could appear to be confident on the outside, but when you dug a little deeper it became apparent they were dealing with some tough issues and putting a brave face on things. Often they just needed someone to ask if they were okay, then listen to them.

Which was exactly what she'd done for Gavin, she remembered with a lurch. Not that he'd appreciated it in the end.

Sighing, she rubbed a hand over her face. Was she setting herself up for more trouble here, getting involved in Julien's drama?

She stared into the mirror, looking deep into her own eyes. No. Because this wasn't going to turn into anything more than a brief encounter—hopefully just one of many connections she'd make during her week here. She was here to socialise and have fun, new experiences this week after all, but that was all it would be.

Pulling a face at herself, she smoothed down her hair then pushed back her shoulders, wishing she'd had something other than her walking clothes to put on tonight. It wasn't that she wanted to impress Julien exactly, but she felt scruffy next to his overt sophistication, and less confident because of it.

Returning to the table, she saw that the waiter had brought their slices of pizza, as well as a beer for Julien and a glass of tap water for her.

Julien looked so strikingly out of place—sitting there on his cherry-red plastic chair in his designer jeans and beautifully cut open-necked shirt, with his golden hair swept back from his face and aviator sunglasses perched on his head as he read something on his smartphone— that she couldn't help but smile.

Taking her seat, she gave him a friendly nod as he looked up to acknowledge her return.

'Great, the food arrived while I was away; I love it when that happens,' she said, picking up her glass and taking a sip of water to cover a sudden bout of nerves at being there with him.

He just looked at her as if she was slightly loopy.

Swallowing hard, she put her glass down and leaned forwards, propping her arms on the table. 'So, tell me, Julien, why did you choose to walk the Amalfi coast?' she asked brightly in an attempt to get the conversation started.

He took his sunglasses off his head and slid them on to his nose so all she could see now was her own reflection in the lenses. 'It seemed like a good place to get away from it all.'

'Apart from all the tourists.' She gave him a smile, which he didn't return.

'I didn't realise how popular this place was.'

'You mean you didn't do your homework? Somehow I find that hard to believe,' she said.

He frowned. 'Really? Why?'

'I don't know... You just seem very—*together*. Very—*businesslike*.'

He huffed out a dry laugh and picked up his beer bottle, taking a long pull. 'Why did you choose to come here?' he asked, gesturing to their surroundings with the neck of the bottle.

She paused, arranging her answer in her mind. 'I've wanted to do this walk for ages and I finally got round to booking it this year,' she said, uncomfortably aware of a jolt of sadness in her chest. She and Gavin had talked about coming here since they'd got together, when things had been good between them. Before he'd started to resent her.

Julien leant back in his seat and studied her. 'Do you often holiday alone?'

'No, just this time.' She took a breath, deciding she might as well be straight with him.

'Actually, I was supposed to come here with my boy-friend, but we split up three months ago. He didn't want to come with his new partner, so I figured, since it was non-refundable, I may as well use it as a chance to get away for a bit.' She was aiming for a breezy and upbeat tone of voice, but from the look on Julien's face she suspected she must have fallen well short.

Still, perhaps her confession would open up an opportunity for him to talk about his own situation.

'How about you? Were you supposed to come here with someone?' she asked, perhaps a little desperately.

He avoided her gaze, looking instead at the waiter who was busying about nearby. *'Non,'* was all he said, picking up his slice of pizza and taking a large bite.

'Oh.' She tapped her toe gently against the plastic leg of the table, then picked up her own slice and studied it, uncomfortably aware that she'd lost her appetite now.

'Well, it's really nice to be here, anyway,' she continued, to cover the now rather prickly silence. 'I haven't had a holiday in a couple of years—if you don't count the four days I spent at my oldest brother's house over Christmas, which wasn't exactly a relaxing break. Three of my brothers have kids—one of them has four boys— so it was more like staying in a soft play gym crossed with a zoo.'

Picking up his beer, Julien took another long pull. 'You don't have your own kids?' he asked.

There was a sharp spasm in her chest. She'd fantasised about her and Gavin having kids, once upon a time. Another thing to mourn the loss of. 'Not yet. Hopefully one day. I'm sure it'll happen when it's the right time.'

He grimaced as if he had a bad taste in his mouth. 'The right time,' he repeated flatly.

'Yeah, I firmly believe that kids turn up when you most need them to.'

Looking over the top of his sunglasses, he gave her a withering stare.

Irritation pricked at her skin. 'So I'm guessing you

don't have kids either?' she asked, determined to ignore his negativity.

'*Non.*' The word was terse and had a definite full stop at the end.

'But you'd like to, one day?'

'Can we change the subject?' he said levelly, but with an undertone of steel.

'Um, sure.' Clearly she'd hit a nerve.

Perhaps it was for the best that they talk about something else anyway. The subject wasn't exactly an inspiring one for her now that she was single.

Indigo nibbled at the crust of her pizza while she thought of a new topic of conversation.

'Your English is very good. Where do you live?'

'In Paris, but I conduct a lot of business in the English language.'

'Oh, yeah?'

For the first time that night he seemed to relax, pushing his sunglasses up on to his head again and sitting back in his chair. '*Oui.* My business acquires and renovates high-end holiday homes in France for clients all over the world. We also source and maintain corporate Parisian apartments for executives to live in whilst they conduct business in France.'

'Nice.'

'I enjoy it.'

'Lucrative.'

'*Oui.*'

'Good for you.'

'What about you? What do you do?' He took another large bite of his pizza.

'I run a café that uses mostly surplus and past *best before date* food from supermarkets and restaurants. We sell affordable meals for people on low incomes so they can come and get a square meal at least a couple of times a week. Since we opened, we've had a lot of elderly gentlemen come in who've lost their wives and have no idea how to cook, so I started running cookery lessons in the evenings aimed specifically at people like them, to give them a grounding in making basic, healthy meals for themselves at home. It's going well so far, but it's been hard work. We rely a lot on donations and public grants so there's loads of form filling and face-to-face negotiating, and quite a bit of pleading on bended knee.'

She took a large bite of her food to punctuate her monologue, not wanting to think about what would happen to the café if the next lot of funding didn't come through.

'I imagine you're very good at the negotiating part,' he said with a twist in his smile.

'Usually,' she said through a mouthful of pizza, smiling back at him with her eyes. It felt good to finally hit on a subject he wanted to talk about.

'It's hard work to keep a project like that adequately funded, though. There's a constant threat of grants being pulled or reduced, so I spend a lot of my time looking for new sources of cash. It's hand to mouth in every way, but we make it work.'

'Did you set it up by yourself?' The last of his pizza disappeared into his mouth.

'Initially, but I have a dedicated team of both paid

workers and local volunteers now.' She took another bite of her own food, aware that she needed to eat quickly now to catch up.

'That's impressive. No wonder you need a holiday.'

'Yeah, I've put in some very long days this past year. It's never going to make me rich, but it makes me happy.' At least it had, until her relationship with Gavin ended because of it.

Julien studied her again, this time with a small pinch between his brows.

'What?' she asked, swiping at her chin, worried that she had cheese strings dangling from it.

'I was just thinking it's good to meet someone with such drive and ambition.'

She smiled back in gratified surprise, feeling warmth pool in her belly. Putting her food back on the plate, she wiped her greasy fingers on the paper napkin next to it. 'Thanks. I've always wanted to run my own business— I hate the idea of working for other people for my entire life.' She took a breath. 'I think I was meant to do what I do.'

He snorted gently. 'You're a strong believer in fate. I suppose you're one of those people who think everything happens for a reason?'

'Sure am.' She stared at her pizza, wondering whether she could force down another bite. 'You've just got to keep positive and everything will work itself out in the end.'

When she looked up at him she was disturbed to see his expression had switched to a mixture of amusement and derision.

She frowned, riled by his change in attitude. 'What's so wrong with that?'

He shrugged and stared off into the distance. 'It's total claptrap.' He enunciated the word *claptrap* with some relish.

'It's not claptrap. It's called having a constructive outlook on life.'

Julien grunted and took another long sip of his beer. 'I suppose you believe in fairy tales too.'

'You must believe in happy-ever-afters if you got married,' she pointed out.

His gaze snapped back to hers. 'Maybe. Once. But divorce will knock that kind of naivety right out of you.'

She jumped as he thumped his beer bottle down on to the table between them, and there was an edgy pause as the word 'divorce' buzzed in the air between them like an irritating fly.

'Why did the two of you split up?' she asked gently, relieved they were finally getting to the crux of the matter.

He sighed and folded his arms. 'You know, I don't really want to talk about it. I came on this walk to forget about what went wrong in my life and look forward to a future on my own.' He over-enunciated the word 'own' this time.

Indigo bristled at his bluntness. 'That sounds kind of lonely.'

'Lonely sounds pretty good to me right now.'

The hollow look in his eyes disturbed her.

'You know, if you *did* want to talk about it, I'd be happy to listen,' she said.

His expression flashed with exasperation. 'I don't need some *amateur* psychoanalysing me this week, thanks.'

The stab of hurt she experienced must have shown on her face, because he gave a guttural sigh and shook his head.

Pushing his chair back from the table, he stood up and pulled a handful of notes out of his pocket, tossing them on to the table. 'I don't think I'm the kind of company you're looking for right now, Indigo,' he said tersely, dropping his glasses back down to cover his eyes. 'It's better if we don't spend any more time together. Enjoy the rest of your vacation.'

Without even glancing back, he strode away, his shoulders hunched and his arms hanging stiffly by his sides.

The whole surface of her skin felt hot and prickly with indignation as she stared after him, his words echoing cruelly through her head.

How rude! She'd just wanted to check he was okay here on his own.

Not feeling lost and alone and isolated.

But okay. Fine! If that was the way he wanted it she wouldn't bother trying to be friendly any more.

Swallowing down the painful lump in her throat, she rummaged around in her bag for her purse.

What was wrong with her? She didn't seem to be able to step away from other people's problems, even on holiday.

She shouldn't be spending her precious free time with someone who had such a cynical view about love either, she told herself, yanking the money out of the notes compartment. She needed to surround herself with positivity and optimism right now.

Slamming her money down on the table next to his, she got up from her chair, set her shoulders back and walked in the opposite direction of the one he'd taken.

From this point on she would do as he asked and make a concerted effort to avoid any further contact with Monsieur Julien Moreaux.

CHAPTER FOUR

On to Praiano. A tough day's walk and the first leg of your journey west...

JULIEN KNEW HE shouldn't have kept on drinking after leaving Indigo at the table, but he'd needed to do something to numb the mortification that had trickled through him like ice water when he thought about how bitter and miserable he'd sounded. The look of hurt on her face after his blunt rejection of her offer of friendship had stayed imprinted on his mind's eye till he'd finally managed to wash it away with his fourth beer.

This was exactly why he'd decided to spend the week on his own. The last thing he'd wanted was to let his frustration over the failure of his marriage ruin the first proper break he'd had in a very long time, let alone affect someone else's holiday.

He took another long pull on his water bottle as he slogged along the rocky coastal path towards Praiano, willing the throbbing pain behind his eyes to dissipate. Because of his hangover, he'd started the walk later than he'd intended, and was paying for it now by having to trek hard through the midday sun to make up for the time he'd lost.

According to the hotel receptionist, there should be a small *tratorria* about an hour's walk from where he was. He was looking forward to eating a nourishing, carb-heavy meal to pick him up and give him the boost of energy he needed to get through the rest of the journey.

He attempted to while away the time by thinking through the next stages of a new build he'd been over-seeing before coming here but, to his chagrin, Indigo's hurt expression kept popping back into his head. The worst thing, he finally accepted as he struggled along, was that he'd found himself beginning to like her as she'd revealed more about herself—particularly when she'd talked with such passion about the café and cook-ing classes she'd set up to cater for vulnerable members of her community.

He couldn't help but compare her to his ex-wife Celine, who, without even discussing it with him, had given up her job as a legal secretary as soon as they were married, spending her days shopping and watch-ing reality TV instead. He'd not made a fuss at the time, thinking she'd probably grow bored after a while, but she hadn't. Instead, she'd looked to him to provide all her entertainment and society, as well as supporting her financially.

Which had been fine for a time.

After years of having his nose to the grindstone and putting his business ventures before his personal hap-piness, meeting the beautiful, wild and carefree Celine had been like being caught up in a cyclone of desire, and his formerly work-orientated life had suddenly become a whirl of new experiences and unpredictable passionate moments.

Until the bad luck that had changed everything for them, and his once happy-go-lucky wife turned into someone he didn't recognise any more.

Pushing against the surge of discontent that continued to live within him, forever threatening to pull him under, he strode on, picking up his pace as the *trattoria* finally swung into view.

He trudged up the steps to the seating area inside, now desperate for some shade and sustenance, and managed to secure a small table near the door, slumping into the chair with a sigh of relief.

A loud squall of laughter floated over from the other side of the restaurant, and he turned around to see what was going on.

There was a large group of walkers all crowded around a table at the back, which heaved with the remains of what had obviously been a hearty lunch.

The only person who didn't have a large empty plate in front of her, but was instead nursing a glass of what looked like water, was Indigo. She was talking animatedly with a ruddy-cheeked middle-aged man sitting next to her, and the rest of the group were leaning in, listening to the story she was telling. There was another roar of laughter as she concluded her tale, and she sat back with a wide, captivating smile on her face, then drained the last of her drink and stood up.

His eyes were immediately drawn to her long, shapely legs as she stepped back from the table, and his heart rate picked up as his mutinous mind conjured up the impression of how they might feel wrapped around him.

He turned away quickly as she went to grab her bag, not wanting her to catch him watching her, aware of a heavy pull of disgust with himself in the pit of his belly.

What was he doing? This was ridiculous. He wasn't going to cower here like an idiot. He looked up as she walked past his table, readying himself to face the music, but she didn't notice him sitting there, her eyes looking a little glazed as she made for the door.

Had she eaten anything since breakfast? He suspected not, judging by what he'd just witnessed, and now she was about to walk for another few hours in the hottest part of the day.

He shifted in his seat, irritated by her foolhardiness, aware of an achy tension in his body. Not that it was any of his concern. She was a grown woman who could fend for herself. If she weren't, surely she wouldn't have come on this walking holiday alone?

Except that she wasn't supposed to.

The thought gave him pause.

But no, she'd made the decision to come on her own and just because they'd shared an association, it didn't mean he should feel responsible for her well-being.

He watched out of the window as she walked slowly away, then turned back to the matter in hand.

Looking after his own needs—in the form of lunch.

An hour later, he was back on the path, trudging towards a viewpoint where he planned to take another quick break and stare out across at the swell of the ocean while he caught his breath.

There was a long bench sitting proudly on the apex of the clearing, shaded by a fig tree, its branches heavy with fruit. And on that bench, stretched out with her head on her rucksack, was Indigo.

Julien came to a sudden halt and stared at her, his pulse rattling through his veins.

She looked exhausted, her face pink and the exposed part of her neck and upper chest glistening with perspiration in the heat.

His heart gave a jolt at the sight.

He really should keep walking and leave her alone to rest; she hadn't seen him standing there yet, so now would be a good time to turn around and keep on going. He could take a break another half mile or so on.

But he didn't move. Something was stopping him. Some misplaced sense of responsibility.

Sighing, he made his way over to her, resigned to checking that she was okay, thereby clearing his conscience.

She sat up quickly when she noticed him approaching, pulling her rucksack on to her knees and looping her arms around it, as if using it for protection against him.

Did she really have everything she needed for the whole week in that small bag? he wondered fleetingly. His own luggage was about three times the size of hers—hence getting it transported by courier from place to place as he progressed along the walk.

'Hi, Indigo,' he said as he came to a halt in front of her.

Her shoulders stiffened and she gave him a curt nod. 'Julien.'

'How are you today?'

'Fine, thanks. You?' From the tone of her voice she was clearly struggling to be polite.

'Hung-over,' he admitted, giving her a rueful smile.

She didn't smile back.

Tense silence crackled between them, and Indigo's stomach took the opportunity to rumble loudly.

'Have you eaten enough today?' he asked, aiming for an airy, upbeat tone but not quite pulling it off.

She tightened her arms around her bag and gave him a level stare. 'That depends on what you mean by enough.'

'Did you eat lunch?'

There was a pause, where she seemed to be arguing with herself about whether to answer him truthfully. 'No,' she said finally.

'Why not?'

'I wasn't hungry.'

There was an edge to her voice that told him she wasn't in the mood to be questioned any more about her choices.

'You mean you didn't manage to lift any extra food from the breakfast buffet?' he joked.

Her chin lifted fractionally and her shoulders tensed. 'That's right,' she said with a sarcastic bite to her voice.

It was the dismissive way she deliberately looked away from him into the distance that finally tipped him over the edge. 'You're crazy, you know that? You can't go walking for hours in this heat without eating enough.'

The look she gave him could have frozen water.

Sighing hard, he rummaged in the small rucksack he was carrying his provisions for the walk in and located his emergency energy bar. Striding over to the bench, he held it out towards her.

'Here, take this.'

She looked at the bar with some disdain. 'No, thanks. I don't need anything from you.'

From the tone of her voice, there was undoubtedly a lot more she wanted to add to that statement. Like exactly where he could stick his cereal bar.

Clearly he'd hurt her feelings last night, but, in his defence, he'd been doing her a favour letting her know right away that she was wasting her time if she was expecting anything more to develop between them this week.

Not that he was going to drag that up again right now.

Sighing with impatience, he dropped the energy bar on to the bench next to her, then stepped back, giving her a reproving look.

Okay, he'd done his duty now—he could walk away with integrity.

But, instead of picking up the bar, she stood up and shucked her rucksack on to her back, ignoring it completely.

'Well, it's time I got on with my walk and left you to enjoy the scenery on your *own*. Enjoy the rest of your vacation, Julien,' she said pointedly, echoing his words to her last night.

He watched her walk away from him, his jaw aching with tension as he fought the urge to go after her and tell her to stop being such a stubborn fool and at least stay and rest for a bit longer, the pressure of the denial restarting the throb of pain in his head.

Stomping into Praiano an hour and a half later, with aching legs and a decidedly damp T-shirt sticking to his back, Julien still hadn't shaken the feeling that he should have done more to convince Indigo to take the food he'd offered her.

His failure to persuade her to let him help had reminded him a little too keenly of the struggles he'd had with Celine at the end of their marriage.

Not that the two things could really be compared.

He'd not seen Indigo again on the route; he'd given her a twenty-minute head start after she'd stormed away, which he guessed must mean she'd made it to Praiano without collapsing. At least that was something.

It took him a couple of minutes to locate his hotel, which was in the centre of the small town, and he was about to stride into the glass-fronted lobby when his gaze caught on a familiar figure limping towards him along the pavement to his left.

Indigo didn't appear to notice him standing there and she stopped a few paces away, wrestling her bag off her back and dumping it wearily on to the floor by her feet to pull out her water bottle.

As his gaze followed the movement, he noticed that the trainers she'd chosen to walk for miles and miles in each day were beginning to fall apart, the rubber cracked and peeling away from the material at the sides of the shoe. Surely they couldn't be supporting her feet and ankles properly, and the soles had to be getting thinner and thinner from the rough ground.

Did the woman have *no* sense? Not only was she putting herself in danger of collapse from not eating enough, she was going to end up damaging her feet, or risk skidding off a cliff walking in such unsuitable footwear.

White-hot anger flashed through him at her stupidity, and he stalked towards her, not sure what he was going to say but knowing he needed to say *something* this time.

'Indigo, what are you doing walking in those running shoes over that kind of terrain?' he ground out, frowning hard and jabbing his finger down at her feet.

She took a small step backwards, the alarm on her face at his sudden appearance quickly changing to annoyance.

'What's it to you?' she asked archly, shooting up an eyebrow. 'For someone determined to spend his holiday alone you've got an awful lot to say about the way I spend mine.'

Julien found himself lost for words. She had a point—what was it to him? He wasn't responsible for her and she'd made it perfectly clear she didn't want or need his help.

But someone needed to point out her recklessness

to her. Apparently she had no idea how to look after herself.

'Trekking so far in those flimsy shoes is going to damage your feet.'

She took a tiny step towards him. 'I really don't need you to tell me what I should and shouldn't do, thanks very much.'

He matched her step with one of his own. 'You know, I think you're the most stubborn person I've ever met. It seems to me you need someone to point out the obvious or you're going to give yourself a serious injury.'

She let out a large huff of breath, her cheeks flaring with colour. 'Not that it's any of your business, but it wouldn't normally be my choice to go trekking in trainers. If you must know, the airline lost my bag which had my walking boots in it!'

He stared at her, perplexed. 'Why don't you buy yourself some more boots? Surely your insurance will cover it?'

There was a dangerous flash in her eyes. 'Just go and buy some more boots? With what? I know it's probably hard for someone like you to understand, but some people don't have extra money just lying around in their back pocket. I have nothing in my bank account at the moment and my emergency credit card and half my holiday money also happens to be in my lost bag!'

He could tell from the look in her eyes that she'd reached the end of her tether. Pain and hunger would do that to you.

It suddenly dawned on him what all her previous strange behaviour had been about: the change in hotel after only one night, the stolen lunch, the determination to eat pizza instead of à la carte cuisine.

Money trouble.

'Why haven't you asked your family for help?' he asked, gentling his voice now. 'Surely one of your brothers will lend you some money to tide you over?'

Sighing, she folded her arms and looked down at her feet, kicking at the ground and wincing. 'Because I don't want to.'

'Why not?'

She looked him directly in the eye again. 'I don't like to rely on other people. I need to know I can survive on my own without any help.'

He gave her a puzzled frown. 'That's impressive. But being able to accept help from others is a skill too.'

She opened her mouth as if to speak, then shut it again, shrugged, then flapped her hand around in an airy manner. 'It's an old habit. It was always do or die in the house where I grew up. Showing any kind of neediness to my brothers was deemed as a sign of weakness.'

This insight into her life disturbed him. 'What about your parents then?'

She paused before she spoke. 'My mum died from breast cancer when I was twelve and my dad passed away a couple of years ago—although, to be honest, he pretty much died when she did, at least his spirit did.'

Her whole posture seemed to shrink in on itself as she folded her arms across her chest. Clearly it was a difficult subject for her to talk about.

'He didn't cope well after she'd gone,' she continued, staring down at the floor, 'so I took over running the household. My brothers certainly didn't have a clue how to do it. Luckily, my mum taught me how to cook before she died and I found I was good at it.' She kicked gently at the ground. 'My dad suffered with bad depression so I ended up staying at home whilst I did my college courses, and then for a few years afterwards.' She shrugged. 'Tough times. But it taught me how to look after myself.'

There was a shadow of sadness in her eyes when she finally looked up at him.

Instinctively, he reached out, giving her arm a sympathetic squeeze. 'I'm sorry.'

'Ah, don't be. I'm okay.'

'That must have been really hard for you.'

She shrugged. 'I survived.'

'No wonder you're so driven.'

Taking a step back, she leant against the wall of the hotel. 'Yeah, well, I wanted to do something good with my life. I wanted to feel like my mum would be proud of me, had she survived. She only made it to forty-four before the cancer killed her. How can that be right? She was a good person. A kind and loving person.'

Her sadness hung thickly in the air between them.

'Some days, life seems anything but fair.'

'Ain't that the truth?'

The haunted look in her eyes broke him.

'Okay, come with me,' he ordered, scooping up her rucksack from the ground and slinging it over his shoulder, then setting off back down the street in the direction she'd come from.

It took a moment for her to come running after him.

'Where are you going with my bag?' she demanded, her breath coming out in short pants after her sprint.

'You'll see.'

'Julien, give it back to me!'

'I will, when we get there.'

'Where?'

'You'll see.'

She growled, low in her throat. 'Now who's being stubborn?'

Luckily, the shop specialising in walking gear that he'd walked past earlier was only another minute's walk away, down the next street, which was a good thing as Indigo was limping hard in her wrecked trainers now.

He ignored her exasperated sigh as he ushered her through the door and into the wonderfully cool air-conditioned interior.

She stopped dead just inside the shop and turned to give him a withering look. 'Julien, I told you, I can't afford to buy new boots right now.'

'I heard you. But you're not buying them. I am.'

Before she could even open her mouth to protest he held up a hand. 'Do not argue with me. I cannot let you walk any more in those monstrosities. It's offending my sensibilities.'

She shook her head. 'Julien, I can't—'

'Quiet, stubborn woman,' he growled in frustration.

Thankfully, she didn't take his tone as an insult, although he was a little perturbed when she burst into laughter instead.

In fact, he started to become seriously worried about her when the laughter seemed to overtake her, bending her double and shaking her whole body as she struggled to get her breathing under control.

When she finally managed to pull herself together, she looked up at him with tears of laughter still in her eyes. 'I'm sorry, I don't know why I'm laughing. I think I'm a bit hysterical. Today has just been a bit *much*, you know? In fact, this whole holiday hasn't exactly turned out the way I expected it to.'

'Yes, this wasn't what I had in mind when I pictured a break either. I was hoping for a little more peace and quiet and a lot less bickering with pig-headed women,' he said grumpily.

This only made her start laughing again, in great gulping gasps.

All he could do was stand there and wait for her to get a handle on it again.

'I have no idea why the state of my feet troubles you,' she said eventually, taking deep breaths to calm herself down, 'but if it means so much to you then I'll let you buy me some boots.' She swiped the tears from her cheeks and held up a finger. 'But you have to give me your address so I can reimburse you after I get home.'

He shook his head. 'There is no need to pay me back.'

This seemed to sober her up pretty quickly. 'Yes, there is, Julien.'

He could tell from the look on her face that the only way she'd let him help her out was if she felt she could even things out later. Which was fine by him. The cost of the boots meant nothing to him, but he knew this wasn't really about the money. It was about pride.

'Okay. Agreed,' he said, giving her a resigned smile. Catching the sales assistant's eye, he waved for her to come over.

'Now, let's get you sorted out.'

CHRISTY McKELLEN

Taking a grim breath, pulling her resigned smile, Claudine slides a casual 'gaze' in a wild climactic conclusion...

'Okay, let's get you sorted out.'

CHAPTER FIVE

Discovering Praiano—a simple town with a big heart. Check out the small pebbled cove, which is especially atmospheric in the evening...

THE NEW BOOTS felt wonderful on her feet.

Despite her protests, Julien had insisted on buying her some specialised walking socks and plasters too, in an attempt to protect her poor blistered skin from more damage. She was now wearing all the things they'd purchased and had dropped her ruined trainers into the shop's recycling bin with a huge sigh of relief.

The day was finally starting to look up.

After finally arriving in Praiano, footsore, disgruntled and almost faint with hunger, she'd hit rock bottom when she'd arrived at her hotel to find her bag still hadn't turned up.

She'd nearly cried, right there at the reception desk.

In fact, she was just on her way to grab the cheapest, most calorific meal she could find in the town centre to try and boost her morale when Julien had shown up out of the blue and marched her over to the hiking store.

Even though she felt hugely uncomfortable about him spending money on her, at that precise moment she hadn't had the strength to put up more of a fight.

That was why she'd given in so easily.

That and the fact she'd been acutely aware of something in his eyes when he'd argued with her—something that made her think he'd needed to win this small battle. Maybe it was just a macho male impulse to assert his authority, but for some reason she didn't believe that was the whole of it. Even though he'd made it clear he didn't want anything more to do with her, he hadn't been able to turn a blind eye when he'd seen how she was struggling.

Just the fact he'd noticed that she was in trouble made her feel like she wanted to cry again, only this time with gratitude. It felt like a long time since someone had looked out for her like that.

Argh! And now she was starting to like him again, when she'd told herself to stay well out of his way.

After exiting the shop with Julien hot on her newly shod heels, they stood awkwardly on the pavement, looking anywhere but at each other. She expected him to make some excuse any second now to get away from the strange tension deadening the air between them, but he didn't move, instead turning to look at her with that perplexed frown of his.

'Why don't you go for a short walk in your boots, to check they're fitting properly?' he said, breaking eye contact to glance down at her feet. 'Just in case you need to take them back. I'm guessing you're walking on to

Positano tomorrow, so you won't have an opportunity to swap them after today.'

'Yes, I am,' she said. 'That's a good idea.' Swinging her bag on to her back, she took a pace backwards. 'What are you going to do?' she asked, trying to make the question sound as casual as possible. What was the etiquette here? Should she invite him to come along? It felt rude to just stride off when he'd gone to the trouble of helping her out. But, then again, would she be putting him in an awkward position where he'd feel forced to reject her again?

'Why don't I come with you?' he said, surprising her. 'The assistant didn't seem to know much English and you might need me to translate again.' He frowned and shook his head. 'At least I'm assuming you don't speak Italian? I never asked.'

'You assume correctly.' It had pleased her to find out she'd been right about his linguistic skills. When the sales assistant had come over and they'd started speaking to her in English and she'd not understood the nuances of what they wanted, Julien had switched to Italian. To her untrained ear it sounded as flawless as his English. Which proved her theory that he'd been speaking her language for her benefit the night they'd shared the honeymoon suite. Something about this discovery gave her a little lift of joy.

'I can order a coffee and ask where the bathrooms are, but that's about the extent of my vocabulary without consulting a phrase book,' she said with a smile.

'*Bon*. I'll come with you then.'

'Don't you want to check into your hotel?'

He shook his head. 'Later.'

'Okay,' she said, shrugging, trying not to give away how pleased she was that he wasn't just going to abandon her now. 'I'm going to grab a sandwich from that shop over there before I die of hunger, but I can eat it while we walk.'

'We can sit down. I'm not in a rush.'

'Are you sure?'

'Yes. Sure.'

So, she bought a panini stuffed with prosciutto and nutty-tasting cheese and the sweetest sundried tomatoes she'd even eaten and sat at a long counter in the shop and consumed the whole thing in about two minutes flat. Julien stood next to her, drinking an espresso, not saying a word about her eating habits, though she could practically hear him thinking the words, *See? You were a fool not to take that energy bar when I offered it to you.*

Maybe she had been a little foolish, but she'd still been angry with him at the time for the way he'd spoken to her the night before, and had chosen her pride over her stomach.

After that they wandered out of the town centre and away towards the cliffs, enjoying the cool breeze coming off the sea. It was still hot, but much more bearable now that the sun had begun to slip down behind the horizon.

'Let's go and check out the beach,' she suggested, fully expecting him to say no and make his excuses to leave now.

He paused for a moment, his expression unreadable,

before nodding slowly. 'Sure,' he said, surprising her again with the warmth in his voice.

They made their way over to where a winding set of steps led down to the small pebbled beach. The sharp, briny smell of the sea hit her nose as they picked their way across to the centre of the deserted cove, the only sound coming from the rush of waves and the melodic tinkle of the stones as the water played back and forth over them.

She stopped near the water's edge and looked out towards the horizon, where the sun was disappearing from view, leaving the soft glow of dusk in its wake.

'Wow. It really is beautiful here,' she said as Julien came to a halt beside her.

They stood side by side and stared out at the gentle swell of the water in silence, listening to the faraway cries of the birds wheeling in the sky above them.

When she turned to glance at Julien, she was surprised to find he was looking at her with a strange little pinch between his brows.

A wave of tingling warmth washed from head to foot, pooling deep inside her as their gazes locked. She knew it was ridiculous to read anything into it, but something felt different between them now, as if a layer of armour had been peeled away.

Clearing her throat, she tore her gaze away and rummaged in her bag, desperate for something to distract her from the fizz of nerves in her tummy, producing her book on walking the Amalfi coast and her eyeliner. 'Here,' she said, thrusting them towards him. 'Write your address inside the front cover, will you? Then I'll know where to send the money.'

Without a word, he took them from her and, twitching his eyebrows at her choice of writing implement, wrote in the book.

She watched him move his strong, blunt-tipped fingers across the page, marvelling at how elegant his writing was.

He was a man of such contradictions.

'Why did you do this for me?' she blurted, unable to keep her speculation to herself any longer.

He glanced up at her, his eyes narrowing in thought. 'I don't like to see anyone in trouble, especially when I can do something to fix the problem easily.'

His choice of the word 'anyone' made her stomach drop a little with disappointment. 'You mean by throwing money at it?' she said, perhaps a little too snippily.

He raised an eyebrow. 'If that's what it takes.'

How lucky to have that luxury, she thought. But she didn't say it out loud. It would only have sounded petty and churlish.

'Well, thank you.' She took the book and eyeliner back from him and slid them carefully back into her bag.

There was an uncomfortable pause where they stood looking at each other again.

Indigo was aware of her heart beating hard against her ribcage as she tried to make sense of what was going on here. Why was he still here talking to her? Was it because he felt sorry for her? She hoped that wasn't it.

'Look, Indigo, I should apologise for being so rude last night at dinner.'

She couldn't meet his gaze, the memory of the humiliation she'd felt burning through her once again. 'Forget about it. It doesn't matter.'

'Yes, it does.' He moved his head to the side, then bent towards her, waiting until he'd caught her eye before he spoke again. 'Indigo, it does. I'm not normally so unfriendly; you've just caught me at a bad time.'

She gave him a shaky smile, cocking her head and splaying out her hands on either side of her. 'Okay, I accept your apology.'

There was relief in his eyes and something else.

Her lips tingled as his gaze dropped to her mouth and her pulse rocketed.

He looked like—

—he wanted to—

—*kiss* her.

The thought lit a fire inside her, burning through her veins and turning her nerve endings into a crackling mass of need.

Ever since she'd laid eyes on him she'd wondered what it would feel like to have those strong arms wrapped around her, holding her close, comforting and sheltering her. And those wide, firm lips pressed against hers, smoothing away her loneliness.

The air felt thick with longing as his eyes met hers again. They seemed to darken as she parted her lips to drag warm, salty air deep into her lungs in an attempt to calm her erratic heartbeat.

Something seemed to be pulling her towards him,

some strange magnetic instinct, and she took a microstep forwards to maintain her balance, raising her hand to his face.

He let out a low, rough breath as her fingers connected with the lightly stubbled skin of his jaw, and then suddenly Julien was no longer there in front of her, but far, far away.

Too far.

'What—?' She blinked in shock, stumbling forwards, dazed by the sudden desertion.

He was standing a few paces back from her now, shaking his head, his eyes a little wild. He held up a hand, his face a picture of remorse. 'That's not what I'm here for, Indigo.' He shook his head, his expression heavy with regret and frustration. 'I'm in no position to—' He waved a hand in her direction, his movements jerky and agitated.

'To what?'

'Do this.'

'I don't even know what *this* is, Julien.'

He took another step away from her and rubbed a hand across his face. 'I need my freedom right now, Indigo. I need to be alone.'

She snorted in angry frustration, every inch of her skin feeling hot and prickly. 'It was just going to be a kiss. A bit of fun. It didn't have to mean anything.'

If only that were true. Perhaps if it were then her voice wouldn't sound as if she'd just been picked up and shaken hard.

He screwed up his face in frustration. 'It's never just a bit of fun though, is it?' There was a look of admonishment in his eyes that made her stomach drop to the floor.

How embarrassing. She'd read the situation all wrong—though, to be fair to her, she hadn't come here looking for romance. She was just going with the flow, enjoying the adventure, seeing where the day took her.

Not that she hadn't considered the possibility of something more developing between them after he'd agreed to come down here with her. His change in mood had made her wonder whether there could be something more to this.

Something exciting. Something good.

But clearly she was wrong.

'What is it you're afraid of, Julien?' she asked, her tone a little defensive as she fought to maintain her pride.

He took another step away from her, rubbing a hand through his hair, messing up the neat waves. He looked back at her with such exasperation on his face it made her want to move towards him and smooth it away.

Which, of course, she couldn't.

Instead, she tried to smile as if it all meant nothing to her, which proved impossible because it felt as though the corners of her mouth were being dragged down by some kind of extreme gravitational force. 'I'm sorry. I didn't mean to pry.'

He looked at her for the longest time, his troubled gaze searching her face as if he wanted to say more but couldn't find the right words. Finally, he held up his hand, as if putting up a barrier between them. 'I'm going to go,' he said, taking a step away from her, his posture dipping a little as the pebbles gave way under his feet. 'It's for the best.'

And then he turned, his shoulders tense and his hands clenched into fists, and strode away from her until he disappeared into the inky-dark night.

CHAPTER SIX

Praiano to Positano—traversing the Path of the Gods. Be aware, this part of the walk includes vertiginous sections with breathtaking views...

JULIEN DIDN'T SLEEP well again.

Only this time his dreams weren't tangled with thoughts of his ex-wife and his failed marriage. Instead, they kept coming back to the intensity of the moment he'd shared with Indigo on the beach. Over and over again, as if the memory was stuck on repeat.

In his half wakeful state the next morning, he relived the overpowering instinct he'd felt to hold her close, to experience the strength of her wrapped around him, to taste her sweetness—only then to feel the wrench of guilt for almost indulging his cravings when he had no intention of following through on his physical promises.

There was no wonder she'd looked so wounded when he'd pushed her away. He'd practically accused her of being the one to lead their strange, lustful dance.

He'd been just as much to blame. More so, probably. He'd wanted her.

But he had no right to indulge his wants. Not in the mindset he was in at the moment.

He'd known at the time that he was going too far—way too far—when he'd agreed to go down to the beach with her, but despite the warnings flashing through his mind, he'd not been able to walk away and leave her.

He'd been greedy for more time with Indigo Hughes.

It had felt so good to be able to take charge of her challenging situation and do something to help. After the sheer frustration of failing to save his marriage, it had fortified something inside him—given him the satisfaction that he hadn't lost his ability to take care of people when they needed help. Even if it had been for a near enough stranger.

Not that Indigo felt like a stranger to him any more. After hearing about how she'd lost both her parents and her struggles growing up in such a tough emotional environment, she'd become vividly real to him now. Which, of course, was part of the problem.

Standing on that beach in the quiet of dusk, watching the day change into another dark, solitary night, he'd wanted her to know what an incredible, impressive and attractive person he thought she was. At that moment making a connection with her had seemed important for some reason.

But, in doing so, he'd nearly stepped over the line and once again proved just how selfish he could be.

Giving up on getting any more sleep, he decided to set off early from the hotel in order to miss most of the other walkers on his way to Positano.

A couple of hours into the walk, he'd been enjoying

getting into the soothing rhythm of it, letting his mind wander freely, when he found himself on a particularly narrow part of the path which began to swing gradually out closer to the cliff's edge. It was only when he dragged himself out of his philosophical thoughts to take proper stock of what he was heading for that he realised the next part of the walk was going to take him past some unguarded sections where the exposed cliff edge fell steeply away from the path, straight down to the rocks below.

A bead of sweat trickled down his spine, followed swiftly by another as he carefully continued on the path, which, to his growing unease, was becoming narrower and narrower the further along it he walked.

He'd never been great with heights, but he'd never before experienced this dizzying horror as he took in the sight of the sea crashing against razor-sharp rocks below him. If only there had been a railing he could touch, to reassure himself there was no way he could stumble and fall down into what seemed in his unsettled imaginings to be oblivion.

His breath came fast now, scything in and out of his lungs and burning his parched throat as his pace slowed to a crawl. A gravitational force seemed to be pulling at him, attempting to draw him closer and closer to the edge as he picked his way along the path. Looking behind him, he wondered wildly for a moment whether he should go back, but the thought of even turning around on the narrow path caused a wave of pure terror to flood through his body and his stomach to lurch, bringing him to the edge of nausea.

It would be so easy to topple to the side and fall. He could picture the air rushing past him, feel the impending doom as he rocketed closer and closer to the jagged rocks, then the unforgiving suck of the sea as it pulled him into its fathomless depths.

His heart was pounding so hard he could feel it in his throat.

Closing his eyes, he grabbed for the foliage that rose to the right of him to steady himself and somehow managed to anchor himself enough to slide down on to his haunches with his back to the rough stone wall, pressing himself hard against it.

The solid feel of rock and earth steadied him and he opened his eyelids a crack to take stock of his situation.

Not good.

He was roughly halfway along the dangerously narrow path, with no easy way forward or back.

He was stuck.

Why the heck hadn't he bought himself a walking guidebook, like the last hotel receptionist had suggested? If he had, he'd have known what he was about to face and could either have taken a longer inland route or skipped this section of the walk completely and taken a bus to the next destination.

But then that hadn't been the point of the trip. He was here to challenge his endurance and push through any personal discomfort until he felt like himself again. Skipping part of it would have felt like cheating on the promise he'd made to himself.

But what a challenge it had turned out to be.

Adrenaline had raised his blood pressure, heating

his body as he fought the flight impulse so that he felt as though he was sitting in an oven—the fierce heat of the sun beating down on his head was not helping his cause.

What felt like an age later, the sound of voices floated towards him from the direction he'd come, and he turned his head to see who it was, humiliation already engulfing him at the thought of what he would look like, hunched over, clinging on to the rock face.

Pretty unheroic, he suspected.

A minute later a group of men that he'd not encountered before walked up to him on the path, all of them giving him an odd look as they picked their way carefully past him.

'*Buongiorno,*' he muttered to them, raising his head and forcing a friendly smile on to his face.

'Everything okay?' one of them asked in Italian as he passed, his brow crinkled with concern.

'Great, fine,' Julien muttered, flapping a hand in the air. 'Just taking a quick break,' he added, quickly lowering his hand again to grip back on to the rocky surface.

The man's frown deepened, but he didn't stop walking, giving a shrug and picking up his pace to catch up with his friends.

Letting out a low sigh, Julien pressed his head back against the wall again and tried to think himself out of his problem. This was ridiculous; he was a grown man of thirty-six, he should not be letting a bit of rock and air defeat him.

Blowing gently first up towards his forehead, then down towards his chest, he attempted to think cooling thoughts to regulate his heartbeat, then, when that didn't work, he tried distracting himself by thinking about work. But his mind kept leaping back to how close he was to the edge, which made him laugh out loud in a maniacal fashion because it occurred to him then that his whole world seemed to be full of edges that he was trying not to fall off at the moment.

Which inevitably made him think about Indigo. He shifted uncomfortably on his haunches as he thought again about the look of hurt in those beautiful eyes of hers—the look he'd caused—and he nearly toppled forwards.

That woman would be the death of him. Literally.

Another age passed while he tried to gather himself enough to stand up and force himself to walk along the rest of the path. It couldn't be that much further until it wound back inland. Could it?

Just as he was about to attempt to heave himself back to standing, the sound of more voices coming towards him made him freeze in dismay.

Taking a deep breath and cursing himself for picking such a popular walking route to be stranded on, he steeled himself to make polite conversation again until they'd gone. He really didn't want to have any witnesses to his humiliation, so he was going to wave them on and wait until they were well out of sight before he made his next attempt at getting off this damn cliff.

He readied himself, fixing a smile firmly on to his face and was about to turn towards the approaching group when he realised with a lurch that he recognised one of the voices.

Oh, no. Please, no. Anyone but her.

After counting to three, which did absolutely nothing to calm his raging pulse, he turned his head to watch Indigo walk towards him, followed by three women he didn't recognise.

His heart sank. Was this karma coming along to kick his butt? Or, since this was Indigo we were talking about—fate?

Her brow creased into a frown as she got nearer to where he was sitting, which wasn't entirely unjustified since he was taking up half of the path so that anyone wanting to journey on would have to step around him, putting themselves in even more danger of slipping off the edge of the cliff and into the sea.

'Julien, are you okay?' Indigo asked, her voice edged with unease. That would be due to the insulting I-want-you-no-I-don't debacle he'd put her through last night.

'I'm fine, Indigo,' he managed to rasp through a throat that had practically closed up with embarrassment.

Her frown deepened, but she kept on walking, stepping past him so that the women close on her heels could get by too.

Thankfully, none of the others spoke to him and he averted his gaze, willing away the raging heat in his face as he counted down the seconds until they'd be out of his sight line and he could make another attempt at standing up and leaving this godforsaken place.

There was a murmur of voices in the distance, which he assumed was Indigo filling the rest of her party in on the tribulations he'd put her through since they'd first clapped eyes on each other, and he dropped his head to his knees and let out a long, low breath.

So this was what payback felt like.

Indigo made it a few more metres down the path—after breezily explaining to the three women she'd made friends with at breakfast that Julien was just another hiker she'd met on the walk—when her conscience refused to let her take another step.

There had been something odd in Julien's expression when she'd walked up to him that had lodged itself in her head, and she couldn't shake the feeling that something had been very wrong, despite his assertions to the contrary.

After the humiliating episode last night she'd been determined to forget about him now and carry on with her holiday in the way she'd planned. She'd be coolly friendly, of course if—no, *when*—they bumped into each other again, but that would be it.

She wasn't going to put herself in a position where she made a fool of herself in front of him again. Because she didn't need an emotional roller-coaster ride like that right now.

She was supposed to be looking after herself this week.

But something about the way he was sitting there still niggled at her.

'I'm going to go back and check that Julien's okay,' she told her new friends, experiencing a dip of disappointment at leaving them when they'd all been getting on so well.

'Okay. Perhaps we'll see you in Positano,' the more senior of the women, Ruth, said, giving her a friendly smile. There was something else in her expression too, as if she suspected there was a little more to Indigo's about-turn than she was admitting to.

Not that it mattered what Ruth thought. Julien had helped her out by getting her the boots she was currently wearing, thus saving her holiday, and she owed him big for that.

He was probably fine anyway and would wave her concerns away in that arrogant way of his, so she'd be able to catch her new friends up again—but she just wanted to make sure.

Julien looked as though he was about to stand up as she made her way back to him along the rough, narrow path. She began to feel foolish for worrying and was about to turn round again when she noticed that the tendons in his hands were white with tension as he clung to the rock behind him, and a sheen of perspiration had broken out across his forehead.

What was going on here? Was he ill?

'Julien? Are you sure you're okay?' she asked as she came within striking distance of him.

He dropped his chin to his chest at the sound of her voice, as if he was exasperated with her for coming back and bothering him.

A sting of annoyance jabbed her, but she didn't back off. 'Are you feeling ill?'

He lifted his head to look at her and she could tell by the expression on his face that her instincts had been right. There was something badly wrong here.

There was a long pause where she worried whether he was even capable of answering her. Then she saw him swallow hard before letting out a long, frustrated sigh.

'I was fine with the first bit of this walk,' he said, his voice sounding strained, 'but then the path got narrower and I started to feel like the ground was sloping downwards towards the drop, which made me dizzy. Logically, I know it isn't doing that, but my brain keeps telling me otherwise. I've never been great with heights, but I haven't been affected this badly before.'

He was afraid of heights? No wonder he looked so distressed.

'Didn't you read about this bit in your guidebook?' she asked, wondering how the heck she was going to help him get out of here. It wasn't as if she could toss him over her shoulder and carry him the rest of the way.

He let out a huff of breath. 'What guidebook?'

'You don't have a guidebook with you?'

'*Non*. I'm—what do you English say?—*winging it*. I wanted to experience this holiday without any expectations.'

She couldn't help but laugh at the superior expression on his face. 'You are the most mercurial man I've ever met,' she said, unable to stop herself from teasing him. After the way he'd acted last night it was somewhat satisfying to get one over on him.

He gave her a rueful grin. 'I'm glad I amuse you.'

She could tell from the shake in his voice that he was genuinely rattled, though. It must be a terrifying thing, believing that you're stuck alone on the side of a cliff face, not able to go either forwards or back the way you came.

That thought galvanised her.

'Okay, this is what we're going to do. You're going to walk on the inside with one hand touching the wall or foliage and I'll walk next to you on the open side. You look ahead, but slightly inland so you're not looking at the drop the whole way along. I'll make sure we stay safely on the path. Okay?'

He stared at her for a moment, then blinked as if her words had taken a moment to sink in. 'Are you sure you want to do that?'

Once again she realised there was much more to his question than its face value. She knew what he was really asking.

Shaking her head, she put her hands on her hips. 'You think just because we had a minor disagreement I'm going to walk away and leave you here?'

His mouth twitched at the corner and he shook his head. 'No. That doesn't seem like the sort of thing you'd do.' He sighed, his exasperation with himself clear. 'Okay. Let's do it.'

'Okay then. Now, give me your hand.'

He looked up at her and frowned. 'What?'

'Don't worry, I'm not trying to seduce you,' she said, laying on the sarcasm. 'It will keep you grounded.'

'What if I fall and pull you over with me? I don't want to be responsible for tipping us both off a cliff.'

She let out a huff of breath at the doubt in his voice, but reined her irritation back in. 'That's not going to happen; I have fantastic balance. Now, give me your hand.'

Taking a breath, he let go of the rocks behind him and lifted his hand tentatively towards her.

She grasped it in one of hers. 'Okay, good. Now stand up slowly.'

He did so, wobbling a little as he righted himself and faced the direction in which they needed to go.

'Great, we're set,' she said, feeling the tension in his grip. 'Just keep looking at the wall and I'll guide us safely forwards.'

They set off slowly, Julien's steps hesitant at first, but becoming more sure as they made their way slowly along the pathway. Their clasped hands grew sweaty in the heat, but she didn't let go of him to wipe them on her shorts. She didn't think he'd appreciate that.

'Talk to me, take my mind off that thousand-metre drop just inches away,' he said when he wobbled a little at one point.

'I think a thousand metres might be a slight exaggeration—'

'It doesn't feel like it to me,' he cut in gruffly.

She bit back a smile. 'What do you want to talk about?'

'Anything. I don't care. Tell me about the people that you're teaching to cook.'

'Oh, my goodness… Well, there are some real characters in my cooking group.'

'I can imagine.'

'There's one guy whose wife left him six months ago after forty years of marriage because she was fed up with him being so insensitive and lazy. He's learning how to cook so he can woo her back.'

'Is it working?'

'It seems so.' She grinned at the memory. 'Apparently his spaghetti *sorry, babe* was a real hit and she's going back this week to sample his apple *turnover a new leaf.*'

She continued to tell him anecdotes about the people she'd come into contact with in the last year, actually starting to enjoy herself as she remembered things she'd not thought about for a while. It reminded her of how rewarding it had felt to make a difference in these people's lives. Even if it was only in some small way.

Julien listened intently, chiming in every now and again with a gruff question or comment, and by the time they reached the end of the vertiginous section and had come out into a wider, flatter path, his voice sounded almost normal again.

She was glad to have been able to help him, even though, as usual, he'd made it unnecessarily difficult for her.

The man was too proud for his own good—but she wasn't going to hold it against him. She knew all about pride.

It occurred to her that if she'd been here with Gavin and it had been her that had been scared of heights he would have lorded that weakness over her—even though he would have disguised it as teasing—and he wouldn't have let her forget about it for the rest of the holiday.

There was no way she was going to do that to Julien, and she felt sure he wouldn't have done it to her if the roles were reversed; he seemed too classy for that.

She awkwardly extricated her hand from his vice-like grip, somewhat disappointed now to let go. It had been nice having that connection with him as they'd talked.

He seemed a little surprised by the loss of her touch and turned to look at her with his brow drawn into a frown.

'Are you okay now?' she asked.

'Yes, I'm fine. My heart doesn't feel like it's going to explode in my chest any more.'

He looked away towards where the azure-blue ocean crashed noisily against the rocks far below them.

She gazed at his profile, taking in the strength of his jaw with its faint show of bristles, noting a small scar where the bone swooped up towards his ear. She wondered briefly how he'd got it, then pushed away the instinct to ask him. It was probably too personal a question and he might get snippy about answering it.

To be honest, she was a little hurt that he wasn't being friendlier to her after she'd just rescued him from certain doom. Not that she'd done it to be lavished with gratitude and praise, but to hear a simple thank you wouldn't hurt. Perhaps his alpha pride had been dented and this was his way of shutting the humiliation of it out.

But, even so—

He turned back suddenly, making her jump a little as the shock of the movement yanked her out of her reverie.

Taking a pace backwards, he folded his arms tightly against his chest.

She tried not to notice how this made the sculpted muscles in his arms bulge in a rather attractive way.

'So you should consider your debt for the boots paid off,' he bit out, his face dark with a frown.

Great. An acknowledgement. Sort of. It wasn't exactly a heartfelt outpouring of thanks, though.

'You do know there are more sheer drops on the next leg of the walk, don't you?' Indigo blurted with a reproachful lift of her eyebrow, unable to keep her annoyance at him spilling over.

His face seemed to pale. 'Really?'

'You know, I'd be happy to partner with you for that bit if you like,' she said loftily, 'just in case you need me to distract you with my witty repartee till we get past them.'

As soon as she'd said the words she regretted them. Not because she didn't want to spend more time with him, but because she knew, deep down, that it wasn't altruism that had prompted her to make the offer; it was because she enjoyed being around him. Even though there was a good chance she was letting herself in for more hurt and rejection here, she couldn't quite tear herself away from him just yet.

He captivated her with his strange mixture of gruff pride and compassion, not to mention the way he made her tummy flip when he looked at her with his impassioned, penetrating gaze.

She wondered again what could have happened to his marriage to make him so defensive.

'Why would you want to do that?' he asked brusquely.

'Because I'm the better person,' she joked, flashing him a grin, which he countered with a raised eyebrow.

She threw up her hands in exasperation. 'Okay, how about we say each day of walking pays off a boot? In my mind, that makes us even.'

'Okay,' he shot back. 'Fine.' He followed the word with a long, agitated sigh and glanced down once more at the sea beneath them. 'Now, let's put some more distance between us and this death trap and get to Positano before nightfall.'

They didn't speak again until they reached the outskirts of the town and checked the details of their lodgings for the night, which suited Julien just fine. After the humiliation of finding himself at such a disadvantage and having to rely on Indigo's goodwill to get him out of trouble, he'd just wanted to sink into his own head for a while.

Not that he hadn't been intensely aware of her presence beside him the whole way there. He'd been impressed with her fitness levels too—she'd not asked to stop once, even after a particularly steep ascent. No wonder she was in such good shape.

He forced the tantalising image of her lean, fit body that followed that thought right out of his head.

'We're staying on the same road,' Indigo said, throwing him an *it must be fate* smile. 'But I'm a bit further down the hill.'

'Bon,' he replied, desperate for some solitude now so

he could get a handle on these frustratingly conflicting feelings she'd stirred up in him.

He was intensely aware that in another life he would have jumped at the chance to make more of their connection—but that he couldn't act on his impulses, not here, not now. It wouldn't be fair to either of them. Despite the whispered demands of his body, his mind kept reminding him he couldn't offer her any kind of emotional commitment.

And from what he already knew of her, he could tell that wouldn't work for Indigo.

But the thought of saying goodbye to her now also twisted something inside him.

They reached the road they needed barely a minute later.

'Well, this is me,' she said, nodding towards the place where she was going to bed down for the night, with its simple crazy-paved stone frontage and garish sign that shouted: *cheap, but cheerful!*

'And that's me,' he said with a nod towards a much grander building sitting proudly a little further up the hill, with clear sea views and an elegant iron-railed terrace for every room.

Only a little further up the road, but worlds apart.

'Indigo—'

'Yes?'

'Thank you for not abandoning me to my fate today.'

He felt like a fool for saying it, but her expression lightened as if she was relieved to finally hear it.

His acknowledgement didn't stop her from winding him up, though.

'That wasn't fate trying to tip you off a cliff, it was just reminding you that you should be nicer to me.'

He rubbed a hand over his face and snorted. She was right, of course; he hadn't exactly been chivalrous about accepting her help. He'd been so embarrassed his manners seemed to have fled him.

'Okay, point taken.' Despite being desperate for some time alone, he knew he should at least attempt to show some appreciation for what she'd done for him today. She'd certainly gone above and beyond the call of duty. 'Can I buy you dinner tonight? To show my gratitude.'

She shifted on her feet, looking uncomfortable. 'You don't need to do that. I think we're even with the boots.'

She wouldn't meet his eye and her body language made him think about how she'd looked on the beach after they'd been so close—so dangerously close—to kissing. The sensory memory was so acute he could have sworn he caught the same briny scent on the air mixed with her sweet floral fragrance.

He shook it off and folded his arms. 'Look, Indigo, what happened last night on the beach—I never meant to lead you into thinking I was interested in a holiday fling. The truth is, I'm not in a good place right now. I've only just signed my divorce papers and, to be honest, I can't see myself wanting another relationship any time soon.'

She looked at him sharply, her brow pinched, and held up a hand. 'It's okay, Julien, I'm not interested in a fling either. I just came here for a break. To walk and see the magnificent scenery. That's all.'

He looked into her wide grey eyes and saw only steady resolve there. 'Okay then.' He cleared his throat, which felt strangely wadded and tight. 'Well, let's meet here at eight o'clock tomorrow,' he said. 'We should bring enough food to see us through to Nerano. Or, if you prefer, I can ask the receptionist where we can find a place to stop for lunch?'

She grinned at his rather clipped tone and rolled her eyes at him. 'Don't worry, I'll bring a packed lunch with me so you won't need to carry me past the finishing line.'

'Good,' he said, with one chastising eyebrow raised.

'Good,' she replied, pressing her lips into a pugnacious smile.

There was a voice in the back of his head warning him again about the wisdom of getting too friendly with her, but he pushed it aside. Neither of them were stupid; they knew what this was.

But, more importantly, they knew now what it wasn't.

CHAPTER SEVEN

Positano to Nerano via Sant'Agata. More vertiginous drops with a ridgetop walk and views for miles. Going for a reinvigorating swim in the ocean is a must at the end of this hard day's walk...

So, WALKING PARTNERS it was.

At least that would mean they could stop trying to avoid each other at every turn when it was clear they were destined to walk this path together, both metaphorically and physically, Indigo mused as she finished her breakfast the next morning.

She'd been really tempted to take him up on his offer of dinner last night, so much so that she'd had a physical pain in the back of her throat as she forced out her refusal, but she knew she had to be sensible here. There could be a danger she was reverting to type and turning him into a project, thinking she could help or even fix him without getting hurt—just like she had with Gavin—and that wasn't something she wanted to put herself through again.

Ugh! Was it going to be like this every time she met someone she was attracted to? Damn Gavin and his ability to make her feel so paranoid. So she liked helping people! What was so wrong with that?

Still, even if Julien had been willing to embark on a holiday fling with her, giving in to her attraction was a definite no-no. She'd be a fool to get entangled with him when he was so emotionally unavailable and she was still feeling sore after being given the boot by Gavin.

This holiday was supposed to be about looking after *her* for a change, she reminded herself for what felt like the millionth time.

After making sure she'd packed everything into her small rucksack, all the while giving herself a stern talking-to about keeping her fascination with him under wraps today, she checked out and left the hotel to meet Julien.

He was waiting for her where they'd agreed to meet the night before, looking just as perfectly turned out as usual, though his eyes were ringed with dark circles and he clearly hadn't bothered to shave. The sight of Julien with rough edges gave her a delicious little shiver of pleasure, which she quickly stamped on before it got the better of her.

Sighing, she tugged hard on her backpack straps to tighten them.

It was going to be a long day.

After a slightly awkward greeting they strode away from Positano, both a little quiet to begin with, but after a few false starts at conversation they fell into a comfortable rhythm, finding a surprisingly diverse array of subjects to chat about, including a somewhat heated discussion about whether London or Paris was the better city to live in.

'But we have amazing markets in London! Like Spitalfields and Notting Hill and the Columbia Road Flower Market,' Indigo interjected when Julien suggested that Paris was the best city in the world for street markets.

'Well, we have the best architecture,' he countered.

'London is full of great buildings, including lots of new ones,' she pointed out. 'The Shard, for example. It's way taller and more impressive than any of the buildings in Paris. Parisians seem to be totally averse to moving with the times and building anything new.'

'Ah, but we have the Eiffel Tower, which beats The Shard hands down for style,' he threw back, as if that answered everything. 'And I would hate to live in a place that was a perpetual building site.'

In fact, they were so engrossed in their back and forth banter about which city ruled supreme that Julien barely seemed to notice when she slid her hand into his as they reached the spot where one side of the path fell away to a sheer drop, as if it was the most natural thing in the world for her to do.

She thought he seemed a little less tense than he'd been the day before as they traversed the exposed section, moving their conversation on to debate the pros and cons of being part of the Euro. He seemed so engrossed, in fact, that Indigo found herself enjoying a sense of achievement at managing to distract him enough for his vertigo to not have been too much of a problem today.

Then later, chatting over lunch, it turned out they were both big fans of psychological suspense and they got into another animated discussion comparing the top writers of the genre, which took till they reached the fortress-like outskirts of Sant'Agata to conclude.

It had been so wonderful to talk about things they both felt passionate about that Indigo arrived in the town having really enjoyed her walk today.

Her hotel for the night was located on the outskirts, to the east of the town, which meant they walked straight past it once they'd left the trail.

'I'm going to use their bathroom to splash some water on my face before I leave you,' Julien said, following her up to the entrance and into the wonderfully cool interior.

'Okay,' Indigo replied, watching him stride away, feeling a mixture of apprehension and regret as she made her way to the reception desk.

Her insides felt twisted. Would this be the last they'd see of each other now that the more perilous parts of the walk were over? She couldn't imagine Julien wanting to continue holidaying with her now that she wasn't needed, not after what he'd told her about wanting time on his own to get his head together. Her stomach clenched with dismay. She'd so enjoyed getting to know him better today and had been surprised and excited by how much their tastes and beliefs had aligned.

They seemed to be kindred spirits.

Had he felt it too?

'Indigo Hughes—I have a reservation here for tonight,' she said absently to the receptionist when he looked up to greet her, her head still full of thoughts about Julien disappearing from her life now. She knew he'd think it was foolish, but she'd begun to wonder whether they'd been thrown together here for a reason. Ever since she'd met him she'd been filled with an unexpected buzz of hope and excitement for the future, which had been sadly lacking in her personal life for some time.

'Ah, yes, Signorina Hughes, I have a bag for you here,' the receptionist said.

She stared at him, her brain taking a while to switch gears and take in what he'd just said to her.

'Did you say you've got my bag? From the airport?' she asked, her voice trembling with excitement.

'Sì,' the receptionist said, leaving the desk to go into a small room behind reception and returning with her rucksack.

Indigo nearly fell to her knees with relief. After surviving with virtually nothing for half her holiday, it was absolute bliss to have her possessions returned to her. She took the large rucksack from his outstretched hands and hugged it to her like a lost child, then dropped it on to a nearby sofa in the lobby and yanked open the drawstring to check everything was still in there.

Julien returned from the bathroom to find her in a state of ecstasy as she rummaged through the bag, having pulled out first her money, then her phone and now her bikini.

'I can finally go for a swim! I've been desperate to get into the sea but I didn't want to scare the other holidaymakers by stripping down to my sensibly supportive but utterly hideous underwear,' she said, grinning at him.

He stood watching her with an amused smile as she continued to pull things out of her bag and hug them to her.

It felt a little like her birthday and Christmas had all come at once.

Except for the rather unsettling fact that she was about to say goodbye to Julien, of course. It seemed like such a shame when they'd just started getting on so well. Though there was always the possibility they might bump into each other again on the route.

'So, I guess you should be okay with the rest of the walk from this point on,' she said, forcing her mouth into a cheery smile. 'I don't think there are any more exposed paths to worry about.'

Crossing his arms, he leant his hip against the backrest of the sofa. 'Actually, I'm hiring a boat from Nerano. I'm going to sail north along the coast and stop off at some of the places of interest along the way.'

The hope she'd not wanted to fully acknowledge vanished in a puff of smoke and was replaced by a heavy thump of disappointment. So this really was it then. There would be no more opportunities to bump into him. She'd so enjoyed getting to know him today. It had been the most fun day she'd had since she got here. She'd loved the way he challenged and argued with her. Gavin had never stood up to her like that; he'd hated any kind of conflict, which, if she was totally honest, had made him rather dull company sometimes.

Julien, on the other hand, fired something inside her like no one else she'd ever met.

'Okay, well, I guess this is goodbye then,' she said, standing up on unsteady legs. 'It's been good getting to know you, Julien.' She held out her hand, hoping the tremble in it wasn't too obvious.

He stared down at it for the longest time, before clearing his throat and looking back up, straight into her eyes.

Her stomach swooped at the intensity she saw there.

'Listen, why don't you come out on the boat with me this evening? As—what do you English say?—a last hurrah? We can weigh anchor just off the coast, then you can swim away from the crowds. It would be good to have company for one more evening, to give me a chance to check out the boat before I set off on my lone voyage.'

She froze and stared back at him, excited by the invitation, but trying not to let it get the better of her. It was just a sail and a swim he was offering her, nothing more, she reminded herself sternly.

'That sounds like heaven, but are you sure you don't want some peace after having me chewing your ear off all day?'

He smiled, his lopsided grin shooting a disconcerting dart of desire through her. '*Non*. I enjoyed our discussions today. It was a nice distraction.' He didn't say from what, but then he didn't need to. He'd already made it plain why he was here. As an escape from bad memories. Just like her.

'Anyway, I need more time to convince you to give

my favourite thriller author another chance,' he continued when she didn't respond immediately. 'I feel I'd be neglecting my duty to you as a friend if I didn't give it at least one more try.'

The word 'friend' jolted her, reinforcing her resolution not to read anything more into this offer.

Despite her concerns, she couldn't bring herself to say no. Not if saying yes meant being around him for a little while longer. She loved the idea that he'd enjoyed her company today and right now she'd take gratification whichever way it came. After Gavin's accusations, it was nice to feel like she had more to offer than just a shoulder to cry on.

'Well, that would be amazing. I tell you what—since the rest of my money's turned up, I'll buy us dinner,' she suggested, needing to retain a modicum of control in their strange non-relationship relationship.

He smiled again, this time with real warmth, the action of it lighting up his whole face. 'Agreed. Then we're even,' he said.

This time she had to force herself to smile back, because, of course, the sad truth was that they wouldn't be.

Not even close.

A couple of hours later, they were sitting at a table in a beachside restaurant with views across its private golden-sand cove, groaning with pleasure after stuffing themselves full of what they both agreed was the best pasta dish they'd had since arriving in Italy.

'I have to try and persuade them to give me the recipe for this so I can teach my evening class how to make it,' Indigo said, looking round to see whether she could catch the eye of the waiter.

'Give it a go,' Julien said with a smile. 'Just widen those amazingly persuasive eyes at him and I'm sure he'll do anything you ask.'

He wouldn't be at all surprised if she managed to do it either. Indigo had such a lovely way about her it was almost impossible not to give in to her charms—as he himself had discovered time and time again this week.

'Ha! If only it were that easy,' she replied, her cheeks flushing.

Looking at her now, he realised that talking and bantering with her today had been the most fun he'd had in a very long time. She'd ignited something in him with her quick wit and ability to best his arguments, and he'd grown to like her more and more as the day had passed.

She was excellent company.

That was why he'd suggested she join him for a swim from the boat when he'd realised they were about to part ways back at her hotel. It didn't seem like the right way to end things after they'd had such a good day together.

And he hated loose ends.

They were both quiet for a moment as they watched the waiter bustling about between the busy tables.

'So where are we picking up this boat of yours?' she asked, turning to look towards where a number of them bobbed out on the open sea.

'Just over there.' He nodded over towards the other side of the cove where small rowboats and motorboats were being rented out to eager tourists.

'You know, I feel like this holiday has turned a corner,' she said, sitting back in her chair with a grin. 'Only a few days ago it was looking like I was going to have to sing for my supper and look at me now. I couldn't ask for more than this.'

When she looked round at him his heart nearly leapt out of his chest at the expression in her eyes. She looked happy. And the thought that perhaps he'd had something to do with that shook him to the core.

Get a grip, man.

'Anyway—' she cleared her throat '—I guess I'd better settle up.' She turned to catch the waiter's eye and make the international hand sign for the bill. 'Then we can go and cool off in the sea.'

That sounded like a very good idea to him right about then.

A short while after that they sat on a white sofa at back of the yacht that Julien had chartered, drinking from bottles of ice-cold beer.

Indigo leaned back against the plump cushions and stared up at the cloudless sky, barely able to believe where she was right now.

'You know, when you said *boat*, I envisaged something more like one of those,' she said, pointing towards a small rowboat being paddled back to the shore by a hot-and-bothered-looking young man while his girlfriend lay back, blithely trailing her fingers through the water.

'This is more like a luxury cruise liner, albeit a miniature one,' she added, flashing him a teasing grin.

She'd been speechless when they'd zoomed across

the water by motorboat towards this sleek, handsome yacht, which she'd assumed must belong to some millionaire playboy.

It had a kitchen aboard, for goodness' sake, and a full-sized bathroom.

And a bedroom.

That last discovery had thrown her for a complete loop.

'So are you going to sleep here tonight?' she asked, trying not to sound as covetous as she felt. It had to be wonderful to be lulled to sleep by the gentle rock and bob of a boat on the ocean. Especially if Julien was there in the bed too.

Don't go there...

'That's the plan,' he replied, taking another long pull on his beer. 'Don't worry, I can take you back to shore in the motorboat any time you want.'

'I'm not worried,' she said. And she wasn't. Not about him getting her safely back to shore anyway. She felt totally safe in his company; there was something very solid and steady about him—reassuring. But when it came to the way she felt about him, the way her heart leapt and her stomach plunged every time he looked at her...well, that was another matter.

And there was something disconcertingly intimate about the two of them being here, alone together, in the middle of the sea.

They sat back, admiring the view in silence, watching the seagulls wheel above them as the sun's final rays transformed into the warm glow of dusk.

'I can't believe they wouldn't give me the recipe for

that dish,' she said for the umpteenth time since leaving
the restaurant, using her annoyance at not being able
to charm the waiter as a way to disguise her twang-
ing nerves. 'And I gave him a really big tip,' she added
contritely.

'Ah, well, you can't blame them for keeping the secret of their success close to their chests,' Julien said,
employing a full-on Gallic shrug, which made her smile.

'Yeah. I guess it's fair enough,' she grumbled. 'I
could probably guess most of the ingredients anyway.
I'm going to have to experiment when I get home.'

The thought of home made her chest contract. She
didn't want to think about leaving here now that she was
having such a good time. Or the fact that she'd probably
never see Julien again once she left Italy.

'How's your beer?' he asked, breaking into her
thoughts.

'Amazing. Best beer I've ever tasted,' she replied
truthfully. She didn't often drink beer, usually opting
for a glass of crisp, dry white wine when she went out,
but it tasted perfect to her right then. In fact, thinking
about it, everything tasted or felt or smelled that much
more intensely satisfying when Julien was around. It
was as if he made all her senses sit up and pay attention. Whenever she was near him she experienced this
constant prickling frisson, as if she was plugged into
a low-level electric socket, which made her heart race
and her limbs twitch. It was as if her body was priming
itself for something to happen. Something momentous
and life-changing.

But she was a fool if she thought it would. The frustration of this awareness only made the restlessness worse. It made her want to leap around or jump off something, just to relieve the tension of her unsatisfied need.

'I've been meaning to ask—why the red hair?' Julien asked, reaching out and smoothing a piece of it between his fingers.

The tingle of awareness grew more intense. 'It makes me feel powerful,' she replied, desperately trying to latch on to some of that power to give her the strength to keep her wits about her.

'That figures. It suits you.' He smiled right into her eyes, making her breath hitch in her throat.

She gave a little cough to clear the tension. 'Thanks. I've wanted to do it for a while, but Gavin, my ex, wasn't keen, so I didn't until just before I came here.'

His eyebrows nearly hit his hairline. 'Really? I was under the impression you don't like to take orders from anyone.'

Huffing out a laugh, she pulled her feet up on to the sofa and hugged her knees to her. 'I don't normally. But whenever I brought it up as an idea he accused me of not taking his feelings into consideration and I felt bad about that.'

She looked away, remembering the frustration she used to feel when Gavin laid on the guilt to get his own way. It nearly always ended up with her giving in to what he wanted when he did that.

That was something she didn't miss.

Come to think of it, the hurt she'd been carrying around at the beginning of the week seemed to be greatly reduced now. Perhaps it had something to do with having something new and exciting to concentrate on.

Or someone.

Stop!

'Okay, I'm going for a swim before it gets too dark,' she said, springing up, unable to sit still next to Julien any longer, making him jerk in surprise.

Before he could say a word, she dashed down the steps to the diving platform, pulled off the towel she'd wrapped around her to cover her bikini and dived into the water.

The shock of the cold water was a delicious relief against her heated skin, and her heartbeat begin to calm as she swam steadily away from the boat, riding the gentle dip and swell of the waves, feeling a corresponding lift in her tummy.

In the distance, the cliffs rose majestically before her, the foliage vividly green against the soft grey of the rock.

It was so peaceful here, on her own in the middle of the sea with the vast sky above her and the undulating water disappearing into the horizon. This withdrawal was exactly what she needed right now to soothe the raging noise in her head.

It had been fine being alone with Julien when they were walking. The constant forward motion and changing scenery had kept her mind distracted from the intensity of his nearness, but now they were stuck in one place together she was afraid she wouldn't be able to hide how he made her feel when she was around him.

Deep inside her head she knew—she *knew*—that Julien wasn't emotionally available right now and that she should accept that as fact. He'd certainly warned her about it enough times, but it didn't stop her from wondering—hoping—*what if?*

When she finally forced herself to look back towards the boat, she saw that Julien was standing on the diving platform, his face turned towards her, shielding his eyes against the last low rays of the sun.

'Are you coming in? It feels wonderful!' she shouted, aware that her pulse had picked up again at the discovery that he'd been watching her all this time.

He paused for a moment and she got the distinct impression he was searching for an excuse not to join her, but apparently he thought better of it, pulling his T-shirt over his head in one deft move and stepping up on to the edge of the boat.

Indigo trod water, feeling her body being lifted and dropped by the gentle waves as she stared in rapt delight at his muscular physique, immensely glad of the cooling effect of the water as her body surged with nervous heat.

He dived in with the same grace he applied to every physical action and swam towards her, powering through the water. When he reached her, he stopped, barely touching distance away and gave her a wide grin.

'You're right; it does feel wonderful.'

She smiled back, wishing with all her heart that it was okay for her to reach out to him, to slide into his arms and wrap her legs around his waist, to ride the waves with him and laugh and play, then kiss him hard, so he'd know how much she was enjoying being here with him. How he'd opened up this whole new sense of excitement for life in her that she so desperately wanted to cling on to.

For this to be *their* holiday.

She longed to ask him how he'd feel about spending the rest of his week with her, but she knew she'd be on dangerous ground. This link between them was so tenuous it would snap as soon as she put any kind of pressure on it.

So instead, in an attempt to relieve her frustration and wipe that easy smile off his face, she drew back her hand and swished a sheet of water at him.

He didn't see it coming and got a face full.

'Right!' he said with an ominous growl after he'd recovered from the surprise of it, wiping the water off his face with an expression that promised retaliation.

She shrieked and swam away from him, turning back to find him in hot pursuit.

They laughed and played like a couple of kids, chasing each other through the water and sending great sprays of water back and forth until Indigo held up her hand in defeat, her eyes now stinging from the makeup she'd forgotten to take off before jumping into the water.

'Ow, ow, ow! My eyes! Wait, Julien, wait, I can't see.' Distracted by the smarting pain, she forgot to kick and dipped down into the water, sucking in a mouthful of it.

Kicking back up in alarm, she spluttered, coughing the water out and wincing at the revolting taste.

'Are you okay?' she heard Julien say, somewhere close by.

She nodded, but proved herself wrong by acciden-
tally taking in another gulp of briny water when she
drew in a breath to try and cough the sharpness out of
her throat, starting to panic as she felt herself sinking
back down beneath the waves again.

'It's okay, I've got you,' he said right next to her now.

She felt his arm slide around her waist and he pulled
her securely against his chest, lifting her further out of
the water. She clung to him, wrapping her legs around
his hips to make it easier for him to swim, and he kicked
hard, quickly taking them the few metres back to the
boat.

Reaching to grab hold of the rail at the stern, he
hauled them both on to the diving platform and they
toppled backwards with the momentum, Indigo land-
ing on her back beneath him.

He looked down at her, his face only inches from
hers, his eyes dark with alarm.

'Are you okay?' he asked, the concern in his voice
making her shiver.

She was suddenly acutely aware of how little clothing she was wearing and how solid and warm the boat's
deck was under her back and how good the hard press
of his body felt between her legs.

All she could do was nod in response.

'You look like a bedraggled panda,' he murmured,
his voice sounding rough and deep as he ran his thumbs
gently under her eyes, wiping the make-up away.

The simple tenderness of this action undid her and,
from out of nowhere, an overwhelming urge to cry hit
her, forcing the air from her lungs and tightening her

throat. But she didn't want to let the tears come. Not like this, not with him looking at her like he was. He'd see it—her vulnerability and need. So, in the absence of a better idea, she raised her head those few precious inches and kissed him.

In her head, she'd meant it to be a kiss of gratitude, an apology to smooth away his worry, an acknowledgement of his act of kindness, but as soon as her lips touched his, she was lost.

She let out a small moan as she registered the firmness of his mouth, then a gasp as his lips parted so she could sweep the tip of her tongue against his.

He tasted so good: musky and seductive and sweet all wrapped up into one delicious essence. Pressing her lips harder against his, she tightened her grip and pulled his body closer to her, so she was hard up against his solid chest, revelling in the strength of him as she wrapped her limbs around him.

She was drowning again, only this time in his scent, turning into a bundle of nerve endings under his touch. Her whole body sang with joy as she felt the power of him surround her, drawing her down deep into the oblivion of the kiss.

Until something changed.

Her heart started to hammer as she realised he was withdrawing from her.

'Wait, Indigo, stop,' he muttered against her mouth, lifting himself away so she had to loosen her grip on him.

Misery sank through her in a heavy wave as she realised what she'd done.

Exactly what she'd been warning herself against for the entire day.

She'd given herself away again.

When she dared to open her eyes, he was shaking his head, his eyes squeezed tightly closed as if he was trying to will away what had just happened.

And then, like before, when laughter had overtaken her, something seemed to snap inside, only this time it was the tears that came, racking her body with brutal sobs.

'I'm sorry, I'm so sorry,' she managed to struggle out between gasps, wishing she was anywhere but there with Julien right then. She hated him seeing her break down like this.

'I guess I'm still feeling a bit raw and lonely after Gavin dumped me like he did. Not that that's much of an excuse.'

His dismayed expression told her everything she needed to know. She'd totally blown it with him now.

'Stay here. I'll go and get us some towels,' he said, getting up awkwardly.

She felt the cool movement of air on her skin as he left her, which was immediately replaced by the hot sting of humiliation.

Sitting up, she rolled on to her knees then carefully got to her feet, not entirely sure her legs were going to hold her up.

No way was she going to cower here like an idiot until he returned.

By the time she walked on to the main deck, he was coming back with two large, fluffy white towels. He handed one to her and used the other to wipe the remaining water from his face.

'Thank you,' she said, wrapping it tightly around her, unable to make eye contact with him.

'Indigo? Are you okay?' he asked quietly.

When she finally plucked up the courage to look at him his expression was dark with frustration.

'I'm just going to go and wash my face,' she said, tearing her gaze away and turning to make her way shakily down to the belly of the boat.

In the bathroom she sat down on the closed toilet seat and dropped her head into her hands.

What a fool she was. And she only had herself to blame. She'd thought she could handle being here with him—that it wouldn't mean anything to her, but it did. It did.

It meant the world to her.

After washing away the remainder of the make-up, she took a deep bolstering breath and left the bathroom, deciding to ask Julien to take her back to shore right now, before things got any more awkward between them—if that was even possible.

She found him sitting on the sofa when she shuffled back on to the deck, his elbows on his knees and his hands clasped in front of him. He hadn't bothered putting his T-shirt back on and his bare chest glinted with water droplets in the final dying rays of the sun.

Another tormenting rush of awareness made her skin tingle from head to toe.

She perched on the edge of the sofa next to him, readying herself to make some excuse about being tired or needing to get up early the next morning so he wouldn't have to feel guilty about getting her off his boat as soon as possible.

Acutely aware that this would be the last time she'd ever see him, she took a breath and turned to face him, her throat tight with sorrow.

'Tell me what happened with your ex,' he said before she had chance to speak, regarding her with a furrowed brow.

She stared at him, wondering whether she'd misheard.

He just looked back at her with an expectant expression on his face.

'Are—are you sure you want to hear it?' she stuttered. *'Oui.'*

His genuine concern lit a fire within her, warming her both inside and out, but still she hesitated, not sure she wanted him to know the full humiliating story.

He held up a finger. 'Wait. I'll get us more beer.'

Returning a moment later with two more bottles of ice-cold beer, he handed one to her and sat back down, clinking the neck of his against hers before taking a long swallow and raising his eyebrows at her expectantly, waiting for her to begin.

She could *not* tell him, of course—could make up some general non-specific story about things not working out between her and Gavin—but she respected Julien too much to fob him off like that.

She took a long drink from her own bottle, then sat back and took a steadying breath, fighting back the nerves in her tummy before she spoke.

'Apparently my ex, Gavin, needed to be with someone who was more grateful to have him as a boyfriend.'

'More grateful?' Julien repeated slowly, looking
thunderstruck.

She sighed and spread out her hands on her lap, staring down at them for courage.

'Yes, well, our relationship was a bit strange. We met
when he needed somewhere to stay after his wife told
him she wanted a divorce, and I had a spare room available, so I offered it to him as a stopgap—as a favour to
a friend of a friend. He was an emotional wreck when
he moved in and I made a huge effort to make him feel
as welcome as possible.' She took a breath. 'We ended
up getting really close and things sort of developed between us…romantically.'

She glanced at Julien but he just nodded.

'I really liked being the one he leaned on for support.
I guess it fed into my need to try and fix people, or at
least make their lives easier. I'd lost my dad six months
before, after years of looking after him, and I felt a bit
adrift. Gavin was the first serious boyfriend I'd ever
had and I really threw myself into being with him.' She
looked away, across towards the darkening horizon.

'I guess I feel drawn to looking after people. It's what
I do. It makes me feel happy. Useful. In control—or
something.' She knew she sounded defensive, but Julien didn't react so she kept talking.

'Everything was okay between Gavin and me until
I started the Welcome Café,' she continued, wanting
Julien to have the whole story before he judged her.

'He wanted to give me advice about how to run it—

he has his own catering business—and he used to get really offended if I didn't do what he suggested.'

Julien went to speak but she held up a hand, asking him to wait.

'To be fair to him, I'd started spending a lot of evenings working late and at the weekends, so I guess he must have felt neglected as well as ignored.' She sighed and rubbed a hand over her face, vaguely aware of how tight her skin felt after her dip in the sea.

'Thinking about it now, I can see the signs I missed. He'd been frustrated with me at the end of last year because he'd wanted me to go to parties and networking events with him, but I'd made commitments at work that I couldn't get out of so I hadn't been able to go to them.'

Balancing the bottle on her knee, she twisted the neck in her fingers. 'Then, three months ago, I found an engagement ring in the pocket of his coat and got all excited about it being for me.' The familiar tension began to build at the base of her spine.

'He walked into the hall while I was standing there with a goofy smile on my face, staring at it. He went totally white. Like all the blood had drained from his face. At first I thought it was because I'd ruined the surprise by finding the ring before he'd had chance to set up the proposal, but the look in his eyes told me otherwise.'

She realigned the bottle so that the label faced her square-on, unable to look at Julien now, humiliation burning her cheeks.

'He'd bought it to propose to the woman he'd been

cheating on me with.' She stared harder at the beer bottle, catching a drip of condensation on her fingertip as it made its way down the neck. 'He said he was going to tell me when he'd figured out the kindest way to break it to me, but I guess fate stepped in and forced his hand.'

She made an exploding motion with her hands. 'And that was the end of our relationship. They're getting married on Christmas Day, apparently. A winter wedding. Very romantic.'

Looking away, she tested the cool base of the empty bottle against the prickling palm of her hand to distract herself from how hot with mortification she suddenly felt.

'He didn't even give me a chance to fix what I was doing wrong—just found someone else and moved on.'

'It sounds like there wasn't anything for you to fix. He was a coward who used you to get back on his feet— taking advantage of your keen sense of compassion— then cheated on you because he's weak and selfish,' Julien said. There was a rough edge to his voice that she hadn't heard before.

Determined not to give in to the humiliation pressing at the edges of her mind, she sat up on the sofa and gave him a smile, which she hoped came across with sufficient sangfroid. 'Yeah, maybe that's how I should look at it.'

He was looking at her now with a strange expression on his face. Something like solidarity. Or affection.

Or perhaps that was just what she wanted it to be.

Oh, how she ached for it to be that. And more, so much more.

'According to him, it was my fault because I'd started to treat him like a project I'd grown bored with.'

'Had you? Grown bored with him?'

'No.' She shrugged, then sighed in exasperation. 'I don't know. Maybe. I never meant him to feel like that. But I guess once he didn't need me as much any more I took a step back. Perhaps he didn't like the fact I stopped doting on him like I had previously.'

'You mean you started concentrating on yourself and the café and he was annoyed that he'd lost your undivided attention.'

'I guess.' The mention of the café reminded her what was waiting for her to deal with when she got back home, making her stomach roll with unease. 'Ironically, I might lose the café soon anyway if we don't get the funding we need. It can't afford to pay me a living wage for much longer if we don't get the grant I've applied for, and there's no way I'm going to fire any of my staff when they've worked so hard to make it a success.'

Putting the bottle back to her lips, she was surprised to find she'd almost finished. Shrugging, she knocked back the last bit, then stared out towards the twinkling lights that had begun to appear through the velvety dusk in nearby Nerano, desperately trying to pull herself together and regain some modicum of pride.

Julien stared at Indigo's profile, transfixed, as she gazed off into the distance, the pain of her admission clear on her face. She looked younger and more vulnerable without the benefit of her make-up, and the sight of it touched something in his heart.

There was a tight pressure in his chest as he reflected on all that she'd told him. She blamed herself for the breakup of her relationship, which was patently ridiculous. It sounded like the guy hadn't been man enough to handle someone as headstrong as Indigo and, instead of having an honest conversation with her, he'd lied and cheated as a way to escape from a situation he couldn't control.

A raging sense of injustice made him move closer to her on the sofa and slide his hand under her jaw, gently urging her to turn back and face him. He wanted to say something, do something to take that look from her face.

'It never would have worked with Gavin, you know,' he said, shocked by the force of his words as they left his lips.

She blanched, her eyes widening, clearly surprised by the vehemence of his statement. 'You don't think so?'

'*Non.*'

'Why not?'

'Because you emasculated him.'

'What? What do you mean?' Pulling away from his touch, she stood up and took a step away from him.

He stood up too and held out a placating hand. 'I mean he sounds like the type of guy that needs his partner to dote on him to make him feel powerful.' He hadn't meant to alarm her, but he could tell from her body language that he had.

She blinked at him, hurt flashing in her eyes. 'You think I took his power away?'

'Not intentionally, I'm sure. Lots of men can't handle being with smart, assertive women.'

'Great. So what you're telling me is that, basically, if I want to run my own business I'm destined to be single forever.'

He made a move towards her, then stopped himself. 'I didn't say that.'

Her foot slid a little on the deck as she took another step backwards. 'I can't change the way I am, Julien.'

'You don't have to.'

He moved so he was standing right in front of her, barely inches away, and waited until she looked him in the eye again before he spoke. He felt a fierce, instinctive desire to let her know what an incredible person she was.

'Indigo, you're a very attractive woman. Clever, courageous, generous. You'll have no problem finding the right person to love you. Your ex was a fool not to appreciate you.'

She swallowed hard. 'You think? None of those things seem to impress you enough either. You can't even bring yourself to kiss me.' Folding her arms across her chest, she stared down at the floor.

He sighed and rubbed a hand over his face. 'That's because things are complicated for me at the moment.'

She raised a hand. 'It's okay, you don't have to make an excuse. I get it.'

'No, you *don't*, Indigo. You don't get it at all. You're the sexiest, most alluring woman I've ever met, but—'

Unfolding her arms, she flung her hands in the air. 'There's always a "but"!'

'Oui.' He lifted a hand to cup her chin again and force her to look at him so she could see the regret on his face. 'There is.'

His heart thumped heavily against his ribs as he stared into her striking eyes, her pupils so blown he could barely make out the dark ring of her irises in the sinking gloom.

It would feel so good to kiss her right now, to take away her pain. But he knew there would be no going back from it, but also no going forward. He shouldn't put her through that, not when she'd been hurt like she had.

So he just stood there like a fool, inhibited by a powerful sense of walking to the edge of a cliff and looking down into the depths, feeling an innate urge to jump.

'Take me back to shore, Julien. It's time we said goodbye,' she murmured, her eyes welling with fresh tears.

Taking a shuddering breath, she plucked at the end of the towel, which was still wrapped tightly around her, lifting up the edge and using it to dry her eyes before looking up at him again.

His heart gave a hard pulse in his chest at the sight of the pain and humiliation he saw in them.

Because of him.

Seeming to read his concern, she dropped her chin and stared at the floor. 'I'm sorry. I think I drank too much after being teetotal all week. And I'm tired. So tired.' She seemed to sag, as if all the fight had left her, and on instinct he pulled her into a tight hug against him, finding comfort in the scent of her that had become so familiar to him over the last few days. Strangely, he felt as if he'd known it forever.

And they fitted so well together. Like two pieces of a puzzle.

Relaxing his hold on her, he moved back a little so he could look into her face.

'Stay here on the boat tonight,' he heard himself saying.

'What?' Her expression was so full of wounded confusion he knew there was no way he could let her leave now. He had this fierce urge to protect and comfort her, even if it was only for one night.

'I want you to stay with me tonight. Let me prove to you exactly how attractive I find you.'

Without letting her utter another word, he bent to claim her mouth with his own, his body shivering with desire as he experienced the incredible soft sweetness of her again.

Now he'd made the decision he wanted her so much it hurt.

Before she could protest, he scooped her up into his arms, making for the steps to below deck where the bedroom was housed.

The sound of her giggle was music to his ears. 'Julien, you don't need to carry me. I can walk!'

He ignored her, striding down to the forepeak of the boat and into the bedroom, where he lay her gently on the bed.

'Let me look after you tonight, Indigo,' he said, brushing the hair away from her face and settling in next to her, dipping his head to claim her mouth once again.

She gave a small groan of need in the back of her throat. 'Yes,' she whispered against his lips, wrapping her arms around him.

And that was all he needed to hear to finally let himself go.

CHAPTER EIGHT

*Nerano to Sorrento. Walking away from Nerano
will be hard, but the cheering lure of Sorrento
calls...*

WHEN INDIGO WOKE up she couldn't quite place where
she was. Opening her eyes a crack, all she saw was a
plain white wall, which swooped up towards the ceiling like a roof in an attic room. Strange. She didn't remember going to bed in an attic.

Coming round a little more, she became aware of
an unfamiliar rocking motion beneath her and a heavy
weight around her waist that pressed gently into her
tummy. Despite her disorientation, she felt curiously
safe and protected.

Even so, something in the back of her brain told her
that this wasn't where she was supposed to be, and as
she shifted a little she felt a warm pressure behind her
sink a little harder into her back.

Okay, that definitely wasn't right.

Holding her breath, she turned over carefully so as
not to disturb whatever was behind her, only to find her-

self face to face with Julien. His eyes were still firmly shut and flickering slightly in REM sleep, his chest bare above the covers.

It all came flooding back to her in one long agonising rush.

She'd totally lost it last night after telling Julien all her sorry woes and he'd felt forced into taking her to bed to comfort her.

Ugh! What a fool she'd made of herself.

Poor Julien. He'd invited her for a sail and swim from his boat and she'd gone all melodramatic talk show on him.

Trouble was, she'd been holding in this guilt—this fear that the failure of the relationship with Gavin had all been her fault—for so long she'd not realised how close to the surface her pain and sadness really was. She'd just kept pushing it down in order to survive, and as soon as anyone had shown the slightest bit of interest in her she'd blurted the whole thing out in one long rambling splurge.

And he'd been so kind about it. In fact, he'd been more than kind, he'd been downright generous in his praise of her. Which had only served to heighten the emotion of it all.

It had been like catharsis, hearing Julien—someone she respected, revered and whose opinion she cared about—tell her it wasn't her fault. It had released something inside her. She'd finally been able to let the shame go and see the bigger picture.

It had brought it home to her what a fool she'd been thinking that Gavin could be someone she could spend the rest of her life with. She'd had a lucky escape when he left her.

Winter Wedding Woman was welcome to him and his inferiority complex.

But watching Julien now as he slept so peacefully, she felt like a fraud. She'd let him think she was distraught about Gavin leaving her, but that hadn't really been it at all. It was Julien she was most upset about. As she'd told him her miserable tale and seen the understanding and support in his eyes she'd known without a doubt that she'd lied to herself about their connection meaning nothing important to her.

She was in love with him.

Truly and desperately.

But of course she knew it was pointless to hope he felt the same way. He'd already backed away from her more than once, citing his need for freedom after his messy divorce, and one night with her wasn't going to change that.

After the pain of Gavin's cruel dismissal she couldn't put herself in a position where she'd be rejected like that again. Not unless Julien gave her a sign that he'd changed his mind about not looking for another relationship, which she was pretty sure he wasn't going to do.

He'd probably only slept with her last night because he'd felt sorry for her and didn't know what else to do when she'd blubbed all over him.

Her whole body flooded with prickly heat at the thought.

Was that all it had been? A kindness to her? Because he *was* kind—she knew that now she'd finally broken through his gruff exterior. But he'd probably regret what they'd done this morning.

She stared into his handsome face, wondering what it would be like to wake up every day and find him lying next to her. To be allowed to reach over and cup his face in her hands and plant a tender loving kiss on his lips. To be grateful every day for his presence beside her.

There was an ache deep inside her ribs that was making it hard to breathe. The hopelessness of the situation made her want to scream with frustration. Why did she have to meet him now? At the worst possible time in his life.

Perhaps because it wasn't meant to be, a small voice in her head warned.

If only he'd lower his defences enough for her to get through to him. But she understood why he was afraid to let her in; divorce could be a soul-destroying experience that could take months or even years to recover from. And with him living so far away from her there would be no opportunity to take things slowly, to try each other out for size, without making a major commitment.

It would be asking way too much of him.

And she wasn't prepared to be just some woman he'd had a fling with on the rebound.

She knew how these things went. He'd forget all about her once he returned to his real life, once the enchantment of the holiday had worn off. She'd just be some girl he once knew for a few days. An interlude. Barely even an anecdote.

Whereas for her, meeting Julien had been the best thing that had ever happened to her.

As if her last piercing thought had penetrated his dreams, Julien's eyes began to flicker open and he blinked hard, his pupils dilating as he stared into her face in confusion.

For just one heart-stopping second she thought he might lean forwards and kiss her, but he seemed to pull himself together and come fully awake, his brow creasing into a frown.

'Good morning, Indigo, how are you feeling today?'

God, she loved how he said her name, as if he was stroking every syllable with his tongue.

A telltale warmth crept up her neck at the rogue thought, continuing upwards to flush her face with heat.

'A little embarrassed if I'm honest,' she said, averting her eyes from his searching gaze.

He shifted back away from her and sat up, swinging his legs over the edge of the bed.

Realising how disrespectful that sounded, she put out a hand to touch the smooth skin of his back, but withdrew it quickly before she made contact. It felt like too intimate a gesture. 'I mean, I'm sorry for crying on you last night.'

Half turning back to face her, he exhaled in a rush of breath and shook his head.

'No apology necessary. I had fun.'

A bit of fun. That was all it had been.

A feeling of cold acceptance flooded through her, as if the remains of her hope was being washed away, leaving her thoughts clean and jagged.

Hardening the last piece of her heart, she leant down and plucked the towel that she'd been wearing last night from the floor and sat up to wrap it tightly around her.

'Well, I suppose I really ought to get back to shore. I want to get to Sorrento before the end of the day so I can have a good look around before setting off for Capri the day after. Could you take me back in the motorboat, please?'

Her words sounded so perfunctory she cringed with unease.

When she turned to look at him he was staring at her in confused surprise, then blinked and nodded as if coming out of a trance when he saw she was looking at him. '*Oui*. Okay.'

'Thank you.'

Not daring to look at him again, she strode quickly out of the room and into the bathroom, where she'd left her clothes the previous evening after getting changed into her bikini, trying to ignore the voices in her head that were urging her to turn around and tell him that she'd changed her mind and that she could stay for a little longer. Just till they'd eaten breakfast together.

Pull yourself together, Indigo, you fool! You're not a couple and you never will be.

Pulling on the dress she'd chosen with such care for their dinner together last night, she turned to the mirror to try and do something with her hair. It was sticking up in all directions after she'd slept on it wet and refused to play ball, so after a minute of fruitless fussing she gave up on it. She was desperate for a shower, but now that she'd made her mind up to go she didn't want to linger. It would only prolong the pain of leaving.

Giving her puffy face one last dismayed look in the mirror, she left the bathroom and made her way to the living area, where she found Julien sitting on the sofa waiting for her.

He stood up quickly when he saw her and walked with her towards the door to the upper deck, neither of them saying a word.

'Wait.' He put an arm across the doorway before she could walk through it, blocking her way out.

Her heart hammered hard in her chest as she looked up into his mesmerising eyes.

'You know, Indigo, if you don't mind missing that part of the walk I can sail you to Sorrento, then pick you up again the next day and drop you in Capri. I'm going that way anyway. You may as well come along for the ride.'

It was so tempting. But what a ride it would be. Just the thought of having to put a brave face on for him, pretending she was fine with them just being casual lovers for the next couple of days, made her shudder with horror.

No, she'd be better to cut her losses now and walk away while she still had some of her wits about her.

'No. Thanks. To be honest, I don't want to miss walking that bit of the track.' She couldn't meet his eyes. 'I only have a couple of days left here before it's time to get back to reality and I'm sure you don't really want me tagging along for the rest of your holiday.'

He was frowning at her now, which wasn't surprising as her voice seemed to have morphed into that of an ailing crow again.

'Are you sure you're okay?' he asked with real concern in his voice.

'Yes. I was just thinking about what you said about Gavin.'

'Oui?' He looked uncomfortable at the mention of her ex.

'I think you're right; it would never have worked out with him long term. I've been so distracted by the pain and humiliation of the way he dumped me I got the feeling muddled with missing him. I need to be with someone who's proud of me for what I've achieved, not jealous of my success. I've been beating myself up about the wrong things. It's time I stopped.'

'Oui.'

'Thank you, for making me realise that.'

'You're welcome. You deserve to be happy, Indigo.'

'As do you, Julien.'

They stared at each other, with the crackle of unsaid words in the air around them.

Say something more, Julien. Please.

But he didn't; he just nodded in a sage kind of way, as if he hadn't heard the underlying pleading in her voice.

So that was it; she had to leave right now, on her terms. It was important for her peace of mind that she kept her control, after having it so savagely ripped away from her in her last relationship.

For her own sense of self-confidence, she couldn't allow Julien to dismiss her too.

'Okay, well, I'm ready to go when you are,' she said overly brightly.

He didn't say another word as they walked up to the deck together. When they reached where the small on-board motorboat was housed, she hung back until he'd released it from its mooring and manoeuvred it down the small slope and into the water.

After climbing in he held out his hand to help her climb in too and she hoped to goodness he wouldn't notice how much she was shaking.

Neither of them said a word as Julien piloted the small craft back to the shore, sending waves of froth into the choppy water behind them.

At any other time she would have loved the feeling of powering through the waves at high speed, revelling in the adrenaline rush of something so alien and excit-ing, but the heavy tug of gloom in her belly cancelled out any enjoyment she might have felt.

Julien drove the boat straight on to the deserted beach and jumped out, pulling it further ashore so she could step out without getting her feet wet.

Hopping out, she turned to face him.

'So, I guess this is it then,' she said, turning to give him a smile that she knew must look incredibly fake.

'Probably not,' he said, dipping his chin and rais-ing his eyebrow, his eyes holding a look she couldn't decipher.

Was he making a joke about their strangely magnetic connection, or was he about to ask to see her again after he'd concluded his holiday?

She drew in a shaky breath, anticipation making a pulse beat hard in her throat.

'Based on our luck so far, we're bound to run into each other on Capri,' he said with a playful lilt to his voice.

She nodded and waited—heart racing, breath stuck in her throat—for him to suggest they made a plan to meet up there.

But he didn't. Instead, he gave her a tight smile, then turned to look back towards where his yacht was anchored a mile or so off the coast. 'Well, I'd better get back and chart my course,' he said, his voice giving no suggestion at all that he was sorry to see her go. 'I only have the boat for three more days then it's back to real life.'

Real life.

Her stomach dipped and her eyes grew hot, but she refused to show him how much it was going to hurt her to leave him like this.

'Okay, well, enjoy the rest of your holiday,' she said, steeling herself as he moved towards her and placed a gentle kiss on each cheek, French-style.

'It was good knowing you, Indigo,' he murmured into her ear, before pulling back and giving her a firm nod.

'You too, Julien.' She was amazed she'd been able to get the words past her throat.

He nodded once more before turning abruptly on the spot and striding away from her.

It felt empty on the boat after Indigo had gone.

Julien paced up and down the deck feeling unsettled about the way she'd left so suddenly.

When he'd woken up to find her watching him with that perplexed expression in her eyes, he'd been worried that he'd made a huge mistake asking her to stay the night, that he'd hurt her more than helped her—and set himself up for more heartache too—and his first instinct had been to gently let her know that it had been a one-time-only thing for him.

He'd been relieved when she'd made the decision to go without him having to say anything, but he'd also been taken aback and a little perturbed by how vehement she'd been about it.

Something about the way she'd sprung out of bed didn't sit well with him.

After that he'd felt compelled to offer her a lift to Sorrento and had experienced a strange sting of hurt when she'd been almost cold in her refusal.

The memory of it disturbed him.

Perhaps she'd been embarrassed about what had happened between them after she'd fallen apart last night.

He wasn't, though. He'd loved the feel of her in his arms and the softness of her pressed beneath him. She'd been so responsive to him, making it clear she'd enjoyed his touch as much as he'd enjoyed hers.

Maybe she was just distracted by the thought of what awaited her when she got home after talking to him about it last night.

It made him so angry to think about how badly her ex had treated her because her strength and tenacity had intimidated him. And he hated the idea that she had to deal with the threat of the business she'd worked so hard to build from nothing being taken away from her all by herself.

She deserved better.

Needing a distraction from his thoughts, he went down into the galley kitchen and fixed himself some breakfast, raiding the ready-stocked cupboards and fridge, choosing sugar-free muesli and strong black coffee to satisfy his appetite. Not that he felt particularly hungry this morning.

After clearing away his crockery, he tried reading one of the books from a shelf in the living area, but he couldn't seem to concentrate on it. He was restless and twitchy. Perhaps Indigo had had a point about not missing today's walk. His body seemed attuned to doing that much exercise now and the lack of it today had left him with an abundance of energy.

Getting up, he went down to the bedroom and made the bed, pausing to skim his fingers over a small black smudge that the last of her eye make-up had left on one of the pillows.

It made him think of the way she'd looked at him through her thick black lashes when she wanted him to agree to something and a sudden, disorientating feeling of loss hit him straight in the solar plexus, taking his breath away.

Like the walking, he'd become so attuned to her presence he appeared to be missing her company.

Which finally brought him round to the real reason he'd felt troubled about her leaving so suddenly.

Waking up in the early hours of the morning to find her warm body snuggled up against his had shaken him.

Lying there under the heavy blanket of night he'd felt such a sense of calm—for the first time in as long as he could remember. He'd rested there, with Indigo in his arms, exulting in the rush and pull of the ocean beneath them, enjoying the gentle melody of the waves against the hull of the boat as he drifted in and out of sleep.

In his half wakeful state, he'd relived the feel of her long, long limbs wrapped around him, and the intoxicating scent of her as he dragged it deep into his lungs and the sweet taste of her in his mouth. He'd wanted her so badly he ached with it, and he'd just taken what he wanted even though he'd known it was a bad idea. An insight that had been reinforced when he'd seen the regret in her eyes the next morning.

It reminded him a little too keenly of all those gut-wrenching mornings, waking up next to Celine and seeing the shuttered look on her face. The cold, blank expression of a woman who despised him.

His failure to make things right between him and Celine still haunted him, even though they were divorced now and she was no longer his responsibility. He'd always been able to fix things before he met her—by finally earning enough money to buy his mother the kind of house she deserved and provide her with a lifestyle that made her happy, by finding jobs for friends who found themselves adrift and in money trouble—but with Celine he'd not been able to find a way to satisfy her. He'd given her everything he could think of and it still hadn't been enough.

It had eaten away at him.

And now he had a new regret.

He'd known, in his heart, that Indigo wasn't the sort of person who would be satisfied with a one-night stand, but he'd gone ahead and let it happen anyway. To satisfy his greedy need.

Slumping down on to the bed, he rolled on to his back and stared up at the ceiling, imagining the vast blue sky stretching out above him, feeling smaller and more helpless than he was comfortable with.

He really didn't want to have Indigo's suffering gnawing away at him too. He could have done so much more to make her happy, but he'd let her go, telling himself it was what she wanted.

She'd needed more from him than a kiss on the cheek and a metaphorical pat on the head.

His hands twitched at his sides as blood rushed through his veins.

There was no way he could leave things with her like this; it would plague him for the rest of his life.

Especially when he knew he could do something to really help and support her.

Sitting up, he took a deep fortifying breath, feeling his energy returning as purpose and resolve flooded his body with adrenaline.

He was going to find her and make things right.

CHAPTER NINE

Sorrento to Capri. It could be a rough ride between the mainland and the island, so be prepared for turbulence on your journey. Don't worry—once you're there it'll all be worth it...

HE'D NOT BEEN able to find Indigo in Sorrento.

It was ridiculous for him to feel miffed about the fact because the town had a population of over fifteen thousand, which no doubt doubled in high season. But after not being able to avoid her at the beginning of the week he'd fully expected to bump into her as soon as he set foot on dry land.

But after a fruitless search through the town, where he felt as if he'd visited every eatery and hotel that Sorrento had to offer, his heart lurching every time he caught so much as a flash of the colour red, he'd finally given up, deciding the best place to catch her would be the small port in Capri where the ferries sailed in from Sorrento on a regular basis.

Mooring the yacht in the marina just to the west of the main ferry port, he holed up early for the evening, determined to get up at the crack of dawn in order to meet the first ferry of the day in case Indigo was on it.

It felt good to have a purpose after spending the rest of the week in a state of disconnected limbo, occasionally checking his work email for news, only to find that everything was running smoothly without him. This had both heartened and distressed him.

He didn't like the idea of not being needed.

The early morning air felt fresh and cool on his skin as he made his way over to where the passenger ferries docked in the marina, armed with a bag full of food and beverages so he wouldn't have to run the risk of missing Indigo in between landings.

When he arrived, the place was only just waking up for business, catering for a few early risers who paced about waiting for the first ferry to arrive and take them back to the mainland.

He could tell from the intensity of the first rays of the sun burning through the low hanging clouds that it was going to be another hot day.

Settling down on to one of the long stone benches that faced out across the water, he took out a book he'd borrowed from his yacht's small library, made himself as comfortable as possible on a seat that wasn't really designed for people to sit on for more than a few minutes and prepared himself to wait until Indigo made an appearance.

Since leaving Julien on the beach in Nerano, Indigo had spent her time making good on her decision to continue the walk to Sorrento. In a stroke of pure luck, she'd bumped into Ruth and her group heading that way too, and was somewhat relieved to find herself warmly integrated back into the group.

She'd needed the distraction after spending the morning in a state of torment after saying goodbye to Julien.

It had taken Ruth a couple of miles' worth of small talk before she finally got round to asking about him, clearly sensing that there was something wrong in Indigo's world but that she wasn't going to bring it up herself.

Indigo had been preparing herself to talk about Julien, but even so, it was still hard to make her story of their walk to Nerano and subsequent night on the yacht sound as inconsequential as she'd wanted it to.

Ruth had not been fooled by her bluster though and had pressed her about their relationship until Indigo had given up on the pretence that he meant nothing important to her and blurted out the whole sorry tale.

'He sounds like he needs more time, love,' Ruth told her as they walked the last leg towards Sorrento.

'Yeah, I know,' she said with a sigh. 'It was just really bad timing.' They walked for another mile or so in companionable silence, with Indigo's thoughts spinning through her head until she couldn't keep it in any longer.

'I just felt like we were meant to meet,' she blurted. 'It was like some force kept dragging us back together. It felt right to be with him, you know?'

'I do,' Ruth agreed. 'My husband and I met in Western Samoa, of all places, after living only five miles apart for twelve years, never having crossed paths before. We kept missing each other, even though we now realise we'd attended quite a few of the same events. He was married to someone else at the time, though, who sadly died after a long illness a year before he and I met each other in Samoa, so it wouldn't have worked out if we'd bumped into each other earlier. It's funny how these things happen. You can't help but suspect there's some kind of benevolent force pushing you together at the right time.'

'Yeah, but if the other person isn't ready, there's only so much magic fate can weave.'

They'd come to a halt on the outskirts of the town at that point and Ruth put a comforting arm around her. 'If it's meant to be, you'll see him again, honey,' she said with a warmth in her voice that made Indigo think of the cuddles her mum used to give her when she was upset about something. From out of nowhere, she experienced a sudden and intense pang of loss. The grief of losing her mother never seemed to lessen, though it hit her less often these days, usually when she was feeling particularly low. This time it had the disconcerting effect of reminding her just how alone in the world she was right then.

Forcing back the tears that threatened to spill over, she hugged Ruth back hard, finally pulling away to give her a grateful smile.

'Thanks for taking me under your wing; I really needed the company today,' she said.

'You're welcome, sweetheart. We're flying back to England tomorrow so I'm afraid we won't be able to continue on your travels with you. I hope you enjoy your time in Capri, though—and that you find what you're looking for,' she said with a kind smile.

Indigo couldn't help but smile back, albeit with a twist of sad scepticism.

'Yeah, you never know,' she said.

And now here she was, stepping off the ferry in Capri into the bright morning sunshine and the first person she laid eyes on was Julien.

He appeared to have been watching the people getting off the ferry and as soon as he locked eyes with her he stood up and started walking towards her.

She came to a sudden halt in shock, feeling the other passengers push past her and hearing the odd 'tut' as she blocked part of the gangway. Her heart hammered in her chest, her senses on high alert as she watched him pushing his way through the crowd.

What was he doing here?

Pulling herself together, she started walking towards him again, feeling the tide of people drawing them ever closer together, until finally they were standing only feet apart, grinning as if they'd not seen each other for a year.

A gentle breeze whipped her hair around her head and she pushed it away from her face with a shaking hand.

'Julien—I thought I'd seen the last of you,' she said, hyperaware of a tremble in her voice. 'Were you waiting here for me?'

'*Oui.*'

She gazed into his eyes looking for a clue as to why, hardly daring to hope that he'd come to tell her he'd changed his mind about being ready for a new relationship, but his expression was inscrutable.

'I wanted to catch you before I leave Capri and sail on to Naples,' he said, taking her hand and leading her gently away from the crowd of people still mingling around the ferry and over towards the quieter side of the port.

So he wasn't staying on Capri? Was he here to try and persuade her to leave with him then? The idea of it made her stomach flutter.

When they reached a small stone bench next to a closed ticket office he let go of her hand and, reaching for her rucksack, lifted it from her shoulder and propped it up against the bench.

The anticipation was killing her. 'What's going on? Is everything okay?' she asked, hugging her arms around her. Despite her conviction they were meant to be together, something in the back of her brain warned her not to get her hopes up, just in case.

'I have something I want to give you.' He moved his hand around to his back pocket, glancing behind him as he removed whatever he had in there.

For one ridiculous, heart-thumping second she thought he was going to produce a ring and she drew in a sharp, shaky breath…

It was a large white envelope.

He held it out towards her, an expectant smile lighting up his eyes.

She tried hard not to let her disappointment show on her face as she stared down at it.

'What's this?' she asked.

'Open it and see.'

Her hands shook as she took the envelope from him and lifted up the flap at the back.

She stared at the contents, a heavy sinking sensation turning her stomach over.

It was money. Lots and lots of money. All in fifty euro notes.

'It's a donation to help with the running of your café. So you can keep working there,' he said, not appearing to notice her distress.

'I felt bad about the way we'd left things after what happened between us,' he said. 'I kept thinking about what a struggle you'll have when you get back to London. I wanted to do something to help you.'

'You came here to give me money?' she asked, her voice barely making it past her throat. Bitter disillusionment coursed through her, causing her eyes to burn with unshed tears and her skin to prickle as if she were being attacked by a thousand bees.

He frowned, looking visibly shocked by her lack of enthusiasm. 'What's wrong? I thought you'd be pleased.'

'Do you even know me at all? Did you really think I wouldn't be offended by you giving me money after I'd slept with you?' Her voice crackled with dismay. 'It's like you're paying me off to relieve your conscience!'

She knew it was a low blow, but she was so angry with him right now. Couldn't he see how humiliating this was for her?

'That's not why I'm giving it to you. *Mon Dieu!* It just means if your grant doesn't come through you can keep working there until you find another source of funding.' His shoulders tensed as he folded his arms across his chest. 'I wanted to do something to help you,' he repeated, in the same tone he'd used with the receptionist on the very first night they'd met, when he'd made it clear how disgusted he was with the lack of service she'd provided.

'I don't want your money, Julien.' This time the words came out loud and clear, thanks to a sudden surge of anger that came rushing up from the pit of her stomach.

He opened his mouth to speak, then looked away as if he'd thought better of it, frowning and shaking his head in confusion.

When he looked back, his expression was shuttered and a muscle flickered in his jaw.

'Where is this coming from, Indigo? Hmm? Why are you so angry with me for wanting to help? Can't you put your stubborn pride aside for a moment and let someone help *you* for once?' He shook his head, his eyes narrowed. 'I don't understand. What is it you want from me?'

How could he ask that? Didn't he know how she felt about him? Wasn't it obvious? 'I want you, you idiot!'

The silence after her outburst seemed to stretch on forever.

Finally, Julien closed his eyes and rubbed a hand over his face, letting out a long sigh.

'When you turned up here I thought you'd come back for me. *Me*, Julien!' Her throat felt painfully tight as she fought back the tears. 'But I guess that makes me the idiot!' A sob broke loose and she clasped a hand over her mouth to stop any more from escaping.

'Indigo—' His expression was full of regret now.

'I just want the opportunity for us to get to know each other better.' She took a deep, calming breath, not wanting to give in to her emotions and ruin any chance she had of making herself heard. 'To give a relationship a chance.'

He was shaking his head now, his eyes a little wild, as if she'd caught him in a trap and he couldn't see any way to escape. 'I can't, Indigo. I'm not ready for that.'

'So you'll just let this amazing connection that we have go? You feel it too, right? Please tell me it's not just me.'

There was another long silence where he stared at the ground. 'It's not just you,' he said finally.

'So why won't you give it a chance?'

'I *can't*, Indigo.'

'What are you afraid of?'

He rubbed a hand over his face. 'I've spent the last two years feeling like I was suffocating. I need my space—to begin to feel like I've got a grip on my life again.'

'And you can't do that and still have some space left for me?'

He spread his hands in mute apology. 'No. I'm sorry.' He gestured towards the envelope still clutched in her hand. 'That's the best I can do right now.'

'Well, I don't want it.' She thrust it back towards him and after a second's hesitation he took it from her.

From the intensity of his frown she could tell that he wasn't prepared to listen to any more of her entreaties.

She opened her mouth to try anyway, but he raised his hand to stop her.

'I can't ask you to wait for me, Indigo, because I don't know when I'll feel ready to have another serious relationship again—or if I'll ever be ready for one.

And, after what happened with your ex, the last thing you need is to embark on something so precarious with someone like me. I don't want to have any part in corrupting that amazing positivity that you have. I'm too bitter and messed up right now. I'd be a danger to you.'

'But you might feel differently one day?' There was a pleading tone in her voice now that made her cringe inside.

'*Oui*, I might. But I can't make that promise and it wouldn't be fair to ask you to wait in the hope things would change for me. I need my freedom right now and you need something I can't give you—stability. Don't wait for me. I'm sure the best person for you will walk into your life when you most need him to.'

'You already did, Julien.' Her voice broke on his name.

He shook his head and backed away from her, the expression in his eyes hard with determination. '*Non*, Indigo. I think you're an amazing woman and at another time in my life maybe we could have had something really special, but not now.'

She moved towards him, desperate not to leave things this way between them. 'You can't beat yourself up forever because of one bad relationship.'

'I'm sorry, Indigo, I have nothing else to offer you right now.' He held up the envelope, then dropped his hand again as if he felt frustrated to still be holding it.

The pause seemed to go on forever as she swallowed and swallowed and swallowed down the pain.

'Okay then, go, if that's what you think is best,' she finally managed to say.

He gave her one last nod, then turned and walked away, taking her very last hope for a future together with him.

She wanted to weep—for what could have been if only they'd met at another time.

How was it possible to feel like this for Julien after such a short amount of time? It seemed incredible that it was only a week since he'd come storming into her life with his reluctant heroism and inimitable strength.

But who you fell in love with wasn't something you could control.

And she had fallen in love with him. Desperately and completely.

But now she had to let him go.

There was something very fitting about the rough assault of waves against his boat, Julien reflected as he fought to keep the vessel on course through a sudden and ferocious storm that had swept in without warning the following day. It harmonised well with the raging confusion of emotions in his head.

This holiday was meant to punctuate a difficult and painful time in his life, to give him a definite end to the way it was then, but, to his utter frustration, it only seemed to have started a new chapter.

During his time with Indigo he'd begun to sense a difference in himself. Somehow she'd managed to pop the bubble that had been preventing him from feeling anything, bringing everything into razor-sharp focus.

The flip side of that was that he now felt everything. So acutely it made his chest ache.

He spent the next couple of days after the storm taking mental breaths whilst gliding slowly through the now peaceful waters, sailing past the looming greatness of Vesuvius, then onward towards his final destination, Naples, where he was to leave the boat and board a plane back to Paris.

Back to reality.

Not that this holiday hadn't been very real. In fact, it had probably ended up being more stressful than a week's work would have been, just for very different reasons.

Or, more precisely, one reason.

Not allowing himself to be with Indigo.

When he'd seen the look of appeal on her face, just before he'd turned away from her, he'd known in that split second what was causing the painful ache in his chest.

Love.

A fierce and irrepressible love for her.

It had shaken him to his core. Which was why he'd walked away and kept on walking until he was back on his boat, then back out to sea, putting a whole body of water between them.

He'd told himself at the time that he was leaving so she didn't get hurt, but he knew he'd only hurt her more. He'd seen it in her eyes and in the slump of her shoulders—the grief for something that could have been so good.

Thinking about it now, he realised he'd treated her with a total lack of respect by trying to buy his absolution.

How could he have thought that the way to make her happy was to give her *money*? How crass and unthinking he'd been. He knew now he couldn't buy her happiness or respect; he had to earn it with his actions, by giving her something of himself.

Which was a terrifying thought after what had happened with Celine. But then wasn't that the point? Real love was never easy; it was complex and sticky and downright rough sometimes.

He knew now that he hadn't been in love with Celine—in lust, sure—and he'd married her because he believed it was the right thing to do at the time. But the way he felt about Indigo wasn't wrapped up in sex or lust or duty; it was based on how he felt about himself when he was with her.

She'd made him come alive.

In the dark hours of the night, tossing and turning as sleep eluded him, he pictured her back in London, filling her days working at the café, laughing and joking with her colleagues, then perhaps going on a date with a man she'd met, the sparkle returning to her eyes as he lavished the praise and attention on her that she deserved.

The thought of someone else taking care of her made his stomach lurch with anxiety.

Indigo would be fine without him because she was a fighter. It was one of the things he loved about her.

But would he be all right without her?

Okay, so meeting Indigo right now wasn't great timing, but then what in life ever really was?

And at least this time being with her would be his choice.

Fuelled by the fervour of his revelation, he quickly plotted a course that would get him to Naples ahead of schedule, then picked up his phone, intent on getting himself out of Italy as fast as possible in order to set a new plan in motion.

He knew now that being here alone had been a pilgrimage to nothing. He'd thought he wanted his freedom—but it didn't feel the way he'd thought it would. It felt empty. And silent. And lonely.

A pyrrhic victory.

He'd thought he could go back to the way things used to be, before Celine, but trying to go backwards was a big mistake.

What he needed was a fresh start.

Finally, there was clarity in his mind. He missed Indigo. He loved her. He'd let her go.

And now he was going to get her back.

CHAPTER TEN

London is a vibrant and forward-looking city,
ever evolving, with an exciting new encounter
just waiting for you at every turn...

One week later

INDIGO WIPED HER hands on her apron and looked round
at the eclectic gathering of local people who had turned
up for her early evening cookery course, despite the
torrential rain.

Her feet throbbed and her back ached from being
on her feet all day, but her insides burned with satisfied warmth as she perused the table full of nutritious,
delicious-smelling food that her class had produced in
just half an hour—which they'd easily be able to rep-
licate at home.

This made all her hard work worth it—the shine
of pride on the faces of people who'd previously not
believed they'd ever have the skills to cook anything
vaguely edible for themselves, let alone something
they'd be proud to share with friends or loved ones.

The kitchen at the back of the café wasn't stocked with enough culinary equipment to be able to teach more than five people at a time, but she was hoping that once the grant came through—she mentally crossed her fingers that it still would—she'd be able to afford to buy more so she could teach a larger group at one time.

'Well, I think you've all done a wonderful job today; it's great to see how much you've improved since you first started coming here,' she said, beaming at them all.

'It's good to have you back, Indigo; we missed your lovely smile while you were off gallivanting in Italy,' Ron, one of the gentlemen who had been coming to her for a couple of months, now called across the room, giving her a cheeky wink. He'd been a morose character when he'd first started coming, due to losing his beloved wife only a short time ago, but he'd slowly made friends and come out of his shell as, week by week, he'd allowed himself to be integrated into the group. She suspected there might even be romance blossoming between him and the only lady currently attending. They often had their heads together, chatting quietly as they worked.

Pushing away a sting of melancholy at the thought of the dire state of her own love life, he returned his wink and gestured towards the table.

'Okay, well, if you want to start tidying away, we're just about out of time. I don't know about you, but I can't wait to get home and eat after being tortured by the smell of your wonderful grub cooking for the last twenty minutes.'

It was hard keeping up a chipper tone of voice when

her heart was so heavy, but somehow she seemed to be managing it.

When the group had asked her about her holiday she'd worked hard to sound breezy and upbeat about it, telling them as much as she could whilst studiously avoiding mentioning Julien's name. She thought she'd pulled off making it sound as if she'd had a fun and re-vitalising time, though.

The bell of the café rang in the distance and she glanced over to her friend and kitchen assistant, Lacey, sharing a questioning smile with her.

'I'll go and see who it is and tell them we're closed,' Lacey said, already walking towards the door.

Grabbing some dirty bowls from the table, Indigo went to stack them in the dishwasher—wanting to pre-empt the tidy-up so she could get home a bit earlier to-night and have a soothing bath—and turned back to see Lacey walk into the kitchen, closely followed by a man.

A man who was tall, with blond hair and mesmeris-ing whisky-brown eyes.

'Julien?' she gasped, not wanting to trust her vision. She hadn't been sleeping particularly well since she'd got back, her mind still whirling with thoughts about him, and she wondered for a second whether her addled brain had conjured him up to torture her a little bit more.

He walked slowly towards her, smiling in that wry way that she knew so well, making her heart beat a little faster with the comforting familiarity of it.

'What…what are you doing here?' she stammered.

'I hear you offer cookery courses to men who no longer have wives,' he said.

She blinked at him, confused by such a strange opening line. 'To widowers usually,' she said uncertainly. There was a beat of uncomfortable silence. 'But I guess we could make an exception for a divorcee,' she finished, not wanting to look rude and uncomfortable in front of her class.

'Is this the young man you met on holiday that you've been avoiding telling us about?' Margery, the lone woman in the group, piped up, her eyes twinkling with good humour.

The whole roomful of people seemed to shift at once as they all turned to look at each other, exchanging knowing glances.

Had they been talking about her behind her back whenever she left the room?

She sighed, feeling trapped and unprepared to deal with Julien's presence here in her kitchen—a place she liked to think of as her personal sanctuary. 'This is Julien,' she said, gesturing vaguely towards him. 'And yes, we met in Italy.'

There was a murmur of friendly greeting from the group.

Turning to face him now, she said with as much assertiveness as she could muster, 'I'm afraid we're just about to pack up for the evening, but if you'd like to come back at another time I'm sure we can talk about finding a place in a group for you.'

There was a glint of determination in his eyes. 'Actually, I was hoping I could walk you home tonight,' he said, moving closer. 'I have some things I need to say to you—and I'd rather not do it in front of all these strange people.' He held up an apologetic hand to the group. 'No offence.'

'None taken,' Margery called from the other side of the room, giving Julien a supportive grin.

'Yes, Indigo, you go,' Lacey said. 'I can supervise the tidy-up and make sure the place is locked up before I leave.'

Indigo opened her mouth to argue but, as one, the whole group shook their heads at her.

'Go and spend some time with your friend,' Ron said, flapping a dismissing hand at her.

Well, it seemed as if she didn't have much of a choice. Clearly, they weren't going to let her stay. So much for her being the one in charge here.

'Okay then,' she said with an exasperated smile, pulling off her apron and going to hang it up on one of the pegs on the wall. She gave her hands a quick wash, then went to fetch her bag and coat from the small office behind the kitchen, taking a moment to drag in some steadying breaths before she went back out there to face whatever was in store for her this evening. No way was she letting herself get excited about him being here. She didn't think she could cope with more disappointment when it came to Julien.

When she returned he was chatting comfortably with Lacey, who was leaning against the counter, looking up at him with big, friendly eyes.

Huh, trust him to charm everyone as soon as he walked in.

'Okay, I'm ready to go,' she told Julien as she approached the two of them, making sure to keep her voice emotion-free. 'Thanks, Lacey.'

'Have a good evening,' her friend replied, giving her a covert eyebrow-waggle.

Indigo scowled back, intensely aware of Julien's presence right there beside her.

'See you next week, everyone,' she called to the rest of the group, hoping to goodness her face didn't look as flushed as it felt. They all responded with a wave and a smile and continued to watch her with interest until she put her hand on Julien's back and ushered him towards the door. There was a gentle hubbub of noise as they walked out. No doubt tongues would be wagging once she'd gone.

Out in the damp night air, she turned to face him and crossed her arms in front of her. It felt so strange to see him here, on her patch. He was as immaculately dressed as always and her tummy tumbled as she fully took him in for the first time since he'd shown up. He looked so darn handsome, standing there as if he didn't have a care in the world. Which she guessed he didn't. She wondered fleetingly whether it was going to be possible to get through this without entirely losing her cool.

'So what's this all about? Why are you here?'

He let out a low breath and looked around him, as if gathering himself for what he was about to say. 'Let's walk, shall we?'

'Can't you just tell me here?' she said, grasping on to the only thread of power she had left.

He crossed his own arms and frowned down at the floor and she noticed for the first time that he had a black shopping bag swinging from one hand. She wondered what he could have in there. It was a strange receptacle for him to be carrying overnight clothes in.

'What's in the bag?' she blurted, unable to keep her curiosity to herself.

'You'll see,' he said, flashing her an enigmatic smile.

'Really? You're not going to tell me?'

'*Non*. You'll have to wait until we're back at your flat and I'm ready to show you. I'm not prepared to do this out on the street either.'

She bristled with frustration. 'And you think I'm stubborn!' Sighing, she took one more look at the determination on his face and gave him a resigned nod, knowing there was no way she could turn him away. Not if it meant she'd finally find out what was really going on with him. It had been eating away at her since she'd last seen him and she needed answers so she could move on.

'Okay, fine, you win.' She gestured for them to start walking. 'It's this way.'

It only took them two minutes to walk to her flat from the café and neither of them spoke a word as they made their way down the noisy main road, stepping around the puddles that the earlier heavy downpour had left in its wake.

'This is me,' she said when they reached the end of her road.

He followed her to her flat—the place she'd moved into after Gavin had left her. Hers was on the top floor of the converted terrace house, which she loved because she enjoyed falling asleep looking at the night sky through the skylight in the sloping attic ceiling.

'I'm at the top,' she said, letting them in through the main door and leading him up the stairs. It took her a moment to get the key to line up with the lock because her hands were shaking so much. He stood so close to her she could smell the wonderfully evocative scent of him and she had to take great gulps of air through her mouth so as not to become too distracted by the urge to turn around and wrap her arms around him and pull him close.

When she finally got the door open, she led him through to the kitchen diner and gestured for him to sit with her at the small dining table that she had set up in the middle of the room.

Blood pulsed in her ears as she waited for him to tell her why he was here.

'Have you heard about your grant yet?' he asked conversationally, throwing her for a loop.

Was he still cross about her refusing to take the money from him? She hoped he wasn't here to try and get her to change her mind. She didn't regret the decision she'd made, firmly believing that things would work out here without his help. Somehow.

She folded her arms. 'Not yet. Soon, hopefully.'

'That must be stressful.'

She shrugged. 'Yes, well, as you know, money and I aren't exactly on speaking terms at the moment.'

He smiled. 'That makes two of us.'

What did he mean by that?

'Are you having financial troubles too?' she asked, confused.

'No. But money seems to be my nemesis at the moment. It makes me do stupid things.'

There was a tense pause while she waited for him to elaborate.

He didn't. Instead, he jumped up and started pacing around the room, moving into the living area and running his fingers lightly over her things, as if wanting to learn them by touch.

'It's a great flat. Exactly the sort of place I imagined you living in. It's very you.'

'Me?'

He nodded, turning to look her in the eyes. 'Sophisticated, but welcoming.'

She couldn't stop the smile from breaking over her face. 'How very kind of you.'

He started pacing around again and she realised with a shock that he was nervous.

Standing up, she took a couple of steps towards him. 'Julien, will you please just spit out whatever it is you've come to say? You're killing me here!'

He stopped moving and turned to face her again, his expression apologetic.

Taking an audible breath, he walked closer. 'Okay, first of all, I wanted to say sorry, about trying to buy my freedom—and your forgiveness. It was a crass and selfish thing to do. I knew how much you needed that money and it wasn't fair to make you choose between that and me.' He snorted gently. 'Not that you did. In your inimitable style you turned your back on both options.'

'I couldn't feel like I was indebted to you, Julien, it would have destroyed any equilibrium between us.'

He nodded, his expression telling her he understood

what she was saying. 'It seems to have become a bad habit with me to throw money at things to try and fix them quickly and without pain. It was ignorant of me to do that and I can see now why you were offended. I apologise.'

A heavy weight seemed to lift from her chest. 'Apology accepted.'

Julien looked at the woman he loved and knew that if he wanted to repair things between them he had to tell her everything. He owed her an explanation after all the strife he'd caused. But now he was here he was having trouble finding the words he needed without making himself sound like the worst kind of low life.

This was exactly why he'd not talked to anyone else when it became apparent that his marriage was over. The shame had stopped the words—kept them lodged inside him, somewhere between his chest and his throat, like a cork pushed too far down to extract.

'I want to tell you why I was such a nightmare to be around in Italy,' he said. 'So you understand that my behaviour was never about something you did or didn't do.'

The apprehension in her eyes made his blood pump faster and he watched with concern as she walked further into the living area and sat down heavily on to her small red velvet sofa as if her legs had suddenly refused to hold her any longer.

'Okay. Go on,' she said quietly.

He sat down too and turned to face her, making sure he had her full attention before he started his sorry tale.

She looked back at him with such apprehension he hoped to God this wouldn't be the last time he'd ever see her after making his confession.

'My ex-wife's name is Celine,' he began, deciding to cover the basic facts first, hoping the rest would flow from there. 'We met at a mutual friend's wedding. Both of us were late and we snuck into the back of the church together and somehow managed to knock over a huge flower display and disrupt the service at a key moment. As you can imagine, that didn't exactly make us popular guests, but it banded us together as social fugitives.'

'Is your mutual friend speaking to you yet?' she asked with a smile in her voice.

He grimaced, too aware of the regret pulling at him to enjoy the gentle joke, but relieved that she felt comfortable enough to tease him still. 'Only just.'

She flapped a hand. 'Sorry to interrupt; do go on.'

'At that point in my life I'd been working so hard I'd not given any of my relationships—with perfectly nice women—a decent chance of surviving and it had begun to occur to me, as I watched all my friends get married and move on with their lives, that I'd put my career before my personal life for too long, and if I didn't do something about it I was going to end up a lonely old man.'

She shifted on the sofa, pulling her legs under her, and he took her cue and settled back, making himself more comfortable.

'Celine made me feel like there could be an exciting future ahead of me and, after our first meeting, we started seeing each other regularly—though when

I say "seeing" I mean we spent a lot of time in bed together. It was a crazy whirlwind of a relationship and she turned my entire world upside down. She had this energy that electrified me: she was wild and spontaneous and creative, all the things I'm not, but she was also highly strung and only seemed to thrive when all the attention was on her. I can see that now, with the benefit of hindsight, though I was blind to it at the time.'

He was quiet for a while as he relived the memory of what he'd thought was the most passionate and extraordinary interlude in his formerly routine life—until he'd met Indigo and realised what passion really was.

'So what happened?' she prompted gently.

He sighed. 'We jumped into getting married too quickly.' He took a breath. 'I thought I was doing the right thing at the time, but it was a huge mistake.'

'What do you mean, "doing the right thing"?' she asked with a careful tone to her voice, which made him think she'd already figured it out.

He turned to give her a sad, knowing smile. '*Oui*, she was pregnant.'

She looked at him steadily for a moment and he saw her throat bob as she swallowed hard. 'Ah. I see. Well, that was honourable of you.'

'Yes, well, my father left my mother after he got her pregnant and she struggled for money and support for years, raising me. It was very tough on her. I didn't want Celine to suffer like that and I wanted to be there for my child. I worked hard for years to be successful so I'd be in a good position to support a family, should

I have one. It didn't happen the way I was expecting it to, but I thought: *so what?* This was my child and I was prepared to make a go of the marriage so we could all be together.'

'So you *do* have a child?' she asked quietly.

He shook his head and averted his gaze, staring instead at a print of Monet's *Poppies* that she had on the wall behind the sofa, finding comfort in the vibrant colours. '*Non.* We lost the baby a few weeks after our wedding.'

When he turned back to look at her, the expression on her face was so full of sympathy it made his stomach drop.

'Oh, Julien, I'm so sorry to hear that.'

He nodded to acknowledge her commiseration. 'It wasn't just the failed pregnancy that wrecked our relationship, though,' he continued. 'It felt to me as though Celine gave up her individuality as soon as we got married, as if she didn't need to try at anything any more. She'd already handed in her notice at the place she worked and I became her whole universe. It was stifling. She wanted my undivided attention and I tried to give her as much as I could, but she'd phone me ten or twenty times a day and turn up when I had important meetings and make a scene if I didn't have time to see her.'

'Was this before or after the miscarriage?' Indigo asked.

'Before. It got even worse after it.'

Indigo didn't say anything, just nodded as if she understood.

'Then, when we lost the baby, she didn't want me to even leave the house. She became obsessed with trying to get pregnant again, to the point where there was no joy in our sex life any more. It was as if she only thought of me as a baby-making machine and would get angry with me if I said I was too tired or not in the mood. When I suggested we should wait a while before trying to get pregnant again, to give us both some time to recover, she was furious with me. So furious.'

He rubbed a hand over his face, feeling the familiar tension mounting.

'I tried to get her friends to talk to her, to give her the kind of support I couldn't,' he said, wanting Indigo to know he hadn't been totally heartless about it, 'but she froze them out, saying they couldn't possibly understand how she felt. She hadn't spoken to her parents in years—she and her father had had some kind of falling out when she was eighteen—so there was no support there either. And she refused to go to counselling. She wanted me to make things better, but I had no idea how to make her happy any more. It got too much. I started working later and later and ignoring her calls, just to get some space.'

The words seemed to be pouring from him now, as if the pressure they'd been stoppered under had finally found a release.

'Then she stopped talking to me, to punish me, I think, and my life outside work became one long, silent nightmare. So then I spent even more time away from the house so I didn't have to face what had gone wrong with my life.'

'Oh, Julien, that sounds horrendous.' She put her hand briefly over his and he found comfort in the warmth of her touch. But only for a moment.

'It wasn't the best year of my life, that's for sure.'

'So who ended it?'

'She did. She told me she wanted a divorce out of the blue one morning, then walked out and didn't come back.'

'That must have been difficult for you.'

'Honestly—I didn't try very hard to stop her.' He sighed and scrubbed a hand through his hair, making it stand on end. 'I didn't love her.'

'Oh, Julien—'

But he didn't want her sympathy right then, didn't feel as if he deserved it. 'She needed more from me. She needed my understanding. I knew she wasn't coping well with the miscarriage, but I kept pushing her away because I didn't know how to deal with everything that had happened either. I failed her.'

He felt Indigo move closer to him on the sofa. 'You mustn't think that. It must have been awful for both of you and it sounds like she fell apart and expected you to deal with everything. You shouldn't feel guilty for not trying harder. It sounds like you did everything you could think of.'

'I offered her a very generous divorce settlement to get it over with quickly. At least she'll never need to work another day in her life. I fixed her with money.' He let out a long, low rush of breath. 'And I feel relieved to be free of her. That makes me a terrible person, doesn't it?'

He glanced over at Indigo and was relieved to see understanding in her eyes.

On his way here he'd been terrified about how she'd take all this. He'd almost turned back a couple of times, but he knew if he wanted her he had to have the courage to tell her everything.

'It doesn't make you a terrible person. It makes you human,' she said, giving his hand a squeeze this time. 'And it doesn't sound like there was much of a relationship to save after you lost the baby.'

He picked up her hand from where it lay in her lap and linked his fingers through hers, feeling her shiver at his touch. The discovery that she felt the same way he did gave him courage.

'*Oui.* It became clear pretty quickly that we didn't have a lot in common after we got married. We thought and reacted to things in completely contrary ways. When we found out she was pregnant I told myself it wouldn't matter that we were so different because we'd have the child to hold us together.'

'It sounds like there was a good chance the marriage wouldn't have worked even if the baby had survived, and then you'd have felt guilty about depriving him or her of a stable family background instead.'

'Perhaps,' he said, letting her words wash though his mind. It felt good to have finally said all this out loud, after it had festered in his head for so long.

'Have you talked to someone? A counsellor or a friend?'

'*Non.*'

'Why not?'

'Because I'm fine.'

'But you lost a child too.'

'I'm *fine*.'

'So I get it now,' Indigo said, screwing up her face in sympathy.

He gave her a puzzled look. 'Get what?'

'The enforced solitude in Italy. You were making yourself walk the coast path alone as a penance—because you were punishing yourself for not doing more to save your marriage.'

'I didn't do a very good job of being on my own, though,' he said, forcing irony into his smile.

'Perhaps that's because, deep down, you know there was nothing you could have done to make things better, but you feel like you should punish yourself anyway.'

'Or I just couldn't keep away from you, no matter how hard I tried.'

'I'm glad you didn't,' she whispered, looking deep into his eyes, and he knew for sure. at that moment, it hadn't been a mistake to come here. She loved him as fiercely as he loved her. He could see it there, written plainly on her face.

And now he wanted to show her how much she meant to him.

'Are you hungry?' he asked. 'You must be after working with food all day.'

'A bit,' she said, giving him a baffled smile.

'Good, because I managed to get hold of the recipe for that pasta dish you liked so much in the beach restaurant in Nerano. I have all the ingredients in there.'

He pointed to the black shopping bag he'd left on the kitchen counter.

She stared at him, clearly shocked at this revelation. 'You persuaded them to tell you their secret?'

'Oui.'

'And you're going to cook it for me?'

'Sure I am.'

She raised an eyebrow at him, the expression in her eyes wary. Clearly, she still wasn't entirely sure what he'd come here for.

'Are you trying to woo me with your culinary skills?' she asked hesitantly, confirming his suspicions.

'You might want to taste my food before you decide whether it's woo-worthy. I'm not as experienced as you. To be honest, I very rarely cook.' He flashed her a smile. 'But I like a challenge.'

'I'm sure it'll be delicious,' she said, her eyes wide with badly concealed bewilderment, 'but I'm happy to lend a hand.' She started to get up from the sofa.

'Non.' He held up a finger, gesturing for her to stay where she was. 'You sit down and relax. I'll fetch you a glass of wine and you can watch me work.'

Indigo watched in baffled pleasure as Julien made a production of opening an expensive-looking bottle of wine, searching through her cupboards till he'd found her paltry selection of glasses, pouring a large measure into one of them and handing it to her, then going back to the counter to unpack the bag he'd brought with him.

There was something wonderful about watching him moving around her kitchen, preparing and cooking a meal especially for her. Being the one who was looked after for once.

'I'm moving to London, Indigo,' he said suddenly as he dropped pasta into a pan of bubbling water. 'I've decided to branch out and set up a new arm to the business that focuses on providing affordable housing for first-time buyers and low-wage families.'

She stared at him. 'Wow, that sounds amazing.'

He was moving? Here, to London? Her heart tripped over itself at the news.

He looked up at her, flashing her a smile. 'You inspired me.'

'Me?'

'Yes, you. After you told me about your community café it made me realise that I've been too profit-focused for too long. I want to make a difference in people's lives too. And that's the best way I can employ my existing skills and knowledge in order to do that.'

'Well, I think that's wonderful, Julien, but I thought you loved living in Paris?'

'I do, but you're not there.'

The shock of his words reverberated through her head, making her feel a little dizzy.

'You'd move here for me?'

'*Oui*. If we're to give a relationship a chance we need to be living in the same city, since we're both very busy people.'

She gaped at him, her mind reeling as a small but persistent bubble of hope pushed upwards.

'Anyway, you persuaded me whilst we were away that London could come a close second to Paris,' he continued, abandoning what he was doing at the counter and walking back over to her at the sofa. 'And it won't take long to travel back there for a weekend when I need a fix. I can introduce you to my favourite parts of the city. I'd like that.'

He sat down next to her, taking her hands.

'But what if it didn't work out between us?' she asked warily, unable to ignore the memory of how badly things had gone with Gavin. She didn't want to feel responsible for Julien giving up everything he loved if it made him miserable.

'Someone once told me that you've just got to keep positive and everything will work itself out in the end.'

'Someone once told me that was total claptrap,' she pointed out.

'That guy was an idiot.'

She closed her eyes and smiled. When she opened them again he was looking at her with an expression of utter seriousness.

'I've had enough time on my own to think about things. When we talked in Capri I was afraid—afraid that I couldn't give you the level of attention you deserve, that I couldn't be positive enough for you, that you'd come to resent me for my dour outlook and selfish moods. I didn't want you to think of me like that. I wanted to be ready and capable of showing you the real me. Not the shell of a man I was when we first met. It nearly killed me, walking away, but I had to be sure I could handle it.'

'And are you?'

'*Oui*. After panicking that I might have lost you, and

realising that would make me so much more miserable, I *know* I can now.'

Indigo swallowed hard, feeling a familiar tightness in her throat, only this time it was from overwhelming excitement.

He leaned forwards, stroking his thumbs over the backs of her hands. 'I've thought about you every single day since I left you, Indigo. Pretty much every minute of every day. What we had felt so right—no matter how much I tried to convince myself it wasn't—and in a way that it never did with Celine, or anyone else I've ever met. As soon as I met you I *knew*.'

'Me too,' she whispered.

He smiled, relief lighting up his eyes. 'I want to be near you so we can make a real go of a relationship. If you want that too. What do you say? Has fate kept my slot open for me?'

She was so excited by what he was saying, but she still couldn't stop a deep-seated worry from tugging at her.

'What is it?' he asked, clearly sensing her indecision.

'I'm worried that I get too argumentative around you and that you'll get fed up with it.'

'You mean your fighting spirit? I love that you stand up for yourself.'

She felt a smile pull at the corners of her mouth.

'But what if I become really self-centred again? I need to be able to concentrate on the café to keep it running and I might not always be around when you need me.'

'You mean you'd put yourself first for once? Instead, of always considering other people's feelings before your own? I think I could handle that.' He flashed her a wry grin. 'I want to be here to support you, Indigo. Not with money,' he added quickly when he saw the look on her face, 'but to be here when you need me. In fact, I'd live in a cardboard box if it meant I could be with you. The money, the possessions, they mean nothing to me; they're just noise. I have far more than I need to be happy and if me having money makes you uncomfortable then you can help me decide where it could best be donated in order to help other people.'

She stared at him. 'You'd be willing to do that?'

'Yes. For the woman I love.'

'Love—?' She could barely say the word as her throat filled with happy tears.

'*Oui.*' He nodded. 'I'm in love with you.'

'Oh, thank goodness,' she said in a rush, 'because I'm in love with you too.'

There was a look of acute happiness in his eyes as he lifted his hand and slid it into her hair, angling her head towards him and crushing his lips against hers, kissing her with such passion it took her breath away.

When he eventually pulled back she almost growled with frustration, until he cupped his palms around her jaw and looked deep into her eyes.

'Yes, I'm in love with you, Indigo. I love you for your strength and your determination. Your generosity when you have nothing left to give. Your kindness to a strange Frenchman who needed someone to take an interest in him and make him feel like he had something left to offer. That's why I love you. Because you remind me of all the good things about me that I'd forgotten about.

You're the person I'm supposed to have my happy-ever-after with. I believe that now.'

'I believe it too.'

'Good.'

He kissed her again, even more thoroughly this time.

'I want it all with you, Indigo,' he said, kissing her nose, her eyes. 'A home, a family…' He kissed her forehead, her cheeks. 'A future.' Her drew back and smiled, deep into her eyes. 'But mostly I want you.'

She experienced a surge of pure joy at his words, knowing for certain now that this was meant to be. That this was fate and she could give him everything he wanted.

And more.

Much, much more.

EPILOGUE

When pondering what to do for your next adventure, you might want to consider something that has it all: excitement, good society and a plethora of opportunities for personal discovery...

Two years later

INDIGO PACED BACK and forth, quickly covering the floor space of the home that she and Julien had bought together after he'd whisked her off to Paris to propose, just six months after moving to London.

They'd fallen in love with the bijou but funky flat situated in a warehouse conversion in Brixton as soon as they'd walked into it. Since moving in, they'd had great fun decorating it simply but stylishly, haunting the antique and flea markets in both London and Paris until they'd managed to put together a collection of furniture that suited and reflected both of their tastes.

With the two of them sharing the mortgage, Indigo had been confident she could comfortably afford her half of the repayment with her wage from the Welcome Café, and she loved walking through the door and knowing that this place was just as much hers as it was Julien's.

It seemed like a long time ago now that she'd been worried about having to give up working at the café, but she still felt grateful every day for the grants that had turned up just in the nick of time, allowing them to expand and, more recently, open up new branches in other parts of the city. Even though she'd known Julien would have stepped in and given her as much money as she needed had the grants not appeared, she would never have taken it from him, needing to maintain her financial independence for her own sense of pride.

As it turned out, he'd needed to invest a lot of it in his not-for-profit affordable housing scheme, which had already brought happiness and security to a large number of people who had previously believed they'd never be able to afford their own home.

She was so proud of him for what he'd achieved in such a short space of time. He'd worked tirelessly to make it all happen and was full of positivity for expansion in the future.

It made her heart swell to see him so fired up and happy.

Even though they both led very independent working lives, they'd made sure they were around for each other whenever support was required—either as a sounding board to bounce ideas off, or just to be there to listen to each other talk about the vexations or achievements of their day.

Since they were both incredibly busy during the

week, they made sure to take regular breaks away from the city at weekends, when they'd walk and camp and explore the most beautiful parts of England, and occasionally other European countries.

It was a solid and equal partnership, with both of them working hard to make sure they communicated any worries or frustrations they had well before they became an issue.

It worked.

But then she always knew it would. Because they both wanted it to.

Indigo could barely believe it had only been two years since they'd first met in Italy. It felt now as though she'd known him forever.

Their wedding, a year ago, had been a joyous affair, with family and friends travelling from far and wide to the beautiful rural estate just outside Paris—which had been loaned to them by a friend of Julien's—to celebrate with them.

Indigo had worried about how hard she might find it, not having either of her parents there to see her get married, and she'd shed a tear for their absence the night before, but she hadn't allowed it to taint her happiness during the day. She knew they were there with her, in her heart.

And she'd had plenty of people who loved her there, rooting for her. All of her brothers had come along with their families in tow, which had made for an entertaining and raucous gathering.

She and Julien had loved every second of it.

Walking into the kitchen, she gave the food in the

oven one last check to make sure it would be ready to serve as soon as Julien walked through the door. She'd been planning this special meal since this morning, wanting to mark the occasion with style.

Even though Julien had insisted on her teaching him how to cook so they could share the task and give her a break from it when she'd been on her feet all day, she still loved to make food for him, just to see the look of delight on his face when she presented him with one of his favourite meals. He was the perfect recipient, making sure to let her know just how much he appreciated her efforts, showering her with affection and love afterwards.

She couldn't have asked for more.

Except for one thing.

She twisted the much treasured wedding and engagement rings round and round on her finger as she waited impatiently for Julien to get back from work and walk through the door.

Since the wedding they'd tried and failed to conceive, each month bringing with it a sense of crushed excitement as the possibility of extending their family failed to come to fruition.

They'd stayed upbeat about it, but she could tell just how much Julien longed for it to happen. She knew exactly how he felt because she wanted it just as fiercely.

Her heart bumped hard against her chest as she finally heard the sound of Julien's key in the front door, and she rushed to meet him, her blood racing with excitement to finally have him home.

He'd barely made it through the door when she

launched herself at him, throwing her arms around his neck and hugging him tightly to her.

'Whoa!' he said, nearly losing his balance, only managing to keep them both upright by grabbing hold of the doorjamb. 'That's quite a welcome. What's this about?'

Pulling away from him, and without saying a word, she reached into the back pocket of her jeans and brought out the little bit of magic she'd been checking and rechecking over and over again all day with a ceremonial flourish.

'Ta-da!'

He stared at it, perplexed, until the penny finally dropped. 'What does it say?' he asked, his voice shaking with anticipation.

She held it closer so he could read the words on the little screen.

'You're pregnant?' he said, his voice lifting with excitement.

'Yes!'

'How long have you known?'

'I did the test this morning.' She could barely talk for excitement.

'Why didn't you call me?' he said, grabbing her around the waist and lifting her up so he could swing her round and round.

'I knew you needed to be able to concentrate on the meeting with your investors today,' she said, laughing with elation at his reaction. 'I was worried you might go to pieces and they'd think you were a bit loopy and refuse to give you the money.'

He laughed and put her down, holding on to her until

he was sure she had her balance, then flapping his hand in that Gallic way she loved so much. 'Go to pieces! Me! Never!' But there was a glint of tears in his eyes now.

Sliding her hands up to cup his jaw, she gently pulled him towards her so she could kiss his eyes, his nose, his mouth.

'You're a big softie really,' she murmured, kissing away a lone tear that had escaped from his eye.

'I'm just happy. I've wanted this so much.'

'Me too.'

He stroked her cheek, looking deep into her eyes.

'I'm so glad my child will have a mother like you.' He kissed her, his touch firm and possessive. 'Someone who is dedicated to bringing happiness to everyone she meets.' He kissed her again, the urgency of it reminding her how loved she was, how wanted. 'Someone who is full of love for others, no matter their situation.' This time the kiss went on and on until she was breathless with joy.

She couldn't believe how lucky she was to have him.

With each other's support and love they'd finally been able to close the book on the regrets of their pasts.

And now an exciting new chapter of their lives was about to begin.

* * * * *

God, he was handsome.

And shirtless.

He wore a pair of dark blue sweatpants and nothing else. She could barely take her eyes off his chest.

Memories came over her. The two of them sitting on the couch in her living room in her Houston condo. Talking. The tall, dark and incredibly hot cop making her feel safe, making her dream of a way out, making her want him like she'd never wanted a man before. One minute he'd been telling her about his cat, Mr. Whiskers, and the next, he'd reached his hands up to her face and looked at her, then leaned in to kiss her, possessively and passionately, and she'd responded. Within minutes they'd been naked and on the soft shag rug.

From the way he was looking at her now, she had a feeling he was remembering, too.

"Well," he said, glancing away. "If you're both all right, I guess I'll leave you alone." He turned to go, but Georgia sensed he wanted to stay, wanted a reason to stay.

She would give him one. And give Operation Dad more time to work.

* * *

Hurley's Homestyle Kitchen:
There's nothing more delicious
than falling in love…

THE DETECTIVE'S
8 LB, 10 OZ
SURPRISE

BY
MEG MAXWELL

First Published in Great Britain 2016
By Mills & Boon, an imprint of HarperCollins*Publishers*
1 London Bridge Street, London, SE1 9GF

© 2016 Meg Maxwell

ISBN: 978-0-263-91986-8

23-0516

Our policy is to use papers that are natural, renewable and recyclable products and made from wood grown in sustainable forests. The logging and manufacturing processes conform to the legal environmental regulations of the country of origin.

Printed and bound in Spain
by CPI, Barcelona

Meg Maxwell lives on the coast of Maine with her teen-age son, their beagle and their black-and-white cat. When she's not writing, Meg is either reading, at the movies or thinking up new story ideas on her favourite little beach (even in winter) just minutes from her house. Interesting fact: Meg Maxwell is a pseudonym for author Melissa Senate, whose women's fiction titles have been published in over twenty-five countries.

For my dear friend Julia Munroe Martin.
Lucky me to have a great friend
and a great writer friend in one.

Chapter One

In the fifteen minutes it had taken detective Nick Slater to go down the street to Hurley's Homestyle Kitchen to pick up his lunch order of a roast beef po'boy with a side of spicy slaw, someone had left an infant in a blue-and-white baby carrier on his desk.

Nick froze in the back doorway of the otherwise empty Blue Gulch Police Station, staring at the baby and mentally taking stats.

Newborn, one month, maybe six weeks old. Boy, according to all the blue. Healthy, from the peaches-and-cream big cheeks and the rosy bow-shaped lips, slightly quirking. Cared for, given the cap and clean outfit, the hand-knit blanket tucked around him in the sturdy, padded carrier. Sleeping—for now.

All that had been on his desk when he left were his frustrating notes on the Jergen burglary case, half-finished paperwork for Farley Melton's seventh disorderly conduct arrest of the year, a "just because" card with two folded twenties and a ten that he was going to send to his sister at Dallas City College, and a scrawled note from himself that he was running out to pick up lunch, back in ten.

Now there was a baby.

"Hello?" he called out, expecting the parent or caregiver or someone, anyone to appear. The Blue Gulch Police Station wasn't very big. Aside from the main room with the long reception desk, and Nick's and the other two officers' desks, the chief had a private office next to the two jail cells and a break room that served as conference room, interrogation room and lunchroom.

"Hello?" he tried again.

Silence.

Nick kept one eye on the baby and walked over to the break room—empty. Chief's office—empty. Jail cells—one empty, one containing the sleeping form of Farley Melton.

Cynic that he was, he walked over to his desk, put the bag containing his lunch on his chair and lifted up the baby carrier to see if the cash was still in the card. It was. He set the carrier back down.

Okay, so the baby's mother came in for some reason to talk to an officer or lodge a complaint, saw no one was around and set the carrier down while she went to use the restroom.

Except both restroom doors were ajar, the lights out.

Nick glanced out the windows at the front of the station to see if anyone was sitting on the steps or the bench. No one.

"Hello?" he called out again, despite the fact that clearly no one was there. Except for Farley snoring in his jail cell and the gentle hum of an oscillating fan in the corner, the office was quiet.

Why would someone leave a baby on his desk—and when no one was in the station? He mentally went down the list of who in Blue Gulch had had a baby recently. The Loughs, who lived a quarter mile from here in the center of town. But they had a girl with blond wisps. Nick eyed the baby; fuzzy dark hair peeked around the baby's ears, just below the blue cotton cap.

Then there were the Andersons, who lived on the outskirts of Blue Gulch and didn't often come to town. They'd had a boy back in June. Had one of the Andersons left the baby on Nick's desk for some reason that even he, seasoned detective, couldn't come up with? Nick grabbed his phone, looked up their number and punched it in.

He heard a baby cooing the moment Mike Anderson said hello.

Nick pretended to be alerting residents about the coyote sightings in his area, which was true, and to be careful, then hung up, racking his brain for who he might be forgetting. Blue Gulch was a small town, population 4,304—4,305, he corrected. If there had been another hugely pregnant woman in town over the summer, he'd have known about her.

Nick stared at the baby. A tiny blue-encased foot kicked out. Then the other. The big cheeks turned to the left. Then to the right.

Little eyes opened just a crack. Then closed again.

And then the first *waaaah*. The baby started sort-of crying, the bow-shaped mouth suddenly opening wide and pouring forth a screeching wail you wouldn't think could come from such a tiny creature.

He glanced at the clock—1:16 p.m. Michelle Humphrey, department secretary, was on her lunch break. Officer Midwell, who was supposed to be manning the station, was probably at the coffee shop for his sixth iced coffee of the day, flirting with the barista he had a crush on. And the chief, nearing retirement, took long naps in his pickup truck in the back parking lot these hot summer days. *You take over for me, Nick, will ya?* was Chief McTiernan's favorite refrain. Nick wasn't much interested in being chief, even for an hour. He liked being a detective, needed to be out in the field.

And besides, Nick was planning on leaving Blue Gulch in the coming weeks. He'd moved back two years ago to take care of his sixteen-year-old sister when their mother died. But now that Avery was in college, living in a dorm, Nick didn't have to live in this town he hated, a place that reminded him of his worst memories on a daily basis.

"Waaah. Waaah! Waaaah!"

Oh hell. He'd have to do something, like pick up the baby.

He reached into the carrier and pulled down the tiny blanket and froze.

There was a note taped onto the baby's pajamas.

Detective Slater: Please take care of Timmy until I can come back for him in a week. I am not abandoning him. I know I can trust you.

What the—

He stared at the note, reading it again, then again. The note was typed on a half piece of plain white paper, *please* underlined in red pen. He read it yet again, hoping his eyes were playing tricks on him, that it said *I'll be back for him in a minute, thanks.* With *minute* underlined in red.

So…a scared mother? A mother who had to attend to some personal business?

Timmy. At least there was a name. A big clue. Who did he know who'd had a baby named Timmy? No one. He glanced at the little guy. Yawning and stretching, unaware that someone else's decisions, actions, choices could change the entire trajectory of his life.

Nick knew about that too well.

Now here was an innocent baby, at everyone's mercy. His, right now. *I know I can trust you…*

Obviously, the mother was someone he knew.

His heart started banging in his chest. *No. Couldn't be. No, no, no.*

His sister?

God, calm down, Slater, he ordered himself. *You just saw Avery off to college less than two weeks ago.* For the past nine months, she'd been the same tall string bean she'd always been. His eighteen-year-old sister wasn't the baby's mother. His heart rate slowed to normal.

So who? Who would have chosen him over the other officers, or over grandmotherly Michelle, or over anyone else she knew? Why him?

Nick Slater wasn't exactly paternal.

What you want doesn't matter! the entire town had heard him shout at Avery a few months ago when she told him in front of Clyde's Burgertopia that she wasn't sure she wanted to go to college after all. And that her boyfriend, Quentin—*Quentin says this, Quentin says that*—thought she should give her singing talent a real chance. Quentin, who walked around spouting philosophy and called Nick *dude*, thought his eighteen-year-old sister, who liked to sing and play guitar, should give up college to sing at the coffee shop for change from people's lattes. Over Nick's dead body—that was *his* philosophy.

He stared hard at the squawking baby. Who the heck left a baby alone? On someone's desk? A hot burst of anger worked its way inside Nick at the utter crud some people did.

You're not just any old someone, he reminded himself. *You're a police officer. And the note is addressed to you.*

Still, he'd have to call Social Services and report it. He shook his head as he walked to the front door and held open the screen, his gaze going over every hiding spot, from the tall oaks that lined the stone path into the building, to the weeping willow. No one was out there. The Blue Gulch Police Department was in the center of town, right on Blue Gulch Street with easy access to a main road leading to the freeway. He glanced out at the small parking area on the side of the office, flanked by evergreens and the green and brown hills, the expanse of the Sweet Briar Mountains that went as far as he could see, reminding him how big the world outside Blue Gulch was.

Whoever had left the baby had left too.

"I'll give you an hour," he said into the air, putting it out there for the child's mother. "Then I'm calling Social Services."

He glanced back at Timmy. He was still crying. *Pick the baby up*, he ordered himself. He took off the blanket. Wedged against the side of the carrier were two baby bottles, one full of formula, three diapers, a small stuffed yellow rabbit with long brown ears and a canister of formula. *Someone cares about this baby*, he thought, quickly freeing Timmy, who struggled to open his eyes.

Nick picked him up. Carefully. The lightness of him was almost staggering. He definitely wasn't more than nine pounds. Nick cradled the baby's neck against his forearm the way he'd learned long ago in officer training, and Timmy stopped crying. Until he started again, a minute later.

A thud and a string of expletives came from the direction of the cells. Farley Melton must have fallen out of his cot again.

"For Pete's friggin' sake, shut that wailing creature up!" screeched Farley, who been brought in two hours ago for disturbing the peace and public intoxication on town property.

Timmy's probably hungry, Nick thought, reaching for the full bottle. He opened it and gave it a quick smell test and it seemed fine, not that he knew what baby formula, fresh or spoiled, smelled like.

With the crying baby in his arms, he headed over to Farley's rectangular cell, just visible from the main room. The skinny, disheveled sixtysomething was sprawled out on the cot, his hands pressed over his ears.

"Hey, Farley, did you hear anyone come in a little while ago?"

"Yeah, you and that screaming kid," was Farley's helpful response.

"No, I mean like fifteen minutes ago. Did you see anyone come in and leave something on my desk?"

"I was sleeping until that wailing started. Now let

me get back to it," he snapped, and was snoring before Nick could turn around.

Nick rolled his eyes, reached into his pocket and pulled out the note. *Please take care of Timmy until I can come back for him in a week. I am not abandoning him.*

A week. Good Lord.

But the underlined *please* in red assured him the mother would be back when she could because of some kind of trouble or another. He glanced at the clock—1:18. Time sure moved slowly.

As Timmy sucked on the bottle, he glanced outside, hoping the secretary would come back. Michelle was great with babies.

Yes! Someone was coming up the walk. Maybe it was Timmy's mother, realizing she'd done a nutty thing and was returning for her baby. Although he wouldn't hand over Timmy so fast—not until he was sure the mother was stable.

He rushed to the window to get a good look at her in case the woman changed her mind and bolted.

He did a double take.

Georgia Hurley was coming up the walk. And considering that her stomach—which he'd kissed every inch of—had been flat as a surfboard just four months ago when he met her in Houston, she certainly wasn't the mother of baby Timmy.

Well, well, so Georgia had finally come home to Blue Gulch.

The woman was so self-absorbed that when her grandmother had gotten sick a few months ago, and the family business, Hurley's Homestyle Kitchen, was in financial jeopardy, Georgia ignored her sisters' pleas to come home and stayed in Houston with her rich boyfriend.

Nick knew all this because four months ago, before he even knew Georgia Hurley existed, her sister Annabel had been worried sick about Georgia and thought she might be in some kind of trouble. *Nothing would keep Georgia from coming home when her family needed her unless something was very wrong,* Annabel had told him. Nick had barely known Annabel, but since he'd been headed to Houston for a police academy reunion, he'd assured Annabel he'd check on Georgia that weekend. Make sure she was okay.

Boy, had she been okay. Checking on Georgia had started with a knock on her condo door in Houston and ended with the two of them wrapped naked in each other's arms, talking for hours about things he never talked about. He'd lost himself in Georgia Hurley that night.

Then, wham, bucket of cold water on his head in the morning. He'd never forget how she acted as if she didn't know him, as if they hadn't just spent the night together, when her slick boyfriend unexpectedly showed up the next morning in his Italian suit and thousand-dollar shoes. The man's sunglasses probably cost more than a year's room and board at Nick's sister's college.

"Oh, him?" Georgia had said to the boyfriend, tossing a glance at Nick in the bright April sunshine in front of her Houston condo. She and Nick were standing on the sidewalk, making a plan for where to have breakfast, when the boyfriend had shown up. The boyfriend Nick hadn't known about. "Just an acquaintance I ran into. Ready, darling?" she'd added, linking her arm with the Suit and heading down the street. She hadn't looked back.

It took a lot to shock Nick. He's been through hell and back as a kid. He'd gotten through raising his teenage sister, the two of them both in one piece. He'd seen the worst of humanity in his first five years as a cop on the force in Houston. Nothing surprised him. Nothing got to him.

But Georgia did. His head, his heart, everything in him exploded like an earthquake in those minutes on that Houston sidewalk, and trying to make sense of it as he drove back home to Blue Gulch had given him a bigger headache.

She'd used him for the night—why, he didn't know. He hadn't been able to figure that out either. What was the point for her? What had she gotten out of it? Hot sex? When she had some six-foot, four-inch, rich boyfriend? Whatever her reason, whatever motivated her, she'd discarded Nick with a lie and walked away. He'd never heard from her again. He'd gone back to Blue Gulch, let her sister Annabel know that Georgia was absolutely fine—without adding that Georgia was a selfish, lying, cheating witch—and gotten back to his life.

Now here she was, walking into his police station. And this wasn't exactly a good time, he thought, glancing down at Timmy in his arms.

He braced himself for her to walk through the door. But no one came in. He glanced out the window and saw her standing in front of the weeping willow and taking a deep breath. Then another.

And from this angle it was pretty clear her stomach wasn't flat, after all. In fact, Nick would say Georgia Hurley was four or five months pregnant.

Chapter Two

For a moment, Georgia Hurley was so dumbstruck with joy at the sight of Nick Slater, even a hundred feet away through a police station window, that she almost missed that there was a baby in his arms. The infant was nestled against his forearm as he held a small bottle to the tiny mouth.

Confused, she stopped in her tracks, eyed him through the leaves of the weeping willow and sat down on the bench by the steps. Based on everything Nick had told her the night they spent together, he wasn't a father. He'd made it crystal clear that he had no interest in marriage or parenthood. That the bachelor life was for him. Clearly, this baby wasn't his. She didn't believe for one second that he'd lied to her, that he was someone's husband, someone's father. Georgia might get people wrong sometimes—oh boy, did she—but what had drawn her to Nick was the integrity, the honesty that had enveloped him the night they met. She'd felt it in her bones, seen it in his face, in his eyes as he'd held her, as he'd made love to her.

·As she'd betrayed him the next morning.

Despite the warm August air, a chill snaked up her spine at the memory. Georgia closed her eyes, her heart clenching as she remembered the look of utter disbelief on his handsome face, her own powerlessness. *He probably hates me*, she thought—for the hundredth time. *How could he not?*

She sucked in a breath and glanced at him again, but his back was to the window.

Go on in, she ordered herself. It was time to right a wrong. Best she could, anyway.

He shifted to the side and she could see he was still holding the baby, a half-finished bottle in his hand. He was very likely watching the baby for someone, a coworker, probably. That he was holding a baby, feeding a baby, was a good sign, she reminded herself, given what she was about to tell him.

A bit more confident, Georgia started toward the steps, but her belly fluttered, and she sat back down on the bench.

That was only the second time she'd felt the baby move and she brought her hand to her stomach, a feeling of utter wonder spreading through her. The first time happened during the long drive from Houston to Blue Gulch, as if the baby were reminding her of what she had to do upon arrival: tell Nick Slater that he was going to be a father.

Just a few minutes ago, the three-hour drive finally over, she'd stopped for a red light on Blue Gulch Street and had been able to see the steeply pitched roof of the apricot Victorian that housed Hurley's Homestyle Kitchen. Home. She hadn't seen her grandmother, her sisters, since Christmas. Tears had stung the backs of her eyes. More than anything she'd wanted to speed over and tell them everything, finally explain herself. But instead of turning left for the Victorian, for her family, she'd made a right for the police station, knowing she should tell Nick first, that she should let go of the secrets she'd been keeping all these months. Including the awful one.

Georgia stood up. *Okay, get in there. Tell him.*

Hello again, Detective Slater. Nick. You may not remember me, but we met in April in Houston, and without even knowing it, you gave me hope, made me dream again. But the next morning I did something terrible and I can finally explain why.

Yes, she would start with that and then tell him about the baby. Or should she start with the news of her pregnancy first? *Anyone can see you're pregnant*, she reminded herself.

Georgia bit her lower lip and sat back down on the bench. She didn't know Nick Slater well. At all, really. But she did know that after hearing the news, he wasn't going to pull her into a hug and swing her in an excited circle and pass out cigars the way impending fathers used to do in old movies. In the few beautiful hours they'd shared, he told her he'd had a rough childhood and then had barely survived the past two years as sole guardian of his now eighteen-year-old kid sister. All he wanted, Nick had told her, was to do his job, catch the bad guys and keep Blue Gulch a safe place to live. He didn't even want responsibility for the cat his sister had taken in against his wishes—and would stick him with when she left for college in Dallas in mid-August.

It was now August 21. Georgia vaguely wondered how Nick was doing with the cat. Maybe the purring bundle of fur had worked its way into his heart and changed his mind about taking care of living, breathing things. But probably not.

Georgia didn't love this new cynical side of herself. She used to be so motivated by possibility, by *you never know*, by the idea that anything could happen. But these days, that was what scared her the most: that anything *could* happen. Now Georgia only wanted assurances and security—nice words that she was afraid had no meaning anymore.

She stood and dusted off her sundress, smoothed her wavy, shoulder-length brown hair and walked up the steps. She took a final deep breath and pulled open the door.

Nick stood there, the baby cradled in the crook of his arm. He was staring at Georgia, his expression stony.

"This is a surprise," he said.

She took in the sight of him, six feet two, the broad shoulders, his intense dark brown eyes, the thick dark hair, his fair skin, a groove in each cheek the only softening of the otherwise hardened countenance of a police detective.

"Me or the baby you're holding?" she asked, not daring to step farther in.

He glanced down at the infant. "Both. I didn't expect to come back from picking up my lunch to find a baby on my desk. And I definitely didn't expect to see you of all people walking through the door."

Wait—what? "You found the baby on your desk?"

He shifted the bottle in his hand. "With an anonymous note saying his mother would be back in a week, that she wasn't abandoning him and could trust me."

She froze. "Could you be the father?"

He stared at her as though that was preposterous. It most definitely wasn't. "No. No chance."

She looked at the beautiful baby in his arms. So sweet and innocent. What it must have taken for this child's mother to leave him and walk away. Georgia could only imagine what the baby's mother was going through. "What are you going to do?"

Nick stared down at the infant. "Give her another half hour before I call Social Services."

"No, you can't do that," she said. "The mother entrusted this baby to you. Something terrible must be happening and she's in no position to care for her child this week."

Nick stared at her. "And you know this because?"

Because I know what it's like to be in trouble. To be threatened. To feel trapped and cornered and have no one to talk to, nowhere to go. God, if Georgia had had a child—a baby—the past several months? She would have had no choice but to have sought a safe haven for the baby.

"I can imagine," she said, aware of his dark eyes on her, assessing her.

"Is there a reason you're here?" he asked. The baby began fussing and Nick took the bottle from his lips, setting it down on the reception desk.

Now was hardly the right time to tell Nick he was going to be a father. He had his hands full—literally.

"Yes, but perhaps I should come back a bit later? Or I could stay and help," she said, her gaze on the squirming infant. Not that she knew more than he did about babies.

He stared at her, the expression stonier than before. "Should you be holding a baby in your condition?"

Her hand flew to her belly. She wasn't sure he'd noticed. Then again, he was a detective. Of course he'd noticed. "I can handle him. Pregnant mothers have been balancing toddlers on their hips since time began."

"I guess," he said. "Oh, and congratulations."

He was glaring at her, she realized.

Oh God. Because he thought the baby was someone else's.

"Nick, I need to explain to you about the morning after—"

"I don't need to hear it," he said. "In fact, I'm pretty busy right now and would appreciate it if you left. I need to call Social Services."

Social Services. Back in Houston, Georgia had an acquaintance who worked for Child Protective Services. She knew the good work they did, how devoted her friend was. And she also knew how babies and children could slip through the cracks. "Do you?" she asked. "Doesn't the note say that she's leaving the baby with you—for a week? That she isn't abandoning him? That she can trust you? Sounds like someone you know. And she's very specific in the note."

As the baby fussed, Nick began pacing back and forth, trying to comfort the little guy. "Someone who didn't sign her name. I have no idea whose baby this is. I can't think of anyone who had a baby boy recently and named him Timothy—Timmy. Anyway, I can't take responsibility for him—I have active cases."

Georgia's heart sank. She wanted the police to be

superheroes. But they were flesh-and-blood men and women restricted by the law, by regulations. That she knew all too well.

"If you could hold him and get him to stop fussing while I make that call, I'd appreciate it," Nick said.

"Of course," she said, reaching out her arms.

He transferred the baby to her, and the sweet weight of him almost made her knees buckle. How heavenly he felt. And a bit scary. Would she know what to do?

The baby squirmed and cried a bit, so she gently rocked him, and he quirked his mouth, then settled down.

Huh. Maybe she could learn on the go. In the field. She could take care of this baby for Nick for the week.

He stood watching her, his phone against his ear. She listened to him report the baby being left on his desk, about the note. "The mother left the baby in my care, so that means I'm his temporary guardian, right?"

Georgia's heart lifted. He wasn't asking Social Services to take the baby and give him to foster care. He was following protocol, but planning to take responsibility for the infant.

"Yes, if she's not back after a week I will call you back," he said, then clicked off the phone. "Good God. I've got exactly a week to track down the baby's mother or Social Services will take him into custody and arrange for foster placement if the mother doesn't return for him by noon next Saturday. And depending on the circumstances of why the mother left the baby with me, the safe haven law won't apply because even though the baby appears to be under sixty days old, he wasn't left at a hospital, an EMS or a child-welfare agency."

Georgia bit her lip. The baby could be taken away

from his mother, who was only trying to protect him from someone—something. Her youngest sister, Clementine, had been a foster child, adopted by the Hurleys when she was eight years old. Georgia knew there were wonderful foster families—like her parents. But there were also bad ones. She couldn't bear the thought of this baby in her arms being placed with strangers.

"How am I going to take care of a baby, do my job and find Timmy's mother all at the same time?" Nick said, and Georgia realized he was more thinking out loud than asking a question.

"I'll care for him for the week," Georgia blurted out. "I'm back now. Home for good in Blue Gulch. And unemployed." *And without a cent to my name.* Not that she planned to get into all that right now. "And I could use the on-the-job training," she added, touching a hand to her stomach.

He was staring at her belly. "How far along are you?"

"I conceived in April. April twentieth to be exact." *The night you changed my life, made me believe in possibilities again, made me determined to find a way out.* She held his gaze and saw the flicker of mistrust in his eyes when he understood what she was saying.

His lower lip dropped slightly. "And yet on April twenty-first, when your rich boyfriend showed up, you acted like we'd just run into each other outside your condo. How are you so sure when you conceived? Or that I'm the father?"

She owed him an explanation. She'd come here to tell him everything. And though the thought of rehashing it, reliving it for the telling made her feel sick to her stomach, she had to do it.

She could still remember the first time she'd seen

Nick, her surprise that someone from Blue Gulch was standing on the porch of her condo in Houston, the immediate pull of attraction to him on all levels, the inability to look away from his face.

Oh, how the sight of him had comforted her. He was from home. He was the police. But she'd been too afraid to tell him anything—about why her sister Annabel had clearly felt the need to have a policeman check up on her. Why Georgia hadn't come home to Blue Gulch when her gram fell ill and Hurley's Homestyle Kitchen was failing. Why the "fancy city businesswoman" had let down her family and stayed put in Houston. Why she hadn't simply sent home a check to pull Hurley's from the brink of bankruptcy.

She'd invited Nick in and they'd talked about Blue Gulch. They'd talked a little about their families—but Georgia realized she'd done most of the talking, needing to feel connected to the Hurleys even if she couldn't be with them. And a glass of wine had led to another, and a kiss had led to Georgia allowing herself the evening with this man. Knowing there wouldn't be a next day or a next time. She'd given herself to the fantasy of it, of him, of what her life might be like if only—

She pushed the thought away. She wouldn't, couldn't think of the past anymore. It was over, finally over. She was safe. She was free. And she was finally home. She'd bring it up only to explain herself to Nick and her grandmother and her sisters. Then she'd lock it up tight. She was going to be a mother and had to focus on that. Not on mistakes, on regrets, on what had been out of her control.

Easier said than done, but Georgia was going to try.

"I'm sure," she said. "I'm pregnant with your child, Nick. Listen, I—"

"I need to get some air," he interrupted, taking the baby back from her.

She nodded. He'd been streamrolled twice in the same half hour.

He closed his eyes for a moment, then started pacing, the baby seeming to like the quick movements. "I need to get some things for Timmy. I'll be taking the rest of the day off."

"Did you hear what I said?" she whispered.

"I heard you. I'll be in touch."

Dismissed, she thought.

She watched him settle Timothy into the baby carrier, taking a frustrated few moments to figure out the five-point harness straps. Then he picked up the carrier and walked out of the station and down the steps without looking back.

Chapter Three

Timmy was fast asleep in the little bassinet Nick had bought at Baby Center. Nick watched the baby's chest rise and fall, rise and fall, and then he tiptoed out of his bedroom, keeping the door just ajar. Timmy had been sleeping for a good forty-five minutes now. Nick had looked in on him eleven times. Still breathing: check.

There at all and not a figment of his imagination or some crazy dream: check.

Keeping him too occupied to fully process that Georgia was pregnant with his child: check.

The moment he stepped back into the living room, the uneasy feeling hit him in the chest, in his throat, in his head. Again. There was a baby in his bedroom, a tiny human he was responsible for. Every time he sat down and tried to focus on how to go about finding Timmy's mother, he would hear a cry or a sound and leap up like a lunatic and rush into the bedroom and find Timmy exactly as he'd been four minutes ago and four minutes before that: sleeping peacefully.

Everything inside him was on red alert for the baby to start crying or fussing. According to the salesclerk at Baby Center, if Timmy cried, Nick should eye or feel the diaper. *Check for diaper rash. Calculate last feeding time and decide if the baby is hungry. If the baby is fed, changed, rash-free and still fussing, pick him up for a burp. If he's still fussy, cradle him upright against you and hum softly.*

Nick wasn't a hummer. He did not hum.

After he'd left the station, left Georgia just standing there like a jerk, he had buckled Timmy in the backseat of his car, driven over to the Blue Gulch Clinic and had Timmy checked over. Perfectly healthy and deemed to be five weeks old. Since Nick wasn't the baby's legal guardian, he couldn't authorize a DNA sample. He'd been hoping he could in order to check that database to possibly find a biological match between the baby and someone he'd arrested—even just as a start. But he'd have to dig through his records and try to figure out some connection between a recently pregnant woman and a case he'd worked. He'd do some investigating, find out someone had a baby five weeks ago named Timothy, and voilà.

Between now and voilà, he had a baby to take care of. He'd barely made it through the past few hours. How would he get through an entire seven days?

I'll take care of him for the week. I could use the on-the-job training.

He really was almost grateful that he had a very immediate problem on his hands—finding out who

Timmy's mother was—so that he couldn't focus on Georgia and her bombshell. Or her job request.

After the clinic he'd driven over to the Baby Center two towns over and asked that helpful clerk for the essentials. A few hundred dollars later, Nick had a few footed onesies, burp cloths, a couple of extra blankets, a big pack of diapers, two huge containers of baby wipes, a baby monitor, a baby swing and a tiny lullaby player that hooked over the side of the basinet. When he found Timmy's mother, he'd let her keep all the stuff if she needed it, or donate it if she didn't. And he would find her—well before the seven-day deadline. He had to reunite mother and child, for both their own good. And for his.

He sat back down at his dining room table with five boxes of case files, representing the past two years as a detective on the Blue Gulch police force, in front of him. Chief McTiernan was way behind the times in shifting to digital records. So somewhere in these files—police reports, notes and documents from various agencies— was the key to Timmy's mother. Nick had made a good impression on someone, someone who'd entrusted him with a five-week-old baby. Someone related to a suspect? A perp? A witness? Someone who *was* a suspect, a perp, a witness?

He finished reading through his last case file— solved a few days ago in less than two hours, almost a record. Bentley, the miniature greyhound that Harriet Culver had adopted from the animal shelter last week, had been dognapped from where she'd left him tied to a pole near Hurley's Homestyle Kitchen while she ran in to pick up a to-go order. An hour later, his investigation led him to the dugout at the middle school baseball field, where eleven-year-old Jason Pullman was hiding with Bentley and teaching him how to play fetch. Apparently, his parents wouldn't let him have a dog, and the greyhound had been sitting there all alone, so… Harriet had settled on the tearful, remorseful Jason doing two weeks of community service by walking Bentley every day after school, if he wanted. He wanted. Case closed.

Nick liked cases like that. Cases with happy endings. Cases without bodies. Without hospital records.

Okay, so someone on the Culver case liked how he'd handled the dognapping and thought he'd be a good babysitter for a week? He looked through the list of witnesses. He'd spoken to the owners of businesses near where Harriet had tied up Bentley. Clyde Heff of Clyde's Burgertopia. Sau Lan of Sau Lan's Noodle Shop. The manager of the general store. The yoga studio. Then he'd forced himself into Hurley's Homestyle Kitchen to talk to Essie Hurley.

If only he'd spoken to Essie first. She'd been in the kitchen making biscuits and had actually seen the boy take the dog and walk off, but hadn't thought anything of it until Nick came by. He'd been avoiding Hurley's these past few months. Even when he'd craved baby back ribs for dinner or those flaky biscuits slathered with apple butter with his three o'clock coffee break. Just the sight of the peachy-pink-colored Victorian reminded him of Georgia. And he'd tried like hell to put Georgia Hurley out of his mind. But because he could have solved the dognapping case in five minutes had he only gone into Hurley's first, he'd decided just this morning to end his boycott of the place and had ordered from there today. His plan was to connect barbecue burgers and Creole-sauce-slathered catfish po'boys with his thankful stomach instead of a particular Hurley with silky golden-brown hair and big green eyes. And a slick, rich boyfriend.

Oh, him? Just an acquaintance I ran into. Ready, darling?

A cold ache seeped into his bones, despite the eighty-five-degree temperature outside.

Nick was "oh, him." Just an acquaintance. After a woman he barely knew had managed to accomplish something no other woman had: made him feel something more than lust, made him open up about himself, which he rarely did. About the childhood he never talked about. What his mother had endured. His mother passing two years ago and Nick moving back home to Blue Gulch to take care of Avery, sixteen and a grieving mess.

For Avery, he'd lived in his childhood home for six months before he couldn't take another second of it, of remembering the constant sound of his rageful father slamming the front door, shouting, his mother fruitlessly trying to calm him down with a ready beer and a plate of meat and potatoes, the kids out of sight, out of earshot, lest they upset him, lest he start using his fists against his wife and the son who'd try to intervene.

Avery had been furious about having to move to a new home in Blue Gulch, not wanting to leave her childhood home, but she was ten years younger than Nick and remembered very little of their father, who'd died when Avery was just five. But Nick had spent fifteen years being afraid of his father, Vincent Slater, career officer on the Blue Gulch police force. The sight of his gun in his holster used to scare Nick to death, that his father would snap and shoot his mother.

When Nick was fifteen, Vincent Slater had been killed in the line of duty, chasing a burglary suspect who turned and fatally shot him. His partner had fired back at the perp and killed him.

Nick could remember his surprise, that you could grieve so hard for someone you thought you hated, someone you'd wished was dead a million times before.

He'd decided to become a cop to try to understand his father better, but Nick was nothing like his dad and he'd understood nothing. Over the years, mostly in Houston, where he'd served for five years until he moved back home to care for Avery, he'd met some hotheaded cops like his dad, but it didn't seem to be the job that had turned them. They'd always been hotheads; it was just their personality. He'd once asked his kind, gentle mother why she'd married Vincent Slater, why she hadn't packed up him and Avery and left, and she'd said sometimes the opposite of what you are draws you, you admire it, and then things turn bad, things turn ugly and you feel trapped for a million different reasons you can and can't explain. *I'm so sorry I didn't do more to protect you* was one of the last things his mother said to him.

Nick's stomach twisted. He was never getting married. He was never having kids.

He stood up, his chest tight.

I'm pregnant with your baby, Nick.

Well, unless Georgia had never slept with the Suit in the thousand-dollar shoes, Nick couldn't understand how she could be so sure.

He wasn't going to be a father until she explained that little mystery. Not that he wanted to hear one damned word from her about it. He got it. Clear as day. Her actions had told him everything he needed to know about Georgia Hurley.

Nick Slater, a father. He closed his eyes and almost laughed—that was how crazy the idea was. Yes, Nick could learn how to change a diaper and remember to point down tiny male anatomy so that he didn't get sprayed in the chest—again. But being a father was about a hell of a lot more than just stepping up, which Nick would do if he really was the father of Georgia's baby.

As he was doing with Timmy. Stepping up. Taking responsibility, despite being 1,000 percent sure that he wasn't Timmy's father. He'd had a long, self-imposed dry spell in the women department until he met Georgia Hurley. And another since her. Whoever Timmy's mother was, she definitely knew Nicholas Slater was not her son's father. She'd chosen him as a safe keeper for a different reason.

The problem here, Nick realized, was that he didn't want to take care of Timmy. He would, but he didn't want to. First of all, he wouldn't be any good at it. Two, something about that helpless, defenseless, innocent baby had his protective instincts on red alert, giving him that unsettled, uneasy, on-guard knot in his chest and stomach. He'd lived with that feeling his first fifteen years of life and the past two, when he and his kid sister would be at each other's throats and he was so damned afraid he'd mess up and Avery would decide to drop out of high school.

So yes, he could take care of Timmy. But he *did* need to hire a full-time caregiver. That way, he could track down Timmy's mother, find out what her situation was, do what he could to help and reunite a mother and child.

The note she'd left made him think she wasn't a nut job or a rage-aholic or an irresponsible, immature shirker.

These days, though, Nick would give his gut, which had always served him well, a D-. Maybe an F.

Someone knocked on the door. He glanced at his watch. Four o'clock. Timmy's mother? Three hours separated from her baby had been enough, maybe. He rushed to the door and pulled it open.

Oh hell. It was Georgia Hurley. She had a big basket in her arms.

"I brought some things for Timmy," she said, gesturing to the basket.

She still wore the pale blue sundress that draped over her curves, her hair now up in a topknot. She was too damned pretty, too damned sexy, even at four months pregnant.

He took it from her, eyeing the pack of diapers and various ointments and burp cloths. "Thanks."

"Can I come in?" she asked.

He stepped aside to let her enter. "Of course."

"Nice place," she said, glancing around.

"I let my sister pick out a lot of the furniture," he explained as he led the way into the living room. "Otherwise those couches would be black leather and not 'eggplant twill,' whatever that is." Letting Avery do the decorating had saved their relationship back then; she'd been less angry about having to move, about not taking most of their furniture. The worn old upholstered recliner his father had fallen asleep drunk in most nights? Not taking it. He had brought over some of his mother's favorite furnishings, but anything that reminded him of his father had gone into storage for

Avery to decide what to do with when she was ready to furnish her own place.

She smiled. "Did she leave the cat?"

He was surprised she remembered that. "She sure did. Mr. Whiskers hates me. He pretty much sleeps all day in Avery's room and comes out twice a day for breakfast and dinner. Sometimes I forget he's even here."

"I had a stalker," Georgia said suddenly, turning away and facing the window that looked out to the side yard. "That morning, the man...that was him."

Nick froze, his blood cold in his veins. He stared at her back, noting how tense her shoulders were. "What? If he was a stalker, then why—"

Georgia turned and sat down on the love seat, taking a small throw pillow embroidered with an owl and clutching it against her stomach. "About eight months ago, my boss was replaced by a man named James Galvestan. He was so impressive. I was doing well at the company, on my way to being promoted to vice president of new business development, and he was my strongest supporter, my champion, crediting me even though I only developed his ideas further. 'You did the work,' he'd say. 'You get the credit.' He was so handsome, so gallant. I fell in love fast." She closed her eyes and shook her head.

"And then," Nick prompted gently, everything inside him twisting at where this was going.

She leaned her head back, letting out a hard breath. "And then he began making it clear he was attracted to me. A lingering look, a hand on my shoulder, moving down my back. I was so flattered, but nervous about dating not only a colleague but my boss. But within weeks, I began noticing how controlling he was. I had lunch with a male colleague with whom I was working on a project—the next day, that man had been transferred. I'd find James sitting in his car outside my house, and when I'd go out to ask him why, he'd say he just wanted to make sure I was safe."

"Or alone," Nick said.

"Exactly. It's as if he was compelled to sit outside in his car and watch, check up on me. Like being with me wasn't the point. Just making sure no one else was. That's when I realized I had to put an end to our romantic relationship. And he got even scarier. He told me we were meant to be, that I was his dream woman, and when we were married, I'd make him the happiest man on earth. The word *marriage* scared me to death. I told him we were through. And he grabbed me and said we weren't through until he said we were through, that I belonged to him. I quit my job to get away from him—that's how freaked out he made me."

"Please tell me you went to the police for a restraining order," Nick said.

"I did. It made him even angrier. He'd come to my condo and by the time the police came, he'd be gone and I'd be unable to prove he was there. The police said that until he physically hurt me in some way, there was really nothing they could do."

Nick knew all about that.

She stood up and walked over to the window, still clutching the pillow. "And then one day I came home and found him in my bedroom, going through my things. He had old address books, letters, keepsakes. He started saying things like 'How nice that your grandmother owns a restaurant in a small town. One phone call and Granny will have an accident, poor thing. And your sisters. I know how much you care about them. Small towns just aren't as safe as they used to be. You never know who's creeping around waiting to attack a pretty redhead like Annabel. Or a dark-haired former foster kid named Clementine.'" Her voice broke and she turned around, her head dropping.

Nick wanted to rush over to her and pull to her him, comfort her, but he knew from experience that when people were telling their stories—whether victims or witnesses or criminals—you had to let them finish, not rush them, not lead them, not hug them. It took everything in Nick to stay seated, to let her finish when she was ready.

She sat back down, the pillow on her lap. "I didn't know what to do. He was threatening me, and the police said they couldn't help me until he actually hurt me— or my family. So I panicked and just went along with him, figuring I could give myself some time to figure out what to do, how to get help."

"Why the hell didn't you tell me?" he asked, his voice practically a whisper. "I was right there."

"I wanted to," she said, finally looking at him. "I wanted to tell you everything. You can imagine how much of a comfort you were. Not only were you a police officer, but you were home—you were Blue Gulch. I let myself have that beautiful night with you, Nick. I was so afraid to tell you for fear of bringing you into it. He'd go after you and God knows what would happen and suddenly your whole world is upended because of me."

"Georgia, I would have taken that risk."

She shook her head. "I couldn't let you."

I was right there. I was right there. The words kept repeating his head. *I could have done something.*

She shifted a bit to face him. "The night we met, he'd told me he was going out of town for a couple of days. When he returned in the morning I panicked and pretended I just ran into you. You have no idea how desperately I wanted to run into your arms and tell you to help me. But I was so scared, fearing for your life, for my family's. For *your* family's. What if to hurt you, he went after your teenage sister?"

Nick dropped his head into his hands. He'd been right there, he thought again and again and again. Right damned there. And he'd let her down.

Just as he'd let his mother down as a teenager, unable to help her, unable to stop his father's tirades and threats.

She closed her eyes for a moment. "I'll never forget the look on your face when I allowed you to believe the night meant nothing to me, that that monster was my boyfriend. I was half numb, half terrified and found myself frozen. But when I discovered I was pregnant, I knew I had to get away before I started to show."

His heart was starting to thud. "You were going to go into hiding?"

She shook her head. "If I ran, it was going to be to you. And that would just bring him right to your doorstep—to your sister's doorstep. I couldn't, wouldn't risk that. I decided to go back to the police and beg for help. But very early that morning, the police came to my door. James Galvestan was found dead in my backyard, having fallen from the roof and twisted his neck. They found all kinds of cameras and surveillance bugs on him."

She stood up and walked to the windows, wrapping her arms around herself. He wanted to go to her, but he stayed put, wanting her to finish, to cry if she needed to.

She turned to face him. "It's a terrible, terrible feeling to be glad someone is dead, Nick."

"I know," he whispered, but wasn't even sure he'd said it out loud. He stood and walked over to her, jabbing his hands in the pockets of his jeans. "I hate that I let you walk away with that monster."

She was quiet for a moment, then said, "The reason I'm so sure the baby is yours and not his is that he refused to consummate our relationship until marriage. He wanted everything to be his version of perfect."

The baby was Nick's.

What kind of father could he be? What the hell kind of detective was he that he missed the signs, thought the worst of her?

"Nick, listen. I want to put all that behind me. For so many months, he controlled me. He kept me from my family, from being able to come home when my grandmother got sick, when Annabel and Clementine desperately needed my help with the restaurant. Early on, before I knew what he was, he'd talked me into investing all my savings into a business venture that ended up not existing, so I'm completely broke. I lost everything. I'm not letting him invade my thoughts anymore. I have a baby to think about."

Their baby. She was carrying his child. Nick Slater was going to be a father. And given everything Georgia had just been through, there was no way he'd let her down. He'd be there for her—as far as he could. He'd make sure she was safe, pay for her health insurance, be an ear, build her a crib—whatever she needed. He never wanted her to feel a moment's fear again.

She put a hand on her belly, then smoothed the blue material and clasped her hands in front of her. "I want to babysit Timmy for you while you work and search for his mother."

The tension was gone from her shoulders, he saw. The shame and sorrow that had clouded her green eyes as she talked about what had happened in Houston— also gone. She was doing everything she could to move on, to not let it infect her. The determination in her expression was impressive.

He wanted to tell her that. He also wanted to put off talking about the possibility of her being his nanny for the week. "Georgia, I—"

"After I left the police station earlier today, I went to see my grandmother and sisters and told them everything," she interrupted. "I let them know I want to focus on the future, not the past. Hurley's Homestyle Kitchen is doing very well now that Essie is healthy again and back in the kitchen. I'm going to be baking for Hurley's, but that will only require my mornings. I need this job as Timmy's nanny because I'm worried about my ability to be a good mother. I was always focused on my career, climbing the corporate ladder, and never thought I had maternal instincts and now here's my chance to learn in the field."

Nick could hear Timmy beginning to fuss. He turned to head down the hallway. "Exc—"

"I'll get him," she said, picking up her basket of supplies and following the sound of Timmy's cries.

A few minutes later she was back with the baby in

her arms. "Wow, I didn't need to use anything I brought. You have everything he needed."

"I drove over to Baby Center after getting Timmy checked out at the clinic. He's healthy. Five weeks."

She smiled. "Well," she said, nuzzling the infant in her arms. "You're all changed, Timmy. Is someone hungry?" she cooed.

The baby cried harder.

"There, there," Georgia said, rocking Timmy a bit. But he still fussed and squirmed.

Her cheeks flamed and she looked as though she might cry. "If you want to hire a professional nanny or someone with a clue about babies, I'll understand."

Nick looked at the case files on the table. Looked at the baby squirming in Georgia's arms. He thought of everything she'd just told him, everything she'd been through.

He watched as she held Timmy up against her chest and gently patted his back and he calmed down, his tiny hand opening and closing.

She smiled and kissed the top of Timmy's cap. "I'll bet you're hungry, aren't you?"

Timmy let out a wail, his little face turning red. Georgia rocked him and he squirmed harder, so she brought him back up against her and patted his back again and he let out a burp, then calmed down again. Then started fussing again.

She needed this. He needed this. So that was that.

"You're hired," he said. "I'll show you the guest room. Are your bags still in your car?"

"Wait. What?" she asked.

"The job is live-in," he said. "I need you round-the-clock."

She stared at him as though he had five heads.

Maybe he did. Georgia—live here? A woman he wanted to grab to him and run from at the same time. A woman he'd said too much to. A woman who'd been through hell and back herself.

A woman pregnant with his child. His child. Would that ever sound right to his ears?

He liked the idea of knowing she was safe in the next room, that a wall separated them at night. No one and nothing would ever hurt Georgia Hurley again.

Especially not him. Which meant keeping his distance. After what she'd been through, the last thing she needed was a man with no interest in love or marriage or family life. He'd support her, support their child, be there as best he could, but Nick knew his limits, knew how shut down, closed off he was.

"Is that a problem?" he asked. "It's just a five-minute walk to Hurley's from here, so you can easily go between there and here. And if I don't find Timmy's mother before she comes back, it'll be just a week that I have responsibility for him."

"Not a problem," she said, lifting her chin.

"So you'll start tonight?"

"I'm here. So I might as well. I'll take him over to Hurley's tomorrow morning while I bake. My grandmother and sisters will go nuts over him."

He nodded. "The guest room is down here," he added, leading the way. "Right next to my bedroom. If you need anything, just let me know." He watched her walk in and look around. "The basics are in here. Bathroom is right across the hall."

He hoped she liked it. The guest room wasn't much, since he and Avery rarely had guests. They had no family except each other. There was a queen-size bed with a dusty-orange quilt embroidered with seashells. Across was an antique bureau with a big round mirror above it. Two windows with a view of the backyard were covered by pale yellow drapes.

"I'll move in Timmy's stuff," he said as she glanced around the room.

"I do like the idea of living with a cop. I know my ordeal is over, but having an officer of the law in the next room is a comfort nonetheless."

"I can certainly understand that." He was glad she still felt that way even though the police hadn't been able to help her. "I'll go get your bags," he added, heading out, his shoulders relaxing just slightly as he left the room. In a minute he was back, set her bags by the closet, then began moving in Timmy's bassinet and everything else he'd bought from Baby Center.

"I can't believe you bought all this," she said, glancing at the blue-and-white gingham bassinet and the pastel mobile suspended above it.

He looked at Timmy, his big cheeks quirking around the yellow pacifier. "I want him to be comfortable."

Huh. He hadn't realized that until he said it. He'd had a few—more than a few—of those kinds of moments with Avery the past couple of years. Moments of... whatever it was called that always caught him by surprise. Tenderness, maybe. He'd certainly experienced it and then some with Georgia in Houston.

His skin felt...tight. "I'll be in the kitchen with the case files and a pot of coffee if you need me," he said quickly, and shot down the hall.

A week of Georgia here. Given everything he'd been

through—everything he was about to go through with Timmy—having Georgia in the next room might be the hardest of all to deal with.

Chapter Four

The baby had woken up a few times during the night, but the last time, at 4:30 a.m., Georgia changed him, gave him his bottle and then very quietly left Nick's house. It was just five o'clock now and except for one lone jogger, she and Timmy were alone on the short walk to Hurley's Homestyle Kitchen, dawn still an hour away. For the first time in months, she felt no fear as she walked, even as the only person out. She was safe. She was home.

The sight of the old apricot-colored Victorian made her heart leap in her chest. She loved this place. And now that she was back and the restaurant's official baker, Georgia felt she was exactly where she belonged.

She quietly opened the gate of the white picket fence and headed up the porch steps and inside, taking in the scent of lemon cleanness—her sister Clementine's doing, she knew—and the faintest scent of barbecue sauce and biscuits, which always permeated the air at Hurley's. She carried Timmy into the big country kitchen and showed him around, including the baking section where all the supplies were kept. They'd be watching the sunrise in that section for the next several days.

She then took him into the hallway and showed him the family photos lining the walls, of her parents and her grandparents and sisters and Hurley's throughout its fifty years. Hairstyles and clothing might have changed, per the photos of customers in the dining room, but the menu was pretty much the same as it always had been. Good, traditional, home-cooked comfort food from recipes handed down through the generations. From steaks and chops and meat loaf and ribs in Gram's amazing barbecue sauce, to macaroni and cheese, and chicken fingers for the little ones, all served with delicious sides—spicy slaw, potato salad, corn on the cob. Hurley's was open Tuesday through Sunday for lunch and dinner and was a Blue Gulch institution. Everyone in town loved Hurley's.

And because of her, because she'd been unable to come home and help back in April, Gram had almost lost the restaurant she'd started fifty years ago. Well, Georgia would never, ever let that happen again. A man would never come between her and family again, between her and her own values again. She knew that for sure because she was done with men, done with romance. She had a baby on the way. Nothing would get in the way of Georgia being the best mother she could possibly be.

Given how not interested Nick Slater was in marriage and fatherhood, Georgia knew she didn't have to worry about falling in love with him. About hoping for something that couldn't be. Because she wouldn't go there in the first place.

Had she thought about him last night as she lay in his guest bed, so aware of him in the room next door? Yes. Had she lain awake, tossing and turning as she remembered how he'd held her, how he'd made her feel, how he'd made love to her? Yes. And knowing he was right next door, in bed, brought back every moment of their night together. But Nick certainly had no romantic interest in her anymore, not after everything that had happened, everything that would happen five months from now. And she wouldn't let herself have any interest in him. They would be coparents. Though Georgia accepted that she'd be doing the lion's share.

Timmy stirred and Georgia moved on down the hall toward the parlor, finding herself lost in memories of her childhood as she looked at all the family photos on the walls and atop the old piano. "Time to start baking," she whispered to Timmy, careful not to wake up her grandmother, whose room was on the first floor, or Clementine, who had their childhood room on the third floor. She brought Timmy over to the big window with its view of Blue Gulch Street and some shops and other restaurants. Then she brought him back into the kitchen and settled him into his carrier on the table by the window, ready to get to work.

The scent of chocolate cupcakes baking brought Gram into the kitchen, followed by Clementine a few minutes later. As it had yesterday, her heart practically jumped out of her chest at the sight of her beloved grandmother, so strong and healthy now, her chin-length

white-gray hair pulled back with two pretty clips. And
Clementine, her youngest sister, in her trademark yoga
pants and long T-shirt and brightly colored flip-flops.

I'm home. I'm really home, she thought as her grandmother and Clementine beelined for the baby on the
table by the bay window.

They marveled over how sweet and precious Timmy
was while Georgia texted Annabel that they were all
in the kitchen if she was available to come over. Annabel texted back Yes!!! Be there in a flash, and ten minutes later, Annabel arrived, her long auburn hair in a
ponytail with three sparkly scrunchies, the work of her
five-year-old stepdaughter, Georgia figured, smiling.

Annabel peeked at Timmy in his carrier and gasped.
"He's so beautiful! Look at those cheeks!"

Georgia laughed. "So pinchable! Not that I would
really pinch them. I just love the baby-powder smell
of him."

Clementine put on a pot of coffee and then she, Annabel and Gram sat at the round table after Georgia
assured them she didn't want help baking. "I hope we
don't wake him up with our gabbing."

"Well, I've only been his nanny for about twelve
hours," Georgia said, "but he seems to sleep like a
champ in three-hour intervals."

Annabel added cream to her steaming blue mug.
"It's so good to see you back here. I still can't wrap my
mind around what you went through in Houston." Annabel's expression turned grim.

Georgia cracked three eggs into the big silver mix-
ing bowl on the center island. She didn't want to talk
about Houston, but she knew her family might need to.
She'd told them everything yesterday after she left the

police station, and their reaction, the fear and worry and sadness in their eyes, brought her to tears now. She blinked them away. It was over; she was here and safe. "Sometimes I can't either. I'm just glad it's behind me and that I'm home."

Essie stood up and walked over to Georgia, wrapping her arms around her granddaughter. "I know why you stayed quiet, Georgia. I understand you were worried about us. And for good reason. But if anything ever happens to any of you," she said, looking at each of her granddaughters, "you speak up. If the police can't help, you bring in your own cavalry—family, friends, people who love you. I know it's easy to say in hindsight."

Each of them promised and Gram sat back down with her coffee, the conversation thankfully turning to Timmy's cheeks again. For Georgia's benefit, she understood. Of all the things Georgia knew for sure, it was that her family knew her inside and out. She'd told them she was pregnant and that Nick Slater was the father. They were giving her space on that too, not peppering her with questions. She sure appreciated that.

She added the cocoa to the batter, closing her eyes and breathing in the fragrant scent that never failed to soothe her. Baking had always had that effect on her— since she was a little girl learning at her mother's hip and then at her grandmother's after her parents had died in a car accident when Georgia was sixteen. Essie Hurley had taken in the three Hurley girls and given them time and space to mourn. Though there were three small bedrooms on the second floor, the three grieving Hurley girls had wanted to share one room, to be close together in the dark of night after having lost their parents, so they'd taken the big attic bedroom. Their beds had been lined up next to one another, with Clementine, the youngest, in the middle.

Like her sister Annabel, Georgia had found herself gravitating toward the kitchen but not watching step by step as Gram made her famed barbecue or pulled pork for po'boys the way Annabel did. Georgia had instead been glued to Hattie's side. Hattie was Gram's long-time assistant who baked for the restaurant. Cakes, pies, tarts, cookies. Back then, though, being a baker or pastry chef wasn't even on Georgia's mind. She had been something of a math whiz and knew she wanted to be involved in business, work in a sky-rise glass building and wear fancy suits with high heels to work the way businesswomen did in movies.

And for a while she'd been happy, working her way up the corporate ladder in Houston. Until she started missing home, missing a quieter, slower, easier, nicer lifestyle. When she'd first gotten involved with James, she thought maybe she was just waiting for the right man. Now she shuddered to even remember that she'd thought he was Mr. Right.

Some judgment.

I promise you, little one, she said silently to her belly. *You come first. I won't do anything that will jeopardize your future or happiness.*

When Timmy started fussing, Clementine gently picked him up from the carrier. Clementine often baby-sat for folks around town and she held Timmy like a pro. "Someone left this tiny baby on a detective's desk in an empty police station," she muttered. "Who does that? Why not leave him with a relative?"

"Clementine, you really can't judge when you don't have all the facts," Gram said, sipping her coffee.

"There has to be a good reason the baby's mother left him with Detective Slater."

Georgia adored her grandmother, who always did the right thing or the fair thing, depending on the situation. She was so grateful for Essie Hurley. Last night, when she'd let her grandmother know that she'd be staying at Detective Slater's house for the week as a live-in sitter, Essie only told her that sounded like a win-win for all parties. If she had anything else to say on the subject, she'd kept silent and would wait until she was asked.

"Left him on his *desk*," Clementine reminded them. "And given what Georgia said about the timing—that he'd gone out for fifteen minutes to pick up lunch— obviously the mother waited until he was gone to leave Timmy. She didn't want to be caught. She wants to be anonymous. Why? Because she's trouble."

"Or *in* trouble," Annabel said.

"I just hate the way babies and kids are at the mercy of adults who don't give a fig or put themselves in bad situations," Clementine said, cradling Timmy close.

Georgia walked over to Clementine and put a hand on her sister's shoulder. Charlaine and Clinton Hurley had rescued Clementine from a bad foster situation when she was just eight years old and were able to adopt her when her birth mother severed her parental rights. That day had been both the best and the worst of Clementine's life, Clementine had once said, knowing her birth mother had walked away for good when she was eight, but allowing her to find a permanent home with the Hurleys, to have two older sisters who adored her. Clementine didn't talk often about her birth mother, who'd been a drug addict back then and who'd relapsed several times since. Her birth mother lived right in town in a small apartment above the library but crossed the street when she saw Clementine or any of the Hurleys coming.

"You know, Clem," Georgia said softly, "you could say the same thing about me. I ended up in a bad situation with my former boss. Was it my fault for falling for him? For not seeing signs? Or was he a master manipulator? I think I'm pretty smart and levelheaded, and even I fell prey. It can happen to anyone. I wish that wasn't true, but it is."

Tears pooled in Clementine's eyes. "I didn't mean—" She looked down at Timmy and kissed the top of his head, covered in a soft knit yellow hat. "I'm sorry. I know you're right. I'm just…angry about how things work sometimes, how things are."

"Well, that's both good and bad," Essie said. "Good if you do something positive with your anger. Bad if you let it seep inside your bones. *Capisce?*"

Even Clementine had to smile. *"Capisce."* She glanced at Georgia. "Are you really home for good? Not going back to Houston?"

Georgia shook her head. "No way. I'm home for good."

"I'm very glad to hear you say that," Essie said. "Because with Hattie gone to help care for her granddaughters, we've sorely needed a baker and I'm overjoyed you've agreed. I do okay and I make a mean biscuit, but no one bakes a chocolate layer cake like you, Georgia."

Georgia smiled, the compliment from her grandmother nestling in her heart. "I'm just glad to finally be able to help out around here."

Over the next few hours, as Gram and Annabel got busy making sauces, from Creole to barbecue to white gravy for chicken-fried steak, and Clementine set up the dining room, Georgia baked two chocolate layer cakes, three pies—blueberry, apple and lemon meringue— and two dozen chocolate-chip cookies. They talked and laughed and reminisced and gossiped and it was as if Georgia had never been gone. Then Gram and Clementine left for the farmers' market, and Annabel headed to the door to get home for lunch.

"Do you instinctively know what to do?" she asked Annabel, who was stepmother to her husband West Montgomery's five-year-old daughter. She and West had married back in April in a business arrangement to save both Hurley's and West's family—but the two had realized how much they loved each other and their marriage became very real. "Or have you had to learn as you go?"

Annabel smiled. "I'd say a bit of both. Sometimes I surprise myself. Sometimes I'm so afraid to say or do the wrong thing. But even when I do, it works out because my heart is definitely in the right place. You know?"

Georgia nodded. "But at least a five-year-old can tell you you're braiding her hair too tightly or whatever. With Timmy—and with my own baby—I'll have to figure it out for myself. What if I figure wrong?"

"You'll do fine," Annabel said. "I don't have experience with babies either, but moms I know always say you'll just figure it out as you go and you can quickly tell the different between cries. One waaah means hunger, another means pick me up, another means wet diaper."

Georgia bit her lip. "Sounds complicated."

Annabel dug into her tote bag and handed over a

thick book. "I almost forgot! I borrowed this for you from West's bookshelves. *Your Baby 101*."

Georgia smiled. "Thanks. I definitely need this." She slipped the book into her own tote bag. "Thanks for everything, Annabel. And for sending Nick Slater to me in Houston in the first place. I'm sorry I worried you. I wish now I'd just told you what was going on."

Annabel nodded. "Well, I understand why you didn't. But who knew that my sending a detective to check up on my older sister would end up with said sister pregnant with his baby? Not me."

They both laughed, but then Georgia's smile disappeared and she wrapped her sister in a fierce hug. "Thank you, Annabel. And I know I've said it too many times already, but I am so sorry. You entered into a business-deal marriage to save Hurley's."

Annabel smiled. "Well, I would have done that if Hurley's had been in the black too. I really married West to stop his former in-laws from trying to sue for custody of his daughter. Now we're all one big happy family, in-laws included."

"I'm so happy for you." Georgia loved the joy she saw in her sister's eyes.

"Now our big happy family is going to get one person bigger," Annabel said, eyeing Georgia's belly. She glanced at her watch. "I'd better run. See you later."

Alone again in the kitchen, except for napping Timmy, Georgia was sliding the last of the pies from the oven when Timmy began to stir and then let out a wail.

Georgia took off her oven mitts and then rushed over to Timmy, scooping him up from the basinet. "I'm here, sweet boy," she cooed. "Let's change your diaper. Hey, I am getting the hang of this."

She glanced at her watch. Just after eleven-thirty. She and Nick hadn't made any kind of plan for today, and for all she knew, he was off investigating Timmy's mother. Or maybe he was home, reading through the case files and using the internet and phone to investigate. She'd left him a note saying she'd taken Timmy to Hurley's and would be back at lunchtime. Maybe he'd be there too. She'd head back to Nick's and see.

It would be good for Nick to spend time around Timmy. Just as taking care of Timmy would teach her the rudiments of taking care of her own baby, perhaps being around Timmy would soften Nick's feelings about fatherhood, get him used to having a baby around.

She could hope, anyway.

Chapter Five

Last night, Nick had woken up to the sound of a baby crying and thought he was dreaming, then remembered. Timmy. And when Timmy had magically quieted down, Nick had bolted up.

Georgia.

Right next door. It had taken him a while to fall asleep, but he did, only to wake up a few hours later to the same cries. Then the same magic quiet. Then he heard the very faint sound of her singing some kind of lullaby.

He hadn't been able to fall back asleep that last time.

He'd wondered what she was wearing. What she was thinking. If he should knock on her door and offer to make some coffee.

But he hadn't gotten out of bed. He'd sat up, consciously unwilling to check on Georgia and the baby.

Which was interesting, considering that he'd hired her as his live-in nanny.

You want her close but not too close, he knew.

He'd heard her tiptoeing around at five o'clock, heard the front door gently click. Then he'd sprung out of bed. In the kitchen he'd found she'd made a pot of coffee and left a note: *Took Timmy to Hurley's to meet the family and start my first morning as baker. Back at lunchtime.*

He glanced at his watch. It was just about lunchtime. For the past several hours, he'd been parked on the living room couch, the box of case files for the past two years on the coffee table. He'd been too distracted to go through the case files last night, but now they were all fresh in his head, his little notebook full of reminders, schedules and any helpful information. This afternoon, he'd start with the most recent and work his way back. First up: a visit to Harriet Culver, whose greyhound eleven-year-old Jason Pullman had dognapped, then the Pullmans. Harriet was in her early sixties, but perhaps she had a relative or a neighbor who liked how he'd handled the case and thought he'd make an excellent babysitter for the week. Or maybe the Pullmans were connected to Timmy—someone who thought Nick had something to do with how Harriet had been so kind to dogless Timmy when it had been Harriet's own doing.

He pulled the next file, shaking his head. Penny Jergen, a twenty-four-year-old local beauty queen with a mean streak whose entire wardrobe, including shoes, were stolen and never found. The only evidence? Ashes from a bonfire in a clearing on the outskirts of town, a glittery pink scarf left behind with a rock holding it down. Clearly, someone wanted Penny to know all her clothes and shoes were dust. He'd never cracked that case, and Penny Jergen glared at him in town. If she'd had a baby and had had to leave her infant with someone, he doubted it would be him.

But he'd add her to the list. She'd been difficult, to say the least, and he'd been kind and patient, since her demeanor had reminded him of his sister when she'd been hurt and angry or frustrated. Maybe someone connected to her liked how he'd handled Penny and that someone was Timmy's mother.

He'd have to backtrack through all these people. He sighed. Sounded tedious and draining. But somewhere in these boxes was the key to Timmy's mother. So he'd do it.

The doorbell rang and he jogged over to open it. It was Georgia with Timmy.

"You don't have to ring the doorbell," he told her, again struck by how damned pretty she was. She wore a denim skirt and a pale yellow ruffly tank top, the swell of her belly even more visible in this outfit. "This is now your home for the week."

"Still seems strange to just walk in." She set Timmy's carrier on the coffee table next to the box of case files. "Any luck on finding Timmy's mother?"

He sat down and slid the Jergen file back into the box. "Not yet. But I have a long list of folks to see today. My not so brilliant plan is to casually 'run into' them and conversationally check up on their cases. I'll look for any signs of nervousness. You can tell a lot by someone's expression, by what they do with their hands."

Though he'd certainly misread Georgia's back in April. He'd tossed and turned last night thinking about it. Why hadn't he recognized what was right in front of his damned face? He'd allowed her to suffer under that man's abusive thumb—while pregnant with Nick's child—for four months. And what if the bastard hadn't gotten himself killed? Georgia had said she'd had enough, that she was going to ask for help, but that hadn't gotten her very far before.

He looked at Georgia's belly. Five months and there would be a little person in her arms, his child, his son, his daughter.

Nick was man enough to admit he'd been scared before in life. But nothing scared him more than impending fatherhood.

"You know," she said, "maybe Timmy and I could come along. It would probably be easier to get a reaction out of someone who was actually looking at her own baby. Or at a five-week-old relative."

He considered that. "I don't know. None of these folks fall into the dangerous category, but I'm not comfortable bringing you and Timmy on police business."

"Unofficial police business, though."

He smiled. "I suppose. I guess it would help. Good thing about a small town is you know where people generally are. Harriet Culver will be having her usual 1:00 p.m. lunch at Hurley's with her sister, Gloria. We'll find the Pullmans at their son's baseball practice at 3:30 p.m. And Penny Jergen works at the coffee shop her aunt owns. She's on till five."

"Where will you find me on Mondays at ten?" she asked with a smile. A beautiful smile. One he hadn't seen since their night in Houston, he now realized.

"Well, you're a newcomer," he said, taking a sip of coffee. "But I'll have you profiled in no time."

She smiled again, but it faltered a bit. "Actually, this Monday at ten I have a checkup at my obstetrician's office." She hesitated for moment and added, "Perhaps you could come with me."

He almost choked on his coffee.

"I can feel the baby kick inside me. It's what made this feel very real for me. I think you'll feel similarly if you see the baby on the ultrasound."

"I don't know, Georgia," he said, turning away, his skin feeling tight again.

"It's okay if you don't want to. The baby will be here soon enough and then it'll be very real. I just thought—"

She'd caught him off guard and he needed a little time to let the idea sink in. Doctor appointments. Ultrasounds. "Well, I'd better double-check my notes before we leave," he said, standing up. "Hopefully, there'll be a table open near Harriet's," he added in a rush, hoping she'd stick to the change of subject.

She glanced at him and nodded. "I could use a shower. Do you mind watching Timmy for five minutes?"

"Of course I'll watch him," he said, glancing at Timmy in his carrier on the coffee table. As she headed to her room, Nick tried to imagine Georgia naked under a spray of water, but visions of photographic evidence of their unborn child flashed in his head instead. He closed his eyes to clear his head. No luck.

He unbuckled Timmy and carefully picked him up, cradling him in along his arm. "Can I do this?" he whispered to Timmy? "Can I go to OB appointments? Can I be a father at all?"

Did he want to see the baby on the ultrasound? Did he want it to feel real? Probably not, not yet. The trouble wasn't going with her to an appointment or seeing the picture. It was how he'd react, how he'd feel. What if it was like a punch in the gut—how inadequate he'd be as a father—and he shut down even more?

What if seeing his baby on that screen undid him emotionally and made him want to be a good father when he knew it wasn't in him?

Maybe he just wouldn't go to the appointment.

But he knew he would. He had to be there for Georgia. Yes, she had family to stand by her, but he was her baby's father.

That meant he had to go.

Sometimes Nick liked the ease of black and white. Until he thought about the things he wouldn't, couldn't do "because he was the baby's father." That was a long list too.

Two hours later, Georgia and Nick arrived at Hurley's Homestyle Kitchen, Nick holding Timmy's carrier. The dining room was full, but there was no line out on the porch, so there wouldn't be much of a wait. Harriet Culver and her sister, Gloria, whom Georgia had known forever because they were Hurley's regulars dating back to when she was a kid, were sitting by the window facing Blue Gulch Street, and two bankers from Texas Trust were just paying up at the table to their left. Perfect.

"Well, hello again, little guy," Clementine said as she came over to where they waited by the front door, smiling at napping Timmy. "Detective Slater," she added. "It'll be just a minute for a table."

A few minutes later, with the table next to Harriet open, Clementine led the way with menus. Nick set the carrier on the chair between his seat and Harriet's table.

Clementine recited the specials and Georgia opted

for the spicy chicken po'boy—major craving—and sweet potato fries; Nick ordered the barbecue burger. Clementine was back in a flash with their iced teas and a small plate of Gram's biscuits and apple butter.

"What a darling little baby!" Harriet said as Clementine left. She and her sister, both tall, imposing women in their sixties with matching gray-blond bobs, gushed over Timmy, marveling at his big cheeks and bow-shaped lips. "I didn't know you and Georgia were married and had a baby. What a lovely couple you are."

Georgia could feel her cheeks pinken. "Actually, Nick and I aren't married. Or a couple. We're babysitting."

"Oh, you're so lucky," Harriet said. "I have four adult children and not one grandbaby yet. I don't even know anyone with a baby, so I never get to babysit and smell that new-baby smell."

Gloria nodded. "Me too. It's awful," she added as Clementine brought over their orders.

Nick leaned close to Georgia. "Guess we can cross off the Culvers from the list. One down, many to go."

"Who's next?" she whispered, so aware of him beside her, the clean, masculine scent, his leg slightly brushing hers once or twice.

Nick took a bite of his burger, then swiped a fry in Creole mustard dipping sauce. "The Pullmans are next. Nice couple with an eleven-year-old son. We have a couple hours before Jason's baseball practice, so eat slowly."

Georgia smiled and dug into her grilled chicken po'boy. "Mmm, this is good. I grew up eating Hurley's po'boys and those sweet potato fries, and all these year later, nothing beats it. Pure comfort food."

He held his burger up, about to take a bite. "Best burger in town, hands down."

She doubly appreciated that, since Clyde's Burgertopia had opened across the street a few months ago and was big competition.

As Harriet and her sister got up to leave, Harriet said, "Detective Slater, I'll never forget how you saved my Bentley. That dog is everything to me."

Nick smiled. "It was a pretty easy case. Eyewitness. Eleven-year-old perp."

"Maybe so," Harriet said, "but all I know is that Bentley was stolen and an hour later, he was back with me. When I lived in another town and my cat was up a tree and couldn't get back down, do you know what the police told me? To borrow a ladder from a neighbor. But you made Bentley a priority. You must love animals."

Georgia held back her snort, thinking of Mr. Whiskers, the cat.

"Anyway, I just wanted to say thank you, Detective Slater. Some people might think Bentley is just a dog, but he's my family. Thank you for what you did for me." Harriet's eyes were glistening.

"You're very welcome," he said, and Georgia could tell by his expression that he was touched.

As Harriet and her sister left, Georgia stood up, on a twofold mission. She could visit her family in the kitchen and give Nick a little time alone with the baby. "I'm going to say hi to Gram and Annabel in the kitchen. You'll be okay with Timmy?"

He frowned as though she'd insulted him. "I can handle him for a few minutes."

"I know," she said. "I just noticed that you'd rather not."

He probably didn't mean to make that so obvious, especially to her. He unbuckled Timmy's harness, carefully picking him up and laying him in the crook of his arm. Timmy's tiny mouth quirked and stretched in a bit of a yawn; then he settled. "I keep expecting him to start screeching bloody murder."

"I guess you're better at this than you realized you would be."

He glanced at her, then at Timmy. "Holding a baby for a few minutes is a lot different than raising one."

Georgia was suddenly aware of nosy eyes on them, so she placed a quick hand on Nick's shoulder and hurried across the dining room into the kitchen.

The moment she came through the swinging *in* door, Annabel said, "Look at that." Her sister took Georgia's hand and led her back to the door, where a little window provided a view to the dining room.

Nick was standing on the balcony just past their table, gently rocking Timmy, and he seemed to be talking to him.

"Didn't you say Nick had no interest in fatherhood?" Annabel asked.

"I want to believe he'll change his mind, but Timmy seems to represent something else for him. Someone left him on Nick's desk. He feels responsible for Timmy. And Timmy will only be with us for a week. Not a lifetime. It's not quite as scary."

"Maybe so, but Timmy's not in his carrier. Nick isn't on the phone, ignoring him. He's got him in his arms. And he's talking to him."

Georgia watched him, her heart clenching in her chest. Maybe it really was possible for Nick to develop some paternal feelings. "I'd better get back," she said to Annabel, squeezing her sister's hand. "And compliments to the chef. Our lunches were amazing," she added before heading back to the table.

Nick was settling Timmy in his carrier when Georgia arrived. "I was just about to come find you. Two minutes seems to be my limit when it comes to holding a baby."

Georgia deflated a bit. She'd had no idea how much she hoped Annabel was right about Nick. But the more time she spent with him, the more she realized Nick meant what he'd told her in Houston. That he wasn't cut out for fatherhood. He'd opened up then because she lived three hours away from him, she knew. She hadn't been someone he could start a relationship with. And she'd just let him talk, openly and honestly, and had given herself to him because back then, it hadn't mattered that marriage and fatherhood weren't in the cards for him. She hadn't seen a way out of her situation, so she hadn't thought Nick's feelings on parenthood would be an issue.

They sure were now.

He seemed to realize what he'd said. "I mean, I'm sure that when your baby's born, I'll be more comfortable."

"Our baby," she reminded him.

"Right."

Oh boy.

Chapter Six

As they approached the middle school baseball field to "investigate" possible Timmy connection number two, Nick noticed Georgia watching the team run laps around the perimeter while the coaches set out equipment.

"My dad helped me practice hitting and catching on this diamond," she said. "I was the worst one of the softball team, but he kept saying if I wanted to be better and practiced, I wouldn't let myself down."

Nick was barely able to look at the field. "Nice advice." He'd played here too during his middle school baseball career, but his dad hadn't been pitching him balls and helping his young mind with wise and loving advice. "My dad was the opposite. He'd come to my games with two six-packs and about halfway through he'd start yelling his head off at me if I made a mistake or at the coach or ref if he thought they had. One time he rushed onto the field and hit me upside my head so hard I saw stars."

Georgia gasped. "And no one did anything?"

Nick shifted Timmy's carrier from his left to his right hand, mostly to give himself a few seconds to compartmentalize all the crud the subject brought up. "He was a cop. And a good ol' boy with a network of powerful friends. He used to brag about how he'd look the other way for the mayor and some of the rich folks in town. 'You rub my back, I rub yours,' he'd say.'" His gut started twisting. Why was he talking about this? Why had he brought this up?

"I'm so sorry you had to deal with that as a kid," Georgia said. "You must have felt so powerless."

That was exactly how he'd felt back then. "I didn't care much about what he did to me. It was my mother I was worried about. By the time I turned fifteen I was six feet tall but still pretty scrawny even though I worked hard at it, and I'd physically step between him and my mother when he started yelling at her and throwing things. I was so scrawny that he'd actually laugh at the notion of me thinking I could stop him, and sometimes that would defuse him."

She stopped dead in her tracks. "Oh, Nick. How awful."

He kept walking, unwilling to let his memories sock him in the gut. He was almost twenty-nine years old. Not some terrified teenager. "And exactly why I have no business being anyone's father. All that, my father, what he was like, that's in my blood. I don't know anything about a loving father-child relationship. I only know a feeling of cold dread at the thought of parenthood."

Georgia kept pace with him. "But you're nothing like your father. You'll be a great dad."

Now it was his turn to stop, and Georgia slightly bumped into the side of Timmy's carrier. "You don't know that, Georgia. If I'd be a great father, I'd have more interest in spending time around Timmy. But I don't. I'm glad you're taking care of him for me. I'll find his mother and then I can leave Blue Gulch once and for all."

Georgia put her hand on his arm, her green eyes widening. "Leave Blue Gulch? You're leaving?"

He hadn't planned on telling her that. Not yet, anyway. "I only moved back here for Avery. She's in college in Dallas. There's no reason for me to live here."

"You'll have a baby born here."

He led her over to a big oak tree behind the bleachers, aware that prying eyes from folks in the stands were on them. He looked directly at her. "I won't abandon you or the baby, Georgia. I promise. But I can't live in town much longer. Everywhere I go, it's one bad memory after another. I can't even unofficially investigate the Pullmans at their son's baseball practice without memory after memory making me sick to my stomach."

She took the carrier from him and set it down, then lurched herself at him, wrapping her arms around him. "I'm just so sorry you feel that way, Nick. You don't have to feel that way, but I understand that you do."

He felt himself stiffen and he stepped back. "Let's go sit near the Pullmans and watch for any kind of reaction."

Her cheeks pinkened and she picked up Timmy's carrier. "Sorry."

He opened his mouth to tell her it was okay, that she'd

misread him, that the feel of her so close to him, her
hands on his shoulders, made him want to grab her tight
and kiss her. But he couldn't do that, couldn't go there
with Georgia. Not after everything she'd been through
the past few months. And not when he'd confuse her
and make her think he was interested in something
more, like romance, like creating a family. He wasn't.

Subject closed. Why couldn't he keep his own
danged mouth shut? Why did he find himself opening
up around Georgia, blabbing things to her he barely let
himself even think about?

They walked to the side of the bleachers where about
twenty or so people were sitting, watching the practice,
which had just gotten started. Jenna Pullman, dognapper Jason's mother, sat in the third row, a Texas Rangers
cap on her blond head and a water bottle in her hand.

"Oh, Detective Slater, nice to see you," Jenna said
as he slid right next to her, Timmy in his carrier between them. "What a darling baby. I didn't know you
were a father."

For the second time, someone mistook him for a father. Based on what the word *father* meant to him, how
completely…alone he felt walking around in his skin,
he was surprised that anyone would think he was a dad.
"Just babysitting, actually." He introduced Georgia, and
listened to Jenna make small talk about how she and her
family had been eating at Hurley's for years.

No reaction whatsoever about the baby. Jenna was
busy watching the practice as her son, Jason, came up
to bat. He struck out and Jenna sent him a commiserating smile, and then she turned back to Timmy. "You're
so precious!" she cooed to the infant. "My sister just
had twins," she added, glancing at Nick. "I love being

back in the baby stage, even as just an auntie. My husband is even worse. He bought each baby a three-foot-tall stuffed giraffe yesterday." She took a sip from the water bottle, then bit her lip and dropped her shoulders, the way people did sometimes when they were about to confess to something. But her attention was taken by a fly ball.

"Your whole family must be thrilled," he said, fishing. *C'mon, you probably have a cousin or friend who just had a baby and is in some kind of trouble and liked how I handled Jason's criminal offense, so your cousin or friend left baby Timmy with me for safekeeping.* Was Jenna about to say that Timmy looked exactly like her so and so's infant? He leaned closer.

"Oh, they are," Jenna said. "It's been a while since we've had newborns on either side, so we're all overdoing it. I wish they lived here in town, but they're over in Bellville. I think Jason has been glad the attention's off him."

So much for the Pullmans being connected to Timmy. "How's Jason doing?" he asked. "Walking Bentley every day?"

Jenna smiled. "He's crazy about that dog. In fact, he's doing such a good job that his father and I are thinking of surprising him with a trip to the shelter for his birthday coming up in November and letting him pick out his own dog. Taking Harriet's dog was wrong and he knows it, but if he can prove that he can be responsible by walking Bentley every day and he has Harriet's forgiveness, I think it might be a good idea."

Nick smiled. "I think that'll be great. Jason's a good kid. Kids make mistakes. Sometimes knowing how to handle those mistakes makes all the difference."

Jenna nodded. "You're absolutely right. I didn't realize that Jason was acting out because of some stuff going on at school. Once you got us talking about what might have led him to take the dog when he knows it's wrong, he really opened up. And now things are so much better. I can't thank you enough for how generous you were with him."

"Sure thing," he said as Jason came up to bat again and hit a double. His mother jumped up and cheered.

"Two down, many to go," he whispered to Georgia.

She offered a smile of commiseration.

He had to be missing something. Something he wasn't thinking of. They'd make their way to the coffee shop next and order iced lattes so they could check Penny Jergen's reaction to Timmy for any telltale signs that she recognized him. If she did, he'd fish for who the baby belonged to. But he had a feeling he wouldn't get anywhere with Penny or the next two people on his list. He was definitely missing something, but what?

"Folks sure do appreciate you around here," Georgia whispered as they headed back toward town.

"Nature of the job. I'm supposed to help and I do."

Still, he did appreciate knowing that what he did made a difference in people's lives.

The next person on his list wouldn't be so full of appreciation, though.

"Ugh, that baby spit up on me last weekend," Penny Jergen practically screamed from behind the counter as Nick and Georgia arrived at the coffee shop, Timmy in Nick's arms. "Keep him away from my silk tank top!"

Relief flooded through Nick. Yes! He wasn't missing something. His idea to go through the cases wasn't needle-in-a-haystack. "You know this little guy?" he said casually, pretending to be absorbed in the display of baked goods to Penny's left. Just in case Penny would realize she shouldn't say a word about who Timmy belonged to, he didn't want to appear too interested in the information.

Penny pushed her long curly blond hair behind her shoulders. "I'm surprised he's not screeching his head off. He's actually kind of cute when he's not wailing."

Nick eyed Georgia. Timmy wasn't much of a screecher. Well, apart from normal. But Penny Jergen would probably think any crying was screeching.

Nick ordered an iced coffee and Georgia chose an iced herbal tea. Penny scowled at Timmy as she grabbed two plastic cups.

"So, when did you get to hang out with Timmy?" he asked as she made Georgia's tea.

Penny glanced at him. "Timmy? I thought his name was Mikey."

He frowned. "Mikey?"

"Duh," she said. "Short for Michael Jr. As in Mike Anderson's new baby."

Nick's hope deflated as if she'd stuck a pin right in him. "Mike Anderson's new baby is very much a redhead like him and his wife."

Penny topped the cup with a lid and handed it to Georgia. "Oh. Well, how would I know? I only went over to their house because I'm pretty sure his wife is the one who stole my clothes and shoes. She hated me in high school and she came in here for a job and didn't get hired and thought I bad-mouthed her. So she stole all my stuff."

Just what Blue Gulch needed. Another detective on

the wrong track. "Annie Anderson is one of the nicest people I know, Penny."

Penny took Nick's ten-dollar bill and glared at him. "If you know so much, then who stole my two-hundred-dollar jeans? Do you know how many stupid lattes I've had to make to earn the money to buy another pair? Not to mention rebuild an entire gorgeous wardrobe. I've had to give up going out three nights a week for the overtime."

Whoever the thief had been, he or she was very good at covering tracks. "The case is still pending," he said. "The minute I have more information, I'll let you know. Keep the change."

She *humphed* at him and turned her attention to the couple who'd just come in.

He held open the door for Georgia. "I'm beginning to think going through my cases to find Timmy's mother isn't going to get us anywhere."

"You'll find his mother," she said, sticking a straw in her cup. "It may take a lot of these visits, but just like you thought you got close here, someone really will recognize Timmy. I'm sure of it."

Nick took a slug of his iced coffee. He wished he had her confidence. Right now he wondered if he'd find Timmy's mother before she came back—*if* she came back.

Timmy was fussing in his bassinet. Georgia eyed the alarm clock on the bedside table—1:23 a.m. She got out of bed in her dark bedroom, amazed that she woke up at his slightest move. *Maybe I'm getting good at this*, she thought. *Caregiving. Mothering.*

"I'm going to do right by you, little one," she whispered, looking down at her belly. "I'm going to work on your father too. I think he's capable of more than he thinks he is. Don't you worry. On your daddy's side, you'll have an aunt Avery. And you'll have two aunts on my side. You already have a wonderful little cousin named Lucy. And the best great-grandmother in the world."

As she sat down with Timmy and his bottle in the padded rocking chair Nick had brought in from Avery's room, Georgia thought about her mother and father; they would have made such loving grandparents. She liked the idea of honoring them by naming the baby after them; both their names started with *C*.

Caitlin, Christa, Charlotte, Caroline, Claire.

Connor, Colter, Christopher, Caleb, Nick.

Nick. She smiled at the idea. She wondered what Nick would think about a little Nick.

Maybe too much for him right now. No *maybe* about it.

"We have to move a bit slowly with your father," she whispered to her belly. "But I think he'll come around."

She hoped, anyway. It had taken her a while to fall asleep, thinking about how blocked he seemed. But then again, he'd asked her to live here, albeit to care for Timmy, but still. He wanted her close, she knew. To keep an eye on her, to protect her. And their child. A man who couldn't be reached probably wouldn't feel that way, wouldn't be able to have them in his home.

There was her stupid optimism, she realized, sitting with her thoughts for a while. Finally, she got up to change Timmy, sprinkling a little cornstarch on his bottom and fastening the fresh diaper around his sweet little belly. But possibility was all she had to go on right now, so she was taking it.

The man definitely didn't realize what he meant to the people of Blue Gulch. He might be uncomfortable here, letting his bad memories take over the good. But there were clearly some wonderful memories too—of cases like the dognapping. He'd made Harriet Culver feel important. He'd helped a family come together. He'd single-handedly gotten his orphaned teenage sister through the last two years of high school and off to college. He'd done good here.

And his baby would be born here. From here.

Revisiting his old cases might turn out to be a great way to show Nick how much Blue Gulch meant to him, that it was his town, that he could change its meaning for himself. There would be good and bad memories everywhere. Blue Gulch was where Georgia had lost her parents in a car accident. But it was also where she'd gotten a new sister—Clementine. Where she'd had her first kiss. Where her family lived. And where she'd raise her child.

As she scooped up Timmy, the canister of cornstarch fell on the floor with a little thud.

The door whooshed open.

"Is everything okay? Did you fall?" Nick asked, his expression intense and frantic. "Did Timmy roll off the changing table?"

She touched his arm. "No one fell. We're fine. I knocked off the cornstarch with my elbow."

He glanced at it and she saw the release of his broad shoulders as his panic abated.

God, he was handsome.

And shirtless.

He wore a pair of dark blue sweatpants and nothing else. She could barely take her eyes off his chest.

Memories came over her. The two of them sitting on the couch in her living room in her Houston condo. Talking. The tall, dark and incredibly hot cop making her feel safe, making her dream of a way out, making her want him as she'd never wanted a man before. One minute he'd been telling her about his cat, Mr. Whiskers, and the next, he'd reached his hands up to her face and looked at her, then leaned in to kiss her, possessively and passionately, and she'd responded. Within minutes they'd been naked and on the soft shag rug.

From the way he was looking at her now, she had the feeling he was remembering too.

"Well," he said, glancing away, "if you're both all right, I guess I'll leave you alone." He turned to go, but Georgia sensed he wanted to stay, wanted a reason to stay.

She would give him one. And give Operation Dad more time to work.

"Nick, would you mind holding Timmy for a minute while I go wash my hands? I'll be back in a second."

He looked from her to Timmy and back again. "Okay," he said, and held out his arms.

She placed Timmy in his arms and he lifted up his forearm to protect Timmy's head and neck. "The more I think about it, the more I think someone must love this baby a lot to have left him with you. It must be killing his mother not to be with this precious treasure right now."

He was looking down at Timmy. When he moved his hand to straighten Timmy's little blue cap, Timmy reached up and wrapped his impossibly tiny hand around Nick's pinky.

She heard his intake of breath and watched a smile slowly soften the hard line of his mouth.

Thank you, Timmy, she said silently, one hand on her belly as she excused herself to the restroom, giving Nick and baby their time together. Just what he didn't even know he needed.

As she walked through the doorway she felt something furry against her leg and looked down to see a small black-and-white cat rubbing against her shin. "Well, hello, Mr. Whiskers," she said, bending down to scratch along the cat's back.

"I guess it's just me she hates," Nick said.

Indeed, the cat rubbed against Georgia's leg again, glanced at Nick, and then padded away.

Nick laughed. "Told you."

Georgia smiled. She'd work on the cat too. Nick would be a master diaper changer and baby burper in days, and he'd have that cat literally eating out of his hand. It was good to have a mission.

Chapter Seven

What Nick wanted to do this morning was get in his car—alone—and drive, blasting the radio or an old Rolling Stones CD and not think about that little hand gripping his pinky last night. Or how Timmy looked right at him with such trust.

I won't fail you, little guy, he'd told Timmy last night. *I'm making sure you're well cared for. Georgia will take good care of you till I find your mother.*

How did he know Georgia would take good care of Timmy, though, really? Instinct. He had faith in her. She'd survived a bad situation and had sacrificed herself and her happiness to ensure the safety of others.

That took courage. Courage she didn't even seem to know she had.

But that didn't mean she had to face being pregnant with their child alone.

He sat down with his mug of coffee on the living room sofa and leaned his head back. That meant going with her to the ultrasound appointment at her obstetrician's office. Go. Don't go. Go. Don't Go.

At just before nine, Georgia came in—and this time she used her key. She wheeled Timmy in the baby carriage, parking it by the front door and lifting out the carrier. As she came into the living room, he realized she smelled like lemon. And there was chocolate in the ends of her hair. He resisted the urge to pull her against him the way he'd wanted to last night.

"Baking frenzy at Hurley's?" he asked, taking a sip of his coffee.

She smiled, setting the carrier down on the coffee table. "Some lemon bars, two kinds of pie and three chocolate layer cakes. Apparently, the two I made yesterday morning sold out after Harold Handleman had a bite and announced how good it was at his rancher association meeting."

His mouth watered. "I'll have to try it sometime."

"You don't think I brought you home a slice?" she asked with a smile, carefully taking a small box out of her tote bag.

He laughed. "I do have a terrible sweet tooth."

"You'd never know it by the sight of you," she said, her eyes sweeping the length of him as her cheeks turned pink. She shot her gaze to his as if determined to make clear she was no longer checking him out.

But instead of letting her off the hook, giving her the out and letting the moment pass into nothing, he held her gaze with exactly what he was feeling right then: desire.

What the hell are you doing, Slater? he chastised

himself. *Playing some kind of flirting game? The woman is pregnant with your child. You're not interested in marriage or fatherhood—beyond living up to your responsibilities. So stop being a class-A jerk.*

He shifted and grabbed his coffee mug off the table. Dammit, this was complicated. When he looked at Georgia, beautiful Georgia, he wanted to be with her in bed, exploring every inch of her. But when his brain caught up to below the belt buckle, he was aware of a lukewarm bucket of water knocking the fantasy out of him.

She lifted her chin and stared at him for a moment, and he got the feeling she could tell he was having some kind of internal war. "My appointment for the ultrasound is in an hour. I'd like to take a quick shower and get the chocolate out of my hair if you'll watch Timmy."

"Of course."

She headed toward the hallway. "Oh," she said, turning back. "I'm sure it'll be fine for me to take Timmy to the appointment so you can get back to work."

Ah, there it was again, something to force his hand. "Well, I wouldn't want you to have to watch Timmy while you're trying to focus on your own baby. I'll go."

She smiled.

Okay, if Nick had known Georgia's entire family would be at the appointment to watch Timmy and to ooh and aah at everything, maybe he would have stayed home. Why had he thought she'd be all alone at the appointment?

That wasn't the point, he reminded himself. The point was for him, as the baby's father, to be present for anything related to their baby.

Georgia lay on the padded table in the large examining room, the doctor scanning her belly, while Nick stood anxiously on one side as her grandmother and two sisters stood on the other side, staring from her to the monitor across from them all.

He heard a communal gasp and looked from Georgia to the screen and almost gasped himself. He could just make out the face, tiny fused eyes, a bit of a nose, a mouth, arms.

"Oh, Georgia," Essie Hurley said, dabbing under her eyes with a tissue.

Annabel slung her arms around Clementine. "We're aunts!"

"Congratulations, you two," Clementine said, looking from Georgia to Nick.

Nick cleared his throat. He offered a tight smile, the collar of his shirt suddenly feeling tight around the neck. Was it hot in here, despite the air conditioner?

He kept his eyes off the monitor.

"If you'd like to know the sex of the baby, I can tell you," the doctor said.

Georgia was looking at him. "Would you like to know? I admit it—I would."

Nick took a deep breath. This was about to go from "baby," the future baby, it, to him or her. Son or daughter. This was about to get very real, as his sister would say.

"Okay," he said, nodding, his stomach uncharacteristically full of butterflies.

"Georgia, Nick," the doctor said, "Unless I'm mistaken and of course it won't be one hundred percent until the baby is born, but I'm very sure you're having a baby…boy."

There was the communal gasp again. Georgia started crying and reached out her hand to him, and Nick clasped it, desperately wanting to pry her fingers from around his and run screaming from the room. Could an adult man do that? Could a law-enforcement official do that? Probably not.

The butterflies swarmed. He would have a son.

Suddenly, Georgia's family was hugging him, hugging each other, hugging the surprised doctor. Nick glanced at Georgia, and the happiness on her face gave him some relief. He wanted her to be happy. Especially because he'd never be the cause of that happiness.

As everyone was about to step outside the room so Georgia could get dressed, Nick's phone vibrated and he pulled it out of his pocket in case it was police business. The chief's number flashed on the screen.

Talk about perfect timing. "I'd better take this," he said. He gave everyone another tight smile. "Congratulations," he said to Georgia. Like a total idiot. And then he fled from the room, his heart beating like mad, sweat breaking out across his forehead as he stepped outside the building.

He gulped in the fresh morning air. Nick with a son. He shook his head, fear crawling around his stomach. He'd been someone's son and only knew his father's heavy footsteps, his father's disappointment, his father's rage. Everything he knew about the father-and-son relationship was inside that strain.

For at least five minutes he stood there practically hyperventilating to the point that he never did answer the chief's call. *Get it together, Slater*, he ordered himself. *Do what you do.* One: assess the situation. Check. Georgia was really and truly pregnant with his child. If he hadn't known that already, the image on the monitor made it crystal clear. Two: come up with a plan of action. Half a check mark—in that he was determined to do right by Georgia and the baby, though "right" certainly had its levels and layers. Three: act. Standing here like a frozen jerk wasn't acting. If he was going to step up, he had to actually step up. He had shown up for the appointment, so there was that. "Act" had the makings of a check mark.

Dammit. He'd return the chief's call, then go back inside. He had to buck the hell up and go back in, be there for Georgia.

She has her family with her. She's okay.

The makings of that check mark on "act" began fading as he held on to that rationalization. He was about to press in the chief's number when he heard someone calling his name. Someone out of breath.

"Detective Slater!"

Nick whirled around. Joe Black, a fiftysomething rancher with a spread about ten miles from here, was running toward him from the police station walkway across the street, panic on his face.

"One of Logan Grainger's nephews is missing!" Joe shouted as he raced over, a bag of supplies from the hardware store in his hand. Joe and Logan had neighboring ranches. "Logan just called me to see if I'd seen the boy on my property. He was doing some fence work and let the twins tag along. Harry was showing him a frog he'd caught, and when Logan turned around, Henry was gone. He looked everywhere. I'm going to check my land." Joe raced for his truck.

Oh hell. The twins were only three years old. Nick rushed to his car and followed Joe back toward the

Grainger ranch, calling the chief and checking in and then calling Georgia.

"I'm sorry I left on you like that," he said. "Turned out to be a problem at the Grainger ranch."

"The Grainger ranch?" Georgia asked, worry in her voice. "Clementine babysits for the twins. Is everything okay?"

"Henry went missing while the boys were tagging along with Logan as he did some fence work. I'm about to gun it to get out there fast. I'll see you and Timmy at home."

He was on adrenaline and what he'd said barely registered, but it sounded funny to Nick's ears, as if she was his wife and Timmy was their baby.

As Nick arrived at the Grainger ranch, about fifty acres heading up to the woods, two patrol cars were there as well as Chief McTiernan's vehicle.

Logan Grainger, the missing boy's uncle and legal guardian, looked distraught. His shaggy dark hair was full of bits of leaves and brush, indicating he'd done some searching already. Tall and muscular, he pounded the hood of his truck with his fist, desperation in his blue eyes. "I need to be back out there looking for Henry, not going over this again," he shouted, getting in his pickup and heading up the dirt road toward where Nick had been briefed that the boy had been last seen.

Nick glanced at his boss, upped his chin at Logan's retreating truck and quickly got back in his SUV to follow Logan. According to the chief's debriefing on Nick's way out here, two volunteer search-and-rescue workers were also out looking, focusing on the hard-to-see places on the other side of the fence near where Henry was last seen.

Logan got out of his truck a mile up and raced along the fence, looking for a child-size tear in the fence. "Here!"

Nick ran over and the two of them pulled the tear wider and they ducked through.

"Henry!" Logan called.

The woods were dense with evergreens, making it difficult to see very far. Nick, Logan and a search party that grew bigger every few minutes started off in opposite directions. Ten minutes later, there was still no sign of Henry. Nick checked in with Logan and the chief by cell phone. The chief had called a neighboring town's police station to borrow their search-and-rescue dog, and the K-9 team would be here in ten minutes.

Everyone was calling for Henry, pushing aside brush and branches to the point that Nick wondered if he'd even hear Henry call out. Could he have tripped and fallen and was unconscious in an area they hadn't yet searched? Why hadn't he come running? How far could a three-year-old have gotten? This made no sense.

"Henry! Honey, can you hear me, it's Clementine!"

Up ahead, coming through a thicket of brush, Nick saw Clementine, Annabel and Georgia taking part in the search. "Timmy's with Gram," Georgia called out as she continued to look carefully around her for the missing boy.

Nick nodded, his mind on the time, years ago, that a teenager had gone missing in the woods not too far from here. Nick had been thirteen and wanted to join the search party that was forming, but Nick's father refused to take part because he was off duty. And halfway to being drunk. Nick had rushed out on his own and searched the woods, his face and hands scratched, but all he'd found were other members of the team. Finally, after two hours, the missing boy had been located, unconscious but alive from a fall. The kid had survived—no thanks to Nick's dad.

Nick pushed aside the memory and scanned the area around him. Logan and the chief were coming from opposite sides of the forest, shaking their heads.

"He has to be around here," Logan said, worry making his voice thick. "He's too little to have gotten very far past where he crawled through the fence opening and not strong enough to push past the brush. He has to be near."

Nick took off his sunglasses, squinting in the sunshine as he did a slow scan to his left. "Hey! There's something glinting under that evergreen," he added, pointing fifty feet to the left. "Something silver."

"Henry's sneakers have silver stripes!" Logan said, racing over.

All of them rushed over to the tree, its thick branches making it impossible to easily get to. A small opening led to what looked like some kind of den for a hedgehog or groundhog or prairie dog where the tree met the denser woods behind it. Logan began tearing apart branches.

Three-year-old Henry Grainger sat inside the little clearing between the opening and the den, just big enough for his hunched-over little body, tears running down his dirty face. His hands were caked with dirt and twigs were stuck in his light blond hair. "Am I in twuble?"

Logan gently helped Henry out and picked him up,

holding him tight, his eyes clenched for a moment before he pulled back a bit and looked at his nephew. "Henry, why didn't you come out when we were calling? We were all looking for you."

Henry's little shoulders slumped. "I wanted to find a frog too. But I didn't."

"You're not supposed to go off by yourself," Logan said. "These are big woods and it's easy to get lost or hurt. Next time, just tell me if you want to find a frog, okay? And if you end up alone in the woods and you hear me calling for you, come on out or shout back, okay?"

"Okay," he said, entwining his arms around Logan's neck. The little boy bit his lip; then his attention caught on Georgia's sister Clementine past his uncle's shoulder. "Hi, Clementine!" Henry called. "I didn't find a frog. But Harry did."

Clementine smiled at the boy, but if Nick wasn't mistaken, she looked on the verge of tears.

"All's well that ends well," the chief said, calling off the search. He thanked everyone for coming out, shook Nick's hand on a job well done, then tipped his hat to Clementine, Georgia and Annabel as he headed back toward the fence.

Nick watched Logan Grainger hug his nephew tight, Logan's eyes glistening. Detective that he was, he caught Logan blink them away, slide a glance at Clementine that was full of tension and then turn away to face the small crowd. He thanked everyone for coming out.

"Detective Slater, I owe you one," Logan said.

"Just glad to see your boy safe and sound." As the search party dispersed, Nick glanced over at Georgia, but she and Annabel were deep in quiet conversation with Clementine, who looked very upset.

Ah. Something was going on—or not—between Clementine and Logan.

"I love you so much," he heard Logan say to Henry, wrapped in his arms. "You and your brother mean everything to me. Don't scare me like that again, okay?"

"Okay, Uncle Logan," Henry said.

As Logan headed toward the fence and crawled back through the ripped opening, a posse had already formed to mend the fence. There was Joe, Logan's nearest neighbor. The owner of the hardware store with wire. Even Officer Midwell, who couldn't seem to concentrate on anything because of his crush on a coffee-shop barista, was rolling up his sleeves, ready to help.

"This town really knows how to pull together," Georgia said from behind him. "I can't believe I ever moved away, that I ever thought I'd be happy in the city. This is what I want. This is what I want for our son."

Our son. Nick thought of that grainy image on the monitor, then stared at the ground, looking over at the tree where Henry had been hiding. What if he didn't have that fierce love in himself that he'd just witnessed in Logan Grainger? What if his son went missing and Nick acted like his own father? What if caring, really caring, wasn't part of his DNA? Yeah, he cared about his sister. But a kid sister wasn't the same as a baby to raise.

He'd learned in dealing with his sister that parenthood—older brotherhood—was hard. That Avery was a separate person with her own ideas, thoughts, opinions and that those didn't necessarily mesh with his own. He said this, she said that and suddenly they were arguing. As if a sixteen-year-old girl should be staying out late and going to parties where who knew what was going on.

"You're too strict for no reason!" Avery would screech, and slam her door, the rattle reverberating in his head for hours.

He just wanted her safe, wanted her to get to adulthood. So yes, he'd been strict. He'd followed something of a rulebook that made sense to him. Unfortunately, that book had made little sense to Avery, so a few times she'd admitted she'd heard through the grapevine that something had happened and she was relieved not to be somewhere Nick hadn't let her go.

He could barely parent a teenage girl for two years. He was going to start from scratch with a newborn? And stay in Blue Gulch?

"See you later at home," he said to Georgia as though she'd been talking about the weather or what she'd baked that morning.

The disappointment on her face poked at his chest. An hour ago, her expression had been blissful, full of wonder, as she'd looked at their baby on the ultrasound monitor, as she'd learned they were having a boy. One conversation with Nick and whammo, strain and sadness. *Jerk*, he chastised himself for the third time that day. He was grateful when she gave him one last look, her chin lifted, then turned and headed back to where her sisters waited for her.

He watched her for a moment, almost unable to tear his gaze away from her, the sway of her hips, the sun shining on her light brown hair. *I'll break your heart*, he thought, wanting to scream it at her back, to tell her to run far away from him. *I'm beyond repair. Stay away for your own good.*

Sometimes he thought she knew that. But other times, like last night, when he'd rushed into her bedroom, when she'd looked at him with such trust, when she'd handed Timmy over to him as though he were the kind of man you handed a baby to, he realized she couldn't know. Because if she did know what a stone wall he had for a heart, she wouldn't try so hard.

Maybe she wasn't trying. Maybe she was just being Georgia—kind, optimistic, making the best.

All he knew for sure was that he was standing on the edge of the forest in front of the fence being repaired, thinking long and hard about a woman he planned to walk away from. Had to walk away from. For her benefit.

He needed to focus on finding Timmy's mother. *Blinders on*, he told himself, forcing himself to turn around.

Chapter Eight

As Georgia walked up the pinecone-strewn ground to where Annabel stood, her heart felt so heavy she was surprised she didn't slump over. Maybe it was wrong to try to show Nick that Blue Gulch was a wonderful place to live, that he could take it back for himself, realize there were many good memories here, that he was so important to this town. She was pushing her agenda on him. But that agenda was about him having his home-town back. And yes, having her son's father live right in town was important to her. What if he went back to Houston? Houston was three hours away.

And reminded Georgia of a time she wanted to forget.

Huh. Clearly, Blue Gulch had the same effect on Nick. Maybe she understood more than she realized. She never wanted to go back to Houston, never wanted to see her old neighborhood or her condo, which she would put on the market when she could deal with it. It was hardly fair of her to expect Nick to stay in town when she couldn't imagine stepping foot in Houston ever again. She'd still work on Operation Dad, though. He might not live in Blue Gulch, but he'd be a daddy whether he wanted to be one or not. So helping him along in that department was a necessity.

"Where did Clementine go?" Annabel asked as Georgia approached. "I figured she'd ride home with us, but I don't see her. She didn't leave with Logan and Henry. So where is she?"

Georgia slowly turned, looking around the woods the way she'd seen Nick do. She spotted the silver-blue of Clementine's flip-flops. Clementine was sitting against a tree, her knees up against her chest, her head against her folded hands.

Georgia and Annabel glanced at each other, then walked over and sat down on either side of her.

"Clem?" Georgia said, putting a hand on her arm. "We're here if you want to talk about it."

Clementine pushed her long dark hair behind her shoulders. "Why do I keep thinking that he's going to change his mind about me? You know the saying 'Dumb is when you keep doing the same thing and expect a different outcome'? That's me."

"Clem, honey, are you talking about Logan?" Georgia asked.

Clementine Hurley was well known for being private. But she had the opposite of a poker face, so she gave her broken heart or her anger or her hope away with her expression, even if she very rarely talked about her love life. Or anything to do with her emotions. Was she involved with Logan? All Georgia knew about him was that he was raising his orphaned twin nephews and working hard to keep his cattle ranch going.

"I've been in love with that man since I started baby-sitting for him," Clementine said. "And I thought there was definitely something between us. But a few days ago, we kissed—for the first time—and the next day he fired me."

"Fired you?" Georgia and Annabel asked in unison. "Why?" Clementine babysat for a few families in town, but Logan Grainger had been a regular customer for months, since he'd taken in the twins.

Clementine shrugged. "All I know is that he got a letter in the mail that upset him. I thought we were finally making a little headway, but after he read that letter he wasn't the same. And he fired me, no explanation."

"Wow, Clem, sorry," Georgia said. "I wonder what the letter was about."

Clementine's expression was so sad that Georgia's heart clenched. "I don't know. Something to do with his family, probably, or the twins? He won't talk about it." She dabbed under her eyes with the hem of her tank top. "When I heard Henry was missing, I got so scared. I love that little boy. I love both the twins so much."

"Maybe you could try talking to Logan," Georgia suggested. "Maybe he's had some time to calm down after getting the letter and he'll be more reasonable."

Clementine perked up a little. "I can try. I'll give him a couple of days to get past today's craziness." She stood up and took a deep breath.

The three Hurley sisters linked arms and headed back toward where Georgia's car was parked. Love sure didn't come easy. Maybe it really was for the best that Georgia was done with it. Even if every time she thought about how done she was, Nick Slater's handsome face flashed into her mind.

What a day. As the summer sun began its descent, Nick sat at the kitchen table, sipping coffee and attacking the slice of chocolate cake Georgia had brought home from Hurley's that morning. Before the ultrasound appointment had twisted his gut in more knots than it had already been. Before a missing three-year-old made him wonder if he'd have the same expression as Logan had when his little nephew was gone. When he'd been found. The cake made Nick think of before all that, so he ate the whole thing, as though he could shift time. As though this morning and yesterday and the day before had been any less unsettling.

Damn, Georgia was a good baker. She was good at everything, it seemed. Babysitting infants. Helping search for a missing kid. Helping him find Timmy's mother. She was also good at driving him wild with desire for her. Sometimes, to clear his head, he'd just concentrate on that, on the sensuality of her pretty face, the almond-shaped green eyes and fringe of long lashes, the long, narrow slope of her nose, her wide, beautiful pink-red mouth. Then there was her body, lush and so irresistible he fantasized about her every night. All day, really.

He could hear her giving Timmy a bath in the bathroom sink, in a little blue contraption he'd bought at Baby Center. He could smell that baby soap from here. He'd always liked that smell. That was something, he supposed, as if "likes scent of baby shampoo" was some kind of plus on the how-to-be-a-father checklist. Groan.

He ate the last bite of cake and drank the rest of the coffee, glancing at his notepad on the table. Many names of possibilities for connections to Timmy had been crossed off.

He was beginning to think he wouldn't track down Timmy's mother before Saturday. What if she didn't come back? What if Child Protective Services came to get Timmy at 12:01 p.m. on Saturday? He'd been hoping to find the mother well before to let whoever it was know she wasn't alone, that he would help, whatever the problem was. She was someone who trusted him, and his gut told him—from how well cared for Timmy was, from the note she'd left, that she'd handpicked him, a cop—that she wasn't a criminal but that she was in some kind of trouble.

Tomorrow he'd "bump" into the next name on his list of cases, local lothario John Martin, and watch for any sign of recognition. But Nick had been all over town with Timmy, and word and gossip spread fast in a small town like Blue Gulch. If anyone knew who Timmy belonged to, no one was saying.

That baby smell he liked was getting stronger and closer. He glanced up to see Georgia holding Timmy along her arm, his eyes open and looking straight at Nick. The slate-blue eyes were curious.

"Would you mind holding Timmy for a bit while I make him a bottle?" she asked.

He stood up, holding out his arms as she transferred the baby to him. He leaned close and breathed in that baby-soap smell. "I guess this is practice for the real thing," he called out toward the kitchen, wanting to acknowledge that morning's ultrasound appointment, the very real baby on the monitor.

"For both of us," she said as she returned with the bottle, which she handed to him—eyebrow raised, but not aggressively, at least.

"Okay," he said. "I can do it. I did that first day when I found him on my desk." He slipped the bottle in Timmy's mouth and the little guy began suckling away, the utter miracle of him, of how tiny he was, how beautiful, almost knocking Nick off his feet. "Hey there," he said. "I'll bet your mother is missing you like crazy."

Georgia gently touched Timmy's little foot. "I'll bet she is."

"There are a couple more people to see tomorrow, related to old cases, but I'll tell you, I'm *really* worried we're not going to find his mother before the deadline."

"Me too," she said, heading into the kitchen. He could hear her filling the teakettle with water. "But I'm already of the notion that nothing is easy."

That was for sure. Starting with how damned attracted he was to Georgia. And how he refused to do anything about it. Though sometimes he had to stop himself from doing anything about it. As she said: nothing was easy.

She returned and sat down beside him on the couch and crossed her legs, slightly facing him. "So, I've been thinking about how things will work once our son is born."

"What do you mean, exactly?" he asked.

The kettle whistled and she disappeared into the kitchen again. "Well, how you plan to be in his life," she called out. "Especially if you're going to move away."

Nick was glad she wasn't in the room to see his expression, which had to match his twisting stomach. Why didn't anything feel right? Staying. Leaving. Not staying. Not leaving. "We'll work it out," he called back.

She came back with a mug of tea and sat back down. He could smell the chamomile steeping. "How about now? You're my baby's father. I need to know how you're going to approach fatherhood."

So much for nonaggression, though she had every right. And if he was honest, he liked that she was demanding to know. She was standing up for herself. Given what she'd been through with that bastard in Houston, she'd been unable to do so for quite a while. Nick owed her a real answer. An honest answer. "I'll be there for you and the baby. That's what I know."

She put down the mug and turned to face him, glancing at Timmy, then back up at Nick. "I want you to know something, Nick, something I believe in with all my heart. And something I've been thinking about since we left the baseball field. *You* choose what kind of father you'll be. Your past doesn't dictate who you are. *You* dictate that."

This was a conversation he didn't want to have right now. Or ever, really. He wanted to get up and go for a run or take a shower. Just disappear and not…deal. But Georgia was staring at him, her expression soft, and he saw something in her eyes that troubled him: hope. *Don't hold out too much of that hope for me*, he wanted to tell her.

Mr. Whiskers, Avery's cat, appeared out of nowhere and sniffed at his feet, then padded over to the window and jumped up on the sill.

He shifted Timmy in his arms; the little guy was almost done with his bottle. "A person's past is a part of him, Georgia. I can't shake off what's gone on in my life. And trust me, I'd like to."

"You're so gentle with Timmy," she said kind of dreamily, looking at the baby in his arms.

Timmy stared up at him, so trusting. Nick wouldn't let him down, but—since he did believe, deep down, that he'd find Timmy's mother—the baby was going home in a few days. This wasn't forever. Nick couldn't do much damage in a week. And it wasn't as though taking responsibility for a baby for a week required a lifetime commitment. His entire life wasn't going to change.

"He's falling asleep," Georgia said, shaking him out of his thoughts. She gently took Timmy from him and brought him into the bedroom, then came back into the living room with a basket of laundry.

And a change of subject, he hoped.

"You really saved the day today," she said, setting the basket on the coffee table and taking out a tiny onesie to fold. "Thank God you saw that flash of silver."

Nick shook his head. "I'm no hero. I just did my job."

"Well, your job makes you a hero."

The last thing he was was a hero. Heroes weren't afraid of babies who weren't even born yet.

"Every day I'm here with you makes me feel stronger," she said, holding his gaze. "I know that the man who tried to take over my life—who did take over my life—is gone. But sometimes when I wake up in the morning, I forget where I am and for a second I feel that same fear. Is that crazy?" She clutched the burp cloth she was folding, tears coming into her eyes.

He leaned toward her, putting his hand on her shoulder. "Not crazy in the slightest. Very normal, Georgia. You went through a very serious trauma. You can't expect to be over it just because the threat is gone. Every day you wake up and feel scared is your brain and body's way of dealing with what you went through. And every moment later, when your mind adjusts to the fact that you're here, that you're safe, that no one and nothing will ever do what that bastard did to you, you'll feel safer every day. Soon enough, you'll wake up the way you did before he ever came into your life."

She closed her eyes for a second, then dropped the burp cloth back in the basket. "I hope so. Before the baby comes. Do you think it'll go away before then?"

He took her hands in his and held them. "Yes, I do. And it would happen without a six-foot-two-inch cop with a gun in the room next door, Georgia. It'll happen because you're strong, one of the strongest people I've ever met."

Both her eyebrows shot up. "Strong? Me? I'm just living day by day, dealing with what comes. That doesn't feel strong. It feels...like coping."

"That's part of being strong," Nick said. "*Not* coping is a different story. Hiding. Staying under the covers. I get why some people are driven to that kind of desperation. But you're here, Georgia. You're full of determination to put your past behind you and move on. To be the best mother you can be. To be hopeful and positive about people and human nature. Here you are, helping me with Timmy, when you've got a lot on your emotional plate. That's strength."

She burst into tears and he reached for her, drawing her against his chest. "So much for strength." She dabbed under her eyes with the burp cloth.

"The strongest people cry," he said. "When you cry,

you're hurting. When you're hurting, you feel. When you feel, you're *alive*." He lifted her chin with his finger and looked at her. "I'm proud to know you, Georgia Hurley."

The tears stopped and she managed a small smile. She reached a hand to the side of his face, her expression a combination of thanks and something he couldn't put his finger on. Her hand dropped to his shoulder, where it lingered.

He loved the feel of her hand on him. He couldn't get enough of the sight of her, the gorgeous green eyes and how her silky brown hair lay against the white V-neck T-shirt that clung to her lush breasts. Flashes of their night in Houston came to him, her body naked and writhing beneath him, on top of him, how passionately she'd responded to him. Suddenly, all he felt was a mad rush of desire and he wanted that feeling to stick around, to obliterate everything else.

He drew her closer to him before he could stop himself, overcome with the urge to kiss her. She leaned back and put her hands on his chest and looked at him again, and whatever he saw in her eyes must have been okay with her, because she leaned in and kissed him.

His hands were in her hair, his mouth fused to hers, and he was unable to get close enough to her. He took off her T-shirt and she pulled off his, and the sight of the swell of her breasts inside that lacy bra almost undid him. Her breasts were amazing the first time he'd seen her naked, felt them pressed against his chest, as he'd run his tongue along the rounded curves, across the taut nipples. But now they were even more lush and he slowly ran his hands up her sides and undid the clasp of her bra, his hands caressing every inch of her, his mouth against hers.

He pressed her down on the couch, vaguely aware that behind her head was the sleeve of a onesie with little blue anchors on it. He felt her hands on his shoulders, lower down his back, up his chest, and he pressed against her, then pulled away and looked at her. "Is it safe? I won't hurt the baby?"

She smiled at him, pulling him back against her. "It's absolutely fine."

He tugged off her skirt, mesmerized for a moment by the white cotton underwear. He kissed her, raising her hands over her head to clasp them in one of his while the other edged down those ridiculously sexy panties. In seconds he was out of his jeans and naked. He needed to be inside her. Now.

She gasped as he entered her and he captured her mouth in a kiss, then buried his face in her neck as he fought for control of the sensations rocking his body. It had been so long. So long before Georgia, so long since.

He felt her nails scrape into his back and suddenly he couldn't control himself any longer. She moaned long and loud, and that was the last straw. Everything inside him exploded and he shuddered, then again, burying his face in her neck, gripping her hair, his breaths coming in ragged release.

But then he felt her arms around his neck, holding him close, keeping him close. And all he wanted to do was get away. His skin began to feel tight. Uncomfortable. Very, very uncomfortable. This was Georgia Hurley, the woman he'd fallen so damned hard for in one night. The woman who was pregnant with his child. And yet he couldn't be what she wanted, what she needed.

He had to get up. He needed air. He needed to gulp some air.

Just stay here, he ordered himself. *Do not move. Do not get up. Just deal with how uncomfortable this feels. Did you or did you not just give Georgia a pep talk on strength? Show some, you damned coward.*

The claustrophobic sensation built until he couldn't take it anymore. His skin itched. His nerve endings prickled. Every rise and fall of Georgia's chest made breathing almost a struggle.

"I think I heard Timmy cry," he said like a jerk, getting up and shrugging into his jeans. He didn't look at Georgia, unwilling to see the expression on her face.

Cold bastard, he told himself. *What the hell is wrong with you?*

He knew what was wrong with him. He'd told her what was wrong with him. But he still felt like hell about it. And he had a terrible, terrible feeling that she did too.

Chapter Nine

For the hundredth time that morning, Georgia called herself a big fool. She stood in the kitchen at Hurley's, washing the last of the cookie trays, scrubbing furiously. She was hurt, yes, but she was more mad at herself. Hadn't she told herself to stay away from Nick Slater—romantically speaking? That he was a brick wall? That he'd told her loud and clear how he felt about love and marriage and family? She wasn't going to get her heart all tangled up with a man who couldn't, wouldn't love her back, who didn't want to marry her or to be a family man.

Yet she had. She shook her head at what a dummy she was. She thought about how James Galvestan, that predator, hadn't announced himself as someone who'd ruin her life. You'd think that a man who'd practically shouted from the rooftops that he was going to break her heart in a million pieces was someone she'd keep her distance from. Instead, she handed over her heart to Nick Slater.

He already had it, a little voice inside amended, cutting her a break. *He had it since the day he knocked on your door in Houston.* Tears pricked her eyes, and Georgia blinked them away, then shut off the faucet and dried her hands. Danged hormones.

She glanced over at Timmy in his carrier on the table. He was awake and alert, watching the pale yellow stars and moons of the little mobile that hung down from the canopy of the carrier.

"Let's get you home and I'll read you a story," she said to him, his slate-blue eyes on her. She couldn't help thinking about his mother, who had to be missing Timmy with every fiber of her being. Just a few days with the little guy and she was hopelessly in love and so attached to him. She couldn't even imagine the pain his mother was going through.

Georgia put back the last of the baking ingredients, and with four pies, three cakes and a few dozen cookies baked and stored for the lunch and dinner crowds, she headed back to Nick's house, wheeling Timmy in his little stroller. She wondered how Nick would act, if he'd say anything about last night.

Across the street she saw the Andersons wheeling their own baby. Little Mikey's red wisps made Georgia smile. Not that the smile lasted long. She couldn't help noticing how Annie's arm was looped around Mike's as he pushed the stroller, how happy they both looked.

Georgia would be pushing her baby stroller alone. Her baby's father wouldn't even be in Blue Gulch.

Fool, she yelled at herself. *When he kissed you last*

night, you should have run screaming for the door. Instead, you kissed him right back and practically tore off his clothes. And spent the rest of the evening alone in her room, save for Timmy, her heart smushed, the sting of rejection as fresh in the morning as it had been when he got up and walked away. And stayed away.

Four months ago, when she'd given herself to Nick, she'd been deeply in love with him. That might sound crazy, but in those hours with Nick, everything she'd ever thought and dreamed about love was how she felt in his arms. Just his face, the look in his eyes, triggered something inside her, made her unable to take her eyes off him. She felt a connection to him that she'd never felt before. And in his arms, she felt safe.

Now she'd let her guard down, had been unable to resist him, and the floodgates had opened. She was deeply in love with Nick Slater and wished with everything inside her that he'd want what she wanted—the family she was offering him.

So keep working on him, a determined voice inside her said. *Keep up what you've been doing. Asking him to hold Timmy. Feed Timmy. Open his floodgates.*

But "Operation Get Used to Fatherhood" didn't seem to be working. Nick meant so much to the people of Blue Gulch, but none of that seemed to matter to him either. He wanted out. He was a lone wolf.

Except weren't wolves pack animals? Didn't they need a pack?

Georgia and their son were his pack.

She wasn't sure how she'd convey that to Nick, but she'd try. Her new motto was "try," wasn't it? You didn't just take your licks. You did something about them.

Chin lifted, Georgia headed up the drive to Nick's

house, stopping short when she realized an unfamiliar car was in the driveway, parked next to Nick's SUV.

Timmy's mother? Had she come back?

Georgia hurried to the door and let herself in.

"You don't understand anything!" she heard a female voice shout.

"Oh, I understand perfectly!" she heard Nick shout back.

Curiosity piqued, Georgia parked Timmy in his stroller by the door, and since he was napping, she let him be. She tentatively walked into the living room.

Nick and a younger female version of himself, both with arms crossed against their chests and matching scowls, stood glaring at each other until they noticed her.

"Georgia," Nick said, "This is my sister, Avery. Avery, Georgia Hurley."

Avery's pretty face lit up. "Oooh, you're a Hurley? Of Hurley's Homestyle Kitchen?"

Georgia nodded. "My grandmother owns it. I'm the new baker."

"I love Hurley's!" Avery said. "I had my first date with Quentin there! I could live on the mac and cheese for the rest of my life."

Georgia smiled. "I did as a kid," She reached out her hand to shake Avery's. Again she was struck by how much they looked alike. Avery was tall and lanky with long, straight dark hair and blunt bangs. Her dark eyes were softer than Nick's, and her complexion even paler. She was startlingly pretty. She wore silver rings on every finger and a long, floaty black skirt with a fitted silver tank top. Her toenails were painted a sparkly, iridescent light blue.

"Key word here is *kid*," Nick said. "You're a kid, Avery. And kids get foolish notions in their heads."

Oh boy. This must be where Georgia had come in. The argument.

"I'm not a kid!" Avery said, hands on hips. "I'm eighteen and know my own mind. I want to sing, Nick. I want to try for a music career. I have to follow my heart."

Nick shook his head. "What you have to do is use common sense. If you want a music career, great, be a music major at college like you planned. You'll become a music teacher. Remember Ms. Finch at the high school? She still walks around town singing. She sings in groups and performs in clubs, but she has a steady, solid *job*."

"Quentin says—"

Nick frowned. *"I don't care what Quentin says!"*

"Yes, Nick, I know," Avery shouted back, narrowing her eyes at her brother. "But I do. He's supportive of my dreams."

Nick seemed to realize his combative approach was getting him nowhere. He let out a breath and walked a bit closer to his sister "Avery, I'm supportive of your dreams too. But I want you to be smart about how you go about those dreams."

Now it was Avery's turn to shake her head. "I have a plan, Nick. I've really thought this through. I know college was important to you and I let you talk me into it. But I don't want to be there. I want to become a country singer. And that means moving to Nashville."

Was that red smoke coming out of Nick's ears?

Georgia cleared her throat. "Nick, Avery, I'm sorry

that I barged in on this family conversation. I should let you two talk privately."

Avery lifted her chin. "I've said everything that needs to be said. Quentin and I are leaving for Nashville on Sunday morning." With that, she walked past Georgia with a friendly nod toward the front door. "Mr. Whiskers," she called out, glancing around. "Where are you, boy? Come say goodbye—for now." The little black-and-white cat ran over and Avery scooped him up and nuzzled him, then she put him down. "Don't worry, Mr. Whiskers, of course you're coming with us when we move to Nashville."

Nick let out a long, hard sigh and turned to face the windows.

"Did y'all know there's a baby over here?" Avery called.

"Yes," Georgia said, walking toward the door. "We're watching Timmy for the week."

Nick walked over to the archway separating the foyer from the living room. "Actually, Avery, we're watching Timmy for the week because Timmy's mother left him in my care with an anonymous note. I have no idea who she is or why she left him with me. All I know is that she's clearly in some kind of trouble, either emotionally or financially or criminally. And running off to Nashville with Quentin the philosopher is going to mean you're out there, no safety net, no security, who knows what can happen? Just like with Timmy's mother."

Avery's face clearly showed her exasperation. "So now I'm having a baby and leaving him with a police detective?"

"One choice leads to another," he said.

Avery frowned. "Yes, my choice to give my dream a chance means it can happen." With that she left.

Nick let out an expletive, then walked back to the living room and dropped down on the sofa, his head back, as he stared at the ceiling.

Oh boy.

"She sounds pretty determined," Georgia said.

"What she sounds is young and silly."

Georgia wasn't so sure about that. But she understood where Nick was coming from. And this was his kid sister. The kid sister he'd raised alone for the past two years, struggling to do right by her. Georgia would need to be careful with putting in her two cents.

"It's not like either of them has anything to fall back on. Quentin works in a bookstore, which he lives above, in a one-bedroom apartment. His parents retired to Washington State, but he insisted on staying here to be close to Avery. He wasn't interested in college and considers himself 'self-teaching.' I'll bet he's been after Avery to quit college since she left." He shook his head, anger in his expression.

She figured she should let him sit with his thoughts, process the whole conversation. "I'll go get Timmy," she said, heading toward the foyer.

He cleared his throat. "Georgia, about last night. I'm sorry if I seemed…"

Cold? Unwilling to let someone in? Unable to break down steel barriers?

She turned and waited, letting him squirm a bit, refusing to say *oh, that's okay* or *I get it*. She wanted him to finish the sentence. She tilted her head.

She watched him clamp his mouth shut. He wasn't going to say anything else. He only wanted to bring it up to apologize for how he'd acted, but there wasn't going to be a conversation.

At least she was beginning to understand how he worked. After last night, how could she not?

"I think I hear Timmy," he said, looking beyond her toward the door where Timmy lay in his stroller.

She almost smiled at how well she could read him. That was something. A smile instead of tears. But man, did she have her work cut out for her. She was not giving up on Nick so fast.

Nick had to get out of his house. Away from Georgia and how he'd handled things last night. Away from worrying about his sister ruining her life. He needed to focus on finding Timmy's mother. He checked his notes, let Georgia know he was going out and walked over to Best Pizza Ever on the far end of Blue Gulch Street, where he knew he'd find John Martin, the owner, making pizzas for the lunch rush. As he crossed the street, he wondered what, exactly, he'd been planning to say to Georgia. *I'm sorry if I seemed...*

Seemed like what? A bastard? He was acting like a real jerk lately.

I don't care what Quentin says!

Okay, that hadn't been so...mature. And he knew saying things like that would only put distance between him and Avery, and he didn't want that. He loved Avery so much. He just wanted what was best for her.

He thought finding Timmy's mother was his most important mission? Suddenly, it had a rival: stopping his sister from making a huge mistake. Running off to Nashville to become a country singer. With her philosophy-spouting boyfriend.

Hadn't he said this would happen over his dead body?

His sister was not moving to Nashville. She was not dropping out of college. It was Nick's duty to make sure she was on a solid path. She needed a safety net beneath her. She needed options. Not chasing some crazy dream.

His phone buzzed and he pulled it from his pocket. Text from Avery: Nick, Q and I think we should all get together and talk. Dinner tonight at Hurley's? The 4 of us? Is Georgia your GF? I like her.

Oh hell, he thought as he pulled open the door to the pizzeria. How was he supposed to talk sense into Avery with "Quentin Says" sitting right there and saying all of it, contradicting Nick? Who would she listen to? Her handsome boyfriend who supposedly knew everything or her older brother who really did know some things about life?

The boyfriend would win.

But maybe Nick—with Georgia's help—could win the boyfriend over to Nick's side. Yes, that was it. The more he thought about it, the more he realized that if he could get through to Quentin, make him see that Avery needed to stay in college, stay on her path, she would have more options down the road. And could always sing in the college chorus.

"Uh-oh," John Martin said the moment Nick walked into the pizza joint. "Someone keyed my car? Egged my apartment door? Wrote *John Martin is a jerk* in lipstick in a bar's bathroom stall?"

Nick raised an eyebrow. John was a twenty-eight-year-old lothario who'd dated most of the town's young single women. With movie-star good looks, dimples and too much charm, John juggled three girlfriends at a time and twice had been punched in the face for getting too flirty with someone's wife. Nick had investigated quite a few vandalism incidents directed at John Martin's belongings, including the big front window of the pizzeria, which had been smashed twice. By a spurned lover once and pissed-off ex-boyfriend of a new girlfriend twice. But Nick now realized that he hadn't gotten a call from John about vandalism or assault in a few weeks. That was a record.

"Actually, things have been quiet where you're concerned," Nick said. "Too quiet." He narrowed his gaze on John. "Don't tell me you've fallen in love and only have one woman in your life?"

John grinned and ladled sauce on the round pizza dough. "I don't know about the love part, but I think some kind of weird sickness has come over me. I met someone and think about her all the time. I don't even want to see any other women."

"Yeah, that's called love," Nick said.

"Really?" John asked, his brow furrowing. "I'm in love? That's what this is?"

Nick half smiled, half rolled his eyes, wondering how John had gotten so far in life. He pulled out his phone and swiped to a photo of Timmy. "Do you recognize this baby?"

John paused in spreading around the sauce. "Yeah."

Nick perked up. "From where?"

"I see that pretty Hurley chick with that baby all the time."

Nick deflated again. "Had you ever seen this baby before seeing Georgia Hurley with him?"

"Don't all babies look alike?" John asked.

"Nope."

"Really?" John asked. "Huh. That's twice you blew my mind today, man."

Nick couldn't help smiling. John was a character, all right. "Are you absolutely positive you haven't gotten anyone pregnant lately? Say ten months ago?" He glanced at John's very blond hair. "A dark-haired woman?"

"I never go anywhere without a condom and a spare," John said, generously layering cheese on the sauce. "I'm very careful." He leaned close. "But do you want to know a secret?"

Nick stared at John, wondering if he was about to admit that Timmy could be his. "The woman I'm dating now has a little girl. They're a package deal, and that's fine with me. Oh man, I really must be in love." He glanced at the clock on the wall. "I just remembered they're coming in after school. I'm gonna make a smiley-face pizza for her."

Huh. Nick always thought nothing could surprise him, and then something always did.

"Ever worry about what kind of father you'll be?" Nick asked before he could stop himself. "Being a bachelor for so long, I mean."

"You kidding me? I'll be the best stepfather in town."

Nick admired his confidence. "How do you know?"

"Well, first of all, I like kids. If I didn't I couldn't own a pizzeria. This place is all kids all the time. Second, yeah, I *do* love Lauren, my girlfriend. I mean, love with a capital *L*, you know? And don't tell anyone this, but I went to her daughter's dance recital at her camp the other day and I swear I got teary. *Me*."

Nick had sat at quite a few of Avery's piano recitals and chorus concerts over the past two years, and he had always felt a surge of pride in his kid sister. Would a toddler concert of "It's A Small World" or whatever little kids sang make him choke up? He couldn't see it. "Maybe you've always been a big softie," Nick said. But he knew that wasn't true. John Martin was anything but. A string of broken hearts was proof of that.

John placed generous rounds of pepperoni on the cheese. "I just met the right woman, I guess. Like everyone says will happen. When you meet the right person, you change because you want to. Because you have to. It kind of happens without your say-so, anyway."

Nick wasn't changing. Was he? "Well, thanks, John. You've been a big help." Maybe not with Timmy's mother, but with…big life questions.

John shot Nick his killer grin and slid the pizza in the oven. "Come back later and I'll hook you up with a slice of sausage and mushroom."

Nick smiled and left, his stomach grumbling but not from hunger. He'd never been looking for the "right person." He didn't want to marry or have kids. But yeah, then he'd met Georgia in Houston and there'd been something between them from the minute she opened the door, some kind of crazy energy, connection. He'd never felt that before. And when she walked away the next morning, hadn't he felt his heart crumble?

Maybe that was why he kept her at such a distance. Not because he didn't want to hurt her—of course he didn't. But because she had affected him that way. She had gotten to him. And no woman was allowed to.

If anyone had told him that John "Casanova" Martin would help him figure out why he was so…on edge around Georgia, he'd have laughed. But now he knew why.

Before Avery had come with her bombshell, Nick

would have told himself he was leaving town soon, anyway. He'd see Georgia through the pregnancy and then
settle back in Houston or maybe Dallas for a change
and he'd keep in close contract with Georgia and come
visit twice a month.

Twice-a-month fatherhood. That didn't sound right.

Neither did all-the-time fatherhood.

Except he'd created a child with Georgia, was bringing a life into this world, and there was no way in hell
he'd shirk his responsibilities or make a child feel that
his father wasn't there for him. That his father didn't
love him.

So now what?

For the time being he had to deal with his sister, set
her straight, get Quentin Says on his side. Then he'd
figure out how the heck he was going to be the father
he *had* to be.

At the square table facing the Sweet Briar Moun-
tain Range in Hurley's Homestyle Kitchen, Georgia
sat next to Nick—who was ramrod stiff, his expression trademark stony—with his sister and her boyfriend
across from them. Annabel was babysitting Timmy at
her home, so she and Nick were off duty baby-wise.

"So we have news," Avery said, pushing her long
dark hair behind her shoulders. She sat up straight and
linked her arm through Quentin's, then leaned over to
kiss his cheek. "We're engaged!"

"No, you're not," Nick said, his voice like ice. "You're
in college. Studying to become a music teacher. That's
what you are."

Avery glared at Nick. She reached into her purse,
pulled out a gold ring with a tiny but lovely diamond

embedded in the setting and slid it on her finger. "I am engaged," she repeated, holding up her hand. "I didn't want you to see the ring before Quentin and I could tell you together. I don't know why I considered your feelings. You don't consider mine."

Georgia eyed Quentin. He didn't shrink from Nick's glowering glare. He sat tall in his chair, his arm around Avery. He and Avery made a beautiful couple. Quentin had a mop of sandy brown hair and clear blue eyes, matching dimples beside his mouth. He was tall and lanky like Avery.

"Dude," Quentin began, looking at Nick. Avery nudged him in the side with her elbow. "I mean, sir." He cleared his throat. "Sir, I know we're young. But I love Avery with all my heart. I've loved her since my junior year. She's the world to me, and luckily she feels the same about me. So we decided to get engaged. Your blessing is very important to Avery."

Nick sipped his water as if to have something to do besides imploding. "Well, she's not getting it. You're both too young to get married. You're eighteen, for Pete's sake. What is the damned rush?"

"There's no rush," Avery said. "We're doing what feels right to us. Nick, I'm engaged and we're moving to Nashville to focus on my career as a country singer. I'd like your support before we go."

Nick turned his glare on Quentin. "And what exactly will you be doing while Avery is auditioning and trying to become a country star?"

"I'll be her support system," Quentin responded. "My cousin lives in Nashville and has offered me a job as a production assistant at the record company he works for. Yes, I'll be starting from the bottom, but

I've always been passionate about the music industry and it's a good in for Avery. Dude, she's *so* talented." He shook his head. "I mean, sir. She really is. I know she'll make it."

"Have y'all decided what you'll have?" the waitress, a sweet young woman named Lizzie, interrupted.

Perfect timing. They all needed a break. Everyone glanced at the menu, but they all knew every dish by heart and exactly what they wanted.

Nick leaned back, his expression still stony. Avery and Quentin ordered the ribs for two. Georgia had a craving for a burger so she went with that, and Nick chose the blackened catfish special.

"Any luck finding Timmy's mother?" Avery asked, a change of subject that was welcome.

"Not yet," Nick said, barely looking at her. "I'm working on it."

"She must think about Timmy all the time," Quentin said. "Avery filled me in. I can't imagine how it must feel to leave someone you love behind."

Georgia glanced at Quentin. He was young, but he seemed smart and kind. What he'd said made her think of herself on that Houston sidewalk, walking away from Nick.

For the next fifteen minutes, there were bursts of stilted silences that either Georgia or Quentin tried to fill by asking innocuous questions, and Georgia couldn't help finding Quentin endearing as he struggled to ask Nick questions about being a detective, only forgetting not to call him *dude* twice more. Nick's answers were brief, but Quentin's interested, intelligent conversation seemed to soften Nick just a bit.

As their entrées arrived, Nick was clearly relieved to

have something to do besides glare at his sister and her fiancé. Avery kept the conversation focused on questions about Timmy and told funny stories about her former after-school job as a babysitter for a six-month-old who had a huge laugh. But every time Avery picked up her fork or her glass of iced tea, her ring flashed, and Georgia would catch Nick glance at it and feel him tense beside her.

Finally, coffee and dessert declined, Avery and Quentin stood up.

Avery smiled at Georgia. "I'm so glad I met you. And thank you for joining us for dinner." She turned to Nick. "As Quentin said, Nick, your blessing is very important to me. But we're leaving on Sunday with or without it." With that she came around to hug Georgia, pressed a kiss to her brother's stony cheek, then took Quentin's hand and they left.

Nick dropped back down in his chair. "How could she do this? How could she ruin her life?"

Georgia sipped her herbal iced tea. "I'm not so sure she *is* ruining her life. She has a dream and she's going for it. That's pretty exciting. And she's engaged. That means Quentin isn't just some boyfriend who'll disappear from her life. They're committed and they have a life plan. Yeah, maybe it won't work out. Maybe she won't become the next big thing. But trying is everything, Nick."

He stared at her as though she'd said the craziest thing he'd ever heard. "You can't possibly think they're doing the right thing."

"Well, I'm just saying they sound mature about what they're doing."

"They're eighteen! Avery belongs in school. She's

going to become a music teacher. She can always go on auditions. But if that doesn't work out, she'll have a steady, secure career doing what she loves."

Georgia put her hand on his forearm. "Like you said, she's eighteen. She has dreams and you've raised her to have confidence."

Nick frowned. "Let's change the subject. To nothing."

Georgia offered a commiserating smile. "How about we go pick up Timmy from Annabel and West's house?"

Nick sighed.

Chapter Ten

Annabel and West Montgomery lived on a ranch about ten miles out from the center of town. As Nick drove up the long drive to the property, Georgia could see Annabel, West and West's five-year-old daughter, Lucy, at the fence of the pony pasture a short distance from the white farmhouse. From the way Annabel's arms were positioned, it was clear she was holding Timmy. A brown-and-white pony sniffed at Lucy's hand, and as the car got closer, Georgia could see the pony gently taking a carrot.

This was what Georgia dreamed of. Family. Georgia, her husband and their son feeding ponies, chasing after the dog they'd adopt from the shelter, going for a walk to the ice-cream parlor. Family. Sure, Georgia and her son would be a family of their own and she'd do all those things on her own. But what she would give to have Nick by her side, their side, part of that family. To her, family and love were such gifts, maybe even more so because she'd lost her parents. But so had Nick. And family represented something very different to him.

She'd learned a long time ago that there was no one way to look at something, one way to be, that there was no "just because." *But to choose to be on your own when you could have...this*, she thought, watching her brother-in-law pull her sister to him for a hug, then swing his daughter up on his shoulders.

"I hear that West's therapeutic riding program for children is going really well," Nick said as they parked. "His little girl certainly looks very happy."

She wondered what he was thinking beyond what he'd said, if it registered that Lucy had lost her mother, that the ponies, along with her father's love and devotion to her, had helped her through that loss. West had started an official program to help other kids and adults, as well. Annabel, who knew what it was like to lose your parents, volunteered in the program. Georgia would like to, as well. Maybe once Timmy's mother was found and Nick's free time was once again his own, she'd bring up the idea of his volunteering in the program.

As West turned toward the car, Lucy excitedly asked to be put down and she raced over.

"Hi, Lucy!" Georgia said with a smile as she got out, holding a big white box containing a strawberry shortcake, a favorite of the little girl's. "Wait till you see what I brought for you all. I baked it this morning."

"Ooh, does it have strawberries in it?" Lucy asked.

"It just might," Georgia said, adoring her new niece. Annabel was crazy about her stepdaughter and working on adopting Lucy with the blessing of Lucy's maternal grandparents.

"Lucy, have you met Detective Nick Slater?" Georgia asked. "Detective Nick is a police officer." The little girl had been a regular at Hurley's Homestyle Kitchen the past few months, but Essie had mentioned that Nick had stopped coming in until very recently. Because of her, she knew.

"I know Detective Nick from our class field trip to the police station," Lucy said. "Plus, I saw him ordering a po'boy from Hurley's the other day when I was there." Annabel had told Georgia that she often picked up Lucy after school and took her to Hurley's for mini cooking lessons as Annabel prepped for the dinner rush.

Nick laughed. "I do love po'boys. Nice to see you again, Lucy."

"Lucy, will you lead the way to your parents?" Georgia asked. "I can't wait to see Timmy. I hope he was a good boy for you and your parents."

Lucy gave a big nod. "He was. I like Timmy. He's so cute."

"Very cute and no trouble at all," Annabel said as the three of them reached the fence. She smiled at Georgia and Nick, then peered down at Timmy nestled in her arms. "I gave him a bottle at five and he's freshly changed. He likes looking at the ponies."

Nick shook hands with West and smiled at Annabel. "Thanks for watching him for us."

"Anytime," West said. Georgia was looking forward to getting to know her brother-in-law better. The Montgomerys were clearly very much in love, and the sight of her sister so happy, the love shining in her eyes as she looked at her husband and stepdaughter, brought a comforting peace to Georgia.

As they left, Annabel and West were watching the ponies graze with Lucy between them. The three were holding hands.

"What a beautiful family," Georgia said, her heart squeezing in her chest. "Annabel is blessed."

Nick glanced over but didn't say anything. Georgia deflated a bit. Nick seemed no closer to becoming a family man than he had when Georgia first came back to Blue Gulch. And what he viewed as his sister's "defection" certainly didn't help him develop warm, fuzzy feelings toward the meaning of family.

Maybe she had to let the fantasy go. She just didn't want to.

After putting Timmy down in his bassinet in her bedroom, Georgia found herself craving a peanut-butter-and-jelly sandwich. Surely, Nick had peanut butter and jelly in his cupboards. If not, she just might have to walk over to the grocery store or go over to Hurley's.

She slipped out of her room and headed down the hall, expecting to find Nick in the living room, going over his notes on his cases, trying to find some connection he'd missed to who might possibly be Timmy's mother.

But the living room was empty. She walked into the kitchen to find him sitting at the table with a cup of coffee and holding a photograph in a frame.

Georgia glanced at it. Nick and Avery at Avery's high school graduation. His sister wore her gold cap and dark blue gown, all smiles. Nick looked very proud.

"From this to Nashville to go after some pipe dream.

Engaged at eighteen." He shook his head. "What did I do wrong? I was too strict, maybe. I should have let her have more of a say, more of her own mind."

Georgia could tell from his expression, the set of his shoulders, that once again, he needed to sit with his thoughts for a moment, process them himself before she jumped in, so she searched the cupboard for peanut butter and found a jar. She got out the bread and found strawberry jam in the fridge. "Hungry?" she asked him.

"Considering I could barely look at my dinner, let alone eat it, yeah," he said. "Extra jelly."

She smiled and got to work, the simple task of making Nick a peanut-butter-and-jelly sandwich oddly fulfilling. "You didn't do anything wrong, Nick. Avery is a smart, thoughtful girl with a good head on her shoulders. And Quentin seems the same."

He rolled his eyes and threw his hands up in the air. "How could you defend that…Svengali!"

Georgia was generous with Nick's layer of strawberry jam, put the two slices of bread together and cut on the diagonal, the way her mother and grandmother always did, then added a handful of red grapes on the side of the plate. "He hardly seems like he wants to control her into his 'creation.' He sounds supportive," she added, bringing two plates to the table. "And he has a good plan. He has a job all lined up in the record business. And that's quite an immediate in for Avery. That doesn't mean she'll make it, but they're not going there blind."

Nick glared at her. "She belongs in college working toward her music education degree. That's how you don't go blindly into the world. You work toward a secure path."

Georgia poured two glasses of iced tea and set them on the table. "Well, that's kind of what they're doing."

"Talking to you is like talking to a brick wall," he grumbled, getting up. He took a bite of the sandwich, then stalked out of the room, leaving the photo of him and Avery on table.

Georgia shook her head at the utter irony, grabbed their plates and followed him. She'd be ticked off at him if the notion of Nick calling someone a brick wall wasn't so ridiculous. "Nick. Eat your sandwich."

He grimaced again and took it, dropping down on the sofa and biting into it. "This is perfect, thanks."

She gave him a soft smile, letting him finish one half before she voiced her thoughts. "I think Avery will be just fine. And you know what? If she's not, she can come home. She can go back to school. She has you, Nick."

He leaned his head back against the couch, the strong column of his neck drawing her gaze. Down his dark green T-shirt along his muscular chest and taut stomach to his old faded jeans. She lingered on his bare feet, then finally remembered to take a bite of her own sandwich. Suddenly her craving for PB&J had morphed into a craving of another kind, of Nick's hands on her skin, his hard mouth against her lips. She'd fantasize but she'd not let it happen again. She'd learned her lesson and then some.

Mr. Whiskers jumped up on the couch and sniffed Nick's stomach, then sat down and stared at him with his amber eyes. Nick reached out a hand to pet him and Mr. Whiskers brushed against fingers. Huh. Just when the cat was starting to warm up to Nick, Avery would be taking him with her.

"Nick, I—" she began.

"Let's change the subject," he said, giving Mr. Whiskers a scratch behind the ears. "Is Timmy sleeping?"

She blinked herself out of her little fantasy. "He was when I put him down. And I don't hear a peep."

He finished his sandwich and leaned back again. "I'm sorry about what I said." He glanced at her. "The brick-wall thing. You're hardly that."

She smiled. "It's okay. Talking things out is good. You're going to get frustrated. That's part of life. You just have to work through it."

"I'm frustrated now," he said, holding her gaze. "Frustrated as hell because I want you so damned much and feel like I'd better leave you alone. You don't want a repeat of last night. Well, after last night, I mean." She noticed his gaze drop along her own body, lingering on her breasts under the white tank top, on where her flippy cotton skirt ended just above her knees.

Georgia took a deep breath, afraid where this was going to go. Sometimes a brick wall was comforting. Nothing was said. Nothing explained. You had to speculate and conjecture. There was always room for hope there.

Now there might not be.

"And last night was a problem because…" she prompted.

He sat up straight and looked at her, his dark eyes intense on her, conflicted. "Because I don't know what I'm doing, Georgia. I don't want to be a father. I don't want to live in Blue Gulch. That's what I know. But I am going to be a father and there's no way in hell I'll let you or our son down. I won't do it. If that means staying in Blue Gulch, so be it."

So he'd be here but miserable? Was that better? What if he never changed? What if he couldn't? What if he looked at their son and felt absolutely nothing except obligation?

Tears stung her eyes, so she closed them, willing herself not to cry. Danged hormones again.

Danged Nick Slater was more like it.

She felt his hand close over hers. Then he was pulling her to him, and the tears flowed down her cheeks.

"Don't cry, Georgia. Please don't cry. I'm sorry. I'm so sorry."

She wiped at her eyes and let him hold her. What was she supposed to say? *I'm sorry you feel the way you do? I'm sorry you're the brick wall? It's okay?* It wasn't okay, because she was madly in love with him and desperately wanted to form a family with this man, the three of them together, learning and growing and changing with the passing days, weeks, months, years.

How had she gone from being determined to focus on impending motherhood to yearning for a future with Nick?

She gasped, realizing what this meant.

She trusted him. She trusted Nick Slater because she loved him.

"You've surprised me constantly these past few days, Nick," Georgia said. "I'm sure you've surprised yourself too."

"I do what needs to be done. I believe in responsibility, in fulfilling my obligations."

The brick wall was back.

He still held her hand, the warmth and strength of it a comfort. "I want to do right by you, Georgia. You deserve that. Especially after all you've been through."

She bristled and pulled her hand away. Obligation again. "I don't need your pity, Nick." She bolted up with her half-eaten sandwich, her appetite gone.

"Georgia, that's not what I meant."

"Yes, it is," she said. She hurried into the kitchen and threw the rest of her sandwich away, quickly washed her plate, then turned to leave, her gaze catching on the photograph of Nick and his sister.

Their time together was coming to an end very soon. Timmy's mother would return on Saturday—Georgia felt sure of it. She would move out of Nick's guest room and into an empty bedroom on the second floor of Hurley's, the one with the lovely fireplace and L-shape, perfect for a nursery. Everything would be okay.

She didn't look at Nick as she headed from the kitchen down the short hall to the guest room. She closed the door behind her, walking up to the bureau and staring at her belly in the big round mirror above it. She stood sideways. She definitely looked pregnant.

No matter what, we'll be fine, she told her belly.

There was a knock on her door. She could pretend she was sleeping. Anything to avoid hearing him say what she didn't want to hear.

"Come in," she said without meaning to.

He opened the door and stared at her, his expression so…tortured she wanted to rush into his arms and assure him that she was okay, that she'd be okay, with or without him.

She wouldn't be so okay without him, though. She was deeply in love with Nick Slater.

He stepped in a bit closer. "I just wanted to say goodnight. My mother used to tell me we should never go to bed angry with each other. Not that I was ever really angry at her. Just the situation. Anyway, she was right. Going to bed angry just makes you fester. I know."

"I'm not angry, Nick," she said. "I just think it stinks that you've given up on yourself."

He frowned. "What are you talking about?"

"You've given up on yourself. You don't think you can be a good father. Just like you don't think Avery can make it in Nashville. You have no faith in yourself or anyone else."

The stony expression she knew so well returned. "I'm not having this conversation," he said, backing out of the room and shutting the door.

Georgia closed her eyes, wondering how much of this she could take before her heart split in two.

Chapter Eleven

Faith, schmaith, Nick tried to tell himself for the hundredth time, but he felt like hell even in the morning. He lay on his bed, hands behind his head, staring up at the white ceiling. He'd hated the look on Georgia's face last night, hated that he was disappointing her. But what was he supposed to have faith in? Burglars and murderers and vandals and pissed-off husbands who keyed vehicles belonging to the men their wives flirted with?

Himself? Ha. That was a scream.

Yeah, he'd gotten Bentley the greyhound back for Harriet Culver. He'd been nice to an eleven-year-old dognapper. He was a cop. His job was to do right by the people of Blue Gulch.

He belonged back in Houston. There his cases were more about danger and murder and armed robbery than about dealing with people. Sure, he interviewed and interrogated, but his job in Houston was evidence based, sizing people up. Here in Blue Gulch, it was too much about the community, too people focused, people he'd come to know. He missed the anonymity of Houston.

Avery had graduated from high school. Whether she went back to college or did go to Nashville with Quentin Says, she wasn't living in Blue Gulch anymore. He was free. He could leave.

Except for his son.

And Georgia.

Was Houston really anonymous, anyway? Neighborhoods had a way of feeling like communities no matter how big the city. And he'd been emotionally invested in one of his last cases there—Eleanor Patterson, a widowed mother in her midforties with a teenage son.

The Pattersons were on his list of people to look into for a connection to Timmy, but they were on the Houston list, which he hadn't planned to start on until he'd exhausted possibilities in Blue Gulch. He almost had. And he and Georgia had walked around town so much with Timmy that someone would have come to him with information about Timmy's mother if someone had any to share. Still, Houston was a long drive from Blue Gulch—three hours. And he'd been gone from the Houston police force for two years now. But maybe someone remembered him and made the three-hour drive to drop Timmy off with him. It seemed unlikely, but anything was possible. That much he knew.

Nick sat up and reached for the top box of case files from Houston—it had long been Nick's habit to copy his own police reports for home records—onto his bed and dug out the Patterson file. Forty-three-year-old Hank Patterson had been found drowned in a river, having fallen out of his boat while intoxicated. Patterson had been known to police for several cases of assault around town and four domestic violence calls to his home, which he shared with his wife and then-fifteen-year-old son. The son had called each time; the mother had not pressed charges, status quo, unfortunately, until his death. The Pattersons had reminded Nick so much of his own past that every time he left their company he'd be in knots.

Hank's wife, Eleanor, had been forty-four then. She'd be forty-six now. Possible, but unlikely as Timmy's mother. He'd spent a lot of time with the Pattersons those first few weeks after Hank's death. Trying to help Eleanor and her son Dylan deal with paperwork and forms, getting Eleanor a job at a veterinarian clinic, checking in on Dylan and dropping off gifts here and there, a basketball, a pair of headphones. They thought of Nick as a trusted friend…someone close to Eleanor Patterson might very well trust Nick with her newborn.

When Nick had come by to tell them he was moving to Blue Gulch, Eleanor looked peaceful and Dylan was shooting hoops with a friend. They looked okay, settled. And Nick had moved on to a new life, to raise his teenage sister in his hometown.

Maybe taking a ride out to Houston today would be good for him, to see if it gave him that old rush it once did when it now represented Team Not Blue Gulch in every way possible. He hadn't been there since April, since the academy reunion and Georgia. Now Houston made him think of that night and suddenly he wasn't sure if it was home anymore, anyway.

He heard a key in the door and headed into the living room, forcing himself to face Georgia and unresolved issues from last night when all he wanted to do was get in his car and drive away.

She parked the stroller by the front door and came in with Timmy cradled in her arms.

God, she was so beautiful. She looked so natural with an infant against her chest. She'd make a great mother. He hoped she'd learned that these past days of watching Timmy round-the-clock. He thought she had no faith in anyone? He had faith in *her*.

His voice wasn't working, or maybe it was his brain that was defective at the moment. All his thoughts were jumbled in his head. He cleared his throat and glanced away, pretending to be absorbed in the Patterson police report in his hand. "I'm going to drive to Houston today and check out a possible connection to Timmy's mother. I'll be leaving in a half hour."

She was silent for a moment, then said, "We'll come with you."

He stared at her, barely able to believe what he'd heard. "To Houston? I thought you said you never wanted to go back."

"I know," she said, lifting her chin. "But I think I should. The first step in taking back control is to go. I loved Houston for a long time until it began to feel like a prison. I'm not giving someone—someone's memory and my own bad memories—the right to determine how I feel about a city. I do want to go."

He winced. He was doing the same thing with Blue Gulch. "You're sure?"

"I'm sure."

He had to hand it to her again.

Georgia found herself quiet on the three-hour drive to Houston. Timmy had slept the entire way in his rear-facing car seat, the champion napper giving her no break in her thoughts, no need to do something like hold him or change him or rock him. She thought she'd be fine, thought she could handle this, that it was no biggie, she'd just go back and face it and be done with it. Except from the moment she got in Nick's silver SUV, strapping the seat belt over her torso, she felt claustrophobic, trapped, headed for certain doom. Maybe she wasn't as strong as she thought she was.

And maybe Nick wasn't as wrong as she hoped *he* was about how Blue Gulch made him feel. If even heading toward Houston could have dread snaking around her stomach, fear crawling up her spine, how must he feel every day in Blue Gulch—where he'd spent the past two years for his sister's sake?

Suddenly, she felt like a heel for jumping to Avery and Quentin's side over Nick's. He had sacrificed quite a bit for his sister and now here Georgia was, discounting his feelings. But then again, it was Avery's life. Nick had stayed in Blue Gulch for Avery because he loved her. And that was unconditional. He had to let her go.

Feeling a little better at having worked that out and realizing she was thinking about Nick's situation with his sister to avoid thinking about her own feelings, her own past, she forced herself to look out the window. The rush of city life with its whirlwind of tall buildings and cars and people just made her wish she was back home.

"You okay?" Nick asked, glancing at her.

She had to be honest. "No. I thought I would be. But I'm not. I don't want to be here."

"I'll turn the car right around and take you home," he said, doing just that at the next light.

She put a hand on his arm. "No, Nick. I need to face

what happened here. Like I said, I need to take Houston back for myself. Not let someone else dictate how I feel about a place I once loved."

"You're brave, Georgia. Braver than I am, that's for sure."

Ha. Georgia. Brave. She didn't feel brave, but she liked hearing him say it.

"Do you want to avoid your old neighborhood?" he asked. "The Pattersons live ten minutes out from that direction, but I can bypass it."

Did she want to see her condo? Where she'd lain awake every night for months worried sick and feeling trapped, racking her brain for how to get herself out from James Galvestan's clutches?

Where she'd met Nick. Where they'd made love. Where she'd walked away from him.

But where she'd conceived their child.

"Let's go past the condo," she said. "I'm not sure how I'll feel, but I think I need to see it."

He nodded and they headed for the historic district. As he drove slowly down her old street, instead of seeing the place where she'd been so terrified, where someone had insinuated himself into her life with threats, all she could think about was Nick inside her condo, how he'd kissed her, touched her, how passionate and tender he'd been at the same time. How was that even possible?

Georgia hadn't had that many boyfriends in her life. There was the high school beau who'd joined the navy and was now married with three kids and a fourth on the way, per his mother, whom Georgia had run into on the street a couple of days ago. Then there'd been a few men in Houston in years past, perfectly nice, attractive, interesting men, but not The One you always heard was possible, The One who made your knees weak, The One you couldn't take your eyes off, The One you couldn't stop thinking about. She'd begun to think that was just something in songs or that only lucky folks found, like her parents. But she'd recognized it the moment she opened her condo door and Nick was standing there.

She looked at his hands on the steering wheel, recalling them on her.

She'd fallen in love with Nick in a single night, then had to let him go the next morning—for four months. Now here he was, beside her—for the time being. There was a chance to help him open up the way he had done that night, when there had been no expectations, when she hadn't been pregnant with his child, when they lived three hours apart. If she could coax the tenderness back out of him, maybe there was a chance for them.

Nick pulled into a space across from her condo and lowered the windows. Georgia peered out at her pretty building with its flower boxes and stately red door. *Nick*, she thought. *All I'm thinking about is Nick.*

Because how I feel about him is more powerful than how powerless James made me feel. Which meant, she realized, her heart twisting, that Nick didn't feel the same way about her. Everything Blue Gulch represented for Nick was stronger than whatever it was Georgia meant to him.

"Shut up, you old fool!" a woman's gravelly voice barked.

Georgia turned to see where the voice was coming from. A gray-haired couple, in their eighties, was slowly walking across the street, the woman using a cane and the man pulling a cart containing two bags of groceries.

"You shut up!" the man said. "You can't even cook a decent steak!"

The woman lifted her cane and poked it in his side. "Well, you can make your own steak tonight!"

"But you make it better than I do," the man whined. "I'm hungry!"

"Fine," the woman said, her voice softening. "I'll make you creamed spinach to go with it."

The man kissed her cheek and the woman half scowled, half smiled as they continued up the street.

Nick shook his head, looking from the couple to the steering wheel. "God, count me out."

"Of?" Georgia asked.

"Growing old with someone. Talking to them like that. Getting poked with a cane."

Georgia couldn't help smiling. "But they made up. He kissed her cheek. She's making him his favorite creamed spinach."

Nick raised an eyebrow. "Yeah, because he wants his steak."

"Or that's their dynamic and it works."

"Why not just be loving?" he asked. "Why not be respectful? Why treat each other like that at all? 'Shut up'? Why talk to your spouse that way?"

Georgia didn't have a good answer for that. She certainly didn't want a relationship like that either, but maybe when you were married for sixty years, you got cranky with each other. Not that her grandparents had done so. Essie and Benjamin Hurley had been married for forty years when Grandpa Ben had died of a heart attack. Georgia had never heard her grandparents talk like that to each other. Sure, they disagreed, they had arguments like all couples, but they treated each other with respect.

Nick needed to see that. Couples who were kind to each other. He had to see love and respect in action. Perhaps she'd invite Annabel and her husband, West, and their daughter to dinner soon, and Nick could have longer than ten minutes to see how wonderfully loving marriage could be.

Perked up, Georgia stared at her condo and knew that love had conquered its opposite. Her feelings for Nick were too strong for anything to topple them.

Love, beautiful love, was possible. Happiness was possible. You just had to watch the signs, know which were red flags waving and run the other way. With James, she'd ignored a few very bright red flags early on before she knew what he was. She'd thought she was the problem. Her lack of experience. Her lack of sophistication. She'd been naive, but those days were over.

The problem with Nick seemed to be that he thought of himself as a red flag.

But she wasn't running. Not from the good guy.

Georgia Hurley: bullfighter. She almost laughed, but her chest puffed out a bit at the thought.

"I'm ready to go," she said, settling back in her seat, her mind at a certain peace. "I'm okay now. Houston is where our child was conceived, Nick. That's what it'll mean to me."

He eyed her, clearly skeptical of her Pollyanna-ness.

"I'm not saying I've magically forgotten what happened here," she added. "How terrified I was. But better, stronger memories were made here, Nick." She put her hands on her belly. "This baby was created here." She smiled and felt a swell of happiness inside her.

He took her hand and looked at her, holding her gaze, his dark eyes soft on her. "I'm glad for you, Georgia. I really am."

She thought he might have turned a figurative corner with his own issues about places and memories and good feelings, good memories outweighing bad, but he slipped his hand away and turned the key in the ignition.

"Let's go visit the Pattersons and see if they recognize Timmy," he said, moving on, which was what Nick liked to do. Move on.

Nick made another left and drove about ten miles to a more run-down part of town. He slowed the car and came to a stop in front of a peeling, two-story small gray house with a chain-link fenced yard.

"You know what I hate about my job?" Nick asked. "The part where you don't know what you're going to find when you knock. I've never gotten used to that."

"You knocked on my door and found me," she whispered.

He looked at her and took a deep breath but didn't respond.

Nick felt something of a shiver as he rang the Pattersons' doorbell. He'd thought Eleanor would have moved from this house after her husband's death, but she never had. For the first few months, she'd said she just needed to adjust to all the changes in her life now that she was a widow and she'd wanted Dylan to stay in the same school. But two years later, she hadn't moved.

Georgia stood beside him, holding Timmy's carrier. Nick wondered what reaction he'd get when Eleanor Patterson opened the door. He had no idea if he was on the right track here, if Timmy were connected to the Pattersons. His gut wasn't telling him anything.

But there was no response from inside. Nick rang the doorbell again. Then knocked. Still nothing.

"Are you looking for Dylan?" a voice asked.

Nick glanced to his left. An elderly woman was leaning out the window of her home next door.

"Well, I'm looking for his mom, Eleanor," Nick explained.

The woman's face fell. "Eleanor passed away about six months ago. A car accident."

Dammit. His shoulders sank, his chest tight. How much did Dylan have to deal with? The boy was only seventeen now if Nick remembered right. "And Dylan?"

"I don't see much of him these days," the woman said. "He graduated from high school a couple of months ago and works in a diner. Short-order cook, I think."

"Do you know which one?" he asked.

"It's right up the street," she said, pointing in the opposite direction. "Neon sign. Can't miss it."

He thanked the woman, and he and Georgia got back in the car, Nick's heart heavy. He shook his head, barely able to believe the hand that poor kid had been dealt. And Eleanor. After everything she'd been through. A damned car accident. He slammed his hand on the steering wheel, his frustration getting the better of him. "I can't believe she's gone. Survived all that and gone."

Georgia finished settling Timmy in the backseat, then slid into the passenger seat and put her hand on his arm. "From what you told me of the case, Eleanor Patterson spent the past two years not being scared anymore—for herself and her boy. At least she had that. You helped her get settled into a new life, a life she was able to enjoy."

He nodded, taking a deep breath and letting it out. "James wasn't quite sixteen when his father died. Now he's lost his mother, who he was very close to, before his eighteenth birthday." He closed his eyes for a moment, sorrow hitting him in the stomach.

"Let's go see if we can find him at the diner," Georgia said.

Nick lifted his head and nodded. He could see the neon sign for the twenty-four-hour restaurant from here. Nick got out and unlatched Timmy's carrier, and he and Georgia walked up the block and across the avenue to the corner diner.

Inside the small restaurant, which smelled like bacon and burgers, a middle-aged waitress carrying a coffee-pot nodded. "Sit anywhere." She glanced at Timmy in the carrier Nick held. "Aw, cute baby."

He gave something of a smile, all he could muster. "Actually, we're just looking for Dylan Patterson." He glanced around. "I was told he might work here."

"He's right back there," she said, pointing to the pass-through between the kitchen and behind the counter.

Nick could see an elbow, a hand flipping pancakes on the griddle. Then he saw a burger get flipped.

"Dylan," the woman called out. "Some folks to see you."

Dylan slid over and poked his head into view. He was a lot taller than he was two years ago, more muscular, but still looked like a kid. He stared at Nick in complete shock, then turned as if running away. Nick heard a screen door slamming shut.

What the...? Did he just run? Nick handed Georgia

the carrier and rushed through the swinging door of the kitchen, then through the screen door to the back alley. He could just make out Dylan hopping a fence.

"Dylan, wait! I just want to talk to you!"

But he was out of sight before Nick could even think about chasing him.

Nick hurried back inside. "Has Dylan been in any kind of trouble lately?" he asked the waitress. "Trouble with the law?"

The waitress shook her head. "Opposite. I'm the manager here, and Dylan is a model kid. Hard worker too. Comes in early every shift, stays late, wants as much overtime as possible."

"Dylan lives alone?" Nick asked.

"He lives with his elderly great-aunt," the woman said. "Ever since his mom passed. Dylan cares for her best he can since his mom died. She's hard of hearing and on the frail side."

Poor Dylan. He'd been practically on his own for the past six months. Nick thanked the manager for her help and let her know that if Dylan came back, she should assure him he wasn't in any trouble, that Nick just wanted to see how he was. After getting Dylan's cell phone number, he and Georgia left.

"Why would he run?" Nick asked as they headed back to the car. "Why would he be afraid of me if he's a model citizen?"

Georgia shrugged. "Maybe we should stay a day or two. You could ask around about him. Speak to his aunt."

Nick nodded and resettled Timmy in the backseat, then opened Georgia's door for her until she slid in and buckled herself in. "Wow, you weren't kidding about being all right with being back here."

"I'm with you," she said, her green eyes on his. "I feel safe."

He held her gaze, unable to look away. A surge of emotion hit him in the chest and it was so overpowering that he closed his eyes for a second. God, what was happening to him?

He certainly couldn't do this without her. On the teamwork front alone, he needed her to watch Timmy, hold Timmy, take care of Timmy. He couldn't poke around on unofficial business with a baby in his arms.

He was aware again of how much it comforted him to have her near, to know she was safe because she was by his side—but this time, there couldn't be secrets. If something was wrong, he wanted to know. She hadn't said a word about the other night, how he'd walked away from her after they made love. That had to have stung, unless he was flattering himself that sex with him meant anything to her. Regardless, he'd acted like a selfish, self-absorbed toad and she hadn't called him out on it. He'd made some brief apology for his behavior and she'd accepted it and they'd moved on. But it had to bother her on some level, right?

Again, maybe he was flattering himself. But he wanted her to speak her mind. If he did something wrong, he wanted to know it, even if it pissed him off. Which it probably would. Nick Slater liked to keep things swept under that ol' rug where all the bits and pieces of his past lay either dormant or festering. Nick mentally shook his head at himself.

He got in the driver's seat and turned to face Georgia.

"You'll tell me if anything is wrong. If anything's bothering you, right? No secrets this time. No matter what."

"Even if it bothers you to hear it?" she asked with a smile.

Again it pricked at him that she seemed to know him so well. "Even if. I'm kind of the king of that lately, wouldn't you say?"

She smiled again and placed her hand on his for just a second. "You sure are. I will admit that I wish Timmy could speak and tell me what he needs," she said as the baby fussed a bit, then settled. "I feel so helpless sometimes. I keep thinking I should have this down by now, but I don't always know what to do."

He stared at her, surprised she felt that way. She seemed like a natural to him. Yes, she was learning as she went, since she had no experience with babies or children at all, but she was doing a hell of a job.

"I guess I shouldn't admit that to my boss," she said.

He raised an eyebrow. "I'm not your boss."

"Well, you kind of are. I'm your nanny. I work for you. You're my boss."

He turned the key in the ignition and pulled out of their spot in front of the Pattersons' house. "I'm no one's boss. Which is how I like it. I don't have any interest in telling anyone what to do or how to do it." Which was why he wouldn't be much of a father.

"But you uphold the law," she said. "It's your job to tell people what to do and how to do it."

"*Almost* a good point," he conceded. "But I'm a detective. I solve crimes. I hunt for clues. I look over evidence. No one reports to me. I like it that way. I'm responsible to my cases. That's as responsible as I want to be."

He thought about adding something so that he didn't sound so…robotic or as though he didn't care. He cared plenty.

She raised an eyebrow. "You sure did tell your sister what to do and how to do it."

"That's different. Avery is my kid sister. I *am* responsible for her. Legal adult now or not," he added as he turned left toward the historic district.

"You do know that love you feel for her, the responsibility you feel, all the stress over her decisions—that's how parenthood feels," she said. "You're already doing it, Nick. A little bossily for someone who doesn't want to be a boss, but quite well. You love Avery. You want the best for her. You *care*."

His chest tightened. Somehow the conversation had morphed from boss to fatherhood. "Taking care of a sixteen-year-old girl for two years isn't the same as parenting a baby into adulthood. And if I did such a good job, then why is Avery marrying at eighteen? Running off to Nashville after some pie-in-the-sky dream?"

"She's engaged because she's in love. Because she believes in love and marriage. Because she found the one—young, but she found him. And she's chasing her dream because she believes in *herself*. I have no doubt you had a lot to do with that."

He leaned his head back against the seat, eyes straight ahead on the road. She just didn't understand. Or he didn't want to hear it. He wasn't sure. But he was almost certain it was the first. "We'll just have to agree to disagree, as they say."

She crossed her arms over her chest. "Except I'm right."

He laughed. "I admit I like your confidence."

"I actually surprised myself with it. What do you know? I'm getting my groove back. In Houston, no less." She sat up straight and lifted her chin. "I know I'll be fine on my own," she said, placing a hand on the swell of her belly. "I've got this," she added—to her belly and not to him.

He looked at her, full of admiration for her strength, full of…disappointment in himself for making her feel that she'd be alone in raising their son. He pulled over into a spot and put the car in park, turning to face her. "Georgia, I'll take full responsibility for our baby. You know that, right? I will not let you or the baby down."

"Meaning you'll sign your name to the birth certificate. You'll fulfill financial obligations. You'll come by a few times a month to see him, since you'll probably be living in Houston."

"I don't know," he said honestly. "I've been thinking about how this will work, but I don't know yet."

She stared at him and let out a frustrated breath. Timmy fussed from the backseat. "I think he's ready for a nap."

Using Timmy's need for a nap or a bottle or a diaper change had always been his old standby for getting out of a conversation. But this time it was Georgia who was weary and done. Not that he knew what else to say on the subject. He really didn't know how it would work, how their "family" would operate.

Family. Would they *be* a family? His son would be his family, of course. And Georgia was his baby's mother, so that made her family.

A twitch started forming in his right temple. He needed some time to himself to *not* think.

"I know a nice hotel in the theater district," he said,

starting up the car again. "I can do some research into Dylan's background and Timmy can get some rest. And you can put your feet up."

She offered a smile. "That does sound good."

I wish I could be what you need, he thought out of nowhere as he continued on down the street.

But he didn't see that happening, even if he willed it to be.

Chapter Twelve

"Enjoy your stay, Mr. and Mrs. Slater," the hotel desk clerk said as she handed Nick two key cards.

Georgia stiffened. Mrs. Slater. She glanced at Nick, who shifted Timmy's carrier in his other hand, then smiled tightly at the clerk. *Mrs. Slater*, she thought again. *Mrs. Slater*.

It had a familiar ring to it, a nice ring, a comfortable ring.

As if there were any ring at all, she reminded herself, glancing at her bare left hand. Nick Slater wasn't proposing. There would be no big happy family. Well, there would be a happy family. And a big one, given her clan. But she wouldn't be Mrs. Slater. She felt bereft all of a sudden as if she'd ever been Mrs. Slater.

Nick slung their just-in-case overnight bags, which had come in handy, on his shoulder and took the carrier, then led the way to the elevator across the marble lobby.

"You're sure you're okay with the one room?" he asked as they stepped inside and he pressed the button for the fourteenth floor. "I can try to find a room for me in a nearby hotel." Because of two conventions being held in Houston, hotel rooms were scarce for the next couple of days.

"You've seen me naked already," Georgia said, again surprised by how bold she was getting. She liked that the old Georgia was coming back. The Georgia who spoke her mind. The cheeky Georgia. "Twice," she added dryly. "So it's okay."

Well, it wasn't really okay. She wanted to share a room with him, but she wanted him to keep his hands off her and on her at the same time. *Not* touch her so that she wouldn't yearn for him, for his love, for a future with him. *Touch* her because she loved him and wanted him desperately.

Was that win-win or lose-lose? Georgia wasn't sure.

His eyes widened at her brassiness, which always seemed to surprise him too, and he laughed. "I'm sure there's a club chair. I'll sleep in that."

She said nothing, but took one of the key cards from between his fingers and slipped it in the door of room 1412. The room was large, the king-size bed dominating. There was the usual desk and chair, a long bureau with a big mirror, an armoire holding a television and a minibar. Nick put Timmy's carrier down on the desk, then opened the heavy drapes, revealing an expansive view of the city. There was indeed a club chair too, which didn't look comfortable.

"You'll be okay on your own?" he asked. "I figure I'll be gone a couple of hours to pay Dylan's aunt a visit.

I recall mention of an aunt on his father's side, but she didn't live with the Pattersons two years ago."

She sat down on the edge of the big bed. "I'll be fine. I'm zonked so will nap when Timmy does." She *would* be fine. Just as she'd told him in the car. She'd be fine on her own because she had to be. Wasn't necessity the mother of invention? Reinvention too.

She'd just prefer him by her side, in general.

I don't know how this will work... She could imagine Nick coming to the house every second or third Friday with a stuffed giraffe or a soccer ball, building a sandbox in the yard, then a play set, then a tree house. A visitor in their lives.

Yeah, yeah, she'd be fine on her own, but the wave of sadness that rushed through at the thought of Nick ringing the doorbell of the home she shared with their child made her very tired.

"If you need me, for anything, just call," he said. He glanced at Timmy, who was looking at his little mobile, then he looked back at Georgia, nodded and left.

She missed him immediately.

Nick drove back to Dylan's house. There was no car in the short driveway, and the curtains at the front windows were closed. Was Dylan inside? Hiding from him? Only one way to find out.

Nick walked up the three steps, expecting the elderly neighbor to poke her head out the window again. It only took a few seconds.

Her gray head appeared. "Did you find Dylan at the diner?"

"I did, thank you. But now I'm here to see his aunt."

Curiosity brightened her expression. "If Dylan's not

home you'll have to knock hard a few times. Helen's hard of hearing."

"Ah, thank you," Nick said, recalling that the diner manager had mentioned that.

He felt bad about pounding on the door, but after two police-level knocks, he heard shuffling feet. The door opened and a frail-looking woman in her eighties wearing a pink sweat suit appeared.

"My name is Detective Nick Slater," he practically shouted. "I'm—"

The woman's face lit up. "Detective Slater! I know who you are. You were very kind to Eleanor when she was having all that trouble with her husband, who was my nephew, God rest his soul. You were kind to Dylan too. I'm Helen Patterson, Dylan's great-aunt."

"Nice to meet you," he said loudly, extending his hand, which she took in both of hers with a warm smile. "May I come in? I'd like to hear how Dylan is doing."

She pulled the door open wide. "Of course. You'll have to sit on my left. I can barely hear a thing out of my right ear." She led the way into the small living room.

As she moved slightly, Nick's gaze landed on a photograph atop the mantel. He froze.

The photograph was of a baby, a newborn, wrapped in the standard hospital-issue striped blanket, a light blue cotton cap on his head.

The baby looked an awful lot like Timmy.

"May I?" he asked Helen, gesturing at the photograph.

"Sure. Such a darling baby," she said, her expression faltering as she sat down on an easy chair.

He glanced back at Helen Patterson as he walked over to the mantel. The woman looked upset. She was shaking her head; then she reached to a basket beside her chair and pulled out a small stuffed teddy bear, her eyes downcast as she clutched it to her chest. Had this frail eighty-year-old managed to get herself to Blue Gulch to leave Timmy on his desk? Highly doubtful. Whose child was he?

Nick's heart lurched as he stopped in front of the mantel and lifted the photograph, studying the baby. Timmy's eyes had turned a bit more blue, less the gray-blue in the picture. The newborn redness in the face was gone. As were the crinkles and wrinkles. But it was Timmy. He had no doubt.

"Ma'am, whose baby is this?" Nick asked.

"Little louder, Detective?" she asked, pointing at her right ear.

"This baby," he shouted. "Who does he belong to?"

"He belongs to me," a male voice said. "I'm his father."

Nick whirled around. Dylan Patterson stood in the doorway to another room, his hands stuffed in his pockets. The teenager glanced around the room, his blue eyes filling with fear. "Where's Timmy? He's okay, isn't he? Why isn't he with you?"

Nick's mouth almost dropped open. Dylan was Timmy's father? What?

He was just a kid himself. So much a kid—in Nick's mind and memory, anyway—that it hadn't even crossed Nick's mind that Dylan Patterson could be Timmy's parent. Though now that he thought about it, he'd been thinking *mother* the entire time. It had never occurred to him that Timmy's *father* had left the baby on Nick's desk. Not once.

Because you're so damned blocked about father-

*hood you couldn't even imagine that a father, a father
in some kind of trouble, would have written that desperate note to you, left the baby on your desk for you
to safe keep for the week. A father.*

"Where is Timmy!" Dylan shouted, tears welling
in his eyes.

"Timmy is fine, Dylan," he assured the young man.
"He's with Georgia—the woman who was with me at
the diner earlier. We're staying at a hotel in the theater
district. Timmy is likely napping right now or else Georgia is giving him a bottle or singing one of her many
lullabies to him."

Nick watched Dylan's entire body relax. The boy shut
his eyes for a second, letting out a very deep breath.
But he said nothing. No explanation.

Helen glanced uneasily from Dylan to Nick. "Dylan's
a wonderful father. But because Dylan is only seventeen
and the sole parent of Timothy, a social worker came
by and said she'd have to determine Dylan's fitness to
care for the baby, since I'm not in the best of health or
able to help much. She said she was backlogged with
cases but would be back in a few days. That was over a
week ago. Every time someone knocks, I think it's her
coming to take Timmy away."

Ah. So Dylan left Timmy on Nick's desk because he
was afraid Social Services would be coming to take
the baby away.

"Okay," Nick said. "Let's back up." He looked from
Helen to Dylan. "Start from the beginning. You're the
sole parent? Who and where is Timmy's mother."

Dylan ran a hand through his mop of sandy blond
hair and stepped into the room, his gaze on the photograph Nick held. "Madeline Connors is Timmy's

mother. She was my girlfriend. We had all these plans to get married and raise Timmy. But the closer she got to her delivery date, the more she changed her mind. When he was born, she said she was too young for marriage or motherhood, that she was only eighteen and had her whole life ahead of her."

Nick sucked in a breath, his heart heavy for Dylan. So young and he'd been through the wringer, one major blow after another.

Dylan walked closer to Nick, clearly not wanting his aunt to overhear what else he had to say. "Madeline thought my mom would be around to help, since she's not close to her parents. But then my mom—" He squeezed his eyes closed, as if willing himself not to cry, not to break down.

Nick's heart clenched. He wanted to pull the boy into a hug and let him cry it out, but he knew he should let Dylan finish his story. "I'm so sorry about your mother, Dylan."

Dylan wiped away tears, taking a deep breath. "My great-aunt is a widow and was living on her own, but that wasn't working out. When Madeline found out Aunt Helen would live with us, it was the last straw for her and she wanted out of the whole thing. She signed away her parental rights." Tears slipped down his cheeks. "How could she do that? How could she not want Timmy?"

"If that social worker comes back," Helen said, "she might take Timmy away."

Dylan nodded, looking from his aunt back to Nick. "That's why I drove to Blue Gulch to leave him with you. I was afraid if you knew the details, your hands would be tied. So I put Timmy's carrier on your desk with the anonymous note, and then I started freaking out that maybe you wouldn't be back for a long time. But I saw the note you left about just going out for ten minutes to pick up lunch. I hid outside until you came back and watched through a window. Once I saw you pick up the note, I ran to my car and drove home."

"Dylan, that was a huge risk leaving him on my desk," Nick said. "I did have to call Social Services. What if they'd come to take him into foster care until his parents could be tracked down?"

"I knew you wouldn't let anyone take him. I knew that if I wrote the note asking you to care for him, I could trust you, that you'd take care of him until Saturday."

"What happens Saturday?" Nick asked. Tomorrow.

His shoulders lifted. "I turn eighteen. I'm no longer a minor. No one can take Timmy away from me after tomorrow. Right?" he asked, his eyes worried again.

"No one is taking Timmy away from you, Dylan. You've got my word on that." He opened his arms and the boy rushed into them, sobbing.

"I miss Timmy so much," Dylan said, his voice breaking. "Leaving him was the hardest, worst thing I've ever had to do. And I've had to do some of the worst things imaginable."

Such as worry about his mother. Such as bury his father. Such as bury his mother. Then he'd been dumped by his baby's mother, was responsible for his elderly great-aunt, and had to take care of a baby on his own—a baby he'd been terrified he'd also lose.

"Everything's going to be all right, Dylan. I'm here for you, okay? You were one hundred percent right—you *can* trust me. We'll get this settled with the social worker—but no one is taking Timmy from you. He's your son."

Dylan calmed down, wiping under his eyes with the bottom of his T-shirt.

There was no way Nick was leaving Dylan here in Houston with all this on his shoulders, eighteen or not. "I have an idea for a fresh start for you and your family. What do you think about moving to Blue Gulch, the three of you?"

He'd have to talk it over with Georgia, about offering Dylan a job in the kitchen at Hurley's, and he'd have to find a home for the Pattersons, but all that seemed the easy part.

"I'd like that," Dylan said, relief flooding his expression. "And I'm sure Aunt Helen would too." They both turned to look at Helen Patterson, who was leaning toward them with her left ear and nodding with a smile. Dylan smiled back at his aunt, then turned to Nick. "Can I come see Timmy? I won't take him till tomorrow—I won't feel safe until I'm legally an adult. But I have to see his face. I have to see my son."

Nick felt a punch to his gut at the longing coating Dylan's voice, but ignored it and pressed a hand on Dylan's shoulder. Would he ever feel that? What Dylan felt for the baby he'd been compelled to leave for a week. What Logan Grainger felt for his missing nephew. "Let's go."

If he was missing that…synapse or whatever the right word was, he'd do his child a terrible disservice, make his own boy feel unloved, unwanted. Something cold slithered up Nick's spine and settled along his neck. Maybe staying away was the right thing to do. Maybe moving to Houston and visiting twice a month would be better than living in Blue Gulch a half mile away when he might as well be hundred of miles away.

He glanced at Dylan as he told his great-aunt they were going to see Timmy and that Dylan would be back in a little while. The boy seemed at once such a kid and such a grown-up that Nick wasn't sure what to think about Dylan Patterson—teenager or adult. He only knew he believed in the young man 100 percent. Why Nick couldn't believe in himself was another question, one with a lot of answers that added up to a big nothing.

"I can't wait to hold my son," Dylan said as he locked the front door and followed Nick to his SUV. "What's that thing people say about your heart walking around outside your body when you're separated from your child—that's true. That's how it feels."

Maybe Nick would find that to be true. For his son's sake, he sure as hell hoped so.

There was a knock on the hotel room door and Georgia ran to open it. Nick had texted her about ten minutes ago to explain about Dylan, the plan to move to Blue Gulch and that he was desperate to see his baby.

The handsome young man in the doorway looked over Georgia's shoulder to see Timmy in his carrier on the desk. He rushed over and unlatched the baby, carefully cradling him against his chest, gently kissing the top of his head. Tears streamed down Dylan's cheeks, and his knees seemed to buckle, so he moved to the bed and sat down, rocking Timmy gently in his arms.

"I missed you so much, little guy," Dylan said, his cheek against Timmy's head. "I'll never leave you again. Never. Starting tomorrow I'm eighteen and no one can ever take you away from me."

Tears pooled in Georgia's eyes. She glanced at Nick and if she wasn't mistaken, his eyes were glistening.

"Dylan, I'm Georgia Hurley," she said, sitting down next to him. "I've been helping watch Timmy for the past several days. I adore this boy."

Dylan ran a finger down Timmy's cheek. "Thank you. Thank you, both of you, for taking such good care of him." He looked at Nick. "I knew I could count on you."

Nick lifted his chin, then nodded, clearly moved by what Dylan had said.

"Dylan, my family owns a restaurant in Blue Gulch," Georgia said. "It's called Hurley's Homestyle Kitchen. Ribs, burgers, chicken-fried steak, po'boys—"

"And the best garlic mashed potatoes in the state," Nick added.

Georgia smiled. "I have no doubt my grandmother Essie will hire you as a cook if you're interested."

"Really?" Dylan asked. "I have two years' experience as a diner cook. I can make anything, from pancakes to steak to special orders too. Gluten-free, egg-free, dairy-free—I'm on it."

She smiled. "I think my grandmother would love to have you as part of the kitchen team. And I think you'll love Blue Gulch. It's a great place to raise a child." She was aware of Nick's eyes on her. She hadn't said that for Nick's benefit and hoped he didn't think she had. Blue Gulch *was* a great place to raise children. She and her sisters had grown up there, running through the woods, spending weekends on Blue Gulch Street, where kids were always welcome in the shops and restaurants, and of course, learning the restaurant business at her grandmother's hip. Her child would. Maybe Dylan's too.

"I could tell," Dylan said, gently rocking Timmy. "The minute I pulled into town last week, I could tell it was a nice place. And since my great-aunt is happy to move to Blue Gulch too, I'll see about selling our house, which my mother left to me." He frowned. "I can't wait to sell that place. I wish I could tear it down myself."

Georgia glanced at Nick. His gaze was soft on the teenager, and Georgia's heart lifted at just knowing that Dylan had a friend and protector and father figure in Nick—yes, father figure, whether he'd like that "title" or not.

Nick walked over and sat down on the other side of Dylan and slung an arm over his shoulder. "I know what you mean. I felt that way about my childhood home with its share of bad memories. I'm not sure if you remember from our talks two years ago, but our childhoods have some unfortunate things in common."

Dylan glanced at Nick, cradling Timmy against his chest. "Are you kidding? I remember every word you ever said to me. If it hadn't been for you, I don't know what would have become of me."

"What do you mean?" Nick asked. "Your mother took good care of you."

"Well, yeah, she did. But you'd been there, you know? You went through what I went through. And you became a police detective on the Houston force. I...wanted to be like you," he added, glancing down.

Nick's his hero, Georgia realized, her heart squeezing in her chest.

Nick tightened his arm around Dylan's shoulder. "I'm proud to know that, Dylan. I'm glad I was there for you. And I'm here for you and Timmy now."

Dylan nodded, then nodded again, and Georgia could tell he was holding back a floodgate of relieved tears.

"I'll help you house-hunt," Nick said. "There are lots of different homes available in Blue Gulch, from apartments in town to houses to condo developments to ranches. In the meantime, you'll all stay in my house."

"I'll help too," Georgia said. "If I could be selfish, I'd love to have you near the restaurant so I could see Timmy often. Hurley's is in the center of town, on Blue Gulch Street, not too far from the police station."

"That sounds good to me," Dylan said. "My great-aunt would like to be able to walk to shops." He shifted Timmy in his arms. "So, um, I'd like to ask one more thing of both of you. If it's too much, I'll totally understand."

"Shoot," Nick said.

Dylan looked at Nick, then at Georgia, then down at Timmy's little blue-capped head. "I, um, was kind of hoping you'd both agree to be Timmy's godparents. I need all the help I can get."

Georgia smiled and touched Dylan's arm. "I'd be honored."

Nick ran a finger down Timmy's little face. "That goes double for me."

Georgia bit her lip, her heart bursting.

As Timmy began fussing, Dylan stood and rocked the baby. Timmy settled down, his eyes closing. "I'd better get Timmy back in his carrier for his nap." With Timmy fast asleep, Dylan gently kissed his forehead, then headed toward the door. "Can we meet in the lobby at six tomorrow morning so I can officially take over as Timmy's dad? I've waited a week—I can wait one more night until I'm eighteen." He glanced at Nick and Georgia. "Six too early? We can make it seven."

Nick laughed. "Timmy's up at five, so six is no problem. We'll be awake."

At the "we," Dylan glanced at Georgia and she could tell he wondered what her and Nick's relationship was all about. *Wish I knew*, she thought.

Dylan smiled. "Aunt Helen and I will pack some clothes and stuff. Once we find a new home in Blue Gulch, I can come back to Houston with a van to move what I want. See you in the morning," he added, then rushed away.

"Wow," Nick said as the door closed behind Dylan.

"Wow," Georgia agreed, tears still stinging her eyes.

Nick moved to the big wall of windows, looking out at the city. "I can't even imagine how alone he must have felt these past five weeks since Timmy was born, scared to death any minute that someone would come take his child away from him." He shook his head. "I wish he'd called me."

"He was scared," Georgia said. "You're the law. A good guy who was there for him and his mother before, but the law."

Nick nodded. "He said he was worried my hands would be tied." He leaned his head back, then turned around and dropped down in the club chair. "Did you see his eyes light up at the idea of working in the kitchen at Hurley's?"

Georgia smiled. "We already have something of a recommendation from his manager at the diner, so we know he's a hard worker and trustworthy. I'm sure Essie will hire him once she hears his story."

Nick looked relieved. "I have a good feeling about how all this will work out."

"Me too," Georgia said. For the Patterson crew, anyway.

"So, about this godfather thing," Nick said. "I've never been one before. What do I do?"

Georgia smiled. "You do what you've been doing all week. Care."

"I couldn't have done it without you."

Georgia froze, suddenly realizing it was over. Tomorrow Dylan and his great-aunt and Timmy would return with them to Blue Gulch. They'd stay with Nick until Dylan found a new home, Dylan taking Avery's old room and Aunt Helen in the guest room. Georgia's old room.

Nick didn't need her anymore. And Operation Dad hadn't cracked him. *She* hadn't cracked him.

Her heart heavy, she turned away, staring out at the tall buildings of Houston.

She could feel Nick watching her. She wanted to get up and run into the bathroom and shut the door for some privacy, but a gray cloud parked itself over her head and she could barely muster the enthusiasm to move.

"You okay?" he asked.

No, she wanted to scream. *No, I'm not. Because I love you and you're...impenetrable.*

But that wasn't really true. He wasn't impenetrable. Bits and pieces had gotten through chinks in the armor around him, but just bits, nothing able to blast through.

"I'm okay," she managed. "Just tired."

"Why don't you lie down?" he suggested. He got up and pulled back the quilt, patting the bed.

Her heart crumpling, she lay down, facing away from

him so he couldn't see her cry. But instead of him walking over to the club chair, she felt him stretch his long form beside her.

That was unexpected.

"If it's all right," he said.

She turned to face him. He lay staring up the ceiling. She studied the planes of his face, his strong nose, the jaw with its sexy five-o'clock shadow, the long dark lashes. "It's all right," she said, turning away from him again. "Stay here with me." *It's our last night together*, she wanted to add, but held her tongue.

He turned and curved against her, his chin resting on top of her head. She felt his hands move onto her shoulders, then up her neck and fist her hair. Then one hand moved lower, slipping around her protectively, possessively. He buried his face in her neck.

She desperately wanted to turn around and rip his clothes off, fuse her mouth to his, feel his hands and mouth everywhere on her body. But in the morning, she'd only be more brokenhearted. It was over. She'd tried, but she'd failed.

At least she'd tried.

"Maybe you should take the chair, after all," she whispered, her voice catching.

He stiffened. "Okay," he said, quickly getting up. "I didn't mean to—" He didn't finish his sentence.

I didn't mean to break your heart. I didn't mean for you to love me.

He'd told her he was going to hurt her. And she'd believed him and jumped in with her whole heart anyway.

Dummy, she told herself.

"I think I'll take a walk," Nick said. "You'll be all right by yourself? I won't be long."

"I'll be fine."

And she would be, she reminded herself. She would be fine. That had become her new motto.

But as she heard him leave, the door whooshing shut behind him, the lock clicking into place, the tears stung her eyes all over again.

"It's just you and me, Timmy," she whispered to the baby, who was fast asleep. "And it's our last night together. Thank you for everything. Thank you for letting me learn on the go. It was an honor."

Timmy's little bow-shaped mouth quirked and Georgia smiled at him, her hands on her belly. She thought about what Dylan Patterson had done, had risked for his baby son. He hadn't been willing to give up.

"Neither will I," she said to Timmy. "Until Nick picks up and moves to Houston, my work here is not done."

With that she felt much better, changed into her pajamas, got back into bed and drifted off to sleep.

Nick sat on a stool at the hotel bar, taking his time with his scotch and helping himself to a handful of almonds in a glass bowl. It was just past nine o'clock, but the bar wasn't very crowded. Nick sat at the far end and there were two empty seats next to him, then a youngish couple making out in between tequila shots and licking salt off the sides of their thumbs. Two very attractive single women, dolled up to the nines with cleavage and lots of leg, were along the perpendicular side of the bar, and the redhead was eyeing him. Every time he glanced in that direction, he'd catch her looking at him, her expression a combination of interest and challenge. *Try to seduce me out of this bar and into my room*, she seemed to be saying to him as she licked her lips, her gaze on him.

He tried to adopt a *no, thanks* expression, shifting in his chair so that he was looking straight ahead at the rows of top-shelf liquor, a mirrored backdrop behind the bottles. He stared at himself, thinking he didn't look particularly happy. Or interested in anyone.

Ah, *he* was the challenge, he realized as the redhead got up and walked toward him, then past him into the ladies' room, her perfume lingering.

He preferred Georgia's soapy scent, which was actually a combination of soap, baby wash and hand sanitizer. He smiled, picturing her up in their room right now, singing Timmy a lullaby or reading him a book about a sheep that liked to laugh. She read that one to Timmy a lot. He imagined her lying on the big bed wearing a T-shirt and those sexy yoga pants.

Georgia was Blue Gulch. This bar, the redhead— who he hoped would keep walking past him when she emerged from the restroom—was Houston. This would be his life. Alone. Nursing a scotch. No daily responsibilities to anyone but himself. Once a week he'd drive out to Blue Gulch to see his son, to make sure Georgia had everything she needed.

How could she have everything she needed if the father of her baby lived three hours away?

He hated when these questions popped into his head. The impossibility of doing the right thing by Georgia, by his son, which wouldn't allow for him to do the right thing for himself.

Which was sitting here in this bar, in this city, a lone wolf. Leaving Blue Gulch for good. Leaving his bad memories there.

Except he'd made new ones. He thought of his sister in her cap and gown, her big smile as she accepted her high school diploma. He thought of young Brian Pullman, hugging Bentley the greyhound with tears streaming down his cheeks. He thought of finding little Henry Grainger. He thought of several other cases that each had restored his faith in humanity just a little bit.

He thought of making love to Georgia on the couch in his living room.

He wanted to rush upstairs, rip off her baby-spit-up-scented T-shirt and very slowly explore every inch of her. Hadn't he called himself every name for a jerk for having done that twice already when he couldn't give her what she really needed? He stayed put.

But when the redhead did come out of the restroom and stopped right next to him, propping a hip on the empty seat beside him and flashing him a very white smile, he told her he had to go, have a nice night, and headed for the elevator.

Upstairs in their room, the lights were out and not a peep could be heard. He looked in on Timmy in the bassinet the hotel had provided them with, then took a quilt from the closet and sat down in the club chair across from the bed, wishing he could slip in beside Georgia and sleep curled around her.

Wake up and invite me in, he willed her, but she didn't stir and he knew staying in the chair was for the best.

He got up and grabbed the extra blanket from the closet and dropped back down in the club chair, trying to get comfortable. He must have drifted off, because the next thing he knew the room was pitch-dark and Timmy was beginning to cry.

"Waah. Waah," Timmy began, and Nick burst out of the chair before the baby could wake Georgia. He settled Timmy in his arms, then headed over to the kitchenette to make him a bottle. "Look at me, the one-handed wonder," he whispered to Timmy, who quirked a lip at him.

With Timmy having his bottle, Nick sat back down in the chair, watching Timmy's little mouth quirking around the nipple. "I'm glad we found your daddy," he whispered. "You're in good hands with Dylan. I believe that. And Georgia and I will have your back. No worries, little guy."

Georgia and I. Interesting. He'd meant that *he'd* have Timmy's back. He. Singular. Lone wolf. Georgia would separately have Timmy's back. Separately.

Timmy finished his bottle and Nick brought him up to his shoulder for a burp. Only took ten seconds. Nick was getting pretty good at this. He stood up and brought Timmy over to the windows, slipping in between the heavy drapes and the filmy white ones, which he pushed aside. Timmy cooed at the lights and action going on outside, even though it was well past midnight. Gently rocking Timmy back and forth in his arms, Nick pointed out the buildings he recognized, then realized the baby's eyes were closed.

He slipped Timmy back in the bassinet, then sat down in the club chair, pulling the extra blanket up to his chest, no idea if he was ever going to fall asleep.

Chapter Thirteen

Timmy's cries woke Georgia at five o'clock. She sat up in bed and stretched, then hopped out and scooped up Timmy, realizing that she felt great. Really great. As in "she got an entire night of sleep" great. Had Timmy slept through the night? At six weeks?

Georgia glanced over at the club chair. Nick was fast asleep, his long, muscular body sprawled out, his face leaning away from her. On the desk beside the chair was a baby bottle with just a drop left in it. Which meant that Nick had given Timmy his 1:00 a.m. bottle.

That was something, she thought as she laid Timmy on the changing pad and quickly changed his diaper, powdering his adorable bottom. She kissed his sweet belly, then changed him into fresh pajamas. "Your daddy will be here soon," she whispered. She walked Timmy around the room, careful not to wake Nick.

"They'll be buddies."

She whirled around. Nick stood up and stretched his arms behind his back, his T-shirt rising to show his six-pack abs.

"Who'll be buddies?" she asked.

"Timmy and our baby. They'll only be several months apart."

She stared at him, surprise bursting inside her. "I didn't think of that, but you're right. They will be buddies." She smiled, loving the idea.

He seemed to catch himself saying something future-oriented and turned away. "I'll head down to the corner store and pick us up some breakfast sandwiches and coffee. Herbal tea for you?"

She nodded, her smile fading as he left. One step forward, two steps back. He was running away again, like last night. She hadn't heard him come in. She must have been exhausted from the whole day, being back in Houston, facing her past in the form of being here at all, stopping in front of her condo, the discovery of Timmy's father. Realizing that today, she'd be going back to Hurley's to live. She wished she had woken up when he came in; she wouldn't have let him sleep in the chair all night. Or at all.

She wondered why he hadn't slept beside her. Because he didn't want to? Because he knew he'd be leaving Blue Gulch soon and didn't want to make her think otherwise? Or because he hadn't wanted to wake her?

Because she'd stopped his roaming hands earlier, she realized. Or maybe the answer was all of the above.

"Wish I knew for sure," she told Timmy, taking him into the big bathroom and setting his carrier on the counter while she washed her face and brushed her teeth. A brush through her long hair helped. She glanced at herself and dug around in her toiletry bag for a little concealer and mascara. Then she scooped up Timmy and headed back in the main room, taking him out of his carrier and bringing him over to the window where the morning sun was just beginning to rise over Houston.

The key turned in the door and Nick walked in, Dylan right behind him. "Look who I found pacing in front of the hotel, waiting for it to be six."

Georgia smiled. "You could have come up anytime. I know how much this morning means to you."

Beaming, Dylan rushed over to Georgia and she transferred Timmy to his arms. He held him close and spun around. "I'm eighteen. A legal adult. Happy birthday to me," he said to Timmy. "Best birthday present I'll ever get is knowing no one can take you from me."

Georgia smiled and put a hand on Dylan's shoulder. "Happy birthday, Dylan."

"Let's go pick up your aunt and head home, then," Nick said.

Georgia knew Nick well enough now to notice he'd stiffened at hearing himself call Blue Gulch home.

Maybe he really was leaving. She could work on him all she wanted. But maybe she'd better accept that in a couple of days, Nick Slater would be gone from her life.

If someone gave Nick a penny for every time he glanced in the rearview mirror to make sure Dylan's old car was still chugging along behind his on the freeway, Nick would be a zillionaire. The boy swore that the car was safe and had been recently inspected, but Nick would have preferred that Timmy and Helen ride with him and Georgia. But Timmy and Aunt Helen were Dylan's family, not his, and so they went with Dylan.

"It feels weird, doesn't it?" Georgia said, peering into the backseat. "I keep expecting to see Timmy's car seat. I keep expecting to hear him fuss."

"Me too. I don't like that Timmy's in Dylan's car. Though I have to say, he seems like a careful driver," he added, peering in the rearview mirror. Dylan stayed in the middle lane, going the speed limit, two car-lengths behind the one in front of him, which was Nick's.

"So I guess when we get to your house, I'll pack up my things," Georgia said.

"Wait, what?" Nick glanced at her. Then he remembered she was only living with him to care for Timmy. "Well, let's get Dylan and his aunt settled into a new home before we make any big changes."

Georgia glanced at him. "Since the Pattersons are staying with you until they're settled, there won't be room for me. I'll just move into Hurley's. I have my pick of second-floor bedrooms."

He frowned. He didn't want her to leave. He didn't want her to "just move into Hurley's." He wanted her in his guest bedroom, maybe forever. Close, but not too close, per his motto.

When Nick pulled into his driveway, Dylan was right behind him. After a call to a real estate agent who handled home rentals in town, the group walked over to Hurley's for lunch, then met the agent at a small, run-down house near the center of town. Dylan had only two requests when it came to a new home in Blue Gulch: it had to be affordable and have a fenced-in yard for the dog he'd always wanted to get, preferably a gentle little mutt from the animal shelter.

Dylan stood on the lawn, Timmy in his arms. He looked up at the house, frowning. "It's not home. I don't even have to go in to know that. I have enough money saved that I can do a little better for my family."

The real estate agent nodded and they all piled in their cars to drive five minutes in the opposite direction to a yellow Cape Cod on Orchard Street that had the plus of being sparsely furnished. The moment the big group arrived at the second house with its white shutters and flowers lining the stone walkway, Dylan looked up at the house, said, "Now, this feels like home even from the outside." He looked at his aunt, who smiled in a way that Nick would only call satisfied. After a short tour, Dylan signed a lease.

"I can't believe this," Dylan said. "From totally hopeless to the opposite. Thank you, Detective Slater. For everything."

"We're friends. So you call me Nick."

Dylan beamed, rocking Timmy as they all headed back to their cars. Dylan and his family would stay at Nick's tonight, and Nick would help the family get settled in the new house tomorrow.

Tomorrow. Tomorrow he'd wake up and Georgia wouldn't be there. Tonight, actually, since Aunt Helen would stay in the guest room and Dylan would take Avery's room. No live-in, round-the-clock nanny required. No…Georgia.

His head hurt. His stomach felt as if he'd eaten something a month old. He needed some sort of plan for how things would work with Georgia now that she'd be moving out. But tonight he'd have guests and tomorrow he'd be busy with the Pattersons and their new home, then finding his sister and talking her out of this foolishness of Nashville and marriage once and for all. He'd happily drive her back to college, where she belonged.

Then he'd figure out if he was moving to Houston, even though he didn't feel much when he was there. It wasn't home anymore. Blue Gulch had morphed back into that these past two years.

But Blue Gulch couldn't be home. Even if it felt like home. Because that didn't make sense. How could it feel like home?

Because Georgia is here. With your baby about to be born in five months. And she's going to need you, you jerk.

Because Dylan and Timmy are here. And that boy is going to need you, you jerk.

Nick glanced at Georgia, who was helping Helen back into Dylan's beat-up old car. What the hell was Nick going to do about all this? He used to be the man with all the answers.

Now he had none.

When they arrived back at Nick's, Georgia quickly packed up her things and put fresh linens on the bed, since Helen would be taking over the room. As she fluffed the pillows, she glanced out the window and saw Nick handing Dylan his iPad on the patio so Dylan could check out available dogs at the animal shelter. Aunt Helen knocked on the guest room door, and Georgia let her in, her heart heavy.

"All ready for you, Helen," Georgia said, smiling at the kind, elderly woman.

"That bed sure looks comfortable," Helen said. "I'd love to take a nap. It's been quite a day."

Georgia smiled and drew the curtains, then closed

the door behind her, her bags like weights in her hands. Nick came in through the sliding glass door to the living room, his gaze on her suitcases. "I guess this is it," she said to him.

Was that a scowl on his handsome face? "Well, not *it*."

Georgia raised an eyebrow. "Timmy's moving out tomorrow. You have no need for a live-in nanny."

"Yeah, but…" He paused. "When Dylan starts working at Hurley's, he'll need a sitter for Timmy. Aunt Helen can't take that on."

Georgia smiled. "I don't have to live here to babysit Timmy, Nick. Timmy won't live here anymore, remember?"

Nick frowned. "Can't we talk about this later?"

Georgia tilted her head. "About what?"

Nick sucked in a breath and let it out. "About what we are going to do."

"*We?* I know what *I'm* going to do. I'm going to keep taking my prenatal vitamins. I'm going to bake every morning for Hurley's. I'm going to drive over to Baby Center and think about our little one's nursery. I've always liked the idea of a sea-inspired nursery. What will you be doing, Nick?"

She had no idea if pushing him was smart, but the hell with it. It was what had come out of her mouth. Nick Slater needed to be pushed. A little, anyway. Not too hard. But pushed.

Mr. Whiskers padded over and brushed against Nick's leg; he'd been hiding with all the newcomers.

"I have to make a call," he said, picking up the cat and giving him a comforting pat before striding out of the room with him.

Her heart clenched. Maybe she'd pushed too far.

* * *

Nick was sitting on the couch in the living room, holding the pillow with the embroidered owl that Georgia had clutched that first day she came here. It was late, past eleven, and the house was quiet. An hour ago he'd passed by Avery's bedroom and heard Dylan reading a Dr. Seuss book to Timmy. He'd stood outside the door, smiling to himself, happy and relieved for Timmy. Tomorrow he'd call Social Services, both in Houston and the more local office he'd dealt with when he first found Timmy on his desk. He'd get everything squared away in the morning, including helping Aunt Helen find local doctors. He wanted the Patterson family to be comfortable here and settled right away so that Dylan could focus on work and Timmy and not have to worry about much else.

He heard a key slide into the lock and bolted up. Georgia? He headed over to the door, but it was Avery who burst inside, tears streaming down her face.

"Avery? What's wrong?" He knew it had to have something to do with Quentin Says.

She started crying so hard she couldn't even get words out. Nick brought her into his bedroom and closed the door, and Avery sank down on the leather love seat under the window.

"Quentin…broke…up…with…meeee," his sister managed to get out before breaking down into racking sobs. Nick sat down next to her and drew her close. But Avery pulled away, her expression a combination of anger and hurt. "Quentin says he doesn't think we should go to Nashville because he can see that the lack of your blessing is tearing me up and he's noticed I haven't been singing all weekend. He thinks we should postpone our engagement." She started crying again, and this time she let Nick hold her close, his cheek on the top of her head.

Well, for once, Quentin Says said it right! Not that Nick was enjoying Avery's pain. Not one damned second of it. But she *didn't* have his blessing. He wanted her back at school where she belonged. Not married at eighteen. Not running around Nashville, singing at clubs when she should be in the library, studying and making new friends.

Avery sniffled, wiping at her eyes. "Quentin says that sometimes if you love someone, you have to let them go. But I don't want him to let me go. I want to go to Nashville. I want to be a singer. I want to marry Quentin."

"Avery, why do you want to marry Quentin? You're so young. You have your entire life ahead of you." He thought of Dylan, also just eighteen, raising a baby on his own, his future plotted out. Father. Responsibilities. Avery had a beautiful opportunity to explore being herself—not being a wife. Not being a this or that. Learning, growing, changing. Not making heavy, adult decisions.

"I want to marry Quentin because I know he's the one. I want to marry Quentin because he makes me feel like I can do and be anything. I want to marry Quentin because I love him so much my heart feels like it's going to burst out of my chest. When I'm with Quentin, I feel more me than I've ever felt. He gets me. And I trust him, you know? For a very long time it was just me and Mama. And then just you. Quentin feels like family, Nick. Like you. Like Mama did. He's my family." She broke down and this time instead of feeling slightly victorious, tears stung Nick's eyes. Dammit.

Dammit! He sat there for a while, just holding his kid sister, all she'd said sinking into his thick skull. She was wiser than he'd given her credit for, more mature than he wanted to believe. He still didn't like the idea of her marrying so young and chasing a dream, but she loved Quentin for the right reasons. For good reasons.

"Tell you what," he said. "How about if I go talk to Quentin?"

She nodded. He also didn't like the idea of his kid sister staying at a boyfriend's—fiancé's—apartment, especially when this was her home. But he'd been the one to send her running out the other day. And she was eighteen. Dammit.

He explained to her about Dylan and Timmy and Aunt Helen, then headed to the kitchen to leave a note for Dylan in case he woke up. His life sure had changed in a week.

Nick jogged the quarter mile to the bookstore and headed down the short cobblestone alley with the entrance to Quentin's apartment. He found Quentin sitting on the front steps, looking miserable, the glow from a streetlamp barely illuminating his face.

When Nick sat down next to Quentin, the boy practically jumped.

"Avery's very upset," Nick prompted.

Quentin crossed his arms over his chest. "All she talks about is how she can't convince you to give your blessing and that she can't see leaving without it. I just know if we did leave tomorrow, when we got to Nashville, she'd be a wreck about it. You're her family, her big brother who raised her when her mother died. What you think means everything to her."

There was so much pain in Quentin's expression. Nick dragged a hand through his hair and looked up at the stars for a moment, wishing life weren't so damned complicated when sometimes it should be easy. Quentin loved Avery. Avery loved Quentin. And here was Nick, in the middle of it. But it *was* complicated.

"All I really care about is that Avery is happy," Quentin said. "And I just know that not having your blessing will eat away at her and she won't put her all into singing or auditioning. So I think if this is something she really wants, she can either do it on her own and not piss you off or stay in school like you want and go on auditions in Dallas." Quentin squeezed his eyes shut and Nick could see he was willing himself not to cry, especially not in front of the big bad ogre known as Avery's Older Brother.

"You really care about her, don't you?" Nick said.

"Like I told Avery, sometimes when you love someone, you have to let them go." Quentin stood up. "I'll come by the house to say goodbye to Avery in the morning." With that, he turned to go inside.

"Quentin," Nick said.

The young man turned around, tears in his eyes.

"That you're willing to sacrifice your own happiness for Avery's future—that says quite a lot."

Quentin just looked at his feet, clearly unable to speak, his Adam's apple moving. Then he went inside.

What the hell had Nick done? The two of them miserable was better for Avery than the two of them together? Not chasing a dream when you were young and fearless enough to go for it was better than chasing it?

If you love someone, sometimes you have to let them go.

Was he supposed to let Georgia go, to be able to find a man who could love her and be a good father to their baby?

Seemed kind of ridiculous when he was right there, the father of the baby. Unable to do the job.

Unable or unwilling?

Hell if he knew. So he was willing to lose her? Had he given up on himself, as she'd said before they went to Houston?

Soul searching sure was the pits.

When he got back to the house, Avery wasn't in his room. She wasn't in the kitchen or outside in the backyard. She wasn't anywhere. And she wasn't answering her phone.

His heart racing, he texted Quentin. Avery's not here. Is she with you?

I wish, Quentin said. But no.

Dammit! Where had she gone? He thought of her friends, but her two best girlfriends were away at school.

He was pacing and frantic that Avery was out walking alone at midnight when he got another text from Quentin.

First place I'd look is under the weeping willow at the edge of your old house—where she grew up. She likes to go there.

The hairs on Nick's neck stood up. The old house? Avery liked to go there? What?

He got in his car and drove the few miles out to the old house. The white clapboard farmhouse sat on three acres. The front door was now painted red and there were window boxes everywhere, flowers trailing, something he kept up—well, paid someone to keep up—in honor of his mother. The weeping willow his mother had loved so much was right at the edge of the property in the front yard, at a good distance from the house.

He was getting good at spotting feet under trees. He could make out Avery's red flip-flops. She sat huddled. "Hey," he said.

"How'd you know I'd be here?" she asked, wiping tears from under her eyes.

"Quentin said you'd probably be here. I didn't even think of it. Guess he knows you pretty well, huh?" If anyone had told Nick an hour ago he'd ever start a sentence with *Quentin said*, he'd have laughed.

She nodded and sniffled, sucking in a deep breath. "How can I accept that it's over between us? I want to move to Nashville, but I don't want to do it alone. Quentin is my rock, you know? He's my support."

I thought I was, he wanted to say, but he realized he wasn't—not solely, anyway. He was her family. He was her father figure. He was her older brother who'd do anything for her except, it seemed, what would make her happy.

"I guess I'm heading back to school in the morning," she said, tears pooling in her eyes. "Maybe you're right—when I graduate I'll be older and more mature and maybe I'll be ready to move to Nashville on my own."

"Actually, Avery, I don't think I'm right at all."

She turned and stared at him. "About what?"

"If you want to marry Quentin and move to Nashville and become the next Carrie Underwood, you have my blessing. The both of you do."

She burst into tears and threw her arms around him. "What made you change your mind?"

"You did. And Quentin did. You love him. He loves you. You two have a sound plan. I might not love the idea of what you're doing, but I support your right—and your courage—to do it." He raised an eyebrow. "That sounds like something a politician would say."

She laughed. "Your blessing means everything to me."

"I'm glad it does, Avery. That means everything to *me*."

"You hate this house, huh?" she said, looking up at the farmhouse.

"Mama raised us here," he said. "So no, I don't hate it. But I do have bad memories of living here. You know all about that."

"I don't have bad memories," she said. "I wish you hadn't sold it, Nick. But maybe one day I can buy it back."

"I didn't sell it," he said softly. "This house belongs to you. I put the deed in your name when you turned eighteen. I've been renting it out to tenants since we left here, but the house is yours. I wouldn't have sold your childhood home, Avery."

Surprise lit her expression. "I should have known that. I'll always have a home, my home, to come back to. If things don't work out in Nashville."

"You'll always have a home to come back to no matter what," he said, hugging her close. "Why don't I drop you off at Quentin's? You can go put your fiancé out of his misery."

She smiled and bolted up, brushing off her shorts, and Nick realized that he hadn't thought of him as Quentin Says. Just Quentin.

"You won't be sad that I'll be taking Mr. Whiskers with me?"

He smiled "Well, I'll admit that the cat and I did finally bond. But he belongs with you."

"You'll see him again," she said. "In about five months. Since I'll be back when my nephew is born."

He stared at her. "You knew?"

She rolled her eyes and smiled. "Nick. Come on. And I really hope with all my heart you put *yourself* out of your misery and propose to that woman."

"Let's go," he said.

Propose to Georgia. He would if he thought marriage to a man like him would be what she needed or wanted. But Georgia wouldn't want to marry him just because he was the father of her child. She wanted a man who could love, who could be the kind of father their child deserved.

And Nick was…he wasn't even sure how to classify himself. Better than he used to be but no one's bargain.

Chapter Fourteen

"Did you talk to Logan?" Georgia asked Clementine, not sure if she should pry, since Clementine hadn't brought it up.

The sisters had been in the kitchen since 6:00 a.m., Georgia making piecrust and thinking about what kinds of pie would go best with today's specials. A cherry pie, for sure. A chocolate peanut butter. Classic apple. And maybe a pumpkin pie just because Georgia loved pumpkin pie.

It had been strange waking up at five-thirty with no one to take care of but herself. No sweet baby to diaper and powder and feed and burp and rock. She'd taken a shower in utter peace, had a moment's panic while rinsing the shampoo from her hair that she'd left Timmy unattended, then remembered. Timmy was at Nick's. With his father. And great-great-aunt. And Nick.

And Georgia had gotten dressed and gone to work—a commute of a staircase, her sister already up and a pot of coffee brewing in the kitchen. If she had to give up her job at Nick's, being at Hurley's sure was a nice place to be instead.

"I tried," Clementine said, sitting at the table and filling all the little ceramic cactus salt and pepper shakers. She sipped her coffee. "I texted and got back 'It's for the best.' That's it. So I called and he said he had some emergency with a calf and couldn't talk, sorry. And then I just drove out to the ranch at a time I knew he'd be there—he's always there at six for dinnertime with the boys, no matter what—and he froze me out, said, 'We're sitting down to dinner. Goodbye, Clementine.' He kind of emphasized the goodbye in a very final way."

"What happened between you two? What is he so closed off about?" Georgia didn't know much about Logan Grainger, but Nick seemed to hold him in high regard. Word was that since Henry had slipped away a few days ago, Logan hadn't let either boy out of his sight.

Tears pooled in Clementine's eyes. "I don't know. I was a good babysitter to the twins. I know they like me. We had one kiss. *One* kiss. I guess it caught him by surprise. But so what? Why shut me out?"

"I wish I knew. I wish I had a crystal ball that could explain everything about two certain men."

"Me too," Clementine said, plugging the last of the shakers and setting them on her tray. "You doing all right? I know you moved in here last night."

Georgia nodded, her resolve to be grateful for Hurley's, for her sisters and Gram, and her job as baker firm in her mind. "I knew it was temporary. I just wish it could have been forever. Not that I didn't want Timmy to be reunited with his family. I just wanted to stay at Nick's forever, our little family together." Her heart clenched and she handled the dough too roughly and knew she'd have to start over. The last thing she wanted was complaints about her pie just when she needed rallying most.

"I don't know Nick well," Clementine said. "At all, really. But I have this feeling, even without a crystal ball, that you two are meant to be. I look at you together and everything feels right in the world. Do you know what I mean? It's how it seems when Annabel and West are together."

Georgia felt tears prick her eyes at her sister's kindness and compassion. "I sure hope so, Clem. But like the song goes, I can't make him love me if he doesn't."

"I'd bet my life that Nick Slater loves you, Georgia." Before Georgia could even process that, Clementine glanced out the window and flinched. "Oh no."

"What?" Georgia asked, following Clementine's gaze. Her birth mother stood across the street by Clyde's Burgertopia, sipping a cup of coffee and looking toward the Victorian.

"Why does she do this?" Clementine asked, looking away. "She isn't interested in a relationship with me, yet she walks by here at least once a day and looks in the window. It's barely six-thirty in the morning."

Georgia took another glance at the tall, dark-haired, fortysomething woman outside, then returned her attention to her new dough for the piecrust. "Well, maybe she's limited, emotionally speaking, in what she can do, yet the need is there in her to see you, to see where you were raised, where you live."

Clementine placed all the salt and pepper shakers on a tray to be doled out in the dining room, then headed over to the utility closet for a sponge and bucket, filled it with water, kneeled down and began cleaning the already clean lower cabinets and their little rooster pulls, which Annabel had told Georgia was a sign that Clementine was bothered by something. Or hurting.

Georgia knew her sister was troubled by her past, by how her mother, a drug addict in and out of rehab over the past thirty years, had refused to sign over parental rights until Clementine was eight, late for adoption. Clem was both glad her mother hadn't wanted to sever those rights and resentful that her mother had kept relapsing, unable to care for her for longer than a few days before Clementine would be shuttled back to another foster home.

"Part of me wants to rush out there and scream, 'What do you want?' And make her talk. But I know she won't. I've tried that many times over the years."

Georgia glanced back out the window, but the woman had moved on and was nowhere in sight. Georgia kneeled down and hugged Clementine tight. "I'm sorry, Clem. You've sure got a lot on your mind right now. Mom and Dad would be so proud of you."

Clementine had tears in her eyes. "Why?"

"You stayed in Blue Gulch despite how hard it is with your birth mother here and unwilling to meet you halfway. You've stayed by Gram's side all these years. You're a really strong person, Clem. Much stronger than you know."

"I feel as strong as this washcloth," Clem said, dropping it in the bucket. "But thank you," she added, her expression softening. "You really think Mom and Dad would be proud?"

Georgia nodded. "I know they would be. I know they *are*."

Clementine bit her lip. "Well, let's change the subject before I start bawling." She stood up and headed to the counter, adding white paper napkins to the yellow wooden holders for the dining room. "Gram said Dylan Patterson is starting today on lunch duty. I'm so relieved that Timmy's reunited with his father. Timmy wasn't abandoned. But many kids are and no matter what, those kids need a guardian angel like Mom and Dad were for me. Like you and Nick were for Timmy."

Georgia smiled. Clementine was working on the requirements to become a foster parent. She had such a big heart. "Timmy's got a great dad. Dylan's a really impressive young man."

"Speaking of impressive men," Clementine said, lifting her chin toward the window.

Georgia glanced out the window to see Nick standing there pointing at the pie she'd just taken out of the oven. He then pointed to his stomach.

She had to smile. God, she'd missed him so much last night. Though she really had been snug as the ol' bug in one of the guest bedrooms in the Victorian with its familiar furnishings. There was something about knowing her grandmother was in her room downstairs and Clementine upstairs that was very comforting. After they'd all cleaned up the restaurant and dining room, they'd gone into the parlor and watched an old Katherine Hepburn movie, complete with popcorn and iced tea, and Georgia's mind had been taken off her heart.

Until she'd gone to bed, wishing Nick were closer. Literally and figuratively.

She held up a finger, covered the rest of the pies, and headed outside to the porch with a slice of chocolate peanut butter and a thermos of coffee. They sat on the swing, and she waited for Nick to say something, about why he was here. But he just gobbled up the pie and drank the coffee.

"Avery's leaving for Nashville today," he finally said. "With my blessing."

She practically gasped. "How did that happen overnight?"

"Long story." He told her all about it. About Avery crying. About Quentin sacrificing. About the weeping willow at the old house. "While I was there, I realized I needed to stop looking at the house as though it was my childhood home where I have so many bad memories. It's Avery's good childhood home. And it's hers. My mother left it to both of us, but I had Avery made sole owner. She grew up there with a different set of circumstances and the house means something different to her. It represents my mother." He winced. "I took that from her. After our mom died, I moved back to that house for six months and I felt like a piece of me was dying every day I was under that roof. But I was wrong to make Avery move."

"I don't know about that, Nick. You kept her in Blue Gulch. If the house was killing you, you had to leave it."

He took a sip of coffee and leaned back on the swing. "I feel like I quashed that last night. I made it Avery's, my mother's, and a lot of my association with it felt lifted off my shoulders. Seems strange that you could have a mental shift like that just like that."

"It was hardly just like that. You were letting Avery go, Nick. You want to keep your sister safe, protect her. But you knew you needed to let her go. And by sitting with her at the house that brings her comfort, you shifted what the house represents. It's Avery's future—not your past."

He nodded, staring out at Blue Gulch Street. Then he turned to face her. "I'm going to stay, Georgia. It's the right thing to do."

The right thing to do. She wanted to take the basket planter of impatiens beside the swing and dump it on his head. "Okay."

"*Okay?* That's it? I thought you'd be happier than okay. How you handled yourself in Houston, seeing your condo, revisiting all that—you made me realize I've been my own worst enemy about my past."

"I'm glad for that, Nick," she said, and she truly was. Even if it her heart was splitting in two. "I need to get back inside. I want to be here when Dylan arrives for his first day."

He was staring at her, wanting her to explain what he'd said or did wrong. *Throw the man a bone*, she ordered herself. Sometimes that armor around his heart shielded his brain too. "I really am very glad that you're taking back Blue Gulch for yourself, Nick. Like I did with Houston. But you'll still be here out of a sense of obligation. First it was to Avery. Now it's to me. And our son."

He looked flabbergasted. "Obligation is about doing the right thing."

"Right."

He was looking at her as if they weren't speaking the same language. And maybe they weren't. Was she

supposed to throw herself in his arms and tell him she
loved him, dammit, and she wanted him to love her
back? That she wanted him to want to live here to be
near her and their son? That it was out of want, out of
caring, out of love? Not obligation.

So she could hear him tell her he was sorry, but he
just didn't, couldn't, wouldn't?

"Goodbye, Nick," she said, and hurried back inside,
leaving him standing on the porch.

The best way for Nick to avoid thinking about things
he didn't understand, like Georgia sometimes, was to
bury himself in work. And both unfortunately and fortunately, he had an immediate case that afternoon that
took his attention. But not for long. Also fortunately
and unfortunately.

"I'll tell ya, Timmy," Nick said, nodding at his computer screen, at the fingerprint match in the database
that linked a suspect to a burglary in John Martin's
very expensive two-seater car. "Sometimes things are
very, very easy." The baby, in his carrier on the side of
Nick's desk, peered at him with his curious blue eyes.

Early this afternoon, John Martin, the former Blue
Gulch lothario slash pizzeria owner, had bought an engagement ring, then tucked it away in his glove box,
locked his car and gone to get his hair cut for the occasion of proposing to his girlfriend this evening. When
John returned to his car, the passenger window was broken and the little velvet box gone. Apparently, John was
so in la-la land over the idea of proposing that he hadn't
paid attention to who might have been skulking around.
A couple of hours ago he'd called Nick in a panic; he'd
paid a lot for the ring and wanted to start being his girl-

friend's fiancé and his little girl's soon-to-be stepfather
and had pleaded with John to catch the perp.

The fingerprint belonged to one of the former boyfriends who'd decked John in the past for "making his
girl cheat." His prints were on the door handle of the
car. On the glove box.

"Timmy," Nick said, glancing at the baby, "this is
one of those easy times."

Except he couldn't exactly go question a suspect
with an infant in his arms, and he was on babysitting
duty, since Dylan was working at Hurley's and Georgia was baking extra desserts for a big rancher association meeting dinner at the restaurant tonight. Maybe he
could drop off Timmy with Georgia. If Georgia were
speaking to him.

*But you'll still be here out of a sense of obligation.
First it was to Avery. Now it's to me. And our son.*

Did she want him to love Blue Gulch? That he'd
never do. Not with his history, no matter how many new
memories he'd made here. Maybe the town wouldn't
represent the terror he'd felt as a kid anymore, but it
would never make his heart light up the way it did for
some people. Like his sister. Like Georgia. Surely she
could understand that.

Nick had to admit that he did feel…less wound up,
less stressed. Less…like the way he always felt. His
shoulders didn't feel as if two lead weights were pressing down on them. No gray cloud above his head. Deciding to stay in Blue Gulch hadn't hurt that bad. He
wanted to be here for Georgia and the baby. So what
was he missing? Why was she out of sorts?

He texted her to ask if he could drop Timmy off with
her while he questioned a suspect. She immediately

texted back a sure, and he had to admit, his heart *did* light up at the idea of seeing her beautiful face.

He scooped up the carrier and Timmy's bag of stuff, then left the station and headed over to the peachy-pink Victorian. As he walked up the steps, he could see Dylan chopping vegetables at the counter in the big kitchen. Essie Hurley was beside him, peeling potatoes. Nick liked the expression on Dylan's face—peaceful.

Not wanting to interrupt Dylan at work, especially with the big boss right there, Nick didn't stop in the kitchen to say hi and instead went inside the parlor where Georgia had said she'd wait for him. She was sitting on the floral love seat, looking…miffed. Again, what was he missing? He was staying in Blue Gulch. Yes, he felt obligated. But at least the feeling of obligation overpowered his old, bad feelings about the town. That was a good thing. And a start.

"Thanks for watching him," Nick said. "I have to get a search warrant and go check out a lead. I'm not sure what time I'll be back."

"That's fine," she said, her expression neutral.

"We're okay, right?" he asked.

She stared at him. "What else would we be?"

Ugh. What wasn't he getting there? He thought he understood Georgia, knew what she needed. He'd worked toward making that happen—he, father of her child, would be staying in town to help raise their son.

She picked up Timmy's carrier and headed out of the parlor. He wanted to run after her, demand to know what was wrong. But he had to get John Martin's ring back. He and Georgia would talk tonight.

If she was talking to him at all by then.

* * *

Nick sat at his desk in the police station, filling out a police report for the Martin burglary and also entering the information into the new digital system he was trying to get going, despite the chief's old-fashioned ways.

Warrant in hand, Nick, with the help of Officer Midwell, had searched Edward Huffingwell's car, finding the diamond ring in two seconds in his own glove box. Huffingwell had said that slick bastard pizza boy deserved all the unhappiness in the world. Now Huffingwell had joined Farley Melton, back for his eighth disturbing-the-peace arrest of the year, in the jail cell.

With that settled, Nick planned to pick up Dylan, who should be just about finished with his lunch shift, and show him around the area: the home goods store for basic necessities for the new house, towels and linens and that kind of thing, plus the shortcut to the supermarket, then a brief tour of Blue Gulch. He hoped Dylan's first morning at Hurley's was a good one, that he was happy, that Essie was happy with him. Based on what he knew about Dylan and the diner manager's glowing review, Nick had a feeling all would be very well for Dylan at Hurley's.

As Nick stood, so did Farley Melton, his gnarled hands wrapping around the bars of the jail cell. "Oh, look, he's back with that screaming baby," Farley said, looking past Nick's desk, a scowl on his lined face.

Confused, Nick turned around to see Dylan, who'd just come through the door with Timmy in his stroller. Perfect timing, Nick thought, not that shopping was one of his favorite things to do. But he wanted to make sure Dylan was comfortable in town, knew his way around, and that his aunt would have comfortable sheets and pillows for her bedroom at the new house.

But then a thought struck him. Nick turned to Farley. "What do you mean *back*?"

"He's the one who left that squawker on your desk last week," Farley shouted, jabbing his finger toward Dylan. "A man can't get a minute's peace in this place. I should file a complaint."

Nick glared at Farley. "You said you didn't see anyone leave the baby!"

Farley shrugged. "I was half-asleep and wanting to get back to it. Just make sure he doesn't start crying." He shot a frown in Timmy's direction and lay down on his cot. Fifteen seconds later, he was making the racket by snoring.

Nick should charge Farley for withholding information. If Farley had told him a tall, lanky teenage boy had left the baby, Nick would have come up with Dylan Patterson in two seconds.

Shaking his head, he turned to Dylan. Was it his imagination or was Dylan looking kind of pale and clammy. "Everything okay?"

"I don't know," Dylan said, his blue eyes looking sort of glassy.

Nick stepped toward him, noting that Dylan looked very pale.

Dylan gripped the stroller bar as if for support. "My shift ended, so I thought I'd take Timmy for a short walk before leaving him with Georgia so we could take that tour around town. But when I started walking, I got dizzy." He let go of Timmy's stroller and gripped the side of a desk for support.

"Dylan?" Nick said, rushing over.

The precinct secretary got to him first and caught him before he hit the floor, but Dylan was limp and unconscious. Nick called for an ambulance, his heart pounding out of his chest.

Nick squeezed shut his eyes and threw up a prayer, then glanced at Timmy, his little mouth quirking up, his white-socked foot kicking out in a stretch.

Please, please, please, let Dylan be okay.

Chapter Fifteen

Georgia, Gram and her sisters were in the bedding section of Baby Center, Annabel oohing and aahing over crib sheets with tiny climbing monkeys. Clementine pointed at a set with seashells against a pale orange background, and they all smiled; the color immediately brought Hurley's Homestyle Kitchen to mind, and Georgia loved the idea of a bit of the sea in her little one's nursery.

"Is it wrong if I buy the same set?" Annabel asked. Very innocently.

Georgia, Clementine and Gram all stared at her. "Wait a minute," Georgia said. "Are you saying—"

"Yes!" Annabel exclaimed. "I'm expecting!"

There was much cheering and hooting in the bedding section of Baby Center. Gram was crying. "Two great-grandchildren! Four generations of Hurleys."

Annabel filled them in on the details—the baby was due in February. Her husband, West, had already put together his daughter Lucy's old sleigh crib and was painting it a pale yellow. Annabel said they'd decided not to learn the baby's gender, but they might be unable to resist knowing when the time came.

Georgia noticed Clementine staring at a big stuffed giraffe. "You okay?" she whispered.

Clementine touched the giraffe's soft fur. "I'm so happy for you and Annabel. But I had this crazy fantasy that I would marry Logan Grainger, that we'd have a whole house full of kids. Now he doesn't even want me two feet near him."

"I'm so sorry, Clem," Georgia said. "There has to be some reason, something that clamped him up tight. This letter you mentioned. Maybe he got some bad news?"

"I wish I knew. But he won't tell me. He won't even talk to me. And I miss the twins."

Why was love so danged difficult? Georgia wished she had the right words for her sister, but she could barely figure out her own love life, not that she had one. "You could try talking to Logan one last time. Maybe invite him and the boys to Hurley's for dinner."

Clementine barely managed a shrug. "I'll give it one last try. Then I think I'd better listen when someone tells me I'm not wanted." Her expression turned sad and grim, but as they heard Gram oohing and aahing over an impossibly tiny onesie that read My Grandmother Rules, Clem smiled. "I love how happy Gram is. I'm just grateful both my sisters are home, that we're all together. I have my family. A little perspective," she added, knocking herself on the forehead.

Georgia smiled. "You always will have your family."

Her cell phone rang. Nick. Before she could even say hello, Nick explained that Dylan had collapsed at the police station and that Timmy was fine.

Georgia's heart started racing. "Will Dylan be okay? What's wrong?"

"We don't know yet," he said. "Can you come?"

"Of course. I'm at Baby Center with my grandmother and sisters, but I'll leave right away." Georgia had driven over herself, since she'd wanted to stop at the maternity shop and buy a few pieces of clothing before meeting her family at Baby Center. She let her grandmother and sisters know what was going on and they all rushed out, Annabel driving Georgia's car with Georgia in the passenger seat so she wouldn't have to drive while so worried.

Twenty minutes later, they were in the lot of the Blue Gulch Clinic, Gram and Clementine pulling up next to them. Inside was Nick, Timmy in his carrier on the chair beside him, and Dylan's great-aunt Helen on the other side, worry etched on her face. Essie immediately sat beside Helen and took her hand, lending some quiet comfort.

"No word yet?" Georgia asked, sitting down beside Nick.

"They're running tests is all I know," he said, dropping his head between his hands. "He's got to be okay. He has to be."

They all glanced at Timmy, so sweet and innocent. So recently reunited with the father who loved him so much.

"Detective Slater?" a doctor said. "Dylan told me that I could relay his medical information to you. He's going to be fine. Low blood sugar is all. He appears to have been under stress lately."

Nick visibly relaxed. "We've got him settled into a good place right now. All that stress is part of the past."

The doctor nodded. "That's what he said. I think it just caught up with him. You can see him now."

Nick thanked the doctor, then walked up to Aunt Helen and sat on her right side to explain the good news. Helen Patterson was so depleted from worry that Essie, Annabel and Clementine offered to bring her back to Nick's house and get her settled and stay with her until Nick or Dylan returned.

Georgia would stay with Timmy. "Tell Dylan I said hi and that I'm glad he's okay," she said to Nick. "And that Timmy is in good hands."

Essie stood up, helping Helen to her feet. "And make sure he knows he's not allowed to come to work for the dinner shift tonight. When he's one hundred percent better, his job will be waiting."

Nick nodded. "He's a lucky kid to have the Hurleys on his team."

"And you," Georgia said, her hand on his arm.

The moment Nick walked into Dylan's room in the clinic, the teenager burst into tears. He was half-reclined on the cot, a lumpy pillow behind his head, and was wearing one of those loose hospital gowns. He grabbed the box of tissues on the bedside table and wadded up a tissue to dab under his eyes.

Nick hadn't been expecting the tears. "Hey, Dylan," Nick said, walking over to the bed and sitting down in the chair beside it. "You're okay. Everything is okay. Timmy is safe and with Georgia. Your aunt Helen was here, and Essie Hurley and Georgia's sisters are bringing her back to my house to rest and wait for you when you're ready to be discharged. Child Protective Services has closed the case. You have a good job waiting for you when you're up for going back. You have solid friends here to support you. Everything's okay."

Tears streaked down Dylan's face. He shook his head. "Maybe they shouldn't have closed the case."

Nick stared at him. "What are you talking about?"

Dylan jabbed under his eyes with the tissue. "Maybe I'm doing the wrong thing, not putting Timmy up for adoption. I'm eighteen. I don't know anything. I don't know what the hell I'm doing."

That explained the stress level spiking instead of settling down. Now that Dylan and Timmy were reunited, the worry of keeping him no longer an issue, Dylan could finally focus on the reality of being a father and was now questioning his ability to do so—well. Plus the stress of having to leave Timmy with Nick, not seeing his infant for a week, then being spooked by the sight of Nick in Houston and suddenly moving to Blue Gulch—it must have all taken its toll on the new eighteen-year-old. He was a kid. A kid with a heap of responsibility on his young shoulders.

"Maybe I should let him go, be raised by a good family," Dylan said, the tears coming again. "I swore I'd never leave him. But maybe I'm doing him a disservice."

"Do you think you can be a good father to Timmy?" Nick asked.

"I know I can."

"How?" Nick prompted, hoping to lead Dylan back to confidence.

"Because I love him. I loved him before he was born. I've loved him every minute of his life. I want to be everything that my father wasn't."

Nick stiffened. Despite having seen his unborn baby on the monitor, despite being overwhelmed by it, Nick didn't feel a connection to his child yet. Because the idea of fatherhood didn't feel real? Or even like a possibility despite being reality? He leaned closer to Dylan, resting his elbows on his thighs, his hands under his chin. "Do you ever worry that it's in your blood?" He wasn't sure he should even put the question out there, but he wanted the answer—for Dylan and for himself.

Dylan sat up, his expression resolute. "No. I'm not my dad. I'm nothing like him. I'm like my mom."

Nick sat back as something gave way inside him. The words were so simple, yet he'd never thought about his own history in the same way. Nick wasn't anything like his dad either; he never had been.

Nick squeezed Dylan's hand for a moment. "I know that. I believe it." He waited for Dylan to catch his breath. "You're taking on a big responsibility."

"Yeah, I am. But I love my son. I'll take parenting classes. I'll do whatever it takes. I won't give him up."

Nick smiled. "There's the self-assured Dylan from Houston. You're not alone. You'll have Timmy's godparents right here. There are already quite a few people who adore Timmy. You'll have support. I never want you to feel alone, Dylan. I will always be here for you."

The boy burst into tears, shuddering sobs racking his body. "Really?" he managed to say.

Nick leaned over and pulled Dylan into a hug. Yes, he was eighteen. A legal adult. And a father. But he was a boy who needed a father figure himself, and Nick was going to be that father figure.

"I'm here for you, Dylan," Nick said. "Always."

Dylan calmed down and wiped under his eyes.

"And so is Georgia and, from the crowded waiting room earlier, the entire Hurley family." Nick leaned back. "I want you to promise me something."

"Okay," Dylan said.

"If you ever have a problem again, you tell me, okay? Because that's what I'm here for. Hell, I already feel like Timmy is my family. That makes you family."

Dylan's eyes filled with tears, and he nodded. Nick pulled him into another hug.

"It's gonna be okay, Dylan."

"I finally believe that," Dylan said.

Avery wanted to have a going-away lunch at Hurley's, and Nick was glad for the excuse to run into Georgia. He'd tried yesterday, after stopping at the Victorian with Dylan to pick up Timmy, but Georgia had been polite and reserved with him and focusing her attention on Dylan and how he was feeling. The teenager was 100 percent better, mentally and physically. Nick had taken them on the shopping trip he'd planned for the day before, and once he got the Pattersons settled into their new home, he'd breathed a very long sigh of relief.

He hadn't even realized how much the past week had weighed on him until 99 percent of it had been lifted from his shoulders. He still felt responsible for not only Timmy but Dylan and his great-aunt too, yet Dylan was of sturdy stock and could take care of himself and Timmy, even if he wobbled now and then, even if he needed a hand and one of Nick's weary shoulders.

He'd texted Georgia before he'd gone to bed last night, a simple Good night, beautiful. Thanks for…everything, and it had taken her a while to text back. Like almost two hours. He'd just gotten a Good night in response. And then had slept as if he were being pecked by imaginary pigeons.

She wanted something from him that he couldn't quite figure out. For him to want to be a father? To feel more connected to her pregnancy? He'd already agreed to attend the next ultrasound appointment. And be her Lamaze coach.

As he arrived at Hurley's, he saw his sister and Quentin at the round table by the fireplace, Mr. Whiskers's carrier under Avery's chair. They were deep in conversation, their faces an inch apart, and the look of utter love on Quentin's face made him stop in his tracks. He knew the guy loved Avery, but seeing it like this, up close and personal, was like a good left hook to the jaw. He was letting his kid sister go, to live her life, to be herself, to find herself. She wouldn't be alone, no matter what. And really, Nick thought, as he finally got his feet moving again, he didn't feel much of a "matter what" because he trusted in Quentin, trusted in their feelings for each other.

All these strange new feelings settled down as he approached the table, truly happy for Avery. He hugged them both, and listened to their excited chatter about Nashville, ate a ton of ribs and still couldn't resist a slice of Georgia's peach pie, just to have a piece of her with him. Finally, he said his goodbyes, to the cat too, foisted a Happy Travels card with some emergency money inside for the two of them and then hugged his baby sister goodbye.

"Next time I see you you'll be a dad," Avery said, wrapping her arms around him. "That's one lucky little guy."

"I'll try my best," he said, realizing how much he meant that.

Avery laughed and looked at him as though he were crazy. "Your worst is still pretty darned good. Granted, I didn't like being told what to do or how to live my life. But it's nice to know you care, Nick. *Really* care. I don't have any family but you. And now Quentin. But you're my big brother."

"I'll always be that," he said, squeezing her into a hug.

"Bye, sir," Quentin said, reaching out his hand.

Nick smiled and said, "I'm not sir to family." Then he grabbed Quentin into a hug too.

As he watched them leave, drive away in Quentin's little blue car with the crazy bumper stickers, his sister's words echoed in his head.

Your worst is still pretty darned good.

He shook his head, the compliment making him smile. He did care. He cared a hell of a lot. About Avery. Quentin. Georgia. Her family. And their baby, who'd be born in just five months.

A gray cloud didn't form over his head, opening up and drizzling on him the way it always did when the idea of himself as a tiny person's father flashed into his mind. There was just a neutrality when there had been cold fear. He'd call that a big improvement.

Out of the corner of his eye, he saw Georgia coming around the side of the Victorian, a big floppy hat shielding her eyes and pruning sheers in her hand. She had on shorts that showed her long, beautiful legs, and a T-shirt that couldn't hide the swell of her belly.

That was his baby. His. A little Hurley Slater was coming into the world and he could either stand here, happy enough that he no longer felt as if he were jumping out of his skin, or he could take the opportunity and run with it.

He was going to run with it. An idea came to him, involving a camera, Blue Gulch and the rest of his life. As Georgia clipped away at a bush without seeing him, he rushed off the porch in the opposite direction, wanting the rest of his life to finally have a chance to get started.

Chapter Sixteen

Nick bypassed a group of day campers walking two
by two to the playground at Blue Gulch Elementary
School, took out his phone and clicked on the video
camera function. He flipped the screen so that it was
filming him.

"Dad here," he said, but his voice was a little wonky
from how not-everyday this was for him, so he restarted
the video and cleared his throat. "Dad here. Hi. I don't
know your name yet. Your mother and I haven't talked
about that yet, but I'll bring that up later today. You
need a name, right? I—"

A little girl stood at the edge of the playground fence
and stared at him, then finally ran off to the tire swings,
giving him the privacy he needed to do this.

He kept the video camera aimed at him. "I'm filming this five months before you were born. One day,

maybe when you're all grown up—your aunt Avery's age now—you'll like the idea of looking back on how you came into the world." He felt like the Grinch on that snowy precipice, his heart growing so big it almost exploded. "I want you to know something. I want you to know that that even before you were born, I loved you."

The floodgates opened and Nick had to sit down on a bench and catch his breath.

It was true. He loved his child. He always had, from the moment Georgia had told him she was pregnant. He'd been afraid, yeah. But that never meant he didn't love their son.

He aimed the camera back on his face. "Dad here again. I've been worried how I'll do—and since you'll probably be watching this when you're graduating from high school or whenever people watch home videos that only families like, you'll be able to tell me how I did."

He paused, clicking off the video and leaning his head back, something daring to sting the backs of his eyes. He clicked Video. "Got kind of emotional for a minute there. I just want to do right by you. I don't want to let you down. I *won't* let you down. Since there's five months till you're coming, I thought I'd show you a little of the town where you'll be born, where I was born, where your mother was born. I'll show you where I grew up and where I went to school, where I had all my firsts."

I'm reclaiming this town for you, little guy, he added silently. *I'm going to see it through your eyes, for your eyes. Life has to be about the present and future, not the past.*

Yeah. It did. And it would be from here on in.

"This is where you'll go for your first day of school,"

Nick said, sweeping the video camera across the front of the Blue Gulch Elementary School. "Right there," he added, zooming in on the bicycle rack, "is where I wiped out in front of every kid on my bus. I had such a bad cut on my leg that kids used to offer me baseball cards to see it." He turned to the left. "And see that tire swing? That's where I made my first friend, a really funny kid named Finn. I should look him up." Nick smiled at the memory of himself and Finn riding their bikes all over town, looking for buried treasure and frogs, like little Henry Grainger.

After the elementary school, he moved to the middle school, where he had had his first awkward kiss, filming under the bleachers where it had happened. Then the high school, where he shared one of his favorite memories, his high school graduation, his mother and sister surprising him with dinner out at Hurley's. He told his son how back then, he had no idea that the girl he'd grow up to marry had been at Hurley's that day.

Nick froze. The girl he'd grow up to marry. *Marry.* He'd thought about it, of course, over the past weeks, ready to cough up Georgia's least favorite word, *obligation*, and commit to her and their child. But he'd known Georgia wouldn't want a husband who operated out of *should*. She was holding out for the real thing.

His heart wobbling, he got back in his car and filmed around town, pointing out some businesses that had come and gone, spending a good ten minutes in front of Hurley's, aiming it up at Georgia's window on the second floor. He probably looked half-crazy, holding up his phone and narrating, but Nick didn't much care.

"Now I want to show you where I grew up," he said into the video camera. He got into his car and drove over to the house that had stopped making his insides seize up—or had since that night he found Avery in the yard under the weeping willow. It was Avery's house now. That was how he would think of it: about its future.

He walked around to the backyard, hoping his tenants wouldn't mind that he was skulking around. There were no cars in the driveway, so they didn't appear to be home. He swept the video camera across the yard. "This is where I'd lie for hours every night with the telescope my mother bought me for my tenth birthday, looking for the Big Dipper and hoping to see some planets. And right there," he added, zooming in on the back porch, "is where my mother would read to me and Avery every night for an hour." He stared at the porch swing, barely focusing on the crack his father had once put into it in a fit. "This will always be Aunt Avery's house, and if she moves back here, if she's not too big a country music star for little ol' Blue Gulch, maybe she'll read to you here too, under the stars."

I'm having a baby, he whispered into the early evening air, and again he felt something shift in his chest—open instead of close, widen instead of tighten.

He had one more place to visit and then he was going to see Georgia Hurley and let her know he was ready to be a father.

Well, well, there was a new text from Nick, this one asking Georgia to meet him on the front porch of Hurley's. She glanced at the time. It was close to 9:00 p.m. and two big parties had come into the restaurant a little while ago to get in before closing. Georgia should be inside helping out in the dining room, walking around with a coffeepot and a pitcher of lemon water, fetching anything the busy waitstaff couldn't get to.

Anything to avoid what she was afraid was coming: goodbye. Nick might be staying in Blue Gulch, but he might as well be half a world away emotionally.

She took off her apron and hung it up on a peg, let her grandmother know she was stepping outside for a moment and steeled herself before opening the front door. She still couldn't get over his last text—from last night. Thanks…for everything.

Thanks for…everything. She was about to give him a piece of her angry mind. She yanked open the door and there he was, standing on the porch so danged handsome with so many shopping bags in his hands that she was surprised he could still stand straight.

She'd spent hours tossing and turning last night, unable to get comfortable, unable to fall asleep. Tears pricking her eyes every time she thought about Nick. *Thanks for everything* was about goodbye. About appreciation of service. About *we're done here.*

Well, dammit, she wasn't done here. This man wasn't walking away until she said her piece. Until he knew how she felt about him. If he didn't feel the same way, fine. Go live a quarter mile away and visit their baby every other day or however they'd work it out. But until she was officially defeated, she wasn't giving up. *Thanks for everything* was close to defeat, but because Nick *was* the brick wall that surrounded him, there was a chance for them. Brick walls could be blasted through. Well, Nick Slater, meet Georgia, the human blowtorch.

Thanks for everything. Good Lord. Was he kidding? How dare he! A fresh round of hot indignation rose in her, and that was it.

"I have something to say to you, Nick Slater."

He stared at her, and there was something different in his expression, something she couldn't pinpoint. "Okay." He let go of all the shopping bags, wedging them over on the porch with his leg so that diners could pass by on their way out.

Okay. Grr, he was impossible! She took him by the hand and led him down the street to a grassy area with a bench. Neither of them sat.

"You listen to me, Nick Slater," she said, jabbing a finger at him. "I don't want you here out of obligation. I want you here because you want to be here. Do you understand what I mean?"

"Ah. So that's what you were talking about. Now it makes sense."

Grr again. "You really couldn't figure that out?"

He looked down, then away, then turned so that she couldn't see his face.

"Nick?"

"I don't want to hurt you," he finally said, turning back to face her. "After all you've been through, you deserve all the happiness in the world."

"And…" she prompted. If he was going to say it, that he didn't love her and it just wasn't going to happen for them in the way she dreamed, she had to give him the chance to say it. Without trying to read his mind. Or project.

"And I love you, Georgia."

Did he just say he loved her? Her hand flew to her mouth.

"I love you. And I'll be there for you and the baby. I promise you that. I've made some kind of breakthrough today—I'm really ready to be our child's father. Not out of obligation—out of want. The baby is coming in five months and I'll be ready. I'm going to be the best father I can be. I'm sorry for all the mixed signals I've given you ever since you came back to town. I could barely resist you because you're so damned beautiful. I thought I needed to let you go. Same way I let Avery go this afternoon."

Oh, Nick.

"But if you'll have me, I promise to always try to be the man, the husband you deserve."

If she'd have him. She almost laughed.

From the pain shadowing his dark eyes, Georgia knew he wasn't completely sure he was up to the task. But he was. Despite everything he'd been through, all the wrongs he made right in their world, he still didn't realize how good a man he was.

"Nick Slater, you once told me to tell you if anything was ever wrong. And something is wrong. Do you want to know what?"

"Of course I do."

Georgia nodded, then waved at Harriet Culver, who was walking Bentley across the street. She waited until Harriet had moved on far enough so that they had some privacy. "Okay, what's wrong can be made right. But it depends on the answer to a question."

Nick's eyes narrowed. "This sounds complicated."

Georgia smiled. "Yes or no isn't complicated. You just say the answer to the question. Oh, and there's no 'yeah, but' allowed. No 'it depends.' Either yes or no, a sentence in and of itself. Okay?"

"This sounds really complicated now, but okay."

She looked at him, at this handsome man, this beautiful person inside and out, and closed her eyes for a second, making a wish in advance on tonight's stars. She opened her eyes. "Do you *really* love me?"

He leaned back a bit, his gaze intense on her. "Yes. I really do."

Georgia's eyes filled with tears. "Another question, then. Are you in love with me?"

He reached for her hand and held it. "Yes. Very much so."

Her heart was bursting. "So what the gobbledygook have you been doing?"

"Well, for the past few hours I was practically buying out Baby Center for our son. Onesies. Baby blankets. Diapers. Burp clothes. A mobile. Two car seats. At least four or five things we probably don't even need, like a baby wipes warmer."

She laughed, happy tears pricking her eyes again.

"But," he said, "you probably mean since you came back into my life." At her nod, he added, "What I've been doing is...worrying. Being terrified. Of letting myself feel anything."

"Love *is* scary," she said. "In a good way. I know, Nick, because I love you so much. So much."

He took her hand and held it. "I love you too. And I don't want to get this wrong." He placed his other on her cheek, the look in his eyes full of tenderness. "I don't want to let you down."

"You just have to love me," she said. "You'll be surprised how much that covers."

He reached for her and she melted against him, so much anxiety and fear and worry flitting away. "I love you, Georgia. Deeply. I have since the first day I met you."

"Me too," she said. "I love you so much sometimes I think I'll explode."

He held her tight, then said he'd stopped at one more shop earlier and pulled a little velvet box from his jacket pocket. "Will you marry me, Georgia?"

She couldn't help the gasp, then brought a hand up to his cheek and looked into his eyes. "Yes, I will."

He slid the beautiful diamond ring on her finger, then kissed her passionately.

"No wonder you haven't found the thief who stole my clothes!" a voice shouted out. Georgia whirled around and there was Penny Jergen, tottering down Blue Gulch Street in three-inch heels, two similarly dressed girlfriends flanking her. She was glaring at Nick. "Too busy kissing women."

Nick laughed. "Just one," he called out. "Woman. Forever," he added on a whisper.

Epilogue

Well, Georgia had tried on her grandmother's beautiful tea-length wedding dress, the one Essie had worn to marry her great love over fifty years ago, the one Annabel had worn to marry her own great love a few months ago, but there was no way that dress, so elegant and simple and lovely, would fit over her belly. Not when she was five months pregnant.

Georgia, her sisters and her grandmother all headed over to Blue Gulch Bridal, Georgia wondering if she'd get the side eye from Marley, the owner, for being pregnant before the wedding. Not in any kind of judgmental way—just a gossipy way.

"I win twenty-five bucks!" Marley said the moment Georgia entered, her family behind her. "I told my sister that Georgia Hurley was knocked up and she said no, she's just been eating for free at Hurley's all day so she started packing on the pounds."

Georgia couldn't help laughing. "Nice to know, Marley. And yes, I have been enjoying quite a few po'boys for lunch, so technically you both win."

A few hugs and congratulations later, Georgia explained that the wedding was this weekend, just days away, and that Clementine had amazing seamstress skills if Marley's usual seamstress couldn't get to Georgia's dress on such short notice. Marley said she'd work her magic and make it happen on time, no worries.

"So, who all is in the bridal party?" Marley asked. "Yeah, I'm nosy, but I want to know."

Georgia smiled. "Well, we decided to keep it simple. My grandmother is walking me down the aisle to my groom, and that's that. My sisters, my matron and maid of honor, are giving speeches at the reception."

"I had ten bridesmaids," Marley said. "I think you've got the right idea.

Georgia's sisters went through the racks, looking for what Georgia had described as her dream dress—a white gown, simple and sleeveless and pretty. Essie was looking through the "mother of the bride" section for her dress, determined to get dolled up, since she hadn't attended Annabel's quickie wedding-of-then-convenience in Las Vegas.

"I think I found it," Clementine said, pulling a gown off the rack. "It's you, Georgia."

Georgia turned and gasped. It *was* her. And exactly what she'd been looking for. Classic and elegant, sleeveless and simple and flowy, with a row of delicate beading at the necessary empire waist, almost like something Audrey Hepburn would wear.

"So beautiful," Annabel said, nodding.

Georgia took the dress into the large fitting room

and removed her tank top and maternity shorts, then pooled the gown by her feet and stepped in and brought it up. So far so good on fit. "A little help zipping?" she called out, and her whole family rushed in.

Essie zipped and her sisters stood on either side of her, staring into the floor-to-ceiling three-way mirrors.

"I'm going to cry," Annabel said, a hand covering her mouth. "I can't speak."

Clementine eyes welled. "Me either."

"You're going to make a beautiful bride, Georgia," Essie said, wiping away her own tears.

Nick stood by the bay window in the dining room of Hurley's Homestyle Kitchen, which had been turned into a wedding hall, complete with a red carpet aisle runner and more flowers than he'd ever seen in one place. He smiled at his sister and Quentin in the front row beside the Hurley family. Then winked at Dylan beside Quentin, Timmy in his carrier on a seat between Dylan and his great-aunt. Logan Grainger and his two cute twin nephews sat behind Dylan.

Nick had spent the past few minutes with not much to do other than look around at the people who'd come to witness his wedding, so he couldn't help noticing how often Logan looked at Clementine's profile, then quickly looked away when Clementine would realize someone was staring at her. He hoped those two figured it out. Nick had spent some time being miserable when the woman he loved was right beside him, and he had a feeling Logan Grainger was doing the same dumb thing.

Not that it hadn't taken Nick some time to figure that out.

Harriet Culver, sitting at the piano that had been

brought in from the parlor, began the traditional wedding march, and everyone turned around to watch Georgia, her face slightly obscured by a white veil, begin down the aisle, her grandmother beside her.

Nick actually gasped, the sight of the woman he loved in a wedding gown, walking to him, almost too much.

He didn't take his eyes off her. As she reached him, Essie pulled back her veil, and Georgia stood smiling at him. He took both her hands in his, and then they turned toward the pastor, both of them ready to start their future as husband and wife, mother and father.

"I just felt the baby kick!" Georgia whispered, but everyone heard and their guests starting clapping.

Nick laughed and put his hand on her belly. He felt a little kick on the side, and his heart almost burst. "I'm glad he's here for this," Nick whispered. "The best day of my life."

* * * * *

MILLS & BOON®

Cherish™

EXPERIENCE THE ULTIMATE RUSH OF FALLING IN LOVE

0516/23

MILLS & BOON®

The Billionaires Collection!

2 FREE BOOKS!

This fabulous 6 book collection features stories from some of our talented writers. Feel the temperature rise with our ultra-sexy and powerful billionaires. Don't miss this great offer – buy the collection today to get two books free!

Order yours at
www.millsandboon.co.uk/billionaires

MILLS & BOON®

Why shop at millsandboon.co.uk?

Each year, thousands of romance readers find their perfect read at millsandboon.co.uk. That's because we're passionate about bringing you the very best romantic fiction. Here are some of the advantages of shopping at www.millsandboon.co.uk:

* **Get new books first**—you'll be able to buy your favourite books one month before they hit the shops

* **Get exclusive discounts**—you'll also be able to buy our specially created monthly collections, with up to 50% off the RRP

* **Find your favourite authors**—latest news, interviews and new releases for all your favourite authors and series on our website, plus ideas for what to try next

* **Join in**—once you've bought your favourite books, don't forget to register with us to rate, review and join in the discussions

Visit **www.millsandboon.co.uk**
for all this and more today!